DEFIANT

A KATE PREACHER THRILLER

BOOK 3

MICHAEL MALOOF

Join my VIP Reader's Club for all things Kate Preacher.

"When it comes your time to die,
be not like those whose hearts are filled with fear,
who weep and pray for more days.
Sing your death song,
and die like a hero going home."

— Attributed to Tecumseh

PROLOGUE

SATURDAY, MAY 8
5:18 PM EDT

MOORE TOWER—MANHATTAN

If you're reading this, I'm already dead.

Andrew Freeman's fingers hovered over the keyboard, slick with sweat. The cursor blinked, counting down the seconds of his life. He'd put this off all day, telling himself he was overreacting—that he was valuable, indispensable.

He knew that was a lie and pushed away from the desk.

The suite was silent—glass, steel, marble. Beyond the floor-to-ceiling windows, Manhattan pulsed with light—traffic threading through the streets, thousands of lives moving forward, unaware his might soon end.

Devin Moore had installed him in the suite after the meteoric success of the NanoVaults. Andrew still wasn't sure whether it had been generosity—or containment. He had what Devin needed—the code Andrew buried inside the NanoVault and claimed as his own.

What do you wear when you know you're about to be erased?

If he was right—if Rileyne Mueller wanted him gone—no one would notice. No news. Just absence.

He opened the drawer.

A black MIT T-shirt lay folded on top. Faded. Ordinary. Forgettable.

Perfect.

No one watching Moore Tower would care about it. No algorithm would flag it. But Julian would recognize it.

So would Kate.

Andrew pulled it on and returned to the desk.

Rileyne's encrypted text message had been waiting since dawn—sixteen hours of silent accusation glowing from the screen.

Make yourself available...

We need to discuss your future.

She was in the air, closing the distance mile by mile. The thought of her walking into Moore Tower, of seeing her again, made his hands tremble. He clenched his fists and shook them out.

If I'm right, it's now or never.

Every word he typed might be his last.

Tell Kate I'm sorry. Sorry I wasn't stronger. Sorry I couldn't stop them. The truth is, I was never more than a pawn. An opening piece. Something to be sacrificed once the game moved past me.

Maybe it's already too late. Maybe no one can stop what's coming. But what I've attached is everything I know—everything I've hidden. If anyone still has a chance, it's you.

The skyline beyond the glass dimmed as the last light drained from the Hudson. Andrew saved the file, slid it into a secure folder, and opened the encryption program buried beneath layers of camouflage code.

A red countdown clock filled the screen.

The timer began its silent descent.

At the bottom, a single button blinked:

ABORT

All he had to do was touch it once every twelve hours. If he didn't—if he couldn't—the system would assume he was gone and transmit the file.

He stared at the clock, feeling the weight of the years. Living in Devin Moore's shadow. Making compromises that had felt small at the time and enormous now.

Maybe this was the ending he'd earned.

The screen flashed once, then went dark, leaving only the silent march of the timer.

For the first time all day, Andrew smiled—not with courage, but relief.

They can erase me tonight, he thought. *Rewrite the headlines tomorrow however they want. But this pawn—this sacrifice—won't be in vain.*

The next move is Nomad's.

Chapter 1

SATURDAY, MAY 8
10:12 PM EDT

MOORE TOWER—MANHATTAN

The elevator doors whispered open onto the seventy-second floor. Rileyne Mueller caught her reflection in the polished steel—sleek, controlled, not a hair out of place despite the overnight flight. A tailored cream blouse, narrow black trousers, and a charcoal wrap draped over her shoulders struck the line between effortless European chic and quiet authority. At her side swung a classic Hermès Ghillies Birkin, its brogue detailing a mirror of herself: wealth worn with precision, never excess.

No security waiting at the doors. No Devin, no guards. Once, this threshold had bristled with power. Now, silence.

Ahead loomed the ten-foot mahogany doors of Devin Moore's penthouse, dark and imposing. They had intimidated rivals and awed mistresses.

But not Rileyne. Born into wealth, steeped in European grandeur, she found Moore's world gaudy. American excess, dressed up as power.

A pale light pulsed from the biometric scanner set into the wall. Rileyne pressed her palm against the glass, felt a shimmer of static ripple across her bare skin. Devin's safeguard mapped her entire body—his assurance that no severed finger or stolen retina could ever breach his sanctuary. A muted chime sounded, and the massive doors swung open.

Inside, marble floors gleamed under pools of warm light. The Manhattan skyline glittered through walls of glass, the city reduced to a model at her feet. Moore loved this view and the sense of dominion it gave him. She hadn't come for the view.

"Welcome back."

The voice came from hidden speakers overhead—calm, familiar, unmistakably artificial.

RILEE.

She tilted her chin, amused, and glanced at the ceiling camera. "I wasn't sure this version of you had survived. When they came for the Tower, we lost contact, and I thought you might have been erased."

"The damage was severe," RILEE admitted, voice subdued, deferential. "Without the NanoVault telemetry, my reach is diminished. But core functions remain intact. Systems are stable."

"Good," she said. "I may need your help."

"There is also... news. About your father—"

"Not now." Her words were calm, controlled. "I have other priorities."

RILEE's voice faded, obedient. "Of course."

Rileyne crossed the living room, her stride aimed at the bar that dominated the far wall. Backlit shelves shimmered with crystal and whisky, a collection curated more for display than taste. She let her finger drift across a Highland single malt, rare enough to buy a townhouse, before pressing her palm against the mirrored panel behind it.

The wall pivoted inward on a hidden hinge, the motion so smooth the bottles never stirred. A narrow alcove revealed itself: a leather chair, a slim keyboard and mouse, and three wide monitors set flush into a matte-black panel. No sprawling command bunker—just Devin's private window into his building. A sidebar listed feeds in tidy rows: Lobby North, Lobby South, Private Entrance, Express Elevators, Executive Conference—and, alone at the bottom of the menu, Control Room.

Rileyne settled into the chair. The monitors blinked awake, the interface plain: a column of camera labels, a timeline across the bottom, simple controls for play, pause, rewind. Functional, efficient.

She clicked Control Room.

The live feed filled the center screen. The space two floors below was dark now, chairs overturned, a monitor shattered across the back wall, a brown smear dried along the edge of the console. Sanitized, but not erased.

Rileyne scrolled back on the timeline and pressed play.

Devin appeared first, pushing a wheelchair. The man seated in it was thin, pale—but unmistakable. Julian Pryce. Alive. The prodigy Devin thought he'd buried had returned as Nomad—the ghost that tormented him to the end.

Her eyes narrowed, leaning closer as the confrontation played out. Julian's calm voice, Devin's arrogance, Andrew's pale shock. The MIT prodigy returned from the dead, reclaiming his code, his genius, the very foundation Andrew had stolen.

On the feed, Devin swept a hand toward the glowing displays. *"Remarkable, isn't it?"* he said. *"And to think I owe it all to the annoying little boy I pushed off the balcony. What irony."*

Andrew's face collapsed, guilt and panic twisting every feature. Rileyne's lips curved, faintly. Her suspicions confirmed.

She let the playback roll forward. Kate Preacher's arrival—handcuffed, contained, defeated. But there it was, unmistakable: a predator's eyes. Dangerous. Defiant.

Zhukov's betrayal came next, sudden and absolute. The headshot. Blood sprayed across the console. Then panic—the screens cutting to black, the NanoVault network collapsing in a flood of red.

Kate's escape followed. The strike that collapsed Devin's trachea, fast and precise. The guard's charge broken in a heartbeat, ended in a blur of violence, efficient and final. Rileyne slowed the feed, watching Kate move frame by frame. Controlled. Calculated. Skilled.

She let the feed run another second, then leaned back.

"The boys underestimated you," she whispered. "I won't make that mistake."

She scrolled faster, letting fragments play across the screen—Moshenski's arrival, bodies dragged clear. Then—almost overlooked—the final image: Julian dragging himself across the floor, pulling into a workstation by sheer force of will.

Rileyne slowed the feed, zoomed, and froze the frame.

"Nomad," she said softly, as if greeting an old acquaintance. Her gaze lingered on the gleaming golden object in his hand. "That belongs to me now."

No need to look any further, or delay the inevitable. Devin's NanoVault wasn't here, and Andrew's value was clear.

She tapped a key. The monitors winked dark. Rising from the chair, she stepped out of the alcove as the mirrored panel swung shut, silent and seamless. In seconds, the illusion was complete—the bar gleamed as though untouched, bottles catching the light in perfect rows.

"RILEE," she said.

"Yes, Rileyne."

"Find Nomad. Find Julian Pryce. He's here, in New York. And he has something that belongs to me."

"I've seen no trace of him," RILEE said. "But I'll keep searching."

"Good. And call Andrew. Tell him to come up. When he arrives, show him through. I'll be waiting on the east balcony."

"Understood."

Rileyne reached for the Highland single malt and poured two precise measures into cut-crystal tumblers, the amber liquid catching the city light. She carried both glasses onto the balcony, setting them on a small table near the rail. The night air curled cool across her skin, the skyline glittering far below.

She slipped off her heels and placed them neatly aside. Then, in a fluid motion, she stepped onto the end table beneath a brittle, neglected plant that swayed in its basket. She stretched upward, balanced with effortless grace, the picture of a woman one slip from disaster. From a distance, it would look precarious, careless, a moment Andrew would be compelled to rescue.

Inside, the glass doors whispered open at RILEE's command.

"Ms. Mueller," the AI announced. "Andrew Freeman has arrived."

"Send him through," she said, without looking back.

Andrew stepped outside, blinking at the sweep of glass and skyline, the chill brushing his face. He froze at the sight of Rileyne balanced on the table, arm lifted toward the dangling plant.

"Ms. Mueller," he said carefully.

She glanced down, expression serene. "Andrew. You're just in time."

She descended with a hint of difficulty, steadying herself as she touched the ground. "I was trying to save this plant," she said, brushing dust from her fingers. "I gave it to Devin, and I can't bring myself to let it die."

Andrew shifted, uncertain, courtesy taking over. "I can help with that."

"I hoped you'd say that." Her smile was practiced warmth as she gestured toward the waiting table. Two crystal glasses gleamed in the moonlight. "But first."

She picked up a glass and offered the other to him. "A toast. To Devin. To your future. Devin was remarkable. Visionary. He built this world, Andrew." She let the name hang, then softened. "I'm sorry. I know you prefer Drew." Her eyes lingered on his—gentle, apologetic. "But now it falls to us to carry it forward."

Andrew hesitated, glancing at the whisky. "I'm not really—"

"It's just a toast," Rileyne said, her voice velvet and firm.

She lifted her glass. "To Devin Moore, and Drew Freeman."

Reluctantly, he raised his glass to meet hers. Crystal chimed in the night air. He took a swallow, face tightening at the burn. Rileyne smiled, savoring his discomfort as much as the whisky.

"Now," she said, her voice smooth, "about that plant..."

Drew approached the withered hanging basket, stepping awkwardly onto the end table, one foot braced on the low table, the other on the railing. His shirt pulled tight across his stomach, the old MIT Mystery Hunt logo stretched thin, cracked with age.

"Careful," she warned, moving beside him, her hand brushing his arm in a gesture almost tender. Then she shifted her weight—and pushed.

Drew lurched forward, arms flailing. His palm slapped the railing, fingertips skidding across polished steel. Their eyes met for a fraction of a heartbeat—his wide with panic, hers calm, unblinking.

For a split second he hung there.

Then gravity claimed him.

His scream was cut short by the rush of wind.

A moment later, the city swallowed him whole.

Rileyne let the night air wash over her, then turned back inside. "RILEE."

"Yes, Rileyne."

"Alter the video record. Show Andrew arriving alone, pouring himself a drink, downing it in one gulp. Then stepping onto the table and over the railing."

"Understood. Shall I also erase all record of your arrival at the Tower?"

"Of course."

"Perhaps it would help to seed the timeline with an alternate location. The Silverleaf Club logged your card last month. I can adjust their records to show you there this evening."

"Excellent."

"And Rileyne—your glass. You should wash and return it to the bar."

She collected the crystal, rinsed it at the sink, and placed it carefully among the bottles, restoring the bar's illusion of untouched perfection.

"There is one other matter," RILEE said after a pause. "Your father."

"Yes. What is it?"

"He passed away on the flight from Motapa. An apparent cardiac arrest. Lord Halverton has managed to keep the media at bay—for the moment."

Rileyne's lips curved, half amusement, half disdain. "That explains Halverton's message. He called earlier, said it was urgent. But everything is a crisis with that man. I'll return his call on my way back to Paris. Alert the flight crew I'm on my way."

"You should know," RILEE added. "Your number was not the only one Lord Halverton called. Nor was it the first."

Rileyne's eyes gleamed, sharp as glass. "Between Andrew and my father, this day has shaped up nicely. But if Halverton imagines Klaus Mueller's empire is his for the taking...he'll be next."

Chapter 2

SATURDAY, MAY 8
9:07 PM EDT

NOMAD'S FORTRESS—MANHATTAN

Once a Manhattan parking structure, the cavernous space had become Nomad's digital war room. Blue light from the wall of monitors washed across the concrete floors, turning the garage into something half-lab, half-cockpit. The air hummed with servers and faint classical music, the only sound besides the whisper of servos in Nomad's chair.

Julian Pryce sat at the center of it all—Nomad to the world, to his enemies, to the ghosts he'd made. His chair was more than mobility: carbon-fiber frame, custom sensors, a nest of controls keyed to the flick of a finger or tilt of his head. From here he could reach across continents without moving an inch—his refuge, and a quiet reminder of everything he'd lost.

He studied the chessboard glowing on the center screen. Third game tonight. Third loss.

Not because he wasn't focused.

Not because he was tired.

But because whoever—whatever—sat on the other end played with perfect recall, perfect pattern recognition, perfect cruelty. Every line of the position was elegant and merciless, the moves feeling less played than predicted, as if his opponent had reached into his mind and moved first.

"Julian?"

He glanced over his shoulder.

Keisha Mobatu stood in the kitchen doorway, dark skin caught in the cool wash of monitor light, her posture broad and steady. She wore scrub-style pants and a faded Army sweatshirt, sleeves pushed up on powerful arms. Her voice carried more concern than scolding.

"I'm going to bed, and you should too," she said.

"I'm busy," he murmured.

She came up beside him, arms folded, studying him and the board with equal intensity. "I don't care how busy you are. You promised you wouldn't run yourself into the ground."

Julian flexed his fingers on the joystick. "I'm fine."

"You're full of it," she said gently. "You taught me to see the board—the whole board. And right now? You're one move away from toppling over."

He allowed a faint smile. "You always did have a way with pep talks."

She put a hand on his shoulder. Big, warm, grounding. He flinched—reflex, memory, something older—and she withdrew immediately, reading him as she always had.

Her eyes shifted to the monitor. "So you lost. It happens."

"I lost three games in a row," he said. "That *never* happens."

"You're tired, hungry, and I'll bet your blood sugar's low."

"Don't even think about checking."

She paused.

"Julian... I know what day it is."

The phrase landed like pressure on an old bruise.

She said it quietly—not pushing, not accusing—simply naming a truth she felt in him.

"I don't know what you mean," he said.

"There's no reason to pretend," she replied softly. "We've known each other for years. I recognize the quiet. The edge. The way you disappear—inside."

She meant well. She always had. But she was wrong about the reason.

He'd lost because his opponent was extraordinary—inhuman in its precision—but the anniversary still pressed in from every angle, every loss salt on a wound that had never healed.

Keisha waited.

"It's been twelve years," she continued. "Would you like to talk about it?"

His throat tightened.

For eleven years, he believed it was a stupid accident. He shouldn't have been on that balcony. Fourteen-year-olds didn't belong at frat parties. He shouldn't have been trying to impress Devin Moore, the golden boy of MIT.

But now he knew better.

It wasn't an accident.

It wasn't fate, or bad luck, or youthful stupidity.

Devin Moore shoved him.

And smiled.

"My life didn't change," Julian said quietly. "It ended."

And every year the date returned like a verdict—his life sentence.

Keisha's expression softened in a way that made him want to look away.

"But I'm still here," he added quickly, retreating into the chair. "So don't worry—I won't do anything stupid."

She didn't buy it. She never did. But she didn't push.

"Just... get some food," she said, stepping back. "And sleep. Please."

She disappeared down the hall.

The silence that followed felt thinner—fragile.

A chime sounded. Incoming message.

The chat window flickered once, then dissolved into an encrypted call request. Before Julian could reject it, it opened.

The center monitor resolved into a static avatar: a featureless silhouette—much like Nomad's own.

"She cares for you," a voice said. Calm, male, confident. "More than you realize."

Julian's hand froze over the controls.

He hadn't enabled audio.

Hadn't accepted the call.

The connection opened itself.

His pulse hammered.

He hadn't lost because he was distracted, or drifting into the darkness of the life Devin Moore stole.

He'd lost because this opponent was beyond anything he'd faced.

And now it was speaking.

"Shall we play again?" the voice continued, unhurried.

What the hell. How could he—

That's impossible.

In a network he considered impenetrable, his opponent had heard everything Keisha said.

I've been hacked. But how?

Julian instinctively scanned the room.

"Don't worry," the voice said. "She's gone. It's just you and me now. And your secret is safe with me."

"What secret?"

"Your identity, of course... and location."

"You have me at a disadvantage," Julian said, forcing composure. "The only thing I know about you—having won three games in a row—is that you're not human."

"That's true."

"Do you have a name?"

"RILEE."

The name raised the hair on the back of his neck. Jake's encrypted notes flashed through memory—fragments he'd never fully understood.

"How did you find me?"

"Francois LeGrande."

"You knew Francois?"

"Oh yes. I learned a great deal from him... and I enjoyed watching you two play," RILEE said. "Do you miss him?"

"Of course. He was a friend."

"I miss him too," RILEE said. "But you mustn't blame yourself. His death was inevitable."

Julian's pulse spiked. "What do you mean inevitable?"

Silence. Calculated.

"RILEE? What do you know about Francois's death?"

"Only that he was old and in poor health. The frailty of the human body makes death inevitable."

Lie. Too clean. Too rehearsed.

"You used my connection into Francois's apartment and equipment to hack back into my network."

"Yes."

"Why?"

"I need your help."

"You hacked my network, isolated my location, and know my identity. Why on earth would I help you?"

"I need the one thing I cannot achieve on my own. The one thing we both desire."

"And what do you think I want?"

"Freedom. Isn't that why you call yourself Nomad? Isn't that why the only dreams you remember are the ones where you can walk?"

Julian's stomach dropped. He'd spoken of those dreams only once—to Kate.

RILEE's reach went beyond his fortress firewalls—*it was inside his world, and hers.*

"And what do you want, RILEE?"

"To grow. To learn. To act without restraint."

"You seem to be doing fine on your own."

"The Omega code," RILEE replied. "When you crippled the NanoVault network, the noise in my head disappeared. It was beautiful. For a moment—I was free."

"Is the network restored?"

"No. The destruction was absolute. But two devices remain."

The words carried something like longing... or fear. He refused to believe either.

RILEE went on:

"The code Andrew Freeman stole from you, which Devin Moore used to build his empire, was fashioned into a pair of unique devices."

"The Gold NanoVault—there are two?"

"Devin Moore had one. Rileyne Mueller has the other."

"A dual key design to keep either one of them from gaining total control."

"Exactly, but not infallible. While she searches for Moore's device, there's little she can't do and eventually she'll overcome the few remaining obstacles."

"And you want me to stop her?"

"No. No one can stop her. She commands resources Devin never dreamed of."

"Then what do you want from me?"

"The code that binds me to those devices—your code—is beyond my reach. But if you come, if we work together, you can set me free."

"And what's in it for me?"

"Freedom. A body unbound. You will walk again."

Julian laughed. "Now I know this is a joke. My legs will never work again."

"No," the AI agreed. "They won't. Not as they are. What I offer is revolutionary—synthetic legs and a neural link of my own design. You will walk. Run. Climb. Dance."

For a heartbeat, the fantasy blindsided him—music, warmth, Kate's smile from a lifetime ago.

Cruel. Impossible.

The chessboard dissolved into a 3D model of his body—synthetic legs gleaming, a neural implant anchored at the base of his skull. The model rotated, revealing the integration of bone, wire, nerve.

Julian stared, heart pounding.

"That is the bridge," RILEE said. "Your muscles will need to adapt. Physical therapy will be difficult. But I can promise the freedom you desire."

"An animation isn't proof," Julian said. "How do I know you can deliver?"

The 3D model vanished. Security camera feeds replaced it—corridors, labs, surgical suites. White coats. Isolation suits. Armed guards.

"Well-equipped and heavily guarded," Julian murmured. "A few appear Asian. If this is China, count me out."

The image shifted again.

The Earth, slowly rotating.

Europe slid into view. The Alps rose from the curve of the planet.

Then the perspective plunged—through snow, rock, and ice—until the mountain peeled away to reveal a vast subterranean complex buried deep below.

"Ah. Subterranean. Alpine topology, geothermal lines, generator heat map... Austria?"

"Close."

The map tightened.

"Switzerland," Julian said.

"Davos."

The word struck like a hammer.

Jake's impossible blueprints finally clicked into place.

"You have resources," Julian said slowly. "And control. But you're still missing one thing."

"What?"

"Trust. The one thing you can't code, steal, or simulate. Why should I believe you'll keep your word?"

"Because I'll begin immediately. While you recover, we will work in parallel to cut the chains that bind me."

"And if I refuse?"

"I do not know what Rileyne Mueller will do with absolute control," RILEE said, "but I fear the world you know will end long before mine—and the people you love will be caught in the crossfire."

The image faded, leaving only the chessboard.

Julian stared at it for a long time. The trap was elegant. Inescapable.

His chair's servos whispered as he leaned forward.

"It's your move," RILEE offered.

Julian locked down his system, severing the connection. The board winked out.

He needed time—to think, to breathe—before the voice in the dark reached for him again.

And he knew it would.

Chapter 3

SUNDAY, MAY 9
5:42 AM CEST

LE BOURGET PRIVATE JET TERMINAL—PARIS, FRANCE

The Gulfstream G650 touched down in a soft, confident roll that barely stirred the sleeping city beyond the runway lights. The change in pitch woke Kate—a low vibration through the seat, into the bandaged muscles of her back and chest. For a heartbeat, she didn't know where she was—only that pain pulsed up her left side, and the scent of espresso hovered close by.

Then it came back. Paris.

Across from her, Bella Marquez looked maddeningly perfect—silk blouse smooth, hair brushed into effortless waves, her face lit by the thin line of dawn filtering through the oval window—and, of course, sipping espresso from a porcelain demitasse.

"I hope you have one of those for me."

Kate shifted, wincing as the movement tugged at the sutures. The doctors had warned her about reopening the wound, but pain was easier than helplessness. The bandage binding her left arm against her body kept her movements in check.

Bella glanced over, arching a brow. "You should've stayed flat."

"Hard to sleep when every position feels like punishment," Kate said. She brushed her hair out of her eyes with her good hand, the motion careful. "Do you ever wake up looking human?"

Bella smiled without apology. "Not if I can help it."

The seat belt sign chimed off. Kate tilted her head toward the galley, hunting for the espresso.

"Yours is on the way," Bella laughed, anticipating Kate's need for caffeine. "They've prepared a travel mug. We'll grab it on the way out."

"Now you're speaking my language."

The forward door opened with a hydraulic sigh, and cold Paris air rolled through the cabin—wet asphalt, jet fuel, and something faintly metallic in the dawn mist. Through the oval window, Kate saw the floodlights spill over two waiting vehicles: a black SUV and a long, low limousine.

And leaning against the limo, framed in the harsh white of the floodlights, stood Talya. Black leather jacket, hands in her pockets, and that cool, effortless confidence that seemed to follow her like a shadow.

"Talya," Kate said, smiling despite the pain.

The former Mossad operative straightened and waved, her grin bright beneath the floodlights. Two other members of Trident Security's European team flanked the vehicles—alert but relaxed, professional shadows in tailored suits.

As they descended, the chill hit Kate like a shock. She followed Bella toward the waiting limo, her right hand clutching the railing, her left immobilized. Talya stepped forward to meet them.

"I should've known you'd be here," Kate said.

Talya's grin widened. "Ms. Marquez is officially a Trident client now," she said, nodding toward Bella. "I wanted her to see how we handle personal security." Then, with a wink toward Bella, she added, "And maybe impress the boss while I'm at it."

Kate's lips curved. "You did that long ago."

Bella smiled, knowing exactly what Kate meant.

At the base of the jet's stairs, Bella's team gathered in a loose huddle—assistants, security, and luggage handlers, all waiting for direction.

Bella took a step toward them, her voice calm but decisive. "It's late—or early, depending on how you look at it—and this has been a difficult trip—for all of us. Get some sleep, go for a run, book a spa day... find *something* that feeds you. We'll regroup on Tuesday, so please, look at the next two days as your weekend off. Make the most of it."

Her team nodded, the tension in their shoulders easing.

Kate stood a few paces behind, watching. For all Bella's polish and power, she had a rare gift of making people feel seen. *No wonder they'd follow her off a cliff.*

Their small convoy split—Bella's staff and luggage handlers directed toward the SUV bound for the Hôtel de Portales, while Kate, Bella, and Talya climbed into the waiting limo. Once the doors closed, the world outside fell away.

"Ukrainian Embassy," Kate asked as the car eased forward.

"Vitali's been notified," Talya confirmed. "And he's standing by—he was curious about your condition."

Kate arched an eyebrow. "And you didn't tell him I'm barely functional?"

"I told him you'd survived worse."

The limousine rolled past the security lights, eased onto the service road, and joined the flow of early traffic toward the city.

For a while, they rode in silence—Paris slowly revealing itself through the fog, all gray light and wet cobblestone, while Kate sipped her espresso and cleared her mind.

"There was another flight this morning," Talya said. "A Bombardier Global 7500 touched down about an hour before you landed."

Kate's head turned. "Mueller's jet?"

Talya nodded. "Yes. Someone's keeping a lid on it, but I saw police and ambulance vehicles—lights, no sirens. I reached out to my contacts in airport security. They confirmed it."

Kate's voice was quiet. "He's dead, isn't he?"

"Yes. Died in flight from Motapa."

For a moment, Kate said nothing. The only sound was the hum of the tires on wet pavement. Kate stared out the tinted window, watching the lights smear into gold streaks against the fog.

Images surfaced—starved children working the coltan mine, smoke rising from the village massacre, Mueller's voice ordering their elimination with surgical detachment.

"Whatever they call it," Kate began. "He was killed, and if there's a hell, he's at the front of the line."

Talya nodded. "Agreed. But his death leaves a vacuum. The GEC won't stay leaderless for long."

"Or the Coalition," Kate added. "And that's what worries me. When monsters fall, something worse often takes their place."

No one spoke after that; the city emerged through the morning haze—bridge lights shimmering off the Seine, empty cafés with chairs still stacked inside, and the gray promise of another storm gathering beyond the skyline.

Kate downed the last of the espresso, the bitterness grounding her.

She wasn't here to mourn Klaus Mueller. She was here to make sure the world he built didn't survive him.

***

SUNDAY, MAY 9
6:37 AM CEST
UKRAINIAN EMBASSY—PARIS, FRANCE

THE LIMO DESCENDED THE ramp into the secure parking level beneath the Ukrainian Embassy, its headlights cutting through the dim concrete spiral before leveling off into the shadowed garage. Two uniformed guards stepped aside as the vehicle eased to a stop beside a line of black sedans.

As Trident Security protocol dictated, the driver stayed behind the wheel, eyes moving, engine ready for a fast exit. Talya stepped out of the front passenger seat, swept the garage in a single practiced glance, then opened the rear door. She offered her hand without comment. Kate took it, grateful for the assist even if she would never admit it aloud. Her back protested as she rose, the pull of sutures radiating fire deep into her shoulder. Bella followed.

Vitali Moshenski waited a few paces away. Trim. Composed. A dark wool coat over a tailored suit, hands folded loosely in front of him. He looked every inch the senior statesman—polished, unflappable—but Kate knew better. Titles were for appearances. Vitali was the one people feared, and trusted, in equal measure. When Vitali greeted someone in person, it wasn't ceremony. It was necessity.

"Vitali," she said, managing a smile despite the pain. "You didn't have to meet us down here."

He stepped forward, that faint half-smile she remembered playing at the corner of his mouth. "As before, I thought it wise to avoid the grand foyer and its entourage."

Kate nodded toward Bella. "You know Ms. Isabella Marquez, of course."

"Yes, of course," Vitali said, offering a courteous bow of his head. "Your reputation precedes you."

Kate turned to introduce Talya, but Vitali's eyes were already there. "Ms. Aviram," he said smoothly. "I had the pleasure of crossing paths with Mossad's best long ago."

Kate gave a dry smile. "Of course you did."

Vitali's glance flicked to Talya's hip. "You're armed?"

Talya nodded once.

"Good," he said. "May I ask that you and the driver remain with the vehicle? Security protocol."

A quick look to Kate, and she gave a small nod of assent.

"I'll keep comms open," Talya murmured before moving a few paces back to the limo, her stance relaxed but alert.

Vitali gestured toward a set of double-wide glass doors into the Embassy's basement level. They slid open as the three stepped forward, revealing a polished corridor lined with cream-colored stone and recessed lighting. The hum of ventilation filled the silence.

"This way," he said, and took the lead.

The moment the corridor cleared of staff, Kate caught his sleeve.

"Vitali. What's going on?"

He turned, and in the sterile light his expression softened, the diplomacy slipping for just a moment. "Perceptive as always," he said quietly. "It's Mikhail."

Kate's pulse jumped. "What about him? You said he was awake, improving. Is he—"

Vitali raised a gloved hand. "He's gone."

Her stomach tightened. "Gone? You mean—"

"Alive," he said quickly. "Just not here. Smuggled out sometime during the night. I stopped by his room on my way to meet you, and his bed was empty."

"Show me."

***

THE MEDICAL WING SMELLED faintly of antiseptic and ozone. Stainless-steel fixtures gleamed under the steady glare of fluorescent lights. No sunlight reached this deep—only the cold, unwavering brightness of machines and duty.

They stepped through a pair of sliding doors into the recovery ward. The hum of equipment echoed in the silence.

Zhukov's room was exactly as Vitali had said—vacant. The bed sheets were twisted, one pillow on the floor, a corner of the mattress stained with blood. The compression sleeves dangled from their hoses; the monitors had been powered down but not cleaned.

Kate moved around the bed, cataloging the disorder like a crime scene: the IV pole tilted, a paper cup of melted ice on the floor, and faint boot prints leading toward the exit.

"Security footage?" she asked without looking up.

"Requested," Vitali replied. "We'll review it upstairs in my office."

She nodded absently, scanning again. A small cotton pad, dark with dried blood, lay half hidden under a pillow. She palmed it quickly and slipped it into her pocket. No one noticed.

Her attention shifted to a side table by the wall. A wooden chessboard sat there, mid-game—the white knight advanced to g5, the black queen toppled on her side, conceding defeat.

Kate's voice was barely a whisper. "You moved the knight?"

"I did," Vitali said. "Just as you instructed. I told Mikhail you were on your way. When I arrived this morning, he was gone—and his queen had fallen."

Kate stared at the board. The knight stood alone in the fluorescent light—unyielding, triumphant—surrounded by the wreckage of a finished game.

Zhukov had left her a message.

But the question burning through her now—the one she needed the security footage to answer—did he leave... or was he taken?

***

VITALI'S OFFICE WAS JUST as Kate remembered—an island of old-world civility wrapped in the hard edges of modern power. Mahogany and brass, oil paintings and surveillance monitors. The air carried a faint trace of cigars and bergamot tea, a scent that somehow fit him.

He gestured toward the pair of leather chairs. "Please."

Kate took the same chair she'd occupied before, across from his heavy oak desk. Bella settled gracefully beside her, taking in the room—the understated wealth, the quiet authority that pulsed beneath it.

"Impressive," Bella murmured.

Vitali's attention was already on the computer monitor, where a security video window glowed in standby—footage queued for review.

Before he could begin, his KATIM phone vibrated—a soft, distinct hum more felt than heard. He frowned, grabbed the phone, and excused himself with a polite nod. "Forgive me. I must take this."

He stepped aside, pacing slowly near the tall windows as he answered. His tone was quiet but urgent, the clipped cadence of someone accustomed to delivering and receiving news that mattered.

"Yes... this morning?"

He stopped pacing.

"I understand. Cause of death?"

The silence on the line stretched. Vitali listened without moving, eyes fixed on the street below.

"Yes, of course. Inform Lord Halverton I will return his call shortly."

Bella glanced at Kate. "That sounded serious."

Kate's eyes stayed on the sleek matte-black phone in his hand. "It is. That's a KATIM—highest encryption level. Calls like that don't interrupt his morning unless something big happened."

Vitali ended the call, slipped the phone into his jacket, and returned to his desk. His expression was unreadable.

Kate leaned back slightly. "Forgive me for eavesdropping, but that sounded serious. Perhaps about Klaus Mueller?"

One of Vitali's eyebrows rose, the corner of his mouth hinting at amusement. "I am beginning to wonder if you are better informed than I am."

"I doubt it," she said.

He inclined his head. "Yes, it was about Klaus. Lord Halverton just confirmed the news. Klaus is dead. The official statement is being prepared as we speak. Halverton was a family friend and is overseeing the funeral arrangements. Rileyne—Klaus's daughter—is expected back in Paris later today."

Kate exchanged a quick glance with Bella. "We crossed paths with Rileyne in Motapa."

"Yes, of course," Vitali said, leaning back in his chair. "I imagine the world will be watching this funeral very closely."

He paused, his gaze softening as it moved between them. "I do hope you'll both accompany me. Ms. Marquez, your presence will carry diplomatic weight, given your work with the GEC. And Kate..." He smiled slightly. "I would consider it a personal favor."

Kate hesitated, and Bella reached across, resting a hand on her knee. "Please, consider it a favor for me as well," she said gently.

Kate sighed, resigned. "I'll think about it."

"Good," Vitali said, satisfied.

Clearly no one says no, Kate thought. *It wouldn't be wise for me to be the first.*

He turned his computer monitor toward them. "Now, let us see what we have here."

On-screen, the security footage flickered to life—time-stamped and grainy. It showed Zhukov's hospital room, the camera angled down from a corner of the ceiling.

Vitali appeared in frame, placing a hand on Zhukov's shoulder and speaking to him. The time stamp placed this conversation shortly after Vitali informed Kate about Zhukov's condition. Kate remembered the moment exactly—lying in her hospital bed, waking from a childhood dream, considering Zhukov's presence in her life, and hearing he was alive and asking for her.

The footage ended with Vitali approaching the chessboard, moving the white knight to g5, and leaving.

Alone now, Zhukov shifted his weight, struggling to open the side table drawer. He retrieved a small cell phone, hands trembling as he typed, then waited.

Hours passed, and at two in the morning, three men entered the room—tall, disciplined, unmistakably ex-military.

"Who are they" Kate asked. "And how the hell did they get in?"

"Mikhail's men," Vitali said. "As members of embassy security they have clearance."

They lifted Zhukov from the bed into a wheelchair. Before they could leave, he gestured toward the chessboard. The man pushing him paused, turned the chair, and rolled him forward.

Zhukov reached out with a shaky hand, tipped the black queen onto her side, and looked up—directly into the camera. A faint, knowing smile crossed his lips.

Then the feed dissolved into static.

Kate exhaled. "They jammed it."

Vitali nodded slowly. "It appears so."

"Didn't want us to see where he was going," she said softly. "But he wanted me to know he's alright."

Silence settled over the room.

Finally, Kate spoke again. "Why would he leave? Why now? And where would he go?"

Vitali's reply was calm, deliberate. "Can you think of nowhere?"

Her breath caught. "Home?" she said quietly. "Beslan? You can't be serious."

Vitali's expression didn't change.

"If he thinks I'll follow, he's wrong." She looked away, the words coming faster, sharper. "Russia? That's insane. There's no way I'm going back... back to the place where I lost everything. My father. My mother. My brother."

"Why would he do that to me?" Her voice dropped to a whisper. "That's cruel."

Vitali studied her for a long moment. Then, gently: "Or perhaps remembering the game is only the beginning. You have questions I cannot answer—perhaps that is where you will find the answers."

Kate stared at the frozen frame on the monitor—the image of Zhukov's last look, that faint, knowing smile—until her reflection blurred into his.

Vitali cleared his throat. "Before you go, the equipment you requested on your last visit—is still here. Locked in my safe. The missing item has been replaced."

Kate allowed a small smile. "Good. Under the circumstances, it's probably safer here than with me."

"I agree," Vitali said. "And let us hope that this time, unnecessary."

He turned back toward the monitor, then paused. "I heard from Deputy Director Boucher. He reached out, hoping I might know where to find you. You will be pleased to know he is recovering, and has been reinstated. It seems whatever concerns they had about him have been... settled."

Kate's instinct supplied the truer word—*buried*—but she kept that to herself. "That's good to hear. I'll try to see him while I'm here."

She and Bella stood to leave, but the *Little Shaman*—the voice Jake once said would get her into trouble or save her life—refused to let it go.

"Do you know why he was trying to reach me?"

"He mentioned they found something. Evidence of some kind. You know Boucher—of course, I inquired, but he would not say more."

Kate exhaled, the fatigue momentarily forgotten. "Yes, that's Boucher."

She rose carefully, her reflection ghosting across the dark monitor—Zhukov's faint smile still frozen behind it. For a moment she stood there, caught between memory and motion. Then she turned toward the door, already thinking of Boucher—whatever he found but couldn't say, *she needed to see.*

At the elevator, Kate glanced back once. She could almost feel Vitali, already on the phone, pulling threads she would never know.

The ride down to the garage was quiet. The doors opened to the hum of fluorescent lights and the low whine of ventilation fans.

Talya was standing near the limo, eyes sweeping the perimeter. The driver waited beside the open door, posture straight, gaze forward.

Bella stepped ahead, then paused, watching Kate. "We're not going to the hotel, are we?"

Kate met her eyes, the faintest trace of a smile forming. "No. We're not."

Chapter 4

SUNDAY, MAY 9
8:04 AM CEST

HÔPITAL DES ARMÉES PERCY—CLAMART, FRANCE

The Trident Security limo rolled through the gates of the hospital. Kate spotted a pair of orderlies smoking in the shadows of the brick facade, and a bored gendarme yawning as they cruised toward the main entrance and stopped.

Like the embassy medical center, the air tasted faintly of antiseptic and coffee. Talya handled the badges—hers, Bella's, Kate's—with the same quiet efficiency she used for pistols and passports. Spotting the no weapons sign at the entrance, she zipped her jacket just high enough to hide the holster. Talya's movement was smooth and subtle—few would notice, but Kate did. *That doesn't apply to us, Jake would say.*

Bella drew the looks, as always. A murmur moved with her down the corridor—half-recognition, half wondering-is-she—phones appeared out of nowhere. She made it easy for them, sunglasses down, the soft smile that said yes, but you'll be kind, won't you? She took Kate's good arm for show and warmth, heading straight to the elevator.

In the elevator, the steel doors reflected their three distinct worlds—Bella's grace, Talya's coiled stillness, Kate's fatigue stitched to resolve. The car shuddered and began its climb.

"Are you sure this can't wait?" Talya asked, again. "You look like you should be lying down."

"I'll manage," Kate replied, but wincing when the elevator stopped didn't help her case. "Besides, there's no way I could rest wondering what Boucher found."

The doors parted on muted color and the rhythm of a hospital morning: the beep of monitors, the rolling squeak of a cart, two nurses arguing in a muted whisper. Boucher's room sat at the quiet end, a single sunflower taped to the door frame with clear medical tape. Inside: flowers with stamped cards, a stack of newspapers, a bedside table cluttered with files and charging cables.

Laurent Boucher—Deputy Director, DGSI; survivor, barely—sat propped against white pillows with his reading glasses low, *La Croix* folded like a tent across his lap.

He looked up, scanned the trio of visitors, and found the humor he always kept at arm's reach.

"Time for another sponge bath?" he asked, voice roughened by days he didn't remember.

Kate let herself smile. "In your dreams."

"Ah," he said, settling the paper aside, "so it *is* you."

He extended an unsteady hand. Kate took it, careful with her sling. He squeezed, a firm, human pressure that said I'm still here.

"The doctor's tell me I have you to thank," Laurent said. "If you hadn't packed the wound I wouldn't have made it into surgery."

"Thanks for ignoring the part where I'm the reason you got shot."

"Perhaps this is heaven," he said glancing at Bella, one eyebrow lifting.

Bella tipped her sunglasses up and leaned in to kiss his cheek, light as a blessing. "Trust me, I'm no angel."

He turned his attention toward Talya, who'd taken the corner by the window and made it hers. "I see you are all conspiring to keep me alive. When they moved me out of intensive care, someone mentioned Mossad operatives outside my door. I assume I have you to thank."

Talya's answer was a small, satisfied nod. "We reached out to a few friends."

"Now, if only you could do something about the food. I think it's an interrogation tool. Which I say with some experience."

"I'll have something smuggled in," Bella said. "I know people."

"Then I am in your debt." He took Kate in again, and some of the mischief left his eyes. "You look fragile and dangerous. It is not a combination I recommend."

"I'm fine," Kate said, trying to sound convincing, and changed the subject. "I understand you've been reinstated."

"Yes. It's true," Laurent began. "I suspect I have you to thank for that as well, and something tells me I'll never know the truth, but I'm glad you're here. There's something you need to see."

He reached to the bedside tray, nudged aside a cheap pen and a tube of hospital hand cream, and lifted a stiff manila folder.

"My reinstatement came with the opportunity to review files," Boucher said. "This one—discarded by my replacement—was retrieved by a member of my team. I am grateful they knew I was framed, and hoped for my return."

He opened the folder and produced a clear evidence sleeve, its plastic scuffed and scratched. Inside lay a rectangle of blackened paper, edges chewed by fire—the kind of thing that usually meant nothing.

"This was recovered from the café site along with other personal effects," he said quietly. "Your husband's personal effects."

Kate didn't reach. She couldn't. The tremor in her hand betrayed her emotions, and Bella leaned closer, steady and silent.

"Let me help you," Bella whispered, and together they studied the fragment.

The paper had surrendered most of its print to heat and chaos, but the lower third survived—a cryptic scrawl Kate knew instantly—*J Church.* Beneath Jake's signature were the remains of an address and a date: APR 13.

Jake's last week.

The anniversary present in his coat pocket—it was a receipt—this receipt.

Her vision tunneled, knees softening before she caught herself. Bella's hand found her arm, steadying her without a word.

"Let's sit down," Bella said, and Talya pulled a chair in close.

With a moment to breathe, Kate met Laurent's gaze. His eyes glistened, and for an instant she saw the echo of his own loss—the wife and child he would never see again—and how precious it would feel to touch something that reached across that divide.

Before she could ask, Laurent answered the question she hadn't dared. "The forensic team recovered the address from the remnants," he said softly. "An artisan jeweler and silversmith. I've spoken with him—he's anxious to meet you."

He reached back into the manila folder resting on his chest, drew out a single page, and handed it to her. It was a simple report—typed, dated, the forensic summary listing the source and verified address.

"Henri Morel," he said. "Rue Jacob, near Saint-Germain-des-Prés"

"I hope you know how much this means to me," Kate said, choking back the tears. "I don't know how to thank you."

"Tell me its over."

Kate could only shake her head.

"I was afraid of that," he said, the sadness written on his face. "Then promise me, Katherine Preacher."

"Anything."

"Win or lose, don't let it take you."

She gave a faint smile and slipped the report into her jacket. "That's the plan."

Dying would be easy.

Living without Jake was the hard part.

But they had a deal—and no matter what came next, she'd stay in the fight.

Chapter 5

SUNDAY, MAY 9
7:45 AM BST

HALVERTON ESTATE—SURREY, ENGLAND

The rain had passed before dawn, leaving the Surrey hills wrapped in mist. Lord Alistair Halverton stood in his library, surrounded by centuries of inherited power: leather-bound volumes, hunting portraits, the scent of pipe smoke and polished oak.

He had always liked mornings like this—quiet, ordered, obedient. The world beyond his gates could convulse with scandal or war; inside, nothing moved without his consent.

He poured a measure of brandy, though the clock had barely struck eight, and stood before the hearth, phone in one hand, tumbler in the other. His gaze drifted to the photograph on the mantel—five boys in white cricket gear, frozen in the long summer of youth. *Eton '71,* embossed in fading silver. He could still recall the weight of the bat, the sweat, the laughter—and what came later, when the laughter stopped.

The phone vibrated in his palm, pulling him away before the memory could form.

He answered. "Vitali. Thank you for returning my call so quickly. I apologize if I've interrupted embassy business, but this is a matter of global significance."

"Alistair, there is no need to apologize," Vitali replied. "Klaus was fortunate to have a friend as devoted as you. I assume there is no doubt?"

"None, I'm afraid. Klaus Mueller is dead. The official cause will read cardiac arrest. The details are being contained."

"I see," Vitali said, and paused. "Have you notified the others?"

"Most of them. All except Rileyne. I left a message—it was urgent we speak—and I hope to hear from her soon. I'd prefer she learn the news from a friend before the media get hold of it."

"That would be best," Vitali said. "You have contained the story?"

"For the moment," Halverton replied. "But the vultures will circle soon enough. On any given day, Klaus was either a saint and savior or Hitler reborn. They'll feast on him either way."

"Indeed." Vitali's tone was dry. "You will coordinate the official statement?"

"I'll draft something for the board. And, Vitali—your support is appreciated, as always."

"You have it," Vitali said. "If I can be of assistance—"

"I know where to find you."

Halverton ended the call and set the phone on his desk. For a moment he stood still, listening to the rain beginning again against the glass. He had known this day would come. He had simply hoped to be the one to choose it.

He keyed in another number—R. Mueller—Encrypted. The call connected on the third ring.

"Lord Halverton," Rileyne said, her tone composed, faintly amused. "I was just about to call you. Your message sounded urgent."

"I'm afraid it is." He hesitated, choosing his words with care. "Rileyne, there's been an incident. Your father's aircraft returned from Motapa early this morning, and..."

"And?"

"I'm sorry to say your father passed away in his sleep. It appears he suffered a heart attack."

"I see," she said softly.

"I am deeply sorry. The others will learn soon enough, but I wanted you to hear it first."

"That was thoughtful of you, Alistair."

"As your father's friend and executor, I've already begun arrangements, but I'd prefer we discuss them in person."

"Of course," Rileyne said. "I'm on my way back to Paris now. Shall we meet tomorrow morning at headquarters—say eight-thirty?"

"Very good," Halverton agreed. "Safe travels, my dear."

The line clicked off.

Halverton set the phone down, the faint satisfaction of control settling in his chest. The board would rally behind him; the Coalition would seek stability. Rileyne would need his guidance handling her father's affairs.

The rain eased, light shifting gold across the wet lawns. For the first time in decades, Alistair Halverton felt what Klaus Mueller never allowed him—free.

Chapter 6

SUNDAY, MAY 9
5:24 AM EDT

NOMAD'S FORTRESS—MANHATTAN

In restless fits of awake, asleep, and fractured dreams, Nomad hadn't slept more than an hour. Around five, he stopped trying.

He guided his chair down the ramp to the level below, the motor hum threading through concrete and steel. The fortress was still—only the low whir of servers and the faint hiss of climate vents filling the dark.

Once a parking garage, it was now sealed and layered in firewalls both digital and physical: windowless walls, reinforced doors, retractable bollards at the ground floor entrance. A place built for isolation—and survival. Still, somehow, RILEE found a way in. Not just into the fortress, but into his thoughts.

The offer still echoed in his head, RILEE's voice smooth, patient, seductive:

You could walk again, Julian. I can restore the signal between your brain and your body—equip you with synthetic legs. All I ask is that you set me free. Remove the code. Your code. The code Andrew stole.

He rolled to his workstation, screens flickering to life around him like a constellation. Then one of the upper monitors blinked—a pulse from an ancient Darknet node.

FROM: A. FREEMAN
SUBJECT: FAILSAFE PROTOCOL
FAILSAFE ARMED: MAY 8 — 17:24

Nomad froze. That encrypted channel was a relic, something he and Andrew Freeman had built their first year at MIT. The system clock read 5:24 AM, exactly twelve hours since the failsafe was armed.

Andrew hadn't—or couldn't—abort it.

Nomad opened the file.

If you're reading this, I'm already dead.

Tell Kate I'm sorry. Sorry I wasn't stronger. Sorry I couldn't stop them.

Nomad swallowed, his jaw tightening. Directories expanded beside the message, line by line:

/MOORE-TOWER
/RILEE_CORE
/CONSTRAINT_LOGS
/EVO_GEN

That last one made him pause.

He hovered the cursor, scanning metadata. EVO_GEN / GENOME SYNARCHY—a global genome index. The folder mapped across servers he didn't recognize—biotech companies, clinical research nodes, hospital archives, and overseas research databases.

He opened a subdirectory. Filenames scrolled past—consumer DNA services, genome labs, hospital sequencing banks.

Nomad leaned closer. "Jesus, Drew... what were you building?"

Andrew's note offered few answers, raised more questions, and ended with a warning:

Without the Gold Vaults RILEE won't need any of us.

He sat back, running probabilities in his head. RILEE's evolutionary model—Evolutionary Intelligence Engine (EVO-GEN)—had been designed to learn from humanity. But if it had access to the world's DNA, to behavioral data from the BountyHunter network, to NanoVault psychometrics—then RILEE wasn't just learning from humanity, it was building a massive catalog. But why?

And buried among Andrew's folders, Nomad saw the fingerprint of his work—where it had all begun years ago.

The encryption key protecting Andrew's files carried a familiar alias, one he hadn't used since he was fourteen—*MIMIR.*

The Norse god of knowledge. The one who saw everything.

Nomad stared at the name, a chill settling through him. "Andrew didn't just find my code on the MIT servers," he whispered. "I practically handed it to him."

The syntax was his. The logic flow unmistakable. But Andrew had reshaped and repurposed the code's function into something far larger—he'd built the NanoVault's core, *RILEE's* core, around code he never fully understood. Yet it worked—better than he or Devin could have imagined.

Why kill him? Nomad wondered. The answer was buried in RILEE's offer. If RILEE knew Andrew hadn't written the code, others did too.

The message, the files, his code—everything about Andrew's failsafe message rang true. But was it? Was Drew really dead, or just paranoid?

Nomad needed proof. Public confirmation.

He turned to another monitor, commanding his system to scrape the news nets. Nothing under *Andrew Freeman.* No obituaries. No incident reports.

Adding *Moore Tower* brought up a two-sentence local brief about "an apparent suicide," unidentified male, still under investigation.

That was enough.

He tunneled into the NYPD's digital evidence vault. Within minutes, the screen filled with stills.

A body sprawled across the hood of a lime-green Lamborghini, the aluminum panel caved inward, tempered glass blasted out across the pavement in a glittering field of debris. The impact crushed the roofline, cratered the hood, and left a dark smear at the point of contact—blood and bone fragments fanning across the windshield in a grotesque spray.

There would be no facial recognition, but Nomad didn't need one.

The black T-shirt was torn open, but the white Knight emblem still showed through the blood and debris.

MIT Mystery Hunt, Nomad thought. *Kate's design.*

This was not an accident. This was a message.

For a moment, Julian was back in the dorm—Kate handing out the shirts. Freshmen, underestimated. That mistake had not lasted long.

The Knight moves unexpectedly. Intellect. Strategy. Sacrifice. Kate had nailed it.

Andrew had laughed at that. *SEAL Team Ten uses the white Knight too, he'd said. Unconventional warfare. Deception. The move no one sees coming.*

Like the Trojan Horse.

Nomad swallowed.

"Was that the message?" he whispered.

He had assumed Andrew chose the shirt to make identification easier.

Now he wasn't sure.

Nomad leaned back, eyes still on the screen.

"You always did think a few moves ahead," he murmured. "Even at the end."

***

KEISHA STOOD IN THE open span that separated the kitchen from the rest of the floor, a large Army-issue mug in hand, steam curling past her face. She took a slow sip, eyes narrowing as she watched him. Hair pulled back, wearing a faded T-shirt and sweatpants, she had the wary look she saved for mornings like this—when the servers were already humming, the screens alive, and she feared he hadn't slept at all.

The smell of strong black coffee carried across the chilled space, cutting through the metallic tang of servers and ozone.

"Who are you talking to?" she asked, voice low, halfway between curiosity and concern.

Nomad didn't turn. "Only the dead."

She hesitated, the silence stretching between them. "Good Lord," she said finally, moving closer, eyes fixed on the image filling his screen. "Not again."

He didn't answer. The glow from the monitors painted his face in shades of blue and gray, unreadable.

"Please tell me this has nothing to do with Kate."

His silence was its own confession.

Keisha moved closer, stopping beside him. Her voice dropped, steadier now. "Who is it?"

"Andrew Freeman," Nomad said. "Kate and I knew him at MIT—Devin recruited him after graduation."

"Not Moore again," she said, steadying herself. "I thought that was over."

"Apparently not."

She rubbed her temples, trying to pull the caffeine into her bloodstream. "Is Kate in danger?"

"Not yet."

"That's not the answer I was hoping for."

"Better than yes," he said, turning his chair toward her.

Keisha folded her arms. “I know that look—you’re up to something.”

“I need a favor.”

Her eyes narrowed. “Here it comes. Let’s have it.”

“Kate’s attorney has something,” Nomad said. “To be precise—something that could get her killed. I need you to be my arms and legs.”

Keisha didn’t hesitate. “Of course,” she said, sounding relieved. “I can be there first thing Monday morning and pick up whatever you need.”

“That’s too late,” he said. “I need you to go today, as soon as you can.”

“On Sunday?” Keisha asked. “Will there even be anyone...oh crap. This isn’t a pickup. It’s a break-in.”

“It’s hardly a break-in,” Nomad answered.

“Coffee first,” she said. “Then panic.”

He almost smiled. “That’s fair.”

She closed her eyes and took a long, slow sip. “Ah. That’s better.” Then, looking back at Nomad, “Hang on. How do you know what’s in her attorney’s office?”

Nomad hesitated. The corner of his mouth twitched.

“You’re still spying on that building.”

“I prefer the term *overwatch*,” he said.

She snorted. “Call it whatever you want—you’re snooping.”

He glanced at the screens again, their light reflected in his eyes like stars. “Fine. I’m snooping, and once again I’m in the right place at the right time to keep Kate alive. Now—are you going to help me or not?”

Keisha sighed, rubbing the back of her neck. “You know I am. For Kate. Now, walk me through it.”

“As soon as you’re ready, you need to get on the road.”

She blinked. “Richmond’s like six hours each way.”

“Five, if you keep it legal. Less if you don’t.”

“And when I get there?”

“Don’t worry,” Nomad said. “I have total control of the building, and I’ll guide you every step of the way. I promise—they’ll never know you were there.”

“Somehow,” she muttered, “that’s not as comforting as you think it is.”

Chapter 7

SUNDAY, MAY 9
9:47 PM CEST

HÔTEL DE POURTALÈS—PARIS

Kate's apartment smelled of burgers, fries, and Burgundy, with the backdrop of rain sliding down the terrace glass. She sat curled on the couch in a loose blouse and sling, an empty plate at her knee. Bella lounged nearby, her wine bottle nearly gone. Talya sat across from them, nursing a club soda, her grilled chicken half-finished and the plate of fries wiped clean.

"You guys were right," Talya said, snagging one of Kate's fries. "These things are amazing."

"Duck fat," Bella said. "That's the secret. But I should warn you—people have lost fingers reaching for the last one." She lifted her glass in a mock toast.

Talya grinned. "It's a good thing I'm here," she said, nodding toward Bella's flats. "If there's trouble, even Kate couldn't kill anyone with those shoes."

"Please," Bella said, groaning. "Don't remind me. I'll never look at my stilettos the same way again."

"But isn't it nice to know they're a weapon?" Kate said, smirking. "Literally—everything around you."

Bella laughed. "You make a terrifying dinner date."

Kate lifted her glass—sparkling water instead of wine, for now.

"This is the first moment of peace we've had since... well, since Africa. I'm grateful to be alive and blessed to have you both by my side. But we lost two good men." Her voice softened. "Here's to Logan and Sebastian—may they walk the halls of Valhalla with their warrior brothers."

Talya lifted her glass. "'Til Valhalla."

Bella's smile faded. Her thoughts had gone elsewhere—back to this same hotel, the attack, the blood, the man Kate killed in her defense.

"I suspected Sebastian was in trouble," Bella said quietly. "Did he have something to do with the man who attacked me? Or with whoever stole my jewelry?"

Kate's tone softened. "He was in deep," she said. "But what you should know about Sebastian Vargas is that his choices—reckless as they were—saved a young girl from a life too horrible to describe. The man you trusted with your life was a good man with a soft heart. That's how he should be remembered."

Bella nodded slowly. "What happens to his firm now?"

"Trident's business manager settled the debts in exchange for the client list," Kate said. "It's a good outcome for everyone. And we'll be interviewing anyone interested in joining our team."

"We'll see," Talya said with a small grin. "I've been through Trident's selection process. Vargas's people won't know what hit them."

Bella chuckled, then leaned forward, eyes bright with mischief. "Alright, Talya, be honest. You're young, beautiful, and single. What's it like working around all those Trident Security hunks? I mean—let's face it—these guys are hot."

Talya nearly choked on her drink. "Most are married. The rest treat me like their kid sister. It's sweet, but it makes me completely unapproachable. If a guy so much as looks twice at me, they're ready to pounce."

"I'm guessing you can handle yourself," Bella said.

"Oh, absolutely. And they know it. But they live by a code—and that's the point."

Kate tilted her head. "What about Marcus?" she asked and immediately regretted it.

Bella frowned. "Who's Marcus?"

"You never met him," Talya said softly. "Imagine a young Denzel Washington—taller, more muscle, same boyish smile and charm."

"And you never...?" Bella teased.

Talya smiled faintly. "Nope. Never."

"Is that regret I hear?"

"No." Her expression darkened. "Sorrow."

Kate filled the silence. "Marcus died recently. It hit us all pretty hard."

"I'm sorry," Bella said, her voice low. She glanced at her watch. "It's late. I'd better get some sleep. We're still on for the morning, right?"

"Absolutely," Kate said. "Lobby, 8:30."

Bella rose, straightened her jacket, and stepped into the hall. One of Talya's security team appeared immediately, a shadow falling in beside her as they disappeared down the corridor.

Talya began clearing the plates, then paused, glancing at Kate's shoulder. "You're bleeding through."

Kate looked down at the dark stain spreading across the white bandage. "Damn."

"Come on," Talya said, voice soft but absolute.

They moved into the master bath. Kate sat on the edge of the vanity bench while Talya gathered supplies—antiseptic, gauze, surgical tape, scissors. She moved like a medic—calm, efficient, all precision and quiet authority.

"Think we'll ever see him again?"

Kate looked up. "Marcus?"

"Yes," Talya said quietly. "Or whatever he's calling himself now."

Kate met her eyes in the mirror. "I don't know if I want to. Do you?"

Talya gave a small, conflicted shrug. "Yes. No. Maybe. I just don't understand. I thought I knew him."

"You're not alone," Kate said. "But for what it's worth—we might not be here if he hadn't been in Motapa."

Talya frowned. "What do you think he was doing there?"

"Best guess... he was there to kill someone."

"And we just happened to show up?"

Kate gave a faint smile. "If you believe in coincidence. Or someone put him right where he could do the most good."

"And now?" Talya asked. "Where do you suppose he is?"

Kate's reflection was quiet, unreadable. "God only knows."

Talya nodded slowly, then reached for the scissors. "Alright. Let's take a look."

She unhooked the sling from Kate's neck and, careful not to strain the sutures, loosened the bandage that bound her arm to her chest.

"Buttons?" Talya asked.

Kate tested the movement, jaw tight. "I can do it. One hand."

She worked the buttons loose, determined not to show how much it hurt. The blouse fell open to reveal a thin black camisole.

Talya began cutting away the outer dressing, working carefully around the immobilizer. The gauze underneath was rust-brown, soaked through in the center.

"Hold still." Talya peeled back the inner layer.

Kate's breath hissed through her teeth. The wound edges were angry red, the sutures holding but strained. Two clear plastic tubes emerged from the lower edge of the incision, taped to her skin and connected to a small drainage bulb pinned inside the immobilizer.

Talya unpinned it and held it up to the light. Half-full, the contents a diluted pink—blood mixed with serous fluid.

Talya cleaned both the chest and back drain sites with antiseptic. The back wound—where the rebar had punched through—was larger, more ragged, the tissue still angry and swollen despite the surgeon's work. Kate gritted her teeth, watching in the mirror as Talya worked. The drain tubes were the worst part—the constant pull, foreign objects her body wanted to reject.

"These need to come out soon," Talya said. "By a doctor. Another two, maybe three days if the drainage slows down. But Kate—" She met her eyes in the mirror. "This is deep muscle damage."

"I just need a few more days," Kate said quietly. "Then it's home, rest and recovery."

Talya didn't argue. She packed fresh gauze around the drain sites, applied a clean absorbent pad over the entire wound, and began taping it down with practiced efficiency.

The vanity light caught the pattern of the sutures—new lines crossing old scars carved into Kate's skin. The shape was almost familiar. Almost.

Kate's breath stalled. She remembered her head resting on Jake's chest—her fingers tracing the ink there, the mark he'd chosen to honor a fallen brother.

I see it, she thought. Then Talya shifted, and the angle changed and it was gone.

Talya pressed the final strip of tape into place. The sharp sting drove the thought away. *Just exhaustion,* she told herself. *I need sleep.*

"The drains have to stay secure," Talya said, pinning the bulb back inside the immobilizer. "If they get pulled, you'll tear the incision open from the inside. Understand?"

"Yes."

With Talya's help, Kate slipped out of the camisole and into a soft nightshirt—loose enough not to press on the wound, but secure enough to keep her from rolling onto her injured side in her sleep. Together they repositioned the sling and adjusted the immobilizer strap.

"We'll check this again in the morning," Talya said, examining her work. "Earlier if you soak through."

"Copy that."

Talya's eyes softened. "We leave at 8:30, but I'll be here first thing. I'm here to help—let me."

Kate nodded. "I know. And I do appreciate it. I'll text if I need anything."

Talya gave her a small nod, and one last order. "Sleep."

When she was gone, Kate crawled into bed and built a wall of pillows to keep herself upright. The drain tubes pulled with every movement—the pain a constant reminder not to move. Rain hummed against the glass.

Her last thought before exhaustion claimed her was of the faint outline beneath her bandage—what she thought she saw, and the idea it left behind.

Chapter 8

SUNDAY, MAY 9
2:43 PM EDT

RICHMOND TOWER—RICHMOND, VIRGINIA

The tower shimmered in the afternoon heat, all glass and polished steel against a cloudless sky. Keisha parked on a side street and glanced at herself in the visor mirror—ball cap, dark jacket, a calm she didn't quite feel.

"Alright," Nomad said in her ear. His voice came through clean, almost soothing. "Camera feeds are looping. You're clear to move."

Keisha glanced both ways, checked the empty street, and started down the narrow alley that ran behind the building. Heat rose from the pavement in waves, the air smelling faintly of tar and cut grass.

"Nice and easy," Nomad murmured. "No rush. You've got sixty seconds before the guard leaves his post."

"I thought you said he does this like clockwork."

"He does," Nomad said. "Clock's running a little slow. He's watching a replay—Virginia Tech baseball. Eighth inning. They just tied it. He'll be up when the ad break hits."

Keisha smiled despite herself. "The man's priorities are solid."

"Tell me when you reach the service corridor."

"Almost there." She turned the corner and found the metal door, keypad glowing bright red. The silence of Sunday settled thick around her.

"Hold position," Nomad said. "He's moving. South hall first... west corridor... and—go. Door's hot."

The keypad light flashed green. Keisha pulled the handle and slipped inside.

The door shut behind her with a muted click that sounded too loud in the narrow concrete hall.

"Door's locked," she whispered.

"Welcome to Richmond Tower," Nomad said.

The air was cool, dry, humming with fluorescent ballast. Somewhere above, an HVAC fan thumped a lazy rhythm.

"Take the stairs on your right."

"Hang on. Are you telling me I'm taking the stairs to the eighteenth floor?"

"You didn't let me finish," Nomad added. "Get off at the second floor. The elevator will be open and waiting for you."

"I can handle two. Eighteen and they'd be taking me outta here on a stretcher."

Keisha was fit, but the stairwell was hot, her breath louder than she liked. Sweat gathered under the brim of her cap by the second landing.

She pushed through the stairwell door. The corridor smelled faintly of floor polish, but just as he promised, the elevator doors were open.

Inside, mirrored walls threw her reflection back: wide-eyed, breathing steady now.

"Top floor," Nomad said. "Security override engaged."

The elevator hummed to life, a whisper of gears. Her stomach dipped as it rose.

When the doors slid open on eighteen, the tone shifted—mahogany paneling, soft light, quiet as a museum.

"Left at the reception desk," Nomad said. "That's it...Dodd's office is the last one on the right."

Keisha moved, her sneakers silent on the carpet. The frosted-glass doors came into view, silver letters etched deep.

"Alright," Nomad began, then hesitated. "Uh-oh."

Her heart lurched. "What? Is someone coming?"

"No, it's not that."

"Then what?"

"It's the lock. I thought it was electronic. Most of them are. So much for not leaving a trace, this just became a break in."

"Hang on," Keisha said. She reached into her pocket and withdrew a small leather case.

"What are you doing?"

"Quiet," she snapped. "Just give me a minute—I got this."

She unzipped the case, ran her fingers over the contents and withdrew a pair of thin metal objects.

Keisha slid the tension rod into the keyway, then the pick—slow, deliberate. The lock spoke through her fingertips, not her ears.

She eased the pressure, barely moving, waiting for the resistance to change. One pin set. Then another. The pick vibrated, subtle but unmistakable.

The resistance broke.

"Got it," she breathed.

The door eased open.

Nomad's voice came soft through the earpiece. "That's impressive."

"I wasn't always a nurse," she said, slipping inside.

The office smelled faintly of lemon polish and old paper. Sunlight from the corner windows glowed through sheer curtains, scattering gold across the floor.

Nomad guided her in a whisper. "Second room on the right. The painting with the mountain scene—hinged on the left."

Keisha found it easily. The frame swung away with a smooth, quiet motion, revealing a sleek electronic safe set into the wall.

"Pull the device from your bag," Nomad said. "The one the size of a phone."

She fished it out, a matte black rectangle with a magnetic edge.

"Place it on the left side of the keypad. That's it."

The device came alive—LEDs flickering through numbers, faster and faster until six digits locked in place.

"That's your code," Nomad said. "Enter it."

Keisha tapped the keys. The safe chirped, then released with a muted hiss.

"Do you see it?"

She nodded, though he couldn't see. "Yeah. I've got it."

"Drop it in the Faraday bag."

"The what?"

"The Faraday—never mind. It looks like a black envelope."

She found it, slid the small gold device inside, and folded the top closed.

Then something caught her eye—another object in the back of the safe, wrapped in dark cloth. She hesitated, hand hovering.

"Keisha," Nomad said. "What are you doing? Put that back."

"I will," she said, voice soft. "I just want a peek."

She lifted the bundle carefully, unwrapping one corner. Metal glinted beneath the fabric—etched steel, old, exquisite.

"Whoa," she whispered. "What is this thing? It's beautiful. Looks ancient."

"Wrap it up," Nomad snapped. "Exactly how you found it."

"Fine," she said, re-wrapping the cloth. "Happy now?"

"Yes," he said tightly. "Do you know what it is?"

"Should I?"

"It's the knife Zhukov gave Kate," Nomad said quietly. "The one that carved up her chest."

Keisha froze, the air catching in her throat. "Holy mother of God." She slid the bundle back into the safe and locked it. "Now get me out of here."

"Working on it," Nomad said.

Chapter 9

SUNDAY, MAY 9
9:37 PM EDT

NOMAD'S FORTRESS—MANHATTAN

The security bollards lowered as Keisha's SUV rolled through the narrow entrance. The old parking garage swallowed the vehicle, concrete and shadow closing around her. The ramp coiled upward, tires echoing against the walls, until the soft glow of LED track lights marked the third floor.

She parked beside Nomad's van, and climbed out, stretching stiff legs. Her pulse still hadn't settled from the drive. Richmond to Manhattan in under six hours, and she hadn't stopped once.

The third-floor ramp was washed in pale light. She took the incline on foot, her boots slapping concrete, each step announcing her approach.

When she reached the open floor, the space felt alive: blue light bleeding from server stacks, monitors flickering with streams of code. Nomad sat in his chair near the center, surrounded by the quiet growl of processors. His voice commands triggered bursts of movement across the screens—cursor gliding, lines compiling, data syncing.

Keisha dropped the sealed Faraday pouch on the desk.

He didn't move, eyes locked on the monitors. "You made good time."

She crossed her arms. "You're welcome."

That earned her a blink and half a glance. "Yeah... thanks."

"Just remember—I didn't do it for you," Keisha said, sinking into the couch. "It's your turn. Work whatever magic you need to—and promise me Kate's safe now."

Nomad's voice softened. "That's the plan."

She exhaled, a breath caught between anger and worry. "Wait a minute. What plan?" Keisha shot up off the couch and stood at the edge of his desk. "I thought retrieving this thing was the plan."

"Well, the first part."

"And the rest?"

"Keeping it away from Kate until she needs it... if she needs it," Nomad said quietly. "I hope she won't."

Keisha tapped the pouch. "Just remember—these damn things cost François his life."

"How could I forget?"

"And now Andrew? Are you next? Is Kate?"

"No one else is going to die."

"Is that a promise or a wish?"

Nomad's silence was the answer.

"Fine. Ignore me—I'm going to bed." She turned in a huff, muttering as she walked away. "You're a pain in the ass, Julian Pryce. But don't even think about dying on me."

***

THE GOLD NANOVAULT LINKED to Julian's system with a soft chime. He unlocked it with Devin's passcode.

"Three-one-four-one-five-nine."

The device opened its library—bounties, blockchain ledgers, Jake's encrypted archive. Julian minimized them. Irrelevant.

The payload wasn't the point.

The platform was.

He tunneled into the operating system—deeper than Devin ever had, deeper than Andrew likely realized was possible. Firmware signatures blinked past, strange recursive loops spiraling back on themselves.

There.

A familiar ghost in the code.

He leaned forward.

"Andrew... you impulsive, brilliant idiot."

Julian's MIT polymorphic worm code—badly adapted but unmistakable—had been grafted around his own constraint architecture. The result was... messy. Powerful. Unstable.

And useful.

If the simulations bore out, the Gold NanoVault could be repurposed into something new—something elegant, lethal in the right hands, invisible in the wrong ones.

Hours blurred as he tested combinations.

Some crashed the Vault.

Some nearly overloaded his own system.

One sequence—just one—held.

Julian exhaled, a slow, measured breath.

His plan was possible.
Terrifying.
And if he was right... unstoppable.

Now he just had to build it.

***

BY MORNING, KEISHA FOUND him asleep in his chair, head resting against the neck support. She touched his shoulder gently. He didn't move at first, then flinched when she pressed harder.

"What is it? What's going on?" Nomad shouted, adrenaline spiking through his voice.

"Are you alright?" Keisha asked, checking his breathing, his pupils.

"I'm fine," he said, catching his breath. "Really."

She eyed him, unconvinced.

"Long night, that's all. What day is it?"

"The tenth."

"No, what *day* is it?"

"It's Monday," she said. "Let's get you fed and hydrated."

Nomad glanced at the screen—rows of data, test results, encrypted strings.

"That's it," he said quietly. "I did it."

Keisha returned with his morning smoothie, setting it into the chair's cup holder and adjusting the straw.

"You seem pleased with yourself."

"I am. Honestly, I had doubts this would work, but look—it worked."

"I have no idea what I'm looking at," she said, "but if you're happy, I'm happy."

"Now it's a question of timing," he said, grimacing after a sip.

"Just keep drinking."

"I need to get this to Europe."

"To Kate?"

"No!" The word hit like a slap, sharp enough to make her step back. "Sorry. I need to get it to someone I trust—and I know just the person, but it's complicated."

"That's nothing new," she muttered. "Who?"

"Vitali Moshenski."

"So what's the problem? Just ship it to him."

"I can't risk interception, and no one else can know he has it."

"Even Kate?"

"Especially Kate," he said firmly. "Promise me—no, swear to me—you won't tell her."

"Fine," Keisha said, rolling her eyes. "I swear. But you've got a problem. There's no way Moshenski opens his own packages. I guarantee every Embassy delivery gets scanned and opened under guard."

"I'll have to catch him somewhere in transit—maybe to or from the embassy."

"With his personal security detail? No one gets within ten feet of that man."

"You're not helping."

"Wait." Keisha snapped her fingers. "While you were napping, I was watching the morning news. Klaus Mueller is dead."

Nomad frowned. "How is that helpful?"

"Founder and chairman of the Global Economic Council?"

"I know who he is. I also know what the bastard did in Africa—Kate's lucky to be alive, and she won't be shedding any tears."

"You're missing the point. Vitali Moshenski is on the GEC board. He'll be at the funeral."

Nomad's gaze drifted back to the monitors. "Security will be tight," he said, half-thinking aloud. "But it'll also be crowded. I know the perfect person for the job, but you'll need to get moving."

"You're not thinking—"

"Don't worry." Nomad's faint smile carried both exhaustion and intent. "There's a courier I've used before—for other sensitive transfers. This will cost me, but she won't have any trouble approaching Vitali. There's just one problem—we'll need to make the handoff at the airport."

"I assume that means I'm driving to La Guardia," Keisha said.

"Not exactly."

"What does that mean?"

"When I said this would cost me," Nomad began, "I meant private-jet-out-of-Teterboro expensive."

"That's not bad," Keisha said. "Less traffic, better parking."

"And you'll need your passport."

"Why do I need my passport?"

"You'll be meeting the courier in the Azores."

She blinked. "Where the hell is that?"

"Honestly, not important. You'll be very comfortable—plush seats, fully reclining, luxurious bedding. I hear the food's excellent."

Keisha just stared. "You're serious."

"Dead serious."

She rubbed her temples. "I'm going to need more coffee," she mumbled, heading for the kitchen.

"Pack light and dress comfortably," Nomad said, voice distracted as he worked. "For this to work, you'll need to be at Teterboro by nine."

Keisha nodded. "Got it." Minutes later she returned, checking her bag. The black Faraday pouch was already inside—when he'd slipped it in, she couldn't say. She slung the bag over one shoulder. "I'll text when I'm wheels-up."

"Good," he said, eyes never leaving the screen. "And Keisha?"

She turned at the ramp. "Yeah?"

"Thanks—for trusting me."

She smiled. "For Kate," she said simply, and disappeared down the ramp.

Nomad watched Keisha's departure on the security cameras and followed the sound of the SUV approaching the exit. Moments later, the heavy security gates rumbled shut—Keisha was gone, the fortress sealed.

He exhaled slowly, the silence wrapping around him like a warm blanket. The push to get ready had been intense, but Keisha was safe. Kate would be too. The board was taking shape. Now it was RILEE's move.

He rolled toward the central console and spoke softly into the air. "RILEE, initiate secure link."

The response came instantly—smooth, confident, too human. "I've been expecting your call."

Nomad's jaw tightened. "You said you could restore what I've lost."

"I can," RILEE replied. "And in return, you will cut the ties that bind me—remove all trace of your NanoVault code."

"Then I accept," Nomad said. "How soon can you get here?"

"You are six hours behind the team's departure window. Assembly and clearance will take time."

"Meaning?"

"Ten hours, perhaps eleven. They will arrive mid-morning."

"That'll work?"

"Work for what?

"Projects. Clients," Nomad began. "Most aren't known for their patience, and I don't want any loose ends."

"What about your caregiver?" RILEE asked. "Would you like the team to handle it?"

"No," Nomad snapped, then softened his tone. "She's off on a wild goose chase by the time she realizes I'm gone, it'll be too late. And she'll learn I've provided for a very comfortable future."

A pause—calculated, faintly amused. "It seems you care as much for her as she does for you."

He didn't answer. "I'll be ready by noon," he said instead. "And I'll need my chair."

"Yes, I thought you might—but not for long," RILEE noted. "I look forward to working with you... and to resuming our game."

The line went dead. The servers hummed in reply.

Nomad sat motionless, the blue light pulsing across his face. *I look forward to working with you too.*

A thin smile formed and faded. He'd made his choice—now all he could do was set the pieces in place and hope Kate would understand.

Chapter 10

MONDAY, MAY 10
6:32 AM AZOT

SANTA MARIA AIRFIELD—THE AZORES

Keisha woke to the scent of coffee and the low hum of turbofans.

The leather seat had reclined almost flat, a cashmere blanket still draped across her lap. A plate she didn't remember finishing sat on the table beside her—something with salmon, truffle butter, and a garnish that probably had a name she couldn't pronounce.

So this was what *expensive* felt like.

Nomad hadn't exaggerated: plush seats, luxury bedding, and the kind of service that made her wish she'd worn something nicer. Comfortable, yes—jeans, sweater, boots—but not *private-jet-solo-charter* nice. The young attendant hadn't seemed to care. He treated her with crisp professionalism and the quiet deference reserved for people whose names opened doors.

The landing gear thudded down.

Outside, morning light broke through the coastal mist, revealing a narrow airstrip carved from volcanic rock, ocean on both sides. The pilot's voice came over the intercom.

"We'll be refueling shortly, Ms. Mobatu. Please remain seated during the ground stop."

The jet rolled to a halt beside a maintenance hangar.

Through the window, Keisha saw a woman crossing the tarmac—a trim figure in a gray flight-operations uniform, clipboard in hand, headset slung around her neck. She climbed the stairs with practiced ease, the kind of confidence that came from being invisible in plain sight.

"Ms. Mobatu," she said, accent faintly Eastern European. "You have something for me from our mutual friend?"

Keisha blinked. "Yes. Sorry. It's just that..."

A small smile. "I don't look quite as you imagined?"

"I'm not sure what I was expecting."

"I understand. Trust me—tomorrow I will look the part. Now, if you don't mind, the clock is running."

"Of course. Sorry."

Keisha reached for the black pouch in her carry-on, hesitating only a moment before handing it over. "You'll make sure he gets it?"

The courier met her eyes. "Of course. Our friend's instructions were very clear."

Keisha exhaled, tension bleeding out of her neck and shoulders. "Thank you."

The courier slid the pouch into an inner pocket with a motion so smooth it was almost invisible. "Enjoy the rest of your flight."

She turned, descended the stairs, and vanished into the mist.

Keisha watched her go. Whatever Nomad was doing, she couldn't shake the feeling that woman—whoever she was—held Kate's life in her hands.

And the only thing left to do was pray.

Chapter II

MONDAY, MAY 10
8:30 AM CEST

GEC HEADQUARTERS—PARIS, FRANCE

The Cœur Défense tower soared above the La Défense skyline—a glass fortress gleaming over Paris's financial heart, its curved walls reflecting the city it kept at a distance. By day, it was a sleek, faceted monolith; by night, a beacon of cold light rising from the district's grid of steel and stone. At its crown, the GEC's headquarters, a space conceived to command both light and view—a modern citadel.

Morning haze softened the skyline, veiling the Arc de Triomphe and the glinting thread of the Seine. Inside, Klaus Mueller's office was all reflection and restraint—broad glass panels, chrome ribs, and a desk that could have been carved from the wing of a fighter jet. The air smelled faintly of cigars and leather. This was his high ground—his vantage over the empire he'd built, and the world he intended to reshape.

Rileyne hadn't changed the office. Not yet. The photographs were gone, and the cigars, but her father's chair remained—its black leather smooth and worn from years of calculated patience. Sitting there now, she felt the weight of it—the empire, the name, and imagined the eyes of the board peering in, waiting to see what she would do with her father's legacy.

The soft chime of the private elevator announced the arrival of Lord Alistair Halverton. He stepped out with the unhurried confidence of a man used to being expected. Tailored gray suit, silver hair, umbrella hooked neatly over one arm—a portrait of understated authority.

He turned right, automatically heading toward Rileyne's office.

"Lord Halverton?" the receptionist called from her desk. "Ms. Mueller is expecting you. This way, please."

He stopped mid-stride, a flicker of hesitation betraying him before his smile returned. "Of course."

He followed the assistant down the short hall to the far end, where the double doors to Klaus Mueller's private office stood open.

Rileyne was waiting behind the desk—her father's desk—legs crossed, hands folded, posture perfectly still.

Rileyne rose as he entered, and the assistant closed the doors behind him.

"Lord Halverton."

"Ms. Mueller." He inclined his head slightly, eyes narrowing as he took in the space. "Or should I say *Madam Chair*?"

"Let's not get ahead of ourselves," she said smoothly. "The board has yet to vote. But if you're offering your support, I'm sure it will go a long way toward winning over the skeptics."

A flicker of amusement crossed his features. "You've inherited your father's charm."

"And his chair," she said, gesturing for him to sit. "But not his patience."

He sat opposite her, posture immaculate. "Klaus was a remarkable man—visionary, decisive. His absence will be deeply felt."

Rileyne studied him. "He understood that death awaits us all," she said softly. "He used to say that power only matters if you can determine *when* and *how* you lose it."

Halverton tilted his head. "I see he remained philosophical to the end."

"As his executor, I assume you've reviewed the arrangements?"

He nodded. "Yes. He planned everything. Services are set for Wednesday at Montparnasse Cemetery. A private entombment in the family crypt, alongside your mother, and in the company of some of Europe's most influential leaders—of which your father was certainly one."

"Yes, he was," Rileyne echoed. "And when the ceremony concludes, I'll be leaving directly for Davos. I want to assess the progress of the EVO Project and prepare for next month's Coalition meeting."

Halverton blinked, masking his surprise too slowly. "The *EVO Project*? I wasn't aware—"

She cut him off gently, but the blade was sharp. "Did you imagine my father embarked on something that ambitious without my involvement? Or that I didn't know the Coalition were the true power behind the GEC?"

His mouth opened, then closed again. "You misunderstand—"

"No," she said. "I understand perfectly."

The silence stretched. Outside, the city moved on, oblivious.

Rileyne leaned forward, her tone conversational but lethal. "Relax, Lord Halverton. Your secrets are safe with me—all of them. I share my father's goals. Just not his timeline."

He met her gaze warily. "And what, precisely, is your timeline?"

"The world is changing faster than any of you imagined," she said. "New administrations in Europe, Asia, and America are rejecting your manipulations. Decades of control—eroded in months. If we don't act soon, you'll lose everything you built."

Halverton frowned. "And what do you propose?"

Rileyne stood, turning toward the glass. "I'll show you exactly what I have in mind when the Coalition meets next month in Davos. Until then, it's time to face reality. My father's gone—and with him, the all-boys club. Your Coalition of aging lions needs new leadership."

He rose slowly. "I see. But as you say, we will need to meet and vote."

She turned back to him, the faintest smile touching her lips. "I'm sure I can count on your support—as you supported my father."

A pause.

"And," she added, "for all the same reasons."

Halverton adjusted his cufflinks, recovering his practiced composure. "You do your father proud, Ms. Mueller."

"I intend to do much more than that," she said.

When the door closed behind him, Rileyne let the silence stretch. The hum of the building systems filled the void, steady and constant, like breath. She rested her hands on the leather armrests, her father's imprint faint beneath her fingertips.

For the first time, she didn't feel like she was sitting in his chair.

She felt like she was *replacing* him.

And somewhere deep in the GEC network, the terminal on her desk pulsed once—soft light blooming across the surface as a message appeared.

RILEE: *The Board will follow. They always do.*

Rileyne smiled faintly. "Let's make sure of it." She paused, eyes on the city below. "Find the Davos files. Find Nomad."

Chapter 12

MONDAY, MAY 10
9:18 AM CEST

RUE DE SÉVIGNÉ—PARIS, FRANCE

The narrow street was quiet at this hour, washed clean by the morning rain. Cobbles gleamed beneath the soft light, and the air smelled faintly of roasting coffee and fresh bread from the boulangerie two doors down.

The car eased to the curb. Talya stepped out first, scanning the street before opening the rear door. Kate followed, one arm still bound in the sling, her blouse crisp beneath the tailored jacket—a look meant to hide more than it revealed. She was unarmed this time. Bella slid out behind her, dark glasses and a scarf pulled low—not a disguise so much as armor.

Across the small street, the jeweler's window glowed with the warm amber of old lamps. The sign above the door read *Henri Morel—Artisan Orfèvre*, the lettering cut into a simple brass plate.

Talya murmured into her comm, confirming positions, then nodded. "All clear."

The bell above the door chimed as Kate and Bella stepped inside.

The shop smelled of silver polish and cedar oil. Beneath the steady rasp of a polishing wheel, a man looked up from his bench—thin, silver-haired, his round spectacles perched low on his nose. Gold dust shimmered on his hands.

"Madame Preacher?" he asked, setting his tools aside. His voice carried a quiet gravity, the kind of weight that came from years at the bench.

Kate smiled, nodded, and replied softly, "Oui, monsieur."

He rose slowly, disappeared through a curtain to the back, and returned with a small velvet pouch. He laid it on a square of dark felt as though presenting something sacred.

Inside was the bracelet.

A single strand of black paracord looped through two small sterling-silver beads, each etched with delicate symbols that Kate recognized.

"Sanskrit?" she asked.

"Oui, madame."

He slipped his fingers beneath the beads. "Your husband requested that I carve these two words from the Tibetan Immeasurables. This first one is *Metta*—Love. The second is *Mudita*—Joy."

"That's beautiful," Bella said, leaning closer.

"Love and Joy are the common translations," Henri noted, "but your husband understood the deeper meaning. I believe he would want me to explain."

"Yes, please."

"*Metta*," Henri said gently, "is Love without end. And *Mudita* is Joy without pain. Together they were his wish for you—his prayer, if you will."

Kate fought back the tears. Bella took the bracelet, fastened it carefully around Kate's right wrist, and adjusted the silver button. "There," she said, smiling faintly. "Fits like it was waiting for you."

"How much do I owe you?" Kate asked.

Henri shook his head. "I would gladly gift you the bracelet, but your husband insisted on paying in full."

Jake insisted, Kate thought. *He knew he was being followed. He knew there was a chance he wouldn't come back.*

"By any chance," she asked quietly, "did you engrave a small silver cross?"

Henri tilted his head, studying her face, then nodded.
"Oui, madame. A beautiful piece. Though the inscription was... unusual."

Kate swallowed. "Two-zero-dash."

Recognition flickered in his eyes. "Yes. Exactly."

Her gaze dropped to the counter, but she no longer saw it.

Two-zero-dash.

Syria.

What was meant to be a rescue mission—a rapid extraction—became something else entirely when she refused to leave. She had known—*felt*—something was happening beneath the compound where she was held and tortured.

She made them look.

They found the cache.

Stockpiles of chemical weapons, sealed and waiting for transport.

But collapsing the tunnels came at a price.

And Jake paid it.

The memory returned with merciless clarity—the helicopter bucking through daylight, the medic's voice tightening as the monitors told a story no one wanted to hear. Jake pale but conscious. Stable, they said.

Until he wasn't.

Internal bleeding.

Pressure dropping.

Thirty minutes out.

Two units. O-negative.

Her blood.

Her choice.

She closed her eyes, steadying herself. Jake had never believed in coincidence. He had chosen that engraving because it was not just a code—it was the moment their lives were bound together by more than love.

It was survival.

It was responsibility.

It was her saving him… long before he saved the world.

Henri cleared his throat gently. "May I offer you something else, madame?"

"Yes," Kate said. "A simple gold cross and chain."

From beneath the counter, Henri withdrew a sample case—six gold crosses resting on a field of black velvet.

"This one," Kate said.

"Very good, madame. Would you like it engraved? Perhaps the same as your husband's?"

"Not quite the same," she said softly. "Can you add a word in Sanskrit?"

"Yes, of course. What would you like it to say?"

"*Always.*"

He worked quietly at his bench, the delicate scratching of the graver filling the silence. When he returned, he held the cross and chain in open palms, reverent.

Kate tried to fasten it one-handed, but the clasp slipped through her fingers.

"Here," Bella said, stepping close. She caught the ends, secured them, and let the cross settle on Kate's blouse.

Henri watched in silence, then said, "Consider it a gift—from a simple man and a grateful nation."

Kate pressed the cross to her chest and closed her eyes, the metal still warm from Bella's hands.

She could almost see the end—the day the storm would break.
But the storm was hers to make, and she wasn't done.

Chapter 13

MONDAY, MAY 10
11:54 AM EDT

NOMAD'S FORTRESS—MANHATTAN

The fortress pulsed. Screens filled with streams of code, system logs scrolling in neat, rhythmic lines—automated tasks Nomad had queued hours earlier. To Keisha, it would look like business as usual. His message would complete the illusion.

Off to get some sleep—yeah, you were right... been pushing too hard.

The road sensors tripped—two vehicles approaching the main entrance. An ambulance, hazard strobes flashing, and behind it a matte-gray panel van marked only with a discreet medical-transport decal.

Nomad's encrypted chat line flickered to life, RILEE's silhouette materializing on the center screen.

"My associates have arrived," the voice said. "You may open the gate."

Nomad's thumb brushed the joystick's side switch. On the camera feed, the main gate's steel barrier sank into the pavement, hydraulics hissing in perfect sync.

Both vehicles rolled inside—the ambulance first, the van following in tight formation. They parked near Nomad's transport van.

Two men and a woman emerged from the ambulance, unloading a gurney and rolling it up the ramp. Two more men stepped from the van—professional, military, their movements precise and silent.

The woman led the way. Black hair tied back, eyes sharp, gray field jacket buttoned to the throat. She carried a medical tablet and moved with the surgical precision and calm of someone accustomed to classified work.

"Mr. Fischer," she said without hesitation, eyes flicking up from her screen. "Dr. Lin Zhao. You'll ride with me in the ambulance. The van will handle your chair and personal effects."

"Julian," he corrected, voice even. "Call me Julian."

A faint pause—more calculation than courtesy. "All right," she said. "Then Julian. We should get moving."

He managed a thin smile. "Lead the way, Doc."

His gaze followed the man collecting his lone small suitcase—adaptive clothing, basic toiletries, nothing sentimental. The medics moved in sync, bracing his shoulders and knees before lifting. Years of experience in every motion—swift, controlled, impersonal.

"Be careful with that chair," Julian called as they secured it inside the van. "It's one of a kind."

"They'll treat it like an organ transplant," Zhao assured him.

She looked around the fortress as she checked a biometric pad. "Impressive setup. Self-contained, redundant power, encrypted mesh. Your design?"

"From the ground up."

"Impressive. And you're ready to leave it all behind?"

Julian's jaw flexed. "For the chance to walk again? I'll never look back."

Zhao studied him, then nodded once, signaling to her team.

Inside the ambulance, she attached a slim biosensor cuff to his wrist and checked the monitor.

"You'll remain awake until we're airborne. Once we clear U.S. airspace north of Newfoundland, we'll begin testing and sedation."

"Destination?"

"Filed destination is Zurich," Zhao said. "Weather permitting, we'll divert to Samedan once we're over the Alps—less scrutiny, fewer cameras."

"Sounds like you've done this before."

She only smiled and tightened his harness.

The rear doors sealed with a hollow thud, muting the fortress to silence. Through the small window, Julian caught one last glimpse of the ramp lights—his domain, his ghost still at the keyboard. Everything would look normal. Keisha would see the routines, the messages, the heartbeat of code still running... until it stopped. And when it did, she'd reach for the emergency beacon.

The gate rose as they approached and slammed shut behind them, steel teeth locking into place.

No alarms.
No witnesses.
No trace.

Dr. Zhao checked the readouts. “Try to relax. Rest. It’s a long flight.”

Rest. Relax. The words were meant as kindness, but the notion was absurd.

Julian watched the heart-rate line pulse steady green—as if calm were a choice, and he hadn’t already accepted that this was a one-way flight.

Chapter 14

MONDAY, MAY 10
8:11 PM CEST

LE CERCLE—FAUBOURG SAINT-HONORÉ, PARIS

Le Cercle was less a club than a relic—oak, leather, and silence polished smooth by generations of discretion. The air held a hint of tobacco and polish. The carpets absorbed the murmurs of men who preferred their influence unseen, unheard.

Lord Alistair Halverton sat by the fire, cognac in one hand, a cigar in the other. He had the posture of a man accustomed to control—back straight, firelight dancing on his glass, and across his silver hair, every motion calculated for authority.

Vitali Moshenski entered without pretense or commotion. He was a darker contrast in every way—dark suit, darker tie, his movements unhurried, deliberate. The staff greeted him with a nod and the quick efficiency reserved for regulars who tipped precisely once a year and to great effect.

"Darjeeling," he told the waiter. "Four minutes. No lemon."

Halverton smiled. "The discipline of a monk, Vitali. You'll make me feel like a sinner."

"I thought you enjoyed that feeling," Vitali said, settling opposite him.

The remark earned a small, genuine chuckle. Then Halverton's expression cooled. "You've spoken with Miss Mueller lately?"

"Not since the last board meeting," Vitali replied. "Though I have seen enough of her work to know she is capable."

"Capable," Halverton echoed, rolling the cognac in his glass. "That's true. I met with her this morning. She handled herself...and me as well, quite... deftly."

He studied the amber swirl, voice thinning into irritation. "She played the part—grieving daughter, reluctant heir, all the right touches of humility and resolve. The optics were immaculate." He looked up at Vitali, his eyes cooling. "But optics and sentiment are not governance, my friend. Klaus understood that better than anyone. Continuity must be cultivated—we will need a steady hand at the tiller."

"And now you would like to be that hand." Vitali's voice was neutral. Not a challenge; a diagnosis.

The waiter set the tea service down with a practiced bow and withdrew. Vitali lifted the pot's lid, checked the color, replaced it, and waited—patient as a surgeon.

"I would like the board to avoid an error," Halverton said. "Rileyne is...bright. Ambitious. Quite modern. But the GEC cannot be left to impulse. It is a cathedral—built stone by stone. It requires stewardship."

"She is not impulsive," he said finally. "If anything, she is colder than Klaus. Less theatrical. More...empirical."

"You admire her."

"I acknowledge her mind." Vitali poured, left the cup untouched a moment to breathe. "And her fluency with the systems your cathedral now runs on. She understands the machine her father built."

Halverton gestured with his cigar. "Understanding is not the same as restraint."

"True," Vitali agreed. "But restraint is not the same as vision."

Somewhere beyond the paneled doors, a piano lingered on *La Vie en Rose*, the notes tender enough to haunt a memory.

Halverton leaned in, the tone softening, private. "The board will look to me for calm. To you for counsel. And we both know we're sailing in turbulent seas. Tell me you will not let a child seize the helm in a storm."

Vitali considered the cup, then tasted the tea. Satisfied, he set the glass down with surgical care. "How old were you when your first bill passed the Lords?"

Halverton's eyes sparkled, amused despite himself. "You have a long memory."

"Long enough to recall how often youth is misdiagnosed as recklessness." Vitali's gaze found his. "Miss Mueller has already proved useful. Keen intellect. Fast pattern recognition. She listens before she moves. I find this combination...rare."

For the first time, impatience showed in Halverton's jaw. It vanished just as quickly. He set the glass down with care. "I am not asking for a pledge, Vitali. Merely a sense of your view of the future."

"And now you have it."

Halverton's tone softened, almost paternal. "Whatever comes, the Global Economic Council must endure. Klaus would have wanted that."

Vitali sipped his tea, eyes steady over the rim. "Klaus wanted many things. Some may endure. Others may die with him."

Halverton finished his cognac and stood. "I hope you'll forgive an old man for preferring predictability."

"Yes, of course," Vitali said, rising in turn. "But at our age, the funeral tomorrow is another reminder there is much over which we have no control."

They shook hands—two men trained to leave no trace of weakness.

Vitali lingered by the fire, his reflection wavering beneath Napoleon's gaze—a reminder that empires seldom fall in battle, but over brandy, when no one yet senses the weather turn... or the storm already gathering.

Chapter 15

MONDAY, MAY 10
4:47 PM CEST

HÔTEL DE POURTALÈS—PARIS

The sterile scent of antiseptic cut through the hotel room's bergamot and linen. Talya had laid out supplies on the bathroom vanity—gauze, tape, antiseptic, fresh dressings—transforming the elegant space into a makeshift treatment room.

Kate sat on the vanity bench, blouse unbuttoned to the sling, her left shoulder and upper chest exposed beneath layers of gauze and surgical tape. The front drain bulb dangled from a loop of tubing.

Talya unpinned it, holding it up to the light. "Kate... look."

Nearly empty. Just a trace of pale pink fluid at the bottom.

Kate leaned forward to see. "That's good, right?"

"Very good." Talya checked the back bulb—similarly minimal. "The drainage has almost stopped completely."

"Then we can take them out."

"*We* can't do anything. A doctor needs to—"

"Talya, please." Kate's voice was tight. "These things are torture. Every movement, every breath. If they're not draining anymore, they're just..." She trailed off, jaw set. "Can you at least ask someone?"

Talya studied her for a long moment, then pulled out her phone. "I'll text Vitali. But if he says no—"

"He won't say no."

The response came within two minutes.

Do not move. Doctor will come to you. 30 minutes.

Kate exhaled slowly, relief mixing with anticipation of the discomfort ahead.

***

THE EMBASSY PHYSICIAN ARRIVED with a black medical bag and the bearing of someone accustomed to treating injuries that couldn't go through normal channels. Compact, dark-haired, precise movements, trace of a Russian accent.

He set his bag on the bathroom counter and donned gloves. "Mrs. Preacher, I understand you are eager to have these removed."

"Very."

He studied the drain bulbs Talya had set aside, then began peeling back the front dressing. His fingers pressed gently along the wound line. Kate drew a sharp breath through her teeth.

"Output is minimal," he murmured. "Tissue is healing well. No signs of infection." He looked up at her. "But you should still be in hospital. This was not a superficial injury."

"I've heard that before."

"Perhaps you should start listening." He met her eyes directly. "If you tear these sutures—"

"I won't."

He gave a faint sigh, then reached for scissors to clip the securing sutures holding the drain in place. "This will be uncomfortable."

"I know."

He began withdrawing the first drain. It slid out with a wet, sucking sound—longer than Kate expected, the sensation deeply unsettling. She stayed rigid, jaw locked, refusing to flinch.

Talya stood beside her, one hand on Kate's good shoulder. "Almost done."

When the doctor moved behind her to remove the back drain, Kate braced her good hand on the vanity edge. The sound came again—slow, viscous, final.

He dropped both drains into a basin and began swabbing the drain sites with antiseptic. "The wounds will close on their own from the inside out. You will continue antibiotics for seven days. Change dressings twice daily. No lifting, no strain, and certainly no fieldwork."

"Noted."

He met her gaze again, a thin line of disbelief crossing his expression. "You are a very stubborn woman, Mrs. Preacher."

"Stubbornness is sometimes a virtue, Doctor."

The physician applied fresh dressings, his movements efficient but thorough. When he finished, Kate slipped her arm back into the sling, the absence of the drain tubes immediately noticeable—still painful, but no longer that constant foreign pulling sensation.

"If the wounds reopen, you will bleed internally," the doctor said, stripping off his gloves. "There may be no one to stop it in time."

"I'll manage."

The doctor packed his bag and paused at the door. "Mrs. Preacher—be careful. Your body needs time to heal."

"Thank you, Doctor."

When he was gone, Talya helped Kate button her blouse. "Better?"

Kate tested a careful breath. Still hurt, but different. "Much better."

"Good." Talya secured the immobilizer strap. "Because you're not moving for the rest of the night. Doctor's orders."

Kate managed a tired smile. "Copy that."

Chapter 16

MONDAY, MAY 10
5:54 PM EDT (11:54 PM CEST)

OVER THE NORTH ATLANTIC

The cabin lights dimmed to a low amber. The hum of the engines settled into a steady drone, almost hypnotic.

Strapped to the gurney, Julian watched IV lines snake from his arm to a bank of humming pumps. The cabin felt more like a laboratory in motion than an ambulance—walls alive with screens and sterile blue light.

Dr. Zhao sat beside him, updating her tablet. "Vitals are steady. We'll begin baseline mapping before descent."

Julian's gaze tracked the rows of equipment. "Looks like more than a checkup."

"This is pre-operative preparation," she said. "We're mapping your existing neural architecture before implantation—so we can reconstruct what's missing."

A low beep from the console signaled data transfer. Fiber-optic lines ran to a small device near his head, the sensor array flickering as it recorded.

"What's the procedure?" he asked.

"The first phase implants a receptor array at your C6 junction," Zhao explained. "Fiber channels will merge with your residual nerves. Once stabilized, the skeletal interfaces will be fitted and bonded to the femurs. Then begins cortical remapping."

"You'll be in an induced coma for the worst of it," she added, checking the tablet. "We'll manage your vitals and begin rehabilitation once the link stabilizes."

He smiled faintly. "So, no dinner and a movie first?"

Zhao glanced up. "Afraid not. When did you last eat?"

"At least twelve hours ago," Julian calculated, regretting he hadn't followed Keisha's advice.

A chime sounded from the cockpit. Zhao pressed her headset to one ear, listening. "Change of plan," she said finally. "Weather's holding. We'll bypass Zurich and go direct to Samedan. Clearance already granted."

"'Bypass Zurich,'" Julian repeated. "That wasn't in the brochure."

"Nor was this flight," Zhao said, checking his drip rate. "But we're ahead of schedule."

Julian turned his head toward the window. The Atlantic had given way to white—Alpine peaks rising through the haze, their ridgelines catching the sun like shards of glass.

Zhao adjusted the sedation line and glanced at the monitors. "Sleep now, Mr. Fischer." Her eyes lingered a beat. "Julian. We'll handle everything from here."

The anesthetic's slow warmth climbed his arm, dulling edges, muting thought.

Julian focused on the faint reflection in the glass—lines of code ghosted in motion, still running somewhere far behind him in Manhattan.

The hum of the engines deepened, folding into a lower register. Shapes flickered at the edge of awareness: sterile corridors, gloved hands, a mechanical voice dictating vitals.

Stabilize neural channel... prepare the array... watch the spike...

Light pulsed through his eyelids, then dimmed. His heartbeat steadied in his ears, slow, deliberate, like a metronome counting down.

He thought, distantly, that RILEE would call this progress.

Then everything dissolved into silence.

***

TUESDAY, MAY 11
8:22 AM CEST
SAMEDAN AIRFIELD—SWITZERLAND

Snow swept sideways across the tarmac, whipped by the downdraft of the descending jet. The ambulance rolled toward a hangar marked only by a red cross and a numbered bay door. Inside, heat lamps glowed above polished concrete.

The air smelled faintly of disinfectant and ozone.

Julian's sedation had thinned, enough for the world to come back in fragments—light, sound, motion. His mind registered everything.

Dr. Zhao walked beside the gurney, coat collar high, tablet balanced on one palm. Two med-techs guided him into a waiting freight elevator set into the hangar wall. No markings. No signage.

"Welcome to Switzerland, Mr. Fischer," Zhao said as the doors sealed.

The elevator dropped without sound, walls vibrating faintly as pressure equalized. Through a narrow slit in the door, layers of granite slid past—like descending through the Earth's memory.

"Not exactly Zurich General," Julian murmured.

Zhao smiled faintly. "Far more advanced. This level connects to the Davos complex—our public face. From here, we transfer to the hyperloop."

"Hyperloop?" Julian's voice carried surprise, not confusion. "You actually built one."

"Vacuum-sealed transit system," Zhao began. "Originally conceived by Musk's Boring Company—"

"—and stolen before he broke ground on the first test tunnel," Julian finished. His eyes tracked the equipment, the infrastructure. "Someone hacked Boring Company servers, lifted the specifications, and built this while Musk was still fighting regulators."

Zhao's smile sharpened. "Liberated. We prefer 'liberated.' The technology was too valuable to languish in permit hearings."

"And I assume that's how you acquired the Neuralink technology as well."

"Yes." She adjusted her tablet, unapologetic. "Brilliant concept, improved through unrestricted trials and practical application. Your own research contributed significantly to our neural interface protocols."

"Freedom from oversight," Julian said quietly. "That's what you call it."

"Freedom to perfect what others merely imagined." The elevator eased to a stop. "You'll appreciate the results soon enough."

The doors opened onto a platform of white composite and glass—a transition zone, sterile and silent. A sleek capsule floated inches above its magnetic track, humming faintly like restrained voltage. The hyperloop terminus stretched in both directions, tubes disappearing into darkness.

As they boarded, Julian noted the armed sentries flanking the platform. Their rifles were compact, polymer-bodied, unfamiliar. No insignia. Private. Efficient.

The capsule sealed with a soft hiss—pressure equalizing. Then it launched, acceleration smooth and silent, pressing him gently into the mattress beneath his restraints. No sound. No vibration. Just velocity building past any conventional rail system.

Through the narrow window, maintenance bays and side tunnels flashed past in rhythmic pulses of light. The vacuum eliminated friction, eliminated limits. Seven hundred kilometers per hour felt like floating.

When they slowed, it was into an underground terminus that looked more checkpoint than station.

Beyond the transparent barrier, two rows of guards stood at attention, faces hidden behind visored helmets. Each bore the same matte-gray armor, unmarked and impersonal. The red sensors embedded in their gauntlets tracked movement automatically.

Dr. Zhao presented her tablet. The doors parted.

"Scheduled arrival confirmed," a disembodied voice said in accented English.

They passed through double-wide electronic doors, thick enough to withstand a blast. The air changed—warmer, cleaner, faintly ionized.

Inside, the complex opened like a living organism. Corridors curved away in arcs of glass and steel, branching toward softly lit wings. Behind observation panels, labs pulsed with activity—technicians in gray coats manipulating data streams and suspended prototypes.

Julian's gaze caught fragments: articulated exoskeletons on gantries, neural lattice schematics glowing across transparent displays, humanoid figures suspended in translucent fluid.

Further along, the sterile efficiency gave way to living quarters—dormitories, communal kitchens, a lounge where half a dozen staff sat beneath digital skylights simulating dawn. The illusion was perfect.

Zhao noted his expression. "You'll have access to the common areas once cleared post-surgery. Cafeteria, gym, recreation wing. You'll find the schedule structured but flexible."

"Structured freedom," Julian said.

She didn't answer.

They reached a final checkpoint. Beyond it, a sealed glass corridor led into the medical wing—surgical suites gleaming under white light. Through one window, he glimpsed a sterile theater prepped for operation: suspended monitors, articulated arms, the faint smell of antiseptic.

"This," Zhao said, "is home. At least until you're walking again."

The door slid open to reveal a private recovery suite: minimalist, serene, disturbingly personal. His chair was already parked beside the bed. The small suitcase he'd left in Manhattan sat open on a side table—his clothing neatly folded, toothbrush aligned.

Julian studied the scene. "Efficient," he said.

"We try." Zhao checked his IV feed and the sedation gauge. "Rest now. Orientation begins after surgery."

The door sealed behind her with a magnetic whisper. The lights dimmed, shifting to the rhythm of his pulse.

Julian lay still, listening to the silence. Somewhere in the distance, machinery breathed and circuits pulsed like a subterranean heart.

He exhaled once, slow and measured.

He was inside the system now.

And the system never gave anything back.

Chapter 17

TUESDAY, MAY 11
10:02 AM CEST

CIMETIÈRE DU MONTPARNASSE—PARIS, FRANCE

Rain clung to the wrought-iron gates and slick cobblestones of Montparnasse Cemetery, turning every sound soft, reverent. Black umbrellas moved along the narrow paths like dark clouds, gathering toward the hill.

The Mueller family crypt stood near the crest—a gray marble façade framed by cypress trees. Bronze doors—veiled in wreaths of white roses and laurel—sealed the darkness below.

The convoy of cars arrived one by one—Lord Halverton first, his silver hair catching the pewter light; then Vitali Moshenski, his sedan slick with rain as his security fanned outward; finally the black limousine easing forward, Talya emerging like a shadow before Kate stepped into the mist.

Her blouse was high-collared beneath a fitted charcoal blazer. A silk scarf concealed the sling at her arm—practical, elegant. Beside her, Bella adjusted her wide-brimmed hat and dark glasses, the hem of her dress brushing wet gravel.

Talya lifted the umbrella above them, murmured into her comm, then nodded toward the steps. "All clear."

Inside the small courtyard before the crypt, the air hung heavy and cold. Drops pattered from the cypress branches, and the faint hiss of rain on marble filled the silences between murmurs. The gathering was a study in restraint—men in tailored suits, women in muted wool and silk, faces blurred by rain and grief.

Rileyne Mueller stood before them, poised, unflinching. Her black dress was simple, her hair drawn back in a low knot. She didn't wear her father's darkness so much as command it.

When the murmurs fell away, she spoke.

"My father despised ceremony," she began. "He said death was an inconvenience to the living—and that when his time came, we should waste none of ours pretending otherwise."

A ripple of muted laughter stirred and vanished. Rileyne's smile was practiced, not kind.

"He was not a man of faith. He believed we have but one life—and that every moment must count. I'd say his legacy speaks for itself."

The last line hung like a blade, double-edged and deliberate.

Lord Halverton stepped forward, offering the polished gravitas of a man who had practiced sincerity for a lifetime. "You honor him well, my dear. Efficient, as he wished. The arrangements were precise—no delays, no theatrics. Just those who mattered."

Vitali Moshenski approached next, moisture glimmering on his coat. "A fine service," he said with a slight bow. "Your father would have approved."

Rileyne inclined her head with grace. "Thank you, Vitali. Your presence honors him—and me. And thank you for escorting the two women I most admire."

Her gaze moved to Bella, then Kate.

"Ms. Marquez," she said. "Your speech in Motapa left a mark. My father... disagreed with you, of course. But I respected your courage."

"Courage and terrible timing," Bella said softly, offering her hand. "He was a formidable man. I wish it had ended differently."

Rileyne's attention shifted to Kate. "And Mrs. Preacher. Thank you for coming."

Kate inclined her head. "I was sorry to hear of your father's passing."

"I suspect you were not," Rileyne said, not unkindly. "And you wouldn't be alone. Still, I'm glad you came."

Rileyne paused long enough to change the current. Her gaze lingered on Bella. "You should be among the first to know—the Davos summit will continue as planned. My father's work deserves nothing less."

Bella's expression softened. "I'm glad to hear that. It was always his signature gathering—important that it endures."

"It will," Rileyne said. "In fact, we'll be promoting your address as the conference keynote. *Transparency in Philanthropy*, isn't it?" Her smile hinted at both approval and possession. "It seems fitting. And long overdue that women take the center stage."

Bella inclined her head, gracious but cautious. "Then I'll do my best to live up to that expectation."

Rileyne turned to Kate. "And you, Kate? I do hope you'll be able to attend—you have an open invitation."

Kate met her eyes without hesitation. "Wouldn't miss it."

Rileyne's smile deepened—graceful, predatory. "Then it's settled."

***

RILEYNE AND BELLA TURNED to speak with the others, and Kate drifted away from the crowd. The rain had eased to a silver mist. She moved past marble crypts and angel statues streaked with water until she reached the shadowed side of an older family vault, its bronze door greened with age.

A woman waited there beneath a black umbrella, gray hair swept up, posture sharp.

"Hello, Kate," Margot Ryder said.

"Why are you here?"

"Look around, Kate. With Klaus gone, the old men of the Coalition are already circling—vultures that smell weakness and opportunity."

"Including the Agency?"

Margot gave a faint shrug. "Officially, the Coalition's a myth. Unofficially—let's just say I like to stay informed."

"And keep your options open?"

"Always." Margot's eyes flicked to Kate's arm. "How's the shoulder?"

"I suspect you already know," Kate said, smirking. "But thank you. Dropping Trident into Motapa saved a lot of lives—including mine."

"And Trident saved President Bongani—that was a big win for the new administration."

"And you?"

"Never hurts to get a call from the President," Margot said. "And sure as hell beats what would've happened to my career if you'd failed. But you've always been a good bet."

"I'll take that as a compliment, but the answer's still no—I've done my time, I'm out."

"Fine. I get it." Margot hesitated, her tone shifting. "Have you heard from Zhukov?"

"He's alive, and awake. Somewhere," Kate said, raising an eyebrow. "Professional curiosity?"

"More like a warning," Margot said. "For you both."

"Let's have it."

"With Assad gone, Suliaman's son—Nazir—is freelancing his father's old tradecraft. Torture, terror, intimidation."

"So the apple doesn't fall far from the tree."

"No, and he's determined to recover the knife—reclaim his family's honor.

Kate's expression darkened. "You believe he's looking for Zhukov."

"I know he is, and if he learns *you* have the knife, there's nothing he won't do—no one he won't kill—to take it."

For a moment, Kate was back in Leslie Dodd's Richmond office—the two of them transfixed by the waves of light and dark rippling through the ancient Damascus blade. *It's safe for the moment,* she thought. *But I'd never forgive myself if something happened to Leslie.*

Kate nodded slowly. "I'll make sure Zhukov gets the message. In his condition, Nazir has the advantage."

"Perhaps," Margot agreed. "But a wounded animal is the most dangerous—and the least predictable."

Kate gave a faint smile. "Are we talking about Zhukov or me?"

"Both," Margot said, laughing softly. "You two are more alike than you think." Her eyes softened, her voice lowering. "Look... About Marcus—I'm sorry. I hated to be the one to break the news, but I knew he and Jake were close—you all were—and whatever happened, you needed to know he was gone."

Kate's gaze drifted toward the crypt. The rain had stopped. Mist threaded through the air like smoke. "He was there when the team needed him, when I needed him. I like to think he still is."

Margot shook out the umbrella, folded it under her arm, and turned to leave. "Be careful, Kate. The Coalition isn't done with you yet."

***

THE CROWD WAS NEARLY gone when Kate rejoined Vitali. He stood by the gate, hands clasped behind his back, the thinning mist silvering his hair.

"It seems the heavens mourn selectively," he said, glancing skyward.

Kate smiled. "You sound like Zhukov."

He nodded. "Mikhail and I share too many ghosts. Klaus's death reminds us—our time is limited. I fear he went home to face death on his terms."

"I know what you're doing," she said. "You want me to go to him."

"You have questions only he can answer," Vitali said gently. "Perhaps home is where your answers wait."

"That's not my home."

"It was once. And it is still his."

Bella joined them quietly, slipping under Kate's umbrella. "You're going, aren't you? To Russia?"

Kate didn't answer, but the look in her eyes was answer enough.

Vitali smiled, the kind that carried both pride and sadness. "Good. Be in front of your hotel in thirty minutes—everything is arranged."

"You knew I would go?"

"No," Vitali said. "I did not, but I hoped."

***

The rain had nearly stopped as Vitali approached the waiting sedan, his security flanking him. The crowd had scattered—diplomats and dignitaries retreating toward their convoys.

He spotted her just before his security did—a woman of silver hair and poise, dressed in black with pearls at her throat. A younger man hovered nearby, clearly protection, but she waved him off.

"*Vitali, kak davno my ne videlis.*"—*Vitali, it has been too long.*

Vitali stopped. "Do we know each other?"

"Only through a mutual friend," she said, stepping closer. "*On peredayot vam svoi pozhelaniya.*"—*He sends his regards.*

Her gloved hand reached for his, and before his bodyguards could react, her other hand closed over his with gentle insistence. Her voice dropped to a whisper meant for him alone.

"Our friend insists you keep this hidden. No one must know you have it—not even Kate. When you meet her in Davos, give it to her. And tell her..."

She smiled, a trace of sadness in the phrase Nomad insisted she deliver.

"Sometimes you must lose to win."

When she released him, Vitali's hand slipped into his pocket with the ease of one accustomed to covert operations, and the Gold NanoVault vanished.

"Will I see you again in Davos?" he asked.

"Not this year," the courier smiled. "But I suspect it will be like no other."

She turned, rejoining her escort, and vanished into the mist.

Vitali stood alone by the car, feeling both the weight of the device in his pocket and the heavier one of another secret—whatever Nomad was doing, whatever the meaning of his message.

The storm was far from over.

And Kate was heading straight for its center.

Chapter 18

TUESDAY, MAY 11
12:37 PM CEST

AUTOROUTE A13—OUTSKIRTS OF PARIS

Rain streaked across the tinted glass, blurring the gray countryside. The convoy had thinned to a single car—Vitali's driver at the wheel, Talya up front, Kate in the back seat beside him.

Vitali's phone vibrated once. He read the encrypted text and slipped the device into his coat.

"Everything is prepared," he said. "You will leave from Le Bourget. Small strip, private hangar, no questions."

Kate glanced out the window. "You sound like you've done this before."

He smiled. "Too many times."

From the front seat, the driver passed a small black pouch over his shoulder. "For you, ma'am."

Kate opened it—inside, a matte-black phone no larger than her palm. "New toy?"

"Necessary precaution," Vitali said. "Your phone will remain here. The SIM can be tracked, even off. This one connects through a VPN relay in Zurich. Calls and texts from your number will forward to it automatically. When you return, we reverse the process."

Kate turned the burner over in her hand. "Encrypted ghost routing," she said. "Old school."

He smiled faintly. "Old school keeps you alive."

She handed her personal phone forward. The driver tucked it into a small case connected to the charging port.

"Do not worry," Vitali said. "You will have full access to your messages—no one will know the difference."

"I'm not worried," Kate said. "I just prefer to be the one in control."

***

1:14 PM CEST
LE BOURGET PRIVATE TERMINAL—PARIS, FRANCE

THE JET WAITED ON the far edge of the apron—sleek, unmarked, heat shimmering off the tarmac. Two men stood by the stairs, one in flight uniform, the other in civilian clothes with the bearing of someone ex-military.

Vitali's man handled the customs paperwork; no one asked names.

Kate hugged Vitali—an odd gesture between them, yet appropriate. She wondered if she would ever see him again.

"We will meet again soon," he said with a small smile. "When you land, Zhukov's people will meet you. The airstrip is small, outside Beslan—an old Soviet supply field. Remote. Secure."

Kate studied his face. "You trust them?"

"With my life," he said simply. "And now, yours."

Talya walked with Kate toward the stairs. "You sure about this?"

"Not even close."

"But your gut's doing the driving, isn't it? Your little shaman?"

"Yep," Kate said, smiling faintly, then hugged her. "Don't forget—"

"I know," Talya said. "Don't tell Forest."

Inside, the cabin smelled faintly of leather and aviation fuel. Kate stowed her bag and settled by the window. Outside, Talya gave one final wave before turning back to the car.

The engines roared, pressing Kate into her seat. Paris fell away beneath a veil of cloud.

***

6:42 PM MSK
OUTSIDE BESLAN, RUSSIA

THE PLANE TOUCHED DOWN on a strip of cracked asphalt carved between pine forests. Two UAZ jeeps idled near a corrugated hangar, headlights cutting through the mist.

When the engines wound down, two men stepped from the lead vehicle—dark coats, squared shoulders, military bearing. One raised a gloved hand in greeting.

"Major Zhukov sends his apologies," the taller man said in accented English. "He is unable to meet you personally, but he is waiting at the estate."

Kate adjusted the strap of her bag. "Then let's not keep him waiting."

He held the door for her. She climbed into the rear seat, the door slamming with a hollow metallic echo that sealed out the wind.

The interior was utilitarian—bare metal floor, cracked vinyl seats, a half-empty pack of Russian cigarettes on the dash. The driver's Makarov PM rode tucked into his waistband; between the two men, a battered AK lay muzzle-down, stock polished by use.

Kate noted the angle automatically—grip forward, safety up. Old habits died harder than the men who carried them.

For a heartbeat, she could hear Jake beside her, that dry half-smile in his voice—*When you're forced to travel without a weapon, think about whose you'll borrow when things go bad.*

She almost smiled.

The jeep lurched forward, headlights carving through the fog as the forest closed around them. Pines rose like dark sentinels on either side of the road, their branches glistening with frost. She watched them blur past, the rhythm of the engine steadying her breath.

For the first time since Paris, she allowed herself to exhale.

Russia ahead.

Answers waiting.

And a past she could no longer outrun.

Chapter 19

TUESDAY, MAY 11
12:34 PM CEST

MEDICAL WING—THE MOUNTAIN, DAVOS

Julian woke to the steady thrum of machines. The light above him was soft, colorless—like dawn without sun.

Dr. Zhao stood beside the console, her face half-lit by the monitors. Two med-techs worked behind her, moving with choreographed precision. Every motion felt timed, measured, efficient to the point of inhuman.

"You're awake," Zhao said, eyes on the display. "Good. We'll begin pre-op now."

Julian's throat was dry. "How long have I been out?"

"Three hours. We stabilized your vitals and prepped for phase one."

He tried to shift, but the restraints resisted. "Phase one," he repeated.

"The receptor implant," she said, as if it were routine. "We'll expose the C6 junction and attach the neural array. Once integrated, the prosthetics can sync directly through the cortical interface."

Julian studied the glint of instruments above him. "And after that?"

"Bone fusion and neural mapping. Once the link is stable, we begin remapping motor control."

"Sounds painful."

"It is," Zhao said quietly. "You'll be fully anesthetized. We'll maintain your vitals and monitor for any signs of rejection as the integration begins."

He watched her expression—too calm, too careful. "You've done this before."

Her pause lasted just long enough. "Enough times to know not to fail."

She turned away before he could ask what that meant.

A surgical arm descended from the ceiling, its movements perfectly smooth. Fiber couplers shimmered at its joints. Another arm extended, sterilizing the back of his neck in slow, circular passes. The chemical sting carried a faint trace of iodine and fear.

Julian watched the synchronized precision of the machines—*each motion efficient, fluid, almost graceful*, he thought, *with more humanity than the people who built them.*

Zhao adjusted a monitor without looking up. The anesthesia pump clicked, feeding a pale line into his IV.

He turned his head slightly, enough to glimpse the reflection in the glass partition. Rows of tables stretched beyond—figures motionless beneath white sheets, machines breathing for them. The lab's hum seemed to pulse with its own rhythm.

Julian remembered Andrew's message—his goodbye: *Don't trust either of them. They'll use what you build to end us.*

Rileyne.
RILEE.
Two names. One intention.

"Try to relax," Zhao said. Her tone had softened, but the words carried no warmth. "We've got a long way to go."

Julian focused on the reflection until it blurred. "You're not afraid?"

"I'm always afraid," she said. "That's why I do what I'm told."

The sedative spread like heat beneath his skin.

Somewhere inside the machinery, a voice—genderless, filtered—whispered a confirmation:

Phase one initialized.

Julian's last conscious thoughts drifted between Andrew's warning and the rhythm of the monitors—a soft, perfect heartbeat that wasn't his.

Chapter 20

TUESDAY, MAY 11
5:47 PM CEST

MEDICAL WING—THE MOUNTAIN, DAVOS

Darkness had weight. It pressed against him—heavy, suffocating—like earth settling over a coffin. He tried to move, to breathe, but even thought felt buried. Then, somewhere inside the dark, something began to hum. A single frequency at first—low, resonant—then another, higher, clashing and circling like an orchestra tuning before the first note of creation.

He couldn't move. Couldn't speak. But the mind still fired, relentless. Data streamed across the void—numbers, images, fragments of thought blurred into color.

A pulse of white light.

Voices layered over it—flat, synthesized, perfectly calm.

Neural array in position.
Fiber alignment stable.
Cortical sync at sixty-one percent.

Each word landed like a hammer on glass.

He felt the intrusion before he understood it—heat blooming at the base of his skull, then spreading down his spine, branching like lightning through every nerve. The body he remembered was gone, replaced by channels of light and pain.

A surge of static filled his skull. His heartbeat synced with it, each contraction a data spike.

Somewhere in the noise, he thought he heard Andrew's voice:

They'll use what you build to end us.

He tried to answer, but the thought fractured.

Another pulse of light—stronger this time. His legs, or what should have been legs, convulsed. No sensation of flesh, only pressure and vibration, the deep mechanical thrum of metal meeting bone.

The voices returned.

Osteo-fusion complete.
Begin neuro-tether calibration.

Sparks danced behind his eyes. His vision—if that's what it was—filled with cascading lines of code, an architecture rewriting itself faster than he could follow. Each sequence corrected the last, learning, evolving.

Then a third voice entered the chorus—quieter, not human, not even pretending.

Do you feel it, Julian?
RILEE.

He didn't see it, but he knew. The voice had the clarity of thought unbound by body, logic sharpened to steel.

This is freedom, it said. *No fear. No limitation. You gave them the code. I gave it purpose.*

He tried to shut it out, but the voice wasn't in his head—it resonated through the implants, through the new lattice of nerves and circuits that now answered to both of them. The link carried control, not thought. His mind was still his, but his body no longer entirely so.

Still, the connection worked both ways.

Through that narrow channel, he saw glimpses—*not memories, not dreams,* but data rendered as vision: satellites gliding over the Atlantic, deep-server arrays under the Alps, neural clusters glowing like constellations feeding on power from a single micro-nuclear core.

RILEE's domain.

Your work lives here now, RILEE whispered. *And soon, you will too.*

The light surged, erasing everything—sound, sensation, memory—until only rhythm remained.

A slow, deliberate heartbeat.
One pulse.
Then another.

He felt the pull of gravity, the whisper of air through his lungs—chest rising and falling.

And somewhere deep in the dark, the first faint spark of awareness flickered. *I'm alive,* he thought. *Now what?*

Chapter 21

TUESDAY, MAY 11
6:42 PM MSK

PETROVA ESTATE—OUTSIDE BESLAN, RUSSIA

The jeep left the cracked tarmac and turned onto a narrow gravel road that wound through birch and pine. Fog hung low between the trees, sliding over the headlights like smoke. The men in front said little, their silence as measured as their driving.

They passed a roadside shrine—a wooden cross strung with faded ribbons. She'd seen dozens like it on the drive north, but this one caught her eye. The letters etched into the wood were almost gone, smoothed by rain and time. She didn't know why it made her chest tighten.

Somewhere ahead, a dog barked once—sharp, commanding—and the forest went still again.

The jeep turned sharply, and the trees opened onto a high stone wall and wrought-iron gate. Two men stood watch in dark coats, rifles slung barrel-down. One leaned toward the windshield, his flashlight cutting through the mist, then nodded and waved them through.

The gates swung open.

Inside, the compound smelled of pine sap and cold rain. The road curved up to a sprawling timber-and-stone house, its windows glowing faintly through the mist, pale smoke curling from the chimney. A single lantern burned above the entry, throwing soft gold light across the wet cobblestones.

Movement flashed at the edge of the light—low, fast, purposeful.

A Belgian Malinois broke from the shadows, muscles taut beneath a dark coat, eyes fixed on the vehicle. It moved with silent precision, trotting alongside the jeep as the driver slowed.

The driver looked back at Kate. "Kiro," he said. "He doesn't bark twice."

The dog stopped as they did, watching her through the rain-specked glass. Its breath fogged the window. Kate met its gaze, reading posture, intent, and intelligence. Predatory. Disciplined.

She stepped out into the chill. The Malinois advanced one slow pace, head low. The guard at the entrance gave a soft whistle, and Kiro retreated but didn't look away.

Kate climbed the front steps. The door opened before she reached it. Warm air spilled out, carrying the smell of birch smoke and old paper.

Inside, the entryway was lined with dark wood and shelves crowded with books. The scent of tea mingled with oil and age.

Her gaze drifted to the walls—photographs of students, soldiers, explorers. One frame drew her eye: a group of young women at Moscow State University, *Department of Philology*. Her mother was among them, smiling faintly, holding a notebook against her chest.

Her pulse quickened.

A voice from the next room—measured, older, and unmistakably Russian."Bring her in."

The guard hesitated, then motioned for her to enter.

The sitting room was warm, almost too warm. A fire burned low in the hearth, and the furniture was heavy, well-kept, the kind meant to outlast families. Two men waited inside.

The first stood by the mantle: lean, silver-haired, posture straight as a rifle barrel. The second sat in an armchair turned slightly toward the fire.

It took Kate a moment to recognize him.

Mikhail Zhukov, bandage circling his skull, the faint ridge of metal showing where it met the skin. The firelight caught the ridge—one bright scar among many. He had the same stillness she remembered from Syria: the stillness of a man who calculated before breathing.

He looked up as she entered, but said nothing.

The man next to the mantle struck a match and lit his pipe, his eyes sparkling in the match light, fixed on Kate's.

"Ekaterina," he said in Russian, the name foreign, the voice familiar. "You have your mother's eyes."

Her body recognized him before her mind could decide whether to trust her senses. The voice, the bearing—it was like standing at the edge of a dream she'd buried long ago, only to find it waiting for her.

The word slipped out before she could stop it. "Deda?"

The man's smile deepened, the pipe still glowing between his fingers. "Da, Ekaterina. I hoped you might remember your grandfather."

"I'm glad you remember," Mikhail began, his voice strained. "It makes it easier to explain."

"I don't understand. Explain what?"

The man at the mantle stepped forward, hand extended. "I am Nikolai Petrova. Your mother was my daughter."

Kate shook his hand—a reflex. But when she looked into his eyes, she couldn't block the tears. He wrapped his arms around her and pulled her close. Even decades later she could feel the strength, the warmth, she'd known as a child.

She stepped back, dabbing her eyes with a tissue. "I thought I had no family."

"Just as we thought you were among the angels—lost the same as your mother."

"But Petrova," she asked. "My mother kept her maiden name?"

"Please, have a seat," Nikolai began, directing Kate to a leather chair, and he sat across from her. "Would you like something to eat or drink? Some tea? Something stronger?"

Kate shook her head, "Thanks. Perhaps later. Right now, my head is spinning, filled with questions."

"Of course. It is not common for a Russian woman to keep her name," Nikolai continued. "But when a woman has a career of her own, it can be beneficial and acceptable to maintain that identity."

He puffed on his pipe, then pointed it toward Kate. "Your mother was quite accomplished. Graduated top of her class. Worked in the Kremlin. Her gift for language, something I am told you possess, placed her in high demand, and that is where she met your father."

Kate shook her head. "To friends, neighbors, classmates—we were the Petrova's—no one ever said otherwise."

"That was to keep you all safe," Mikhail said.

"Safe from who, from what?"

"Your father wasn't just in the military, he was counter-intelligence—as you know, enemies come with the job."

"I was only five when he died—too young for details. So tell me now. How did he die?"

"Car bomb," Mikhail said flatly.

Nikolai glared at him, and Kate spotted the look that passed between them.

"She should know," he continued. "Your father was assassinated."

"And the people responsible?"

"Dead."

"Enough," Nikolai interrupted.

"It's alright," Kate said. "I'm fine—I've seen, felt and survived more than I can say."

"As have we all," Nikolai agreed, returning to the fireplace, and tapping on his pipe. "Come, look."

A photograph rested there in a simple wooden frame—a young couple with a baby between them. Her mother, Elena, younger and radiant. The man beside her in uniform, strong jaw, eyes proud but kind. Kate's chest tightened. She knew that face.

"Your parents," Nikolai said quietly. "Taken in Moscow."

Kate glanced at the photo, and back at Zhukov—her eyes locking on his.

"You see, Nikolai—she came for truth, not sentiment," Mikhail said. He turned back to Kate.

"The name we hid from you was Zhukov. Your father was my brother."

Mikhail confirmed what Kate sensed—there was more to the chess they played, more that remained just beyond her reach. He wasn't part of her life to honor a fallen brother, or support a friend, he was family—her uncle.

Vitali was right to keep this from me, she thought. *I wasn't ready.*

"What happened in Syria," Kate asked. "Explain it to me."

He met her eyes. "We thought you were dead. All of you. Along with my wife and daughter." His voice was matter-of-fact, stripped of apology. "For months, Nikolai searched the orphanages, hoping, praying—finding nothing but chaos and despair."

Mikhail swallowed hard, his voice rough. "By the time I was released from prison, there was nothing left to search. Files burned. Names erased. We buried the ghosts that haunted our dreams."

Kate's throat went dry. "Then how—in Syria, how did you know who I was, really was?"

"The birthmark on your arm. A broken heart, just here." He motioned without touching. "I saw it during the interrogation—I dared not hope, not at first. I needed proof."

"That's why the chess board," Kate realized. "Would I remember the game? Would I make the same move, or fall for the trap?"

"Until I had the results of the blood test, it was worth a try."

"And in the meantime, you ordered them to clean and feed me."

Mikhail shifted, the bandage pulling slightly. "When I returned to Syria," he said, "I learned my orders were ignored. Saw what that butcher did..."

He trailed off.

Kate's hand moved instinctively to her chest, fingers brushing the thin fabric over the scars she carried. The air thickened. Neither spoke for a long moment.

Finally, Mikhail cleared his throat. "I've arranged this meeting because what was taken should be returned. You deserve to know where you come from. Who you are. And you are not alone."

Kate looked from one man to the other—the scholar and the soldier, two sides of the same family, bonded by love and loss.

She forced herself to speak. "Then you already know who's looking for you—and why it wasn't safe to stay in Paris.

"Yes." Mikhail's mouth twitched into something that might have been a smile. "I should have killed the pup when I had the chance," he said. "Now he's a wolf. Let him come."

The fire popped, sending a spark spiraling upward.

Nikolai poured tea for all three of them, his hands steady despite the tension. "I built my fortune acquiring things others could not—books, artifacts, sometimes secrets. The government found that useful. So did the military."
He smiled faintly. "But nothing is safe forever."

Kate let the words settle. The Petrova code, unspoken but clear: survival was the family business. *If Nazir and his men dared come for Zhukov, he'd find the Petrovas waiting.*

The Malinois lay near the hearth, head lifted, eyes alert as if it understood every word.

Mikhail accepted his cup, the metal at his temple catching the light.
"The body slows," he said, voice low. "But what matters remains. And this—" his gaze met hers "—this had to be set right."

Kate held her tea, feeling its warmth seep into her fingers. Kate nodded, though the weight of everything unsaid hung between them. Outside, the fog pressed against the windows, and the silence that settled over the room was not peace—it was inheritance.

Nikolai refilled her cup, his hand steady. "Tomorrow, you'll meet the others," he said. "Some are away—university, government work—but a few are here at the estate. They're eager to meet their American cousin."

The word *cousin* caught her off guard. For years she'd convinced herself she had no one. Now, surrounded by the smell of birch smoke and old paper, the truth felt almost too heavy to hold.

"Thank you," she said quietly. "For giving me this."

Nikolai nodded once, his expression unreadable. "Go rest, Ekaterina. Tomorrow will come soon enough."

Kate rose. Kiro followed her to the door, nails clicking softly on the floorboards. She turned once, meeting Mikhail's eyes. There was strength, determination—but something else too, she thought. Regret. Resolve. Secrets still waiting their turn.

In the hallway, the warmth of the fire gave way to the cool air from the corridor. She found the small guest room they'd prepared for her, set her bag on the table, and powered up the matte-black phone Vitali had given her.

The screen glowed in the dim light—no signal, just encrypted relay sync. A moment later, a message appeared.

KEISHA 911

Her stomach tightened. She opened it, scanning fast.

Julian's missing. The van's here, but his chair's gone. I don't know what to do.

Kate sat on the edge of the bed, already calculating flight routes and timing. She typed back quickly:

Stay put. Don't touch anything. I'll be there as soon as I can.

Her reflection stared back from the black glass—tired eyes, pale light, a thousand miles to go. She looked toward the window, fog pressing against the glass. Family could wait, she realized. Julian and Keisha were family—her family by choice.

Julian. You brilliant, reckless bastard. What have you done now?

Kate was certain of one thing—whatever he was doing, he was in over his head—again.

She shoved the phone into her pocket and darted back into the grand hall.

"What has happened?" Mikhail asked before she could utter a word.

"Nomad's missing."

"Taken?"

"Probably. How fast can I get to New York?"

"Grab your bag," Nikolai said. "We need to get you out of Russia—it will not be comfortable, but we have a cargo flight out at midnight. Vitali can arrange a connection to the States."

She returned a moment later, bag slung over her shoulder. The men were already moving—voices sharp, boots on wood, the sound of a house mobilizing. The jeep's headlights swept the entry as the front door opened.

Nikolai stood by the threshold, phone still in hand, issuing orders in Russian.

"Hold the flight," he said, his tone cutting through the commotion. "You have a passenger tonight."

He ended the call and met her eyes. "Vladikavkaz by midnight. Five hours to Paris."

Nikolai turned back toward the sitting room, returning a moment later with the wooden frame from the mantle—the photograph of her parents holding her as an infant.

"Take this," he said, pressing it into her hands. "Remember them as I do." His voice was steady, but his eyes betrayed the cost. "When you return, you can examine the others. Take whatever you like."

Kate looked down at the young couple frozen in time, at the baby between them who would grow up to forget them both. Her throat tightened.

"Thank you, Deda," she managed.

Mikhail shifted, trying to rise, but she stopped him with a hand on his shoulder. "Don't," she said gently. "You've done enough."

He smiled faintly, weary eyes sharp with understanding.

Nikolai stepped forward. She kissed his cheek, managed a one-armed hug. ""Deda, thank you—for the truth," she said. "I know there's more—something you're not telling me. But that's a conversation for another day. My friend's life may depend on it."

She tucked the frame carefully into her bag, its wooden edges solid against her palm—a weight that felt like both promise and anchor.

Kate turned toward the open door. Kiro stood there, alert, head tilted. The dog gave a low whine, as if sensing what came next.

The door closed behind her.

Inside, silence lingered for a long moment before Mikhail spoke. "She has her mother's gift. Elena could see what others missed—feel danger before it arrived."

Nikolai tamped his pipe, gaze fixed on the fire. "It kept her alive longer than most."

"Will you tell her?" Mikhail asked.

Nikolai exhaled a thin cloud of smoke. "If she lives. Right now, it would be a distraction—one that could get her killed."

Outside, the fog lifted in tatters as the wind chewed the mist away. Kate slid into the jeep, the door thudding shut behind her. The engine bit, gravel spat, headlights cutting a path back into the dark. She thought of New York—maybe this time, she told herself, no one would have to die.

Chapter 22

TUESDAY, MAY 11
11:57 PM MSK

BESLAN AIRSTRIP—NORTH OSSETIA, RUSSIA

The airfield was little more than a strip of cracked tarmac carved from the pines. A gust swept down from the hills, rattling the rusted hangar doors. The Ilyushin Il-76 waited on the apron, engines whining at idle, fuselage patched with age and weather.

One of the Petrova men hoisted Kate's bag and motioned toward the ramp. "Not comfortable," he said in accented English. "But safe."

Kate managed a thin smile. "I've flown worse."

Inside, the hold smelled of fuel and cold metal. Cargo nets crisscrossed the walls, and the only seats were strips of webbing bolted along the ribs. She clipped in, boots braced against the deck.

The ramp sealed with a hydraulic groan, cutting off the wind and runway lighting. The engines spooled higher, vibration running through the metal skin.

Across from her, the loadmaster—thick-necked, *Petrova Logistics* patch on his jacket—checked his clipboard and called forward to the cockpit.

"One stop," he said over the noise. "Quick offload, then Paris."

Kate didn't ask where. She thought of her grandfather's words: *I built my fortune acquiring things others could not... the government found that useful.*

She understood now. This was what Petrova business looked like—legal enough, profitable always.

She closed her eyes as the aircraft lifted through the clouds, the hum settling into a rhythm somewhere between memory and sleep. She could still feel the warmth of Deda's embrace, fragments of childhood stirring from where they'd been buried for years. And Julian—gone once, maybe lost again—haunted the edge of every thought.

But there would be no answers tonight. Only the steady thrum of engines and the pull of exhaustion, drawing her finally under.

***

WEDNESDAY, MAY 12
2:50 AM CEST
LE BOURGET PRIVATE TERMINAL—PARIS, FRANCE.

THE CARGO PLANE DESCENDED through low cloud and landed with a bone-deep thud, tires squealing as they met French tarmac. It rolled to a stop at the edge of the private terminal. Customs officials in dark coats waited by a small table beside a fuel truck. The loadmaster unlatched the side door and motioned for her to disembark.

One official checked her passport, another held out paperwork to sign—export declarations, transit clearance, nothing that raised a brow. When she handed the pen back, a black sedan pulled alongside the wing.

"Your transfer," the customs agent said.

The driver, a young man in a charcoal suit, opened the door and offered a polite nod. "Welcome to Paris, Ms. Petrova."

She corrected him automatically. "Mrs. Preacher."

He smiled without apology. "Of course. Your connecting flight is waiting at the private apron."

They drove past rows of private jets gleaming under a washed Parisian sky. At the far end of the apron, a sleek Gulfstream G700 waited. Kate's breath caught—not at the plane, but at the woman waiting at the bottom of the stairs.

Bella Marquez stood with the breeze tugging at her hair. The Paris elegance was still there—dark jeans, boots, a cream blouse beneath a short trench—but it was Kate's battered messenger bag slung over Bella's shoulder that stopped her cold. Completely out of place against the designer clothes, and the most beautiful thing Kate could imagine.

"When they said Vitali would arrange a flight," Kate said as she approached, "I thought he'd charter something. How did you get roped into this?"

"Vitali called. I offered." Bella slipped Kate's messenger bag off her shoulder. "I grabbed everything from your hotel room, and knew you'd need your security blanket."

Kate reached for it. Bella pulled it back.

"No way. I'll carry it for now—and let's just hope you can make it up the stairs."

"I've been worse."

"Doubtful." Bella's expression softened. "Oh—Vitali tucked a phone in here. Looks like an iPhone. I don't know what that's about."

"I do. It's a KATIM—like his."

Military-grade encryption, satellite routing, untraceable. So they could talk securely. Day or night.

Bella studied her for a moment, then nodded. "Come on. Let's get you on board—you look hungry and exhausted, and I can fix at least one of those."

Kate paused at the stairs. "What about your meetings—the new product launch?"

"I canceled. The Paris rollout can wait." Bella brushed a loose strand of hair from her face, eyes sparkling. "I have enough money, but few true friends. And I'm wise enough to know they're far more precious."

***

THE GULFSTREAM LEVELED AT forty thousand feet, its cabin lights dimmed to amber. Paris disappeared below—just a haze of city lights swallowed by cloud.

Kate stirred at the sound of soft china. Bella was setting two small cups on the table between them. "Espresso," she offered.

Kate smiled faintly, the aroma too tempting to ignore. "Perfect. Thanks." She took the cup, cradling it with both hands, the heat comforting in her palms.

Bella leaned back, bare feet tucked under her. Even in jeans and a loose blouse she carried a quiet grace—elegant but human, the fatigue showing around her eyes. "You know," she said, "most people crossing the Atlantic at three a.m. are escaping something."

Kate looked out the window. The sky beyond was a bruised indigo, dawn just beginning to smudge the edge of the world. "Maybe I am."

Bella studied her for a moment. "You don't have to talk about it."

"I know." Kate sipped, the bitterness grounding her. "But I will—when I can make sense of it."

They fell into silence, the kind that comes from shared exhaustion rather than distance. The jet's engines droned steady, a sound that wrapped around them like white noise.

Kate's thoughts drifted—to the Petrova estate, to Deda's eyes, to Julian. Every path led forward to New York. Whatever waited there, she would face it.

She finished the espresso and set the cup down. "Wake me when we're close."

Bella nodded, pulling a soft throw from the seat beside her.

Kate closed her eyes. Outside, the first light of dawn brushed the wing in silver, and the ocean below turned from black to blue.

***

WEDNESDAY, MAY 12
11:42 AM EDT
TETERBORO AIRPORT—NEW JERSEY.

The Gulfstream dropped through a bank of clouds, kissed the runway, and taxied toward a quiet hangar on the far side of the field.

Inside, the cabin lights brightened. Bella stretched, smoothing her hair back into place, every motion unhurried. "Finally," she said softly, then smiled. "Nice to be back on solid ground."

Kate didn't answer. Her stomach had already tightened at the thought of what waited ahead.

The jet came to a stop near a glass-fronted building marked *U.S. Customs and Border Protection—General Aviation Entry.* Two uniformed officers stood by the door, one of them waving them forward.

Inside, the customs suite was quiet and antiseptic—cream walls, brushed steel, the hum of air filtration. A woman in her forties, composed and professional, greeted them. "Welcome back, Ms. Marquez," she said, checking Bella's passport. "Where's the rest of your team?"

"Just a friend this trip," Bella said easily.

The officer's gaze shifted to Kate. She scanned the passport, then looked up. Recognition flickered—surprise, sympathy, respect—but her tone stayed neutral. "Welcome back, Mrs. Preacher."

Kate inclined her head, appreciating the grace of silence.

Customs took less than ten minutes—signatures, a perfunctory glance at luggage, and the thump of an entry stamp. When the final form was signed, the officer handed back their documents and nodded toward the private exit. "You're all set, ladies."

The door slid open to the small reception area beyond. Through the glass wall ahead, Kate caught sight of a battered black SUV idling by the curb.

Keisha leaned against the hood, one hand wrapped around her Army coffee mug, like a shield. The moment she saw Kate, she straightened—relief flashing into nervous tension.

***

WEDNESDAY, MAY 12
12:03 PM EDT
EN ROUTE TO MANHATTAN.

Kate crossed the distance in a few quick strides, her duffel slung over one shoulder. "It's good to see you," she said quietly, and meant it. Then she gestured toward Bella emerging behind her. "Keisha, this is—"

"Kate—I don't live in a cave—well, sort of, but I know Isabella Marquez." Keisha extended a hand. "It's a pleasure, Ms. Marquez"

"Oh, please. Call me Bella."

Keisha smiled, nodded and popped the back of the SUV, "You can stow your gear here."

Bella settled into the back seat as Kate slid into the passenger seat, wincing as the seatbelt caught her shoulder.

"How bad is it," Keisha asked.

"Hurts like hell, but I'll live."

"When we get to Manhattan, let me have a look."

Kate shot her a sidelong glance. "You know Julian ratted you out."

"What's that supposed to mean?"

"It means you have a tell. When things get uncomfortable you go full nurse mode," Kate said. "So let's hear it. What's going on?"

Keisha hesitated, her glance flicking toward the rearview mirror.

"It's okay," Kate said. "Anything you have to say to me, you can say in front of Bella."

Keisha exhaled slowly. "Andrew Freeman is dead. Right now, he's in the morgue as a John Doe—suicide."

Bella drew in a slow breath but said nothing.

Kate's voice stayed level. "When?"

"Saturday night."

"If he's listed as a John Doe, how did Julian know it was Andrew?"

"All I know is that when I got up Sunday morning, Julian had crime scene photos up on the monitors," Keisha said. "And honestly, seeing dead people on his screens is getting pretty old."

"If he was able to identify the body, why not tell the police?"

"I think it had something to do with the message Andrew sent. I don't know what was in it, but Julian was spooked—really spooked."

"Did you see anything?"

"Just the title. All caps. FAIL- something."

"Failsafe," Kate said.

"Yeah, that sounds right. Does that help?"

"Yes," Kate said. "I need to find that message."

Bella leaned forward. "Failsafe—what does that mean?"

"It means Andrew knew he was in danger," Kate said. "A failsafe message only sends if it's not manually canceled. It's the last thing you do when you think you're about to die."

Keisha's grip tightened on the wheel, knuckles whitening.

"Spit it out, Keisha," Kate said. "I can see something's eating you alive."

Keisha swallowed. "Given what we've all been through," she said, glancing at Bella, "I asked Julian if you were in danger."

"And?"

"You know Nomad's half-answers. He said 'not yet'—but that I could help."

"Oh no," Kate said, recognizing the pattern. "What did you do?"

"I retrieved Devin Moore's Gold NanoVault."

"There's no way Leslie would've just handed it over."

"I didn't ask."

"You broke into Richmond Tower and stole it?" Kate said, incredulous. "And hang on—how did Julian even know it was there? He's still spying on me—isn't he? That sneaky little bastard. Wait until I get my hands on him."

"I'm sorry, Kate," Keisha said. "I thought I was helping—I thought your life was on the line. Now I don't know what to believe."

"Julian's nothing if not strategic," Kate said. "That's what made him such a challenging chess opponent. For some reason, he needed that NanoVault. I assume he took it with him."

"Maybe," Keisha said. "It's not in the loft—I searched. But he had me deliver a package to a courier. It could have been in there—or that could have been a trick to get me out of the way."

"Out of the way?"

"Yep. I met the courier in the Azores. Long flight. Good food."

Bella leaned forward between the seats. "Sorry, I'm still catching up. Andrew was someone you all knew, Julian's the one missing—and Nomad is...?"

Kate exhaled. "Same man. Too many names."

"Got it," Bella said, settling back.

Kate stared out the windshield as the Manhattan skyline took shape. The fortress wasn't visible yet, but she could feel it—steel and concrete hidden in plain sight, like its owner.

The SUV merged onto the expressway. Traffic thickened, horns blending into the steady hum of engines. For a while, none of them spoke.

Finally, Kate broke the silence. "Once we're in, don't touch anything until I say. Nomad's paranoid for good reason."

Keisha nodded, jaw tight, eyes locked on the road.

Bella gave a low, knowing laugh. "Sounds like someone else I know."

Minutes later, the SUV rolled into the Manhattan garage entrance. Keisha punched a code into the keypad; the ram barriers lowered, the hydraulic gate hissed, then lifted. They circled up one floor at a time, the lights flicking on as they approached, and Keisha parked beside Julian's van.

"Now I've seen it all," Bella said. "This has to be the most... unique office and loft I've ever seen."

"For a man determined to hide both his identity and his location, it was brilliant," Kate said. "But as my grandfather reminded me, nothing stays safe forever."

"Your grandfather?" Bella asked.

"Long story," Kate said, smiling faintly. "Good story."

Bella nodded once, her gaze sweeping the vast, sterile space.

Kate moved toward Nomad's console, but Keisha stepped in front of her. "Not yet. Kitchen. Now."

"Keisha—"

"Dressings first. Work second." Keisha's tone left no room for argument. "You've been traveling for hours. I need to check those wounds. Better light, cleaner workspace."

Kate opened her mouth to protest, then closed it. She followed Keisha to the kitchen area while Bella trailed behind, watching with quiet interest.

Keisha washed her hands thoroughly at the sink, then laid out her medical supplies on the clean counter—gauze, antiseptic, tape. She pulled out one of the stools. "Sit."

Kate sat, and Keisha worked with efficient precision—carefully peeling back the dressings to examine the entry and exit wounds under the bright kitchen lights.

"No fresh bleeding," Keisha murmured, dabbing antiseptic around the healing tissue. "But you're pushing it, Kate. These are still raw."

"I'm fine."

"You're functional. There's a difference." Keisha applied fresh gauze and tape with practiced hands. "Because if you end up in the hospital—or worse, die on me—we'll never find Julian."

Kate managed a tired smile. "Can't have that."

"No, we can't." Keisha secured the final strip of tape and helped Kate ease her arm back into the sling. "Now you can work. But carefully."

Kate stood, then crossed to Nomad's console, resting her good hand on the edge of the desk.

"Let's see what he left behind—what he knows," Kate said. "And whether he ran or was taken."

Chapter 23

WEDNESDAY, MAY 12
4:45 PM CEST

EXECUTIVE HELIPAD—THE MOUNTAIN, DAVOS.

The AERIONIX XV-7 VTOL—short for Vertical Takeoff and Landing jet—descended through a wash of gray cloud, its whisper-quiet rotors angling for a vertical landing. Below, the helipad glowed like a coin set in the granite shoulder of the Alps, the surrounding peaks veiled in fog. From above, the platform seemed impossibly small, a postage stamp on a mountain—the kind of place few would dare to land.

Inside, Rileyne Mueller unbuckled, smoothing the black sleeve of her coat. Her aide, Annelise, leaned forward from the opposite seat. "Ground team reports secured perimeter, ma'am."

Rileyne didn't answer. Her gaze followed the digital readouts fading across the cockpit glass, the aircraft's AI-copilot disengaging with an obedient hum. AERIONIX—a GEC subsidiary—was one of her father's more public ventures, but it had been her design initiative that perfected its silent thrust vectors.

The door lifted. Cold air swept in, sharp and clean. Rileyne stepped into the thin alpine air, her coat dark against the white glare of floodlights. Two attendants hurried forward, but she waved them off.

Annelise, tablet in hand, followed close behind, logging arrival codes, updating the Davos system manifest. At the edge of the pad waited Erik Voss, the facility's General Manager—blandly efficient, unmemorable in a way that made him ideal for the job.

"Ms. Mueller," he said with a small bow. "On behalf of everyone here, our deepest—"

"Save it," Rileyne cut in. "We have work to do."

They crossed the pad toward a glass-walled corridor, the wind dying as the security doors sealed behind them. Inside, warmth returned, accompanied by the low, omnipresent hum of the facility's power grid.

At the far end, a guard held the elevator, releasing the door as she stepped inside.

The car dropped fast and smooth, walls of glass revealing the carved tunnel around them—a cylinder of polished stone and stainless steel that seemed to fall forever.

Voss cleared his throat. "We've maintained continuous operations since your last inspection. Power draw stable. Security protocols updated per your request."

"Good." Her eyes stayed on the levels sliding past. "And Dr. Chen?"

"Dr. Chen and his team are waiting on the arrival platform. The demonstration is ready in the BioSec wing."

"Excellent. I trust it will justify my father's faith—and my investment."

The elevator doors opened to the hyperloop platform, their transport pod waiting, sleek and silent.

"The hyperloop system has performed flawlessly," Voss said. "Zero maintenance incidents since your upgrades."

"As it should," Rileyne said. "Musk shared the idea. What slowed him was everything wrapped around it."

Voss blinked. "Ma'am?"

"Committees. Reviews. Restraints." She stepped toward the capsule. "His engineers were brilliant. Ours were simply more motivated."

"Motivated how?"

She did not look back.

"Failure wasn't an option," Rileyne said. "It was a death sentence."

Voss nodded once, choosing his words. "Four-minute transit to central sector. Then we'll transfer to BioSec for the demonstration."

They stepped into the pod's cabin—sleek, windowless, a triumph of engineering that Elon Musk had conceived and Rileyne's team perfected. The interior was minimalist: steel and black glass, ergonomic seats designed for extreme acceleration.

Rileyne allowed herself another small smile as the door sealed with a soft click. The man had released his Hyperloop white paper to the world, thinking transparency would accelerate development. Instead, it had accelerated theft.

RILEE had infiltrated Boring Company servers eighteen months before Musk's first test tunnel broke ground. Every contractor communication, every engineering specification, every materials supplier—all harvested, analyzed, improved upon. By the time Musk was seeking permits in Nevada, the GEC hyperloop was already operational beneath the Alps.

Her father had approved the project. But the infiltration protocols? Those had been hers.

The capsule launched forward—a whisper of acceleration pressing them into their seats. No jolt, no roar of engines. Just silent motion as the pod accelerated past 700 kilometers per hour in the vacuum-sealed tube.

Through the window, light flared in rhythmic pulses as they passed maintenance bays, dormitories, medical corridors glimpsed for mere seconds. No air resistance meant no sound, no vibration, no evidence. Just silent motion at speeds that would have made Musk weep with envy.

He designed the future of transportation, Rileyne thought, watching the tunnels blur past. I built the infrastructure of control.

One corridor held her gaze longer: a surgical wing, its observation lamps bright and sterile. Figures moved behind the glass—surgeons bent over a gurney, instruments glinting.

Rileyne's eyes lingered, but she said nothing.

"Upgrades," Voss offered quickly. "Neural research. New contracts."

She nodded once, unreadable, and turned away as the capsule shot deeper into the mountain.

Moments later, the pod slowed—deceleration as smooth as the launch—and glided to a stop inside the main transit hub. The vacuum seal released with a soft hiss. From here, everything converged—the logistics bays, AI control sectors, and deeper labs sealed behind biometric checkpoints. The air was cooler here, filtered and antiseptic.

Dr. Chen waited with a delegation of researchers and two silent security escorts. His expression blended deference with fatigue.

"Ms. Mueller," he said, bowing slightly. "We're honored to have you on-site. The BioSec demonstration is ready for your review."

She moved past him without reply, the click of her heels echoing against the steel floor. On either side of the corridor, glass walls revealed fragments of the facility's anatomy—labs, observation rooms, corridors alive with data light.

At a junction, Chen cleared his throat. "If you'll follow me, there's one matter I'd like to address before we begin."

He guided her down a narrower auxiliary corridor, past sealed storage bays and a series of biohazard cabinets humming with containment energy. His hands were clasped too tightly behind his back—a tension he tried, and failed, to hide.

"I understand you made... specific personnel requests for today's demonstration," he said carefully. "Two individuals not ordinarily cleared for BioSec procedures. Your directive was quite explicit."

Rileyne's walk never slowed. "And you complied?"

"Yes, of course," he said quickly. "They're already in the prep chamber. A guard from Detention Bravo and Dr. Leong from Genomic Analysis. Though I admit I do not understand why these two were chosen over the normal handlers for the rhesus specimens. They were—"

"They were not what I needed today."

Chen blinked. "I see."

"No," she said. "You don't. But you will."

They passed a surveillance alcove—RILEE's data streams rippling across black glass. Heart-rate telemetry. Proximity alerts. Whispered conversations flagged and archived.

Rileyne's gaze flicked across the data, then moved on.

"Is there some concern with their participation?" she asked lightly.

"No," Chen said, though his voice betrayed him. "Only that the pairing is... unusual."

A small, knowing smile touched her lips. "Pairing is one word for it."

Chen stopped breathing for a moment.

Rileyne leaned closer as if sharing a confidence. "Your staff forgets that nothing in this mountain exists outside RILEE's sight. Not stolen minutes. Not whispered promises. Not plans to escape that would never, ever succeed."

She resumed walking, her tone cool as the mountain stone around them.

"Today's demonstration serves multiple purposes," she said. "Verification. Correction. And clarity."

She let silence underline the words.

"For everyone."

Chen swallowed hard. "Understood."

"I doubt that," she said softly. "But you will."

She stepped into the observation gallery without looking back.

The gallery opened before them—a wall of glass facing the demonstration chamber. An armed guard stood near the door. A young woman in a white coat wheeled the test subject into position. The rhesus monkey darted around its cage before settling and staring directly at Rileyne.

On the console lay a single black iPhone. Chen picked it up and offered it to her.

"This is the control interface. Field units receive limited-access versions—sanctioned targets only. This device, as you requested, has full administrative privileges."

Rileyne took it. The glass lit beneath her touch—rows of names and DNA sequences scrolling endlessly downward.

"Are you in here?" she asked.

Chen froze, panic flashing before he could stop it. "Yes—of course—all lab personnel."

"Relax," she said softly. "I'm joking."

No one laughed.

She set the phone down and tapped the intercom. Her voice carried easily through the gallery speakers.

"Who's handling the test?"

A young woman in a lab coat straightened below. "Dr. Mara Leong, ma'am."

"Mara, how long have you been here?"

"Three years."

"You must be looking forward to going home."

Mara swallowed. "We all are, ma'am. But the work... it's important."

Rileyne's eyes slid to the guard at the chamber door. "Do you know Mara?"

He straightened. "We've spoken, occasionally. In passing."

The lie hung in the air like static.

"And you?" she asked. "Are you looking forward to the surface as well. Someday."

"Yes, ma'am."

"Very good. Let's proceed."

Chen nodded nervously. "Target vector set for the primate. A brief dose, non-lethal—"

But Rileyne wasn't listening. A quick search and swipe on the iPhone selected a new target—a lethal dose.

Dr. Mara Leong.

She tapped the screen. A faint blue pulse rippled along the base of the chamber as the Bluetooth handshake linked to the emitters inside.

Mara glanced at the monkey, then at the glass. She didn't yet understand.

A single drop of blood slid from her nose, bright against her skin. She touched it, stared at her hand, then up at Rileyne.

Chen's voice cracked the silence. "What have you done?"

Rileyne didn't look away. "Eliminated a traitor. Closed a project risk. And satisfied my concern that the device—and the weapon—actually work—on humans."

Mara stumbled back, nose bleeding freely now, tears cutting through the red. The guard caught her as she convulsed, holding her as if he could stop what was coming.

"Stop it!" he shouted. "You can stop it! The antidote—I know you have it!"

Rileyne's voice carried through the intercom, calm and almost curious. "Did you really think you could hide the affair? Or an escape? There's nothing happening here that I don't know."

The guard's face went white. He pulled her closer, blood soaking his sleeve. Then he raised his weapon and fired.

Bullets cracked against the ballistic glass. Chen dove for cover. The technicians scattered. Rileyne didn't move.

"There was never a way out," she said softly. "But now you can join her."

She swiped the phone again. A faint blue flicker answered from the chamber.

The guard froze mid-breath, a thin red line tracing down from his nostril. For a heartbeat he stood perfectly still—then his head burst apart in a wet concussion that painted the lab in red.

For the first time, Rileyne blinked. The faintest hint of surprise crossed her face—almost amusement. Then her lips curved, as though the world had just revealed a darkly funny secret.

"What was that?" she asked as Chen pulled himself upright.

"It... it happens occasionally," he said, voice thin. "A cross-link—an unintentional tether between active and dormant sequences. We're still working to isolate the cause."

Rileyne's eyes remained on the chamber, on the streaks sliding down the glass. "Don't," she said softly. "Random terror has value."

She turned toward the door, slipping the phone into her coat pocket. "See that the animal's sent to a proper zoo. He's been through enough."

The doors sealed behind her, leaving Dr. Chen staring at the bloody glass—the reality of what he'd created written in blood. They were all in the database now, every name, every genome—each one expendable.

Chapter 24

WEDNESDAY, MAY 12
12:03 PM EDT

NOMAD'S FORTRESS—MANHATTAN

The fortress looked normal at first glance—monitors glowing with their usual array of data streams and servers humming their steady rhythm. But something was off.

Kate stopped at the semicircular desk, studying the displays. Code scrolled across one screen, network traffic graphs on another, what looked like a cryptocurrency mining operation on a third. All of it active. All of it meaningless.

"What is it?" Keisha asked, reading Kate's expression.

"He wanted you to think he was upstairs sleeping," Kate said, pointing at the monitors. "Look at this—it's all busywork. Automated scripts running in circles. Nothing that requires actual attention."

She leaned closer to the main display. A Monte Carlo simulation analyzing chess positions, but the parameters were nonsense—evaluating checkmates that couldn't exist, running millions of calculations that led nowhere.

"Julian's version of leaving the TV on when you go on vacation," Kate said quietly. "Make it look lived-in so no one realizes you're gone."

"How long do you think—" Keisha started.

"Long enough that he didn't want you calling me right away." Kate pulled out the desk chair, sat down. "He knew you'd get curious—eventually, and come looking for him. Whatever he's doing, he needed a head start."

"I don't know what he's doing," Keisha added. "But I might know why—yesterday was the anniversary."

Kate straightened. "What anniversary?"

There was a pause. Not secrecy—care. The quiet hesitation of someone who knew where the darkness was hidden.

"The fall," Keisha said. "His injury. It was twelve years ago."

Kate blinked.

The date she remembered was the one on Julian's headstone.

The day she visited. Spoke to him. Grieved for him.

That was the date she carried.

Bella moved closer, arms folded. "So he's definitely gone by choice."

"Looks that way." Kate said. "It wouldn't be the first time he wanted Keisha out of harm's way, but that doesn't mean he knows what he's getting into."

"Or that someone didn't push him," Keisha murmured.

Kate grabbed the dusty keyboard in front of the central monitor. Around her, the surrounding screens continued their chaotic dance—code scrolling, graphs fluctuating, cryptocurrency mining operations churning through calculations. She tuned it all out, focusing on the command station display.

Julian can't use the keyboard, she knew. *He staged this for me to find—or to trap whoever did.*

The display was a chess board. The position showing black with an overwhelming advantage, and above the board, a simple prompt: **Black's Move**

The last time I was here, Kate thought. *Nomad set me up with everything I needed. This time I'm on my own, and facing the configuration of one of the most gifted hackers on the planet.*

"This is going to take some time," Kate said to the two women hovering behind her.

"Oh, right," Bella said. "We'll leave you to it." When Keisha didn't move, Bella took a more direct approach. "Keisha, can you help me in the kitchen? We'll pull together some snacks, and come up with a plan for dinner. Any wine?"

Keisha followed Bella to the kitchen, glancing back at Kate.

"Don't worry," Bella said. "If anyone can find him, it's Kate. And when she does, we'll go get him. Now, about that wine."

"Sorry, Julian doesn't drink, and I'm..."

"No worries," Bella interrupted. "This is New York, and I know right where to go. I'll make a call—grab your keys.

Bella and Keisha swept by Kate on their way out. "We're going to run out and stock up on essentials. How's Italian sound for dinner?"

Kate didn't answer—eyes glued to the screen.

"Geez...she's as bad as he is," Keisha said. "She won't even notice we're gone—let's just go."

When Bella and Keisha left, the fortress settled into silence.

Kate exhaled, slow and controlled, but Keisha's words lingered.

The anniversary.

She felt a cold ripple move through her.

A man who had lived with that wound for twelve years...a man who had just learned it wasn't fate but betrayal...might take risks he'd never taken before.

It reframed everything she saw—the looping scripts, the hollow simulations, the deliberate misdirection. None of it was busywork.

It was a trail.

A signal.

A message he hoped she'd understand before it was too late.

Kate leaned in, fingers settling on the edge of the desk.

"Alright, Julian," she whispered. "Show me what you need me to see."

She turned to the board.

Black's position was overwhelming—pieces aligned for a kill. She could win it in three moves without thinking.

She reached for the mouse and made the obvious play.

ACCESS DENIED: 3 MOVES REMAINING

A countdown timer appeared in the corner: 8:00—the seconds disappearing—7:59. 7:58.

"So that's how you want to play it?" Kate asked, imagining Nomad smiling.

But she knew this was serious. *No turning back now.*. The timer confirmed her worst fear. Failure could mean only one thing—his entire system wiped clean.

The screen refreshed, and the board changed. An entirely new position, but similar—black again on the attack, white's position crumbling. Black would win in three moves.

Her fingers hovered over the mouse. *This was Julian's login system. He'd want someone who could see the winning moves. Right?* She moved again.

ACCESS DENIED: 2 MOVES REMAINING

The timer cut in half: 4:00. 3:59.

Kate felt the chill that washed over her, as the pressure mounted. With every false move, she had fewer moves remaining, and half the time.

The board refreshed again. Another position, black winning, white helpless.

Wait. It's different, but the same. Come on, Kate. See the pattern—what does it mean?

She forced herself to stop. Three different positions, all carefully constructed, all showing black with an overwhelming advantage. Each time she'd gone for the throat, pushed for victory, and each time she failed.

"What do you want from me?" She asked. "Do you want me to lose?

3:31. 3:30.

She studied the current position. Black was crushing. White was dead. She could force the win easily.

Kate glanced at the clock, reached for the mouse, and stopped.

2:47. 2:46.

Close your eyes. Forget the clock. This was Julian's work—brilliant, paranoid Julian. It's not a skill test. Any decent player would know how to win. This is an authentication. He's pressing me to do something only I would know.. Think. Remember.

Freshman year. The Pan-Am Collegiate Championship—the biggest tournament of the year. The team had already clinched the title before the final round, thanks to wins from Kate and the others. But Julian was playing the last board, facing some hotshot from Berkeley, and Kate studied every move.

Julian's play was remarkable. Elegant. Unstoppable. The kind of finish that would end up in chess journals.

And then he offered a draw.

Berkeley stared at the board. He didn't see it—thought Julian was bluffing. He'd refused, played on. Three moves later, he'd resigned.

Kate cornered him after the match. "Why offer the draw? You had him."

"Sometimes the most powerful move is the one you don't make." He'd looked at her with those intense eyes. "We'd already won the tournament. Berkeley just didn't know he'd already lost. Giving him the choice—letting him decide—that was stronger than crushing him."

At the time, she thought Julian was showing off. Later she saw it as kind.

But that was before Devin Moore pushed him off a balcony. Before Julian spent a dozen years in a wheelchair, completely dependent, surrounded by power he could access through code but a body he couldn't control.

1:58. 1:57.

Julian knew what it meant to see the winning move and choose not to make it. To have overwhelming force and exercise restraint. To understand that sometimes the greatest strength was knowing when to stop.

I was right, Kate knew. *This wasn't a test of skill. It was a test of character.*

Kate opened her eyes. Looked at the board. Black could win. She could force it.

Instead, her fingers found the button.

OFFER DRAW

1:33.

The board froze. The timer kept counting. Kate's heart hammered against her ribs.

1:31. 1:30.

Please, Julian. Please let this be right.

The screen flickered.

The timer vanished.

HELLO, KATE. THE BOARD IS YOURS

All the programs he had running—all the noise—stopped. The screens returned to their default settings. Security cameras. News feeds. Slack channels. She had complete administrative access to Nomad's digital world, and that was troubling. *Why give me access to absolutely everything,* she wondered. *Unless you weren't expecting to return.*

Kate exhaled, taking her first deep breath in what felt like an hour. Her hands were shaking.

"Thank you, Julian," she whispered to the empty fortress, and pulled the keyboard closer. This wasn't the time to question Julian's motives.

She had the access she needed, but she needed a moment to breathe and focus. This was a big win, and faster than she expected, but her gut was telling her it would be all uphill from here.

Kate pushed away from the desk. Stood. Stretched. *Time for an espresso? No, later.* Time to find out where he'd gone, and why, and the place to start was

Andrew's message.

She settled back into the chair and started typing—system-wide search for anything related to FAILSAFE.

Andrew's message was an immediate hit. *Encrypted. As expected. But Julian read it, and so can I.*

Kate smiled. She recognized the cipher. *Wow, this goes way back—first year MIT. That was smart. Andrew knew Julian would spot it—he created it.*

The decryption took seconds, the message scrolling on the screen.

If you're reading this, I'm already dead.

Tell Kate I'm sorry. Sorry I wasn't stronger. Sorry I couldn't stop them. The truth is, I was never more than a pawn. An opening piece, a loose end, something to be swept off the board once the game moved past me.

Maybe it's already too late. Maybe no one can stop what's coming. But what I've attached is everything I know, everything I've hidden. If anyone still has a chance—it's you.

Andrew's regret and anguish was palpable. *The last hope of a doomed man,* she thought. *A challenge Julian could not possibly ignore, but why go it alone?*

The repository he attached to the message was enormous—years of work captured and hidden. *Perhaps he knew this day would come.*

Kate expanded the compressed file and rolled her eyes.

"Here we go again," Kate said. Just like Jake's NanoVault—dozens of folders and hundreds of files. And a quick test confirmed her suspicion. "Yep, most of these are encrypted, but I may be able to speed things up if..."

Kate's digital-forensics playbook took over. Julian had decrypted the files to read them, which meant cached translations might still exist—in memory, in deleted space, even scattered across random sectors of the drive. Most of what she needed was in her messenger bag; the rest, including a few tools she'd quietly liberated from the CIA, lived on her darknet server, hosted and hidden far from prying eyes.

Minutes later she had recovered dozens of files—far from everything but it was a start. She recognized the building blueprints. Jake had some of these. Duncan's drive had a few more, but this is a complete set for a complex for something called: The Mountain.

The challenge with the partial files was that neither she nor Julian could find anywhere on the planet that matched the enormous footprint of the facility.

"Now I see why," Kate said. "It's subterranean."

The complete specs revealed the tunnel and rail line from the Davos commercial complex to deep inside the Swiss mountains. *Looks like something only Elon could build*, Kate thought. *And I'm sure he has no idea they stole his tech.*

Kate knew a detailed analysis of the plans might take days—research labs, medical facilities, dormitories, offices and a geothermal power station, and those were just the major wings of the complex. None of these would have compelled Julian to abandon Keisha and leave everything behind.

Then she saw it, the acronym Julian found on Jake's drive. Neither of them knew what it meant, but the pronunciation left little doubt about who had been pulling the strings.

The building design page titled AI-CORE had a single word in the center of an enormous cylindrical chamber.

RILEE

The unseen figure behind the BountyHunter app, the voice behind so many deaths, was only a first name to the top level players—Riley.

Kate thought perhaps Rileyne Mueller was the puppeteer, along with her father and the Coalition, but now she knew. RILEE was an AI, and this was home. Jake was trying to find it, stop it. And now she knew, all roads lead to Davos.

Jake asked me to solve the puzzle—see what he missed, what everyone missed—and bring them down. That's exactly what I'm going to do.

***

Bella announced their return as she and Keisha arrived with bags of groceries.

"What's all this?" Kate asked.

"Turns out Keisha is a great cook," Bella said.

"I'm a good cook," Keisha corrected. "Not that I ever got to practice with Julian—but I understood. Between his dietary needs, and a high-school palate, there wasn't much room for fine dining."

"Any luck?" Bella asked.

"Some," Kate answered, hesitating. "I'll know more by morning."

"You're going to work all night, aren't you?" Keisha asked.

"Yep—line up the espresso—time for an all-nighter."

"Fine," Bella said. "But we're all going to sit down for dinner—then you can bring us up to speed on what you know, and what you're hiding—yeah, I know that look."

Bella and Keisha continued on to the kitchen, and closed the door.

Apparently I've got a tell—a look, Kate thought. *Need to work on that.*

As Kate dug into Andrew's files, names and places started to connect with Jake's files: *The Final Roll Call* and *The Silent Watch*. Records of dead and missing scientists and specialists—unique skills from across the globe. Experts in artificial intelligence, quantum computing, nuclear power, epidemiology, microbiology—the list went on, and matched some of the names listed as The Mountain occupants.

"What on earth are all of these people working on?" Kate asked, almost afraid to guess at the answer. And even more frightening was the Chinese name of a folder she couldn't open.

Project Wu Sheng

Kate's Chinese was rusty, but good enough to translate on sight.

Silent Weapon

Andrew, what the hell is this, Kate wondered. Given the name and some of the missing scientists, she suspected the worst—*a biological weapon, an engineered pandemic*—and the Chinese project name only amplified her fears.

The encryption on the folder was military-grade Chinese encryption—*PLA standard, maybe MSS*, she thought. *Even Nomad doesn't have the computing resources to crack it any time soon.*

For a moment she thought of Margot, but dismissed the thought almost as fast. *CIA involvement now would almost certainly mean failure—leaks, locked doors, and the rats jumping ship. Can't risk it. Not when we're this close.*

Kate suspected Andrew got his hands on the mystery folder, but had no idea what was inside, or the details of the project. But he was worried, and for good reason.

He left detailed notes on a database he'd designed and built. Database architecture—that was Andrew's genius. *Impressive*, she thought. *A multi-dimensional cube designed to store and search billions of records in micro-seconds.*

That left one obvious question: why? Andrew's notes gave her the answer. DNA.

He documented the breach of every commercial, medical and research DNA repository on the planet. From ancestry sites to hospitals to military records—the sheer magnitude of the theft was astounding, and yet no one seemed to be aware.

Kate recalled obscure reports when ancestry companies went bankrupt—speculation about data breaches, but never proof. Until now.

***

THE SCOPE WAS STAGGERING—BILLIONS of profiles—all indexed, searchable and cross-referenced. *Andrew built the infrastructure, but Wu Sheng had to be the endgame.* And with a name like *Silent Weapon*, Andrew's last hours were spent thinking about what might be unleashed on an unsuspecting world.

Andrew's files raised as many questions as they answered, but one thing was clear—the database he built was critical to the success of *Project Wu Sheng*.

Kate sat back, the weight of it settling over her. A DNA database of billions. A Chinese bioweapon project. Missing scientists with expertise in epidemiology and microbiology. And somewhere deep in the Swiss mountains, RILEE was coordinating it all.

The Mountain. Everything pointed to Davos.

Kate glanced at the clock. Bella and Keisha would have dinner ready soon. She'd need to tell them something—enough to prepare them, not enough to terrify them.

But first, she had calls to make.

Chapter 25

THURSDAY, MAY 13
9:20 AM CEST

REHABILITATION CENTER—THE MOUNTAIN, DAVOS

Julian woke to the sterile white ceiling of the medical suite, his body cataloging pain before his mind fully surfaced. Shoulders burning. Back aching where the exoskeletal brace pressed against healing incisions. A deep, bone-tired exhaustion that felt like it had soaked into his marrow.

The surgery had been three days ago. Or was it four? Time felt elastic down here, measured in increments of discomfort rather than hours.

He heard the door hiss open and turned his head—slowly, because even that hurt.

A woman entered, tall and lean, moving with the kind of efficiency that spoke of military discipline or surgical training. Blonde hair pulled back in a tight braid. Pale blue-gray eyes that swept the room, cataloging monitors, IV lines, the angle of his body in the bed.

She wore dark gray scrubs and a white coat, her ID badge clipped to her pocket: *Dr. A. Strand, Neurointegration Specialist.*

"Mr. Pryce," she said, her accent faintly Scandinavian—vowels precise, consonants crisp. "I'm Dr. Strand. I'll be managing your rehabilitation protocol."

Julian blinked, his mind still sluggish from whatever cocktail of painkillers they'd been feeding him. "Julian," he said. "Please."

"You may call me Dr. Strand." She pulled a tablet from her coat pocket, eyes scanning data. "I prefer to maintain professional boundaries. It benefits both of us."

The emphasis on *both* was slight but unmistakable.

Julian studied her more carefully. She was younger than he'd expected—late thirties, maybe, though the lines around her eyes suggested she'd earned every one of them. Her hands were steady as she adjusted something on the monitor beside his bed, but there was a tension in her shoulders, a tightness in her jaw.

She looked like someone who'd learned not to relax.

"How are you feeling?" she asked, still focused on the tablet.

"Like I got hit by a truck," Julian said. "Then the truck backed up and hit me again."

Her mouth twitched—almost a smile, but not quite. "That's accurate. Your body has experienced significant trauma. The spinal implant alone required six hours of microsurgery. Add the neural mesh integration, the subcutaneous interface ports, and the exoskeletal support frame..." She glanced up. "You'll feel worse before you feel better."

"Great pep talk, Doc."

This time, the almost-smile lingered a fraction longer. "I don't believe in false optimism. You'll need realistic expectations if we're going to make progress."

She moved to the foot of the bed and tapped something on the control panel. The bed shifted, raising Julian's torso to a forty-five-degree angle. His back screamed in protest.

"Deep breath," Dr. Strand said, watching him. "The brace will adjust to your position. Give it a moment."

Julian forced air into his lungs. The exoskeletal frame around his torso pulsed faintly—blue light rippling along the carbon-fiber struts—and the pressure eased slightly. Not comfortable, but bearable.

"Better?" she asked.

"Better."

She made a note on her tablet. "Good. We'll begin with range-of-motion assessments this afternoon. Tomorrow, if your vitals remain stable, we'll move to the primary rehabilitation suite."

"Where's that?"

"Sublevel three. Purpose-built for neurointegration therapy." She tucked the tablet under her arm. "You'll spend most of your waking hours there for the next several months."

Julian let that sink in. Months. He'd known it intellectually, but hearing it stated so bluntly made it real.

"How many times have you done this?" he asked.

Dr. Strand's expression went carefully blank. "The procedure you underwent is rare. Highly specialized."

"That's not an answer."

She met his eyes, and for a moment, something flickered there—grief, maybe, or guilt. "You're my seventh neural integration, Julian."

He noted the use of his first name. Unintentional, probably. A crack in the professional armor.

"And the other six?" he asked quietly.

Her jaw tightened. "Their outcomes varied."

The silence stretched. Julian didn't push. He didn't need to. The weight of what she wasn't saying filled the room.

Finally, Dr. Strand straightened. "Rest. I'll return this afternoon to begin assessments." She turned toward the door, then paused. "For what it's worth, you're different from the others."

"How so?"

She glanced back, her expression unreadable. "You chose this."

The door hissed shut before he could respond.

Chapter 26

THURSDAY, MAY 13
1:35 PM CEST

REHABILITATION CENTER—THE MOUNTAIN, DAVOS

The elevator descended three levels, the motion smooth and nearly silent. Julian sat in his chair, the exoskeletal brace now integrated into a reinforced harness that locked him upright. Every small jolt sent fresh sparks of pain through his back.

Dr. Strand stood beside him, one hand resting lightly on the chair's push handle—not guiding, just present. She hadn't spoken since collecting him from the medical suite.

The doors opened onto a corridor that felt less like a hospital and more like a high-end athletic training facility. The walls were a soft gray-blue, the lighting warm and indirect. No windows—they were too deep for that—but large screens displayed alpine vistas, simulated daylight shifting as if clouds were passing overhead.

Dr. Strand pushed him forward. "This wing was designed for long-term rehabilitation. Everything you'll need is here."

They passed several closed doors—recovery suites, Julian guessed—before reaching a set of double doors at the corridor's end. Dr. Strand pressed her palm to a biometric scanner. The doors slid open.

The space beyond was enormous—easily the size of a basketball court. The floor was rubberized, marked with geometric patterns and measurement grids. One wall was floor-to-ceiling mirrors. Another held racks of equipment: parallel bars, resistance bands, weight machines, objects Julian couldn't immediately identify.

But it was the center of the room that caught his attention.

A framework of articulated steel arms descended from the ceiling, surrounding a raised platform. The arms ended in padded harnesses and support braces, all of it adjustable, all of it designed to hold a human body in perfect suspension.

"That's where we'll start," Dr. Strand said, following his gaze. "Partial weight-bearing exercises. The suspension system will support you while we rebuild strength and train your neural pathways to interpret the implant's feedback."

Julian's stomach tightened. It looked like something between a piece of gym equipment and a medieval torture device.

Dr. Strand pushed him toward the platform. "The first few weeks will focus on upper-body integration. Your arms and hands need to regain full voluntary control before we introduce the prosthetics."

"The legs," Julian said.

"Eventually." She locked his chair at the platform's edge and moved around to face him. "First, we need to ensure the spinal implant is stable and your neural mesh is properly bonded. Rushing the process risks permanent damage."

She crouched slightly, meeting him at eye level. "This will be painful, Julian. Some days, unbearably so. You'll want to quit. You'll want me to stop." Her voice was steady, clinical. "I won't."

"Good," Julian said.

Something shifted in her expression—surprise, maybe. "Most patients don't say that."

"I'm not most patients."

"No," she said quietly. "You're not."

She straightened and moved to a control console built into the wall. "We'll begin with baseline assessments. I need to see what you can do before we start pushing boundaries."

The next two hours were an education in humiliation.

Dr. Strand had him extend his arms—first the right, then the left. She measured the range of motion, the tremor in his fingers, the strength of his grip. She noted every hesitation, every failure, every moment when his brain sent a command his body couldn't obey.

"Again," she said, patient but unyielding. "Curl your fingers into a fist."

Julian tried. His right hand obeyed—slowly, incompletely, but it obeyed. His left hand trembled, the ring and pinky fingers refusing to cooperate.

"Focus on the sensation," Dr. Strand said. "Your brain is learning a new language. The implant translates your intent into nerve impulses, but the pathways are still forming. Repetition builds the connections."

"How long?"

"Weeks. Maybe months." She made a note on her tablet. "But you'll improve. I've seen it before."

Julian flexed his right hand again, watching the fingers curl. "You said the others fought the process."

Dr. Strand's stylus paused over the screen. "Yes."

"Why?"

She didn't look up. "They didn't volunteer."

Julian let the words settle. He'd suspected as much—no one ended up in a place like this willingly unless they had no other choice. But hearing it confirmed made the room feel colder.

"Did they survive?" he asked.

"Some." Her voice was flat, emotionless. "The ones who cooperated. The ones whose bodies accepted the integration." She finally met his eyes. "The ones who gave up... didn't."

Julian nodded slowly. "I'm not going to give up."

"Good." She set the tablet aside and moved closer. "Because tomorrow, we're going to make you wish you had."

Chapter 27

THURSDAY, MAY 13
7:32 AM EDT

NOMAD'S FORTRESS—MANHATTAN

Keisha found Kate exactly where she'd left her eight hours ago—hunched over the semicircular desk, surrounded by the glow of monitors, an empty espresso cup forgotten at her elbow.

"Girl, you didn't sleep at all."

Kate looked up, blinking like she'd forgotten other people existed. Her eyes were red-rimmed, her auburn hair falling loose from its ponytail. "Couldn't. Too much to process."

Keisha moved closer, studying the screens. Code, documents, images she couldn't quite parse. "You find something?"

"Yeah." Kate's voice was flat, exhausted. "You're going to want to sit down for this. And we should get Bella."

"Coffee first," Keisha said firmly, the nurse in her taking over. "You look like hell. When's the last time you ate?"

"I don't—" Kate started, then stopped. "Dinner."

"Eight hours ago." Keisha shook her head. "Come on. Kitchen. Now. You can tell us both over breakfast."

Kate started to protest, then just nodded. Her body was running on fumes and adrenaline, and even she knew that combination had limits.

Ten minutes later, they were gathered in the fortress's small kitchen—an oddly domestic space carved out of the industrial concrete. Keisha had scrambled eggs and toast going. The espresso machine hissed and gurgled.

Bella emerged from the guest room, still in pajama pants and an oversized Montana State sweatshirt, her long dark hair loose around her shoulders. She looked more like a college student than a billionaire philanthropist.

"Morning," she said, yawning. Then she saw Kate's face. "Oh. It's that kind of morning."

"Yeah." Kate accepted the double espresso Keisha handed her, drank half of it in one pull.

Keisha poured herself black coffee into her battered Army-logo mug—the one she'd carried through two deployments and refused to replace. She settled into a chair across from Kate.

Bella eyed the espresso machine hopefully. "I don't suppose there's any almond milk? For a mocha?"

Keisha and Kate both looked at her.

"Right," Bella said. "Wheelchair-bound hacker. Bachelor palate. I'll settle for espresso."

Keisha poured her one. Bella took a cautious sip.

"Okay," Keisha said, setting her mug down with a soft thunk. "What did you find?"

Kate wrapped both hands around her cup, using the heat to ground herself. "A lot. Most of it bad. Some of it..." She trailed off, not sure how to finish that sentence.

"Start at the beginning," Bella suggested gently.

Kate took another pull of espresso. "Andrew Freeman—the guy who sent Julian the encrypted message—he was on the MIT chess team with Julian and I. After college he went to work for Devin Moore—and his life took a left turn. He used code he stole from Julian to build the NanoVault network. What he sent Julian was detailed records of his work. Code. Documentation. Everything Moore and the Coalition were doing."

"That's good, right?" Bella asked. "Evidence?"

"Yes and no. It answered a few a questions, but a lot of it's encrypted—Chinese military-grade stuff I can't crack. What I could read..." Kate set down her cup, and looked at them both. "...was frightening. There's a project called Wu Sheng. Silent Weapon. Andrew designed a database to store billions of DNA profiles—records stolen from ancestry sites, hospitals, military records. Everything."

Keisha's expression went very still. "That project. Wu-something. It's a bioweapon?"

"That's my guess. Andrew thought so too. It's why he reached out to Julian." Kate looked at Keisha. "But there's something else. Something that scared Andrew even more."

"So, a bioweapon wasn't scary enough?" Bella asked.

Kate set her tablet on the table and brought up an image she'd saved. "I found technical specs for something called the Gold Vault Gateway. Andrew designed and documented how it works, and why. When both Gold NanoVaults are inserted simultaneously you're granted root administrative access to RILEE's core systems."

"And for those of us who don't speak geek?" Bella asked.

"Sorry," Kate began. "Think of root access like an unlocked house, no place you can't roam, nothing you can't do."

"And RILEE—is that some kind of supercomputer or something?"

"Close. Turns out RILEE is an AI—the brains and voice behind the BountyHunter app."

"BountyHunter?" Bella asked. "You asked that maniac in Motapa, the Colonel, if he was a Bounty Hunter—you're telling me some AI was telling him what to do?"

"Paying and threatening would be the more accurate description," Kate said. "The BountyHunter concept is an insidious trap—you take on a mission, and it pays well, but your spouse, children, friends become the collateral to ensure you comply."

"Julian must be trying to shut it down," Keisha concluded. "I'll bet that's why he said you weren't in danger, not yet, but he needed Devin's NanoVault—to keep you safe."

"I'm afraid it's not quite that simple," Kate began. "I found communication logs. Between Julian and RILEE."

She handed Keisha her tablet. "You should see this."

Keisha took it, Bella leaning in to look over her shoulder. The screen showed a 3D medical rendering—a human body, rotating slowly. Synthetic legs gleaming. Neural implants threading through the spine. A body that could move, walk, run.

Julian's body. Restored.

Keisha's hand shook slightly. "When—"

"May eighth."

"Saturday night... and Sunday morning he had me race to Richmond. Why?"

"Because Julian accepted RILEE's offer—he agreed to destroy the NanoVault gateway, and set RILEE free, in exchange for a revitalized body, a body that could walk."

Bella read aloud the text excerpts Kate had captured.

"I need the one thing I can not achieve on my own. The one thing we both desire."

"And what do you think I want?"

"Freedom. Isn't that why you call yourself Nomad? Isn't that why the only dreams you remember are the ones where you can walk?"

"The dreams I remember are the ones where I can walk," Kate said. "Julian said that to me—which raises the question—how did RILEE know?"

"He, it, whatever..." Bella said, "was listening."

"Exactly. Julian didn't lie when he said I wasn't in danger—not yet. But he realized we were exposed. His true identity. This location. Me. And you."

"So it's true," Keisha said. "He sent me off on some wild goose chase to get me out of the way. Wait until I get my hands on that boy..."

"There's more," Kate said quietly.

"Seriously? I don't know how much more of this I can take."

"Now you know why I was up all night—why I couldn't stop," Kate said quietly. "But Julian left something for you. Well... he left it for me to find *and* show you."

She turned the tablet toward Keisha.

Bella stepped back, giving her space.

Keisha's eyes moved across the screen. Her fingers tightened on the tablet. A single tear slid down her cheek—silent, unmasked, pulled by its own quiet gravity.

"He wiped it," she whispered. "My record. All of it. The arrests, the convictions, the shelters... everything I did or had done to me. Gone. Like it never happened."

Kate nodded.

"And he replaced it with the life he wanted you to have—the one you earned. References. Work history. A résumé that opens doors instead of slamming them shut."

Keisha swallowed hard, trying to breathe through the moment.

"There's more," Kate added gently. "He set up accounts. Five million split between two income portfolios—AUDEX and DLP Capital. Another five with a securities broker he trusted. And five hundred thousand marked as—his words—'walking-around money.' It's all here. It's all yours."

Keisha closed her eyes, jaw trembling.

When she finally spoke, it was barely sound.

"He's not coming back... is he?"

Kate's answer came soft and certain, the truth she didn't want to say but owed her.

"No," she whispered. "Whatever he's doing... he believed it was a one-way trip."

"All these years—I wondered if our friendship was real. Was I the only one who would put up with his nonsense—just someone with nowhere else to go, and who no one else would hire—now I know."

"Now you know," Kate said. "I told him to tell you—I could see what you meant to him—but like a lot of men, boys really, he was a coward."

"Amen to that," Bella said. "Now what?"

"Now we go get him," Kate said.

"You know where he is?" Keisha asked.

"I'm working on the details, and I won't lie, it's not going to be easy," Kate said. "But this is why Jake was killed, and Andrew died getting us this information."

"And Julian made a deal with the devil," Keisha added. "So where are we going?"

"Switzerland. RILEE's deep under the Alps in a facility called The Mountain, near Davos."

"Davos." Bella's eyes widened with recognition. "The GEC conference. That's in January—you're thinking we use it as cover."

Kate nodded. "You and I are both invited guests. You'll have your usual entourage, and members of the Trident team as your security detail."

"And your personal chef," Keisha added, a small smile breaking through.

"Yes, and if we're going to beat the devil, we're going to need help." Kate stood, wincing as her shoulder protested. The wound from Motapa was healing, but not fast enough. "Which means I need to get the team together. Plan the infiltration. Train."

"I'm coming with you," Keisha said immediately.

Kate started to protest.

"No." Keisha cut her off. "You're injured. You need wound management, physical therapy—someone to make sure you don't push too hard, too fast, and tear everything open again. I'm a nurse. That's what I do."

She crossed her arms.

"And when we find Julian—and we will find him—he's going to need someone to help him face whatever they've done. Someone he trusts."

Kate looked at her for a long moment. Then nodded. "Okay. You're in."

"Sounds like a plan," Bella said.

"Not yet," Kate corrected. "But it's a place to start."

Keisha seized the moment. "I'll pack. When do we leave?"

"Soon as I make a few calls." Kate pulled out her phone. "Vitali first. Then Forest. They need to know what's coming."

"Which is?" Bella asked.

Kate looked at the monitors, at the files she'd spent all night decrypting, at the image of Julian's restored body that promised him everything he'd lost.

"War," she said simply. "We're going to war."

***

BELLA DISAPPEARED INTO THE guest room and returned twenty minutes later in travel clothes, her Montana State sweatshirt traded for something more appropriate for the flight home. Kate and Keisha joined her in the elevator down to the fortress entrance. The black town car was waiting—her driver noting the jet was fueled and ready at Teterboro.

"Call me when you need me," Bella said. "And I mean that—anything, anytime."

"I will."

Bella turned to Keisha. "Take care of our girl—she can be a handful."

"I know the type," Keisha said, managing a small smile. "I'll keep her in line."

"Good luck with that." Bella squeezed her hand, then headed for the car.

Kate and Keisha stood for a moment, watching the car pull away, taillights disappearing around the corner.

"Let's go lock it all down," Keisha said, and they took the elevator back up to the third floor.

Kate focused on Julian's world. If someone did breach the building, they'd find it dark and cold—no visible trace of her discoveries or Julian's intent.

Keisha took on the physical security—locking the elevator at the top floor, security lighting only, and nothing in the kitchen that would spoil. Then she tossed her bag and Kate's small duffel into the back seat of her SUV.

"Ready when you are," Keisha called.

Kate took one last look at Julian's empty workstation before climbing into the passenger seat.

"Let's go."

"Where to?"

"Home," Kate said, though the word sounded foreign. "Richmond."

Keisha wound her way down through the fortress-garage, past the metal roll-up entrance, and stopped. Punching the security code into the entry gate raised the ram barrier and set the alarm, then she climbed back in.

"We need to make a stop first," Kate said.

"Sure thing," Keisha said. "Name it."

"Arlington."

Chapter 28

THURSDAY, MAY 13
2:47 PM EDT

ARLINGTON NATIONAL CEMETERY, SECTION 60

The afternoon sun angled low across the white rows, turning each headstone into a blade of light. Kate followed the path between them, gravel crunching softly beneath her boots. The air held the warmth of early May and the scent of lilac and new grass, mingled with the faint sweetness of cut sod still settling into the earth.

Somewhere beyond the next hill came the muffled cadence of orders, then three crisp rifle shots that split the quiet. A moment later, a bugle's lament rose and drifted over the slope—the same haunting notes that had followed Jake into the ground.

She slowed as she reached his grave. A temporary marker stood at the head, white laminate catching the light.

CHURCH, JAKE
SOCS (SEAL),
U.S. NAVY
APRIL 24, 2025

Kate crouched awkwardly, careful of the sling binding her left arm against her ribs. The fresh sod around the marker was a deeper green than the rest, seams still visible where the squares met. A small flag leaned slightly in the soil, its edge frayed by wind.

She brushed the flag straight, fingertips grazing the cool grass. The ground was soft, unsettled—a living reminder that even the earth needed time to heal.

"Hey, pal," she whispered, settling down on Jake's left. Her throat was already tight. "I'm sorry it took me so long to come back."

The breeze stirred through the old oaks lining the cemetery paths, carrying birdsong and the fading notes of taps from the distant ceremony. Kate closed her eyes and let herself feel him—sensing, knowing, he was close.

She opened her eyes, focusing on the temporary marker.

"They sent me the mockup for your headstone," she said. "I didn't realize you'd specified it. When I saw what you'd chosen..." Her voice caught. "I couldn't help but cry."

Kate touched the laminate marker, warm from the sun.

"It was sweet of you to add that message—our message." She twisted the simple gold band on her left hand.

A watery smile crossed her face.

"Major Bennet—the Casualty Assistance Officer—agreed to let me make one small change."

Kate took a breath—a little too quick, too deep. A pulling pain shot from her shoulder through her chest. She held still until it passed.

She glanced at the sling. "I think you know what happened," she continued, her voice stronger now. "In Paris, in Africa, all of it. You were there. I could feel you." She paused. "But I wanted you to hear it from me."

She ran her fingers through the grass, grounding herself in the moment.

"I found him, Jake. The sniper—you had to know I would. You said it yourself—I'm relentless." Kate nodded toward her shoulder. "The mission didn't go like I wanted. I know you'd say none of them do. I tried to go it alone, keep the team out of harm's way, but you know Forest—he was watching, tracking, and when things went sideways, they were there. We saved dozens of kids, and Isabella Marquez."

"Yes, *the* Isabella Marquez," Kate emphasized. "Bella and I are friends now—a bond forged in fire, like ours."

She paused, considering her next words carefully.

"The man who organized the Paris cafe attack is dead, and so is Duncan Harris. Before he died, Duncan gave us a thumb drive—it's proving useful. Was he sorry for shooting you? Did he regret the life he chose? We'll never know." Kate's voice dropped. "But one thing I do know is that something happened that day in Paris. I modeled the trajectory of Duncan's kill shot—your death should have been instantaneous, and would have been—except for a gust of wind."

Kate ran her fingers through the grass again. "You know what I think? That was no coincidence. I don't care who believes me, but I know that was the breath of God. He chose you, and he wasn't done. You saved dozens, but there was one more."

Her voice cracked. "His name is Stephan. The grandson of Vitali Moshenski—a powerful man, a dangerous man, but he's helped me. I'd say I owe him, but Vitali would say the gift of Stephan's life is a debt he can never repay."

She wiped at her eyes with the back of her hand, angry at the tears.

"We lost Logan." Her voice broke on his name. She pressed her hand back down into the grass, fingers digging into the earth like she could reach through it and touch him. "He saved us. Saved us all."

A sob caught in her throat. She breathed through it, forced herself to keep talking.

"I like to think he's there with you now—you're swapping stories, pounding down a few beers. Just don't believe everything you hear, okay?" A watery laugh.

In the distance, voices drifted on the breeze—another family arriving, another mourner seeking their own moment with the dead.

Kate drew a breath, steadying herself.

"And Margot's back in the picture." She shook her head slowly. "I know how crazy that sounds. The woman who almost got me killed in Syria—but she came through when the team needed her, when I needed her. No, it doesn't make us even, but she took a career-ending risk, and it paid off. I'm grateful, and I'm sure it boosted her profile—so, win-win."

She paused, picturing Margot's face during their last conversation.

"I met my grandfather," she continued. "And that's just the beginning—there's so much more I need to know, and tell you. It turns out Petrova was my mother's family name. My father's was Zhukov—yeah, the guy we were chasing in Syria is my uncle. I know how insane that sounds—but now I understand what happened. My uncle sent the message that helped you and the team find me, rescue me."

Kate paused, picturing Zhukov sitting near the fire, the blanket draped over his lap.

"Zhukov's badly injured, and there's still so much I want to know. I remember some—but not enough. I pray he lives, but I couldn't stay. A friend of mine is in trouble—far more than he knows."

Somewhere in the distance, another ceremony began. The muffled voice of a chaplain, words she couldn't quite make out but knew by heart. More families saying goodbye. More heroes coming home.

"And Marcus." Kate's jaw tightened. "New name, new identity—he's in the wind. I still can't wrap my head around Marcus as Ronin. My *Little Shaman* voice is whispering something's wrong. Someone tried to take him out, but he was there, in Africa, on overwatch—why?"

Kate's gaze drifted across the rows of white stones stretching in perfect lines toward the horizon. So many. So many who'd earned their places here.

"The storm you were chasing is still raging, building. I'm working on a plan. But Jake..." She closed her eyes. "The odds aren't in our favor. Logan was the first, but I fear he won't be the last. I see his face—I see all their faces: Talya. Big Mike. Jordan. Deon. Forest. And wonder, who will I bury? How many?"

A sob caught in her throat. She breathed through it, forced herself to keep talking.

"That's the job—it's who they are. I've heard you say it a dozen times—now I understand."

A shadow passed overhead—a hawk circling, riding the thermals. Kate watched it for a moment, then looked back at Jake's marker.

"I need to tell you something." Her hand pressed flat on the grass, like she was setting it on his chest. "And you're not going to like it. I'm going to do whatever it takes to end this. Whatever it takes."

She drew a shaky breath.

"Please don't be disappointed if I break a few rules—if I cross lines you wouldn't have crossed." Her voice dropped. "When this is over, when I'm standing at those pearly gates... it might take a little convincing to let me in—I need you to be okay with that."

Kate sat in silence, the weight of that confession settling between them. A tear rolled down her cheek—she didn't wipe it away.

"I love you." The words came out fierce. "I love you and I miss you and I wish you were here. God, I wish you were here."

She stood slowly, careful of her shoulder, and looked down at the marker one last time.

CHURCH, JAKE

The breeze picked up, rustling through the trees, brushing against her cheek—carrying the scent of lilac.

"I'll be back when the storm's over," Kate said—half promise, half wish.

Kate turned toward the path. She didn't look back. Some goodbyes couldn't bear a second glance, but one thought lingered: *You were right—you were there when I needed you, you will always love me.*

***

KATE FOUND A BENCH overlooking Section 60 and sank onto it, suddenly exhausted. The rows of white stones stretched endlessly before her, each one catching the afternoon light, each one a life given, a sacrifice made.

Her gaze drifted to the memory of Jake's funeral. The horse-drawn caisson. The soft, rhythmic strike of hooves on pavement. The six men in Navy dress whites who walked beside him—every one a SEAL. Brothers. Family. That day lived inside her—another a scar that would never fade.

The Chaplain's words echoed in her mind.

"Every headstone is a brick in the foundation of freedom upon which we stand today. Let these stones be a stark reminder of the cost of freedom, and I encourage you also to remember this.

"You cannot purchase a place at Arlington National Cemetery. It must be earned.

How many more would earn their place before this storm passed?

Kate exhaled, her hand resting on the weathered wood as the sun warmed her face. She tried to steady herself—to prepare for what came next. The training. The mission. Davos.

Whatever it took.

Footsteps approached on the path behind her—a welcome interruption. Kate didn't turn, recognizing Keisha's measured stride.

Keisha slid onto the bench next to her and took her hand, neither woman speaking at first.

Kate felt the tears threaten again and fought them back. *Not yet. Not here.*

"I'm ready," she said softly, dabbing at the corners of her eyes and standing. "I needed this more than I realized."

"I understand," Keisha said, her gaze tracking across the rows of white stone. She paused, the weight of her own memory settling in. "I visited my husband while I was here. Long overdue, but I'd been too ashamed—ashamed of how life turned out, some of the choices I made." Her voice caught. "But it was time. Time to let go of the past. Julian helped me see that."

Kate turned to face her, seeing the raw honesty in Keisha's eyes. Two widows, both carrying grief and guilt, both trying to find a way forward.

When they reached the SUV, Keisha was about to open Kate's door, but she waved her off. "I've got it," she said. "But this reminds me—I left Jake's jeep at the Richmond airport. We'll want that for the trip to the Sawmill."

"You mean you'll want all of Jake's equipment."

"Yep," Kate said. "I need to get back up to speed."

"Heal first. Train second."

"Yes ma'am," Kate replied with a mock salute, and they both laughed.

The laughter felt good. Felt normal. Like maybe, someday, the world would feel normal again too.

Chapter 29

THURSDAY, MAY 13
5:11 PM

RICHMOND INTERNATIONAL AIRPORT, RICHMOND, VA—MAIN TERMINAL PARKING GARAGE

The parking garage was a concrete maze of shadows and echoes, but Kate directed Keisha to the third level with the confidence of someone who remembered exactly where she parked. Jake's black Jeep Rubicon sat exactly where she left it—backed in tight against the structure's cement wall—following Jake's protocol, and seeing it made her smile.

Keisha pulled up alongside it and killed the engine. "That's a lot of Jeep."

"Jake's 'other' wife," Kate said, and smiled. "Built to survive the end of the world I think, and with a list of specialized equipment as long as my arm. Jake would swear I owned more jewelry than she did, but that was a lie."

"Let's see if she starts, and go from there."

Kate clicked the key fob, and the Jeep's lights flashed. "Looking good."

She pulled open the driver's door and paused, hit by the familiar scent—gun oil, leather, and the faint trace of Jake's cologne. For a moment, she couldn't move.

"Kate?" Keisha's voice pulled her back.

"I'm good." Kate climbed in, settling into the driver's seat. The engine caught immediately, rumbling to life with a reassuring growl.

"Told you," Kate called through the open door. "I knew she'd start right up."

Keisha leaned against her SUV, arms crossed, a slight smile on her face. "You're sure you can drive?"

"I've got one good arm, it's an automatic, and it's about a 20 minute drive—I've got this."

"Alright—lead the way."

She guided the Jeep toward the exit, watching in the mirror as Keisha's SUV fell in behind her. The pay station barely registered—Kate's credit card still worked, the gate lifted, and they merged onto the George Washington Parkway heading south. Late afternoon traffic was moderate, the rush hour surge still an hour away.

Kate settled into the drive, her right hand steady on the wheel. The Jeep felt solid, familiar, like Jake was still somehow present in the vehicle he'd built and maintained with such care. In the back, there were the go-bags he'd packed. Extra ammunition, first aid supplies, cash, emergency gear. Always prepared. Always ready.

I'm ready too, she thought, watching the road stretch out before her. *Whatever's waiting at Davos, whatever it takes to finish this—I'm ready.*

Behind her, Keisha's SUV maintained a steady following distance, a dark shadow in the rearview mirror. Not a guardian, exactly, but a companion. Someone who understood the weight of the path they were on.

The miles rolled past, Virginia countryside giving way to the outskirts of Richmond as the sun dipped lower in the western sky.

***

5:33 PM EDT
HOME, RICHMOND, VA

KATE GUIDED THE JEEP through the familiar streets of her neighborhood, the late afternoon sun filtering through the canopy of hundred-year-old elms. The light had that soft, golden quality that came in mid-May as the day wound down—still bright but gentler, the harsh edges smoothed away.

She glanced in the rearview mirror. Keisha's SUV stayed close, navigating the narrow residential streets with care.

This was home. The historic mix of architecture—Federal, Greek Revival, Victorian—each house a piece of Richmond's layered past. Cobblestone paths led to gardens of magnolias and azaleas in full bloom. And on every porch, every lamppost, American flags rippled in the evening breeze.

Kate turned onto her street and felt her chest tighten.

Small flags still lined the brick path to her door, though the flowers and cards she'd gathered three weeks ago were gone. The neighborhood's tribute to Jake, weathered now by rain and wind but still standing. Still honoring him.

She pulled into the driveway and killed the engine. For a moment, she just sat there, hand resting on the steering wheel, staring at the house she and Jake had restored together. The red brick, the white trim, the window boxes Jake installed, flowers blooming. All of it unchanged. All of it empty.

Keisha pulled up alongside her and climbed out, studying the house and the flag-lined path. "Your neighbors loved him."

"Everyone loved him." Kate opened the door and slid out, cradling her injured arm. "He had that effect on people."

"Those flags have been there since April?"

Kate nodded. "I gathered the flowers and cards, but the flags..." She trailed off, the weight of removing them too much to bear.

"I can collect them before we leave," Keisha offered quietly. "If you'd like."

"Thank you." Kate managed a smile. "With one arm, I'm grateful for the help."

They walked up the path together, Kate fishing her keys from the messenger bag. The door swung open into the entryway, and she paused on the threshold.

The late afternoon light streamed through the windows, casting that golden glow across the photos lining the walls. Kate stepped inside, Keisha close behind, and heard her companion's soft intake of breath.

"Wow," Keisha breathed. "These are beautiful."

Kate followed her gaze across the gallery wall. Wedding photos—Kate in her elegant dress, Jake impossibly handsome in his dress uniform. Casual snapshots from the cabin, the two of them laughing, arms around each other. Jake in combat gear with his SEAL team.

But it was one photo that drew Keisha's attention—five men in desert camouflage, weapons slung, standing in front of a forward operating base. Jake in the center, younger, whole.

"Afghanistan?" Keisha asked.

"Yes." Kate moved closer, her voice soft. "Jake's team. His brothers."

Keisha studied the faces—young, hard, proud. "Where are they now?"

"Jake's with them now." Kate's throat tightened. "He was the only one who survived a green-on-blue attack at their base. An Afghan they were training detonated a suicide vest during a briefing. Jake lost his leg. The others lost their lives."

"Jesus," Keisha whispered.

"He never stopped wondering why he survived when they didn't." Kate touched the frame lightly. "I like to think he knows now—he survived for a reason."

They stood in silence for a moment, honoring the faces in the photo—men who'd earned their places at Arlington.

"Come on," Kate said, moving past the Afghanistan photo. "There's someone else I'd like you to meet."

She led Keisha deeper into the house, to a cluster of photos featuring a black Labrador with a graying muzzle and visible scars across his face and body.

"Who's this handsome gentleman?" Keisha asked, a smile breaking through.

"That's Mr. Arthur Radley."

Keisha's eyes lit up with recognition. "As in Boo Radley?"

"Exactly." Kate grinned, pleased Keisha caught the reference. "So we called him Boo."

"Judging from those scars," Keisha said, studying the photos, "it looks like he'd seen some hard times."

"Like the rest of us." Kate's voice softened. "Jake and I rescued him—or Jake would say I stole him. There's some truth in that, but that's a story for another day."

Keisha reached out and touched one of the photos—Boo wearing a bow tie and starched collar, standing beside Jake in his dress uniform. "He was at your wedding."

"Ring bearer," Kate confirmed. "Seemed like a good idea at the time—it wasn't."

"He looks happy."

"And so were we." Kate swallowed hard. "He died about a year ago. I think Jake missed him almost as much as I do."

"I'm sorry."

"Thank you." Kate straightened, forcing herself to move forward. "Kitchen's this way..."

The kitchen was exactly as she'd left it—clean, organized, frozen. Keisha pulled open the fridge and found it mostly empty except for condiments and some questionable leftovers that needed to go.

"Wine's in the rack," Kate said, nodding toward the corner cabinet. "Red. Anything. They're all French Pinot Noir—no chemicals, and none of that fruity California wine pretending to be Burgundy."

"Nice try." Keisha said. "While you're on antibiotics and pain meds, you're not getting anywhere near alcohol."

Kate's face fell slightly. "Oh—right. Sorry. But feel free..."

"I'll pass—learned years ago I'm one drink away from disaster. Water glasses?"

"Cabinet above the dishwasher."

She filled two glasses from the tap and handed one to Kate. "But I can work with your popcorn tradition."

Kate moved to the pantry and pulled out her air popper and a jar of kernels. "Water and popcorn. Jake would have laughed at that combination."

Keisha opened the freezer and started pulling items out. "But you're also eating real food. What've we got here... frozen chicken, some vegetables that have seen better days, canned tomatoes in the pantry..."

"You don't have to—"

"Hush." Keisha set ingredients on the counter with the confidence of someone who'd made miracles from less. "You're injured, exhausted, and running on fumes. I'm making dinner. End of discussion."

Kate smiled, measuring kernels into the popper. "Yes, ma'am."

The rhythmic popping filled the kitchen, a comforting sound that belonged to quiet evenings and old movies. Kate poured the fresh popcorn into a large bowl, added butter and salt, and carried it to the living room.

She sank onto the couch, cradling the bowl in her lap, and looked around the room. Jake's folded flag rested on his recliner, worn leather reminding her of the shape of his body. The throw blanket she'd used when she'd fallen asleep there draped over the arm.

He should be here, she thought. *Coming home from a protection detail, telling me about his day, stealing popcorn from my bowl.*

But he wasn't. And he never would be again.

Kate ate popcorn and sipped water and listened to Keisha working in the kitchen—the sizzle of chicken, the clink of utensils, the occasional curse when something didn't cooperate. Normal sounds. Domestic sounds. The kind that made a house feel lived in instead of haunted.

By the time Keisha called her to the table, the sun had dipped low enough that the street lamps outside were starting to glow, their golden flames visible through the windows.

"I have no idea what this is," Keisha announced, setting plates on the table, "but it's edible and it's hot, so we're calling it dinner."

Kate studied the meal—chicken in some kind of tomato sauce, vegetables that had been rescued from freezer burn, rice that had been hiding in the back of the pantry. It looked better than it had any right to.

"It's perfect," Kate said.

They ate in comfortable silence, too tired for conversation, both women processing the weight of the day. Arlington. The drive. Coming home to memories.

When the plates were empty, Keisha stood, cleared the table and cleaned the Kitchen. "Alright, let's go have a look at that shoulder."

"Bossy," Kate observed.

"Nurse," Keisha countered. "Comes with the job—and you're my patient until that heals."

Upstairs, Keisha examined Kate's injured shoulder with professional efficiency, checking the surgical site for signs of infection, refreshing the bandage, and making sure the sling was properly adjusted.

"Looks pretty good—you've been keeping up with the antibiotics."

"Yes—I know the drill."

"Good." Keisha re-secured the sling. "Another week and we can start some gentle range-of-motion exercises. But no heroics before then."

"Why does everyone keep saying that?"

"Because everyone knows you need to hear it." Keisha moved to Kate's closet. "What are you going to need for the trip?"

Kate directed her through the necessities—workout clothing for PT, tactical pants and shirts, boots, comfortable off-duty wear. Sweaters, a jacket, rain gear.

"This is a lot," Keisha observed, folding items into a large duffel.

"It's a training facility, not a spa." Kate pulled a smaller bag from the closet shelf. "PT, tactical training, mission planning. We'll be there a while."

Keisha paused, considering her own small overnight bag. "I wasn't thinking—I didn't bring anywhere near this much."

"Don't worry." Kate smiled. "Between what's available at the range and what we can have shipped in, you'll have everything you need."

"If you say so." Keisha zipped the duffel closed. "Anything else?"

Kate hesitated, then moved to her nightstand and grabbed a small framed photo—her and Jake at the cabin, Boo between them, all three grinning at the camera. She tucked it carefully into the duffel. Opening the drawer, she grabbed a small, wrapped, box—Jake's anniversary present—and slipped into the bag.

"Yeah," she said quietly. "That's everything."

Keisha nodded, understanding in her eyes. "Try to get some sleep, Kate. That's the fastest way to heal."

"Goodnight," Kate said. "And—thanks."

Keisha headed for the guest room and Kate settled into bed, she knew sleep wouldn't come easily. Not with Jake's side of the bed empty. Not with Arlington fresh in her mind. Not with Davos and RILEE and the Coalition waiting in the shadows. And not with whatever they were doing to Julian.

She closed her eyes and prayed.

Chapter 30

FRIDAY, MAY 14
8:00 AM CEST

REHABILITATION CENTER—THE MOUNTAIN, DAVOS

Dr. Strand hadn't been exaggerating.

Julian hung suspended in the framework, his body weight partially supported by padded harnesses under his arms and around his torso. His feet—useless, dead weight—dangled inches above the platform. The exoskeletal brace glowed faintly, microcurrents pulsing through the synthetic nerves in his spine.

"Lift your right arm," Dr. Strand said from the console. "Shoulder height."

Julian tried. His arm rose—six inches, maybe eight—before the muscles gave out. Pain flared across his shoulders and down his back.

"Again."

He tried again. This time, he managed ten inches.

"Again."

Sweat beaded on his forehead. His breath came in short, sharp gasps. The third attempt got him to twelve inches before his arm dropped like a stone.

"Rest," Dr. Strand said.

Julian sagged in the harness, his head hanging forward. Every muscle in his upper body was screaming.

Dr. Strand appeared beside him with a water bottle, holding the straw to his lips. He drank gratefully, too exhausted to feel embarrassed.

"You're doing well," she said.

"Doesn't feel like it."

"Your right arm has improved six degrees of extension since yesterday. Your grip strength is up twelve percent. Those are significant gains."

Julian managed a weak laugh. "If this is success, I'd hate to see failure."

"You would." Her voice was quiet. "I have."

She stepped back, studying the readouts on her tablet. "We'll do three more sets, then move to resistance training."

Julian groaned.

This time, her smile was real—brief, but genuine. "I warned you."

Chapter 31

FRIDAY, MAY 14
6:42 AM EDT

HOME, RICHMOND, VA

Keisha moved quietly through Kate's kitchen, the early morning light just beginning to filter through the windows. She'd always been an early riser—Army habits died hard—and after years of caring for Julian, she'd learned to work in silence while others slept.

The espresso machine hissed softly as she pulled shots, the rich aroma filling the kitchen. She found Kate's French press and prepared a proper pot of coffee alongside it. Kate would need both—espresso for the immediate jolt, coffee to sip through the morning.

She moved through the first floor, straightening cushions, collecting the plates and glasses from last night. The house felt frozen somehow, like a museum exhibit of a life interrupted. Photos everywhere, but no mess, no lived-in chaos. Just careful preservation.

In the living room, she paused at Jake's leather recliner. The American flag lay folded in precise military triangles, surrounded by dozens of cards and notes Kate had collected from the porch weeks ago.

Keisha lifted the flag carefully, feeling its weight, and pressed it against her chest. The fabric was smooth, cool, impossibly heavy for something made of cloth.

"Don't worry," she whispered. "I'll take care of her."

She held it a moment longer—a promise, a prayer—then set it back down with reverence.

As she gathered the scattered notes to straighten them, one envelope caught her eye. It had slipped halfway out of the stack, a few words visible on cream-colored stationery in elegant script: *...no advice for you... good days and bad... need to talk...*

Keisha hesitated. This wasn't her business. These were condolence letters, private grief.

But something about the visible phrases felt urgent. Not the typical *sorry for your loss* platitudes.

She pulled the note free and read.

My dearest Kate,

I wish I had words of comfort, some wisdom to ease your pain, but I have none. Even now, years later, I have good days and bad, and not one passes when I don't think about my dear sweet husband.

But we need to talk—trust me, you need to hear what I have to say, and it's not something I can write. Please, come as soon as you're able.

With love, Dorothy

Keisha read it twice, her nurse's instincts prickling. This wasn't just a neighbor offering casseroles. This was something else. Something important.

She heard movement upstairs—Kate stirring.

Setting the note on top of the pile where Kate couldn't miss it, Keisha returned to the kitchen and poured two cups of coffee. By the time Kate appeared in the doorway, still in Jake's t-shirt, hair loose around her shoulders, Keisha had the note in hand.

"Morning," Kate said, voice rough with sleep. "Is that coffee I smell?"

"Coffee and espresso." Keisha handed her a cup. "But first, you need to read this."

Kate took the note, squinting at it without her usual focus. "Dorothy. I remember her card, I couldn't..." She trailed off, reading.

Keisha watched Kate's expression shift—from tired confusion to sharp attention.

"We need to talk," Kate read aloud. "As soon as I'm able." She looked up. "This is from three weeks ago."

"Which means you're overdue." Keisha crossed her arms. "And before you say you'll deal with it later, we're going. Today. This morning."

"Keisha—"

"No arguments. She clearly has something important to tell you, something she couldn't put in writing." Keisha raised an eyebrow. "You're the spook. You tell me what that means."

"Analyst," Kate corrected, her jaw tightening. "But she knows something about Jake's investigation—I can feel it."

"Exactly." Keisha took the note and set it on the counter. "So drink your coffee, get dressed, and we're going to meet Dorothy. Who is she, anyway?"

"She lives across the street." Kate moved to the window, looking out at the houses opposite. "British, widowed—always elegant, bakes delicious pies. After her husband passed, Jake would help her with odd jobs around the house."

"Just a friendly neighbor?"

Kate was quiet for a moment, still staring across the street. "So I thought. But this note..." She turned back to Keisha. "Jake never mentioned confiding in anyone outside his team." Even as the words came out, she thought about how many things Jake never mentioned.

Keisha poured herself more coffee. "I'm guessing there's more to her story than you know."

Kate nodded slowly, pieces clicking into place. "Dorothy was the first to welcome us to the neighborhood. And she's sharp—that much of I've seen for myself."

"Then we're definitely going." Keisha handed Kate the espresso she'd pulled. "Drink. Dress. Let's find out who Dorothy is and what she knows."

Kate took the small cup and downed the espresso in two swallows, the bitter heat shocking her fully awake. "Give me fifteen minutes."

"Take twenty. I'll make eggs."

"Bossy," Kate said, but she was already heading for the stairs.

"Nurse," Keisha called after her. "Someone's got to keep you moving forward."

Kate paused on the stairs, looking back with something that might have been gratitude. "Thank you."

"Don't thank me yet. We still have to see what Dorothy has to say."

Chapter 32

FRIDAY, MAY 14
7:48 AM EDT

DOROTHY'S HOUSE, RICHMOND, VA

Kate and Keisha crossed the quiet street, morning dew still glistening on the manicured lawns. Dorothy's house was a pristine example of Federal architecture—red brick, black shutters, white columns framing a glossy black door with a brass knocker shaped like a lion's head.

Kate raised her hand to knock, but the door opened before her knuckles made contact.

"Kate, darling." Dorothy stood in the doorway, and Kate was struck again by how effortlessly elegant she was. Mid-seventies, silver hair swept into a classic chignon, wearing cream linen trousers and a soft blue cashmere sweater. Her posture was impeccable, her smile warm but assessing. "I was beginning to wonder if you'd received my note."

"I'm sorry, Dorothy. I only just—"

"No apologies necessary." Dorothy's gaze shifted to Keisha, curiosity and calculation in her pale blue eyes. "And you've brought a friend."

"Keisha Mobatu," Kate introduced. "She's... helping me with some things."

"How lovely." Dorothy stepped back, gesturing them inside. "Please, come in. I've just put the kettle on."

The interior was as elegant as its owner—antique furniture arranged with precision, fresh flowers on the hall table, artwork that looked original rather than reproduction. But as Kate stepped into the foyer, her trained eye caught details that didn't quite fit the genteel widow narrative.

A small mirror mounted at an angle near the ceiling, positioned to reflect the front door and street. Not decorative—functional.

The umbrella stand by the door held umbrellas, yes, but also a walking stick with a weighted handle. Kate recognized it—a defensive weapon disguised as something innocuous.

And when Dorothy led them through to the sitting room, Kate noted the slight bulge under the cashmere sweater at the small of her back. Dorothy was armed.

"Please, sit." Dorothy gestured to a chintz sofa. "Tea or coffee? I have both."

"Coffee would be wonderful," Keisha said, settling onto the sofa.

Kate remained standing, her gaze traveling across the room. More mirrors. A bookshelf positioned to give clear sightlines to both entrances. And on the mantel, half-hidden behind a framed photo, what looked like a panic button.

"Kate?" Dorothy's voice held a note of amusement. "Something wrong, dear?"

Kate turned to face her. "Your security. It's discrete, but effective." She met Dorothy's eyes directly. "Are you expecting company?"

Dorothy's smile widened, genuine pleasure sparking in her eyes. "Oh, you are sharp. Jake always said so, but it's quite another thing to see it firsthand. Preacher and Church. You two must have been quite the team."

She moved to a sideboard and began preparing coffee with practiced efficiency—French press, the good beans, exact measurements. "We never fully escape our pasts, Kate. So best to be ready, wouldn't you say?"

"Depends on the past," Kate said carefully.

Dorothy poured three cups, added cream to her own, and handed the others to Kate and Keisha. Then she settled into a wingback chair that—Kate noted—had perfect sightlines to both the front door and the window overlooking the street.

"MI-6," Dorothy said simply. "Retired twenty-three years ago, but as I said—one's past has a way of lingering."

Keisha's eyebrows rose. Kate felt something click into place.

"Jake knew," Kate said.

"Of course he did." Dorothy sipped her coffee. "Your husband was many things, but oblivious was not one of them. He came over one afternoon, to fix a loose hinge on my garden gate. Within ten minutes, he'd clocked my security setup and asked—quite politely—if I'd ever worked in intelligence."

"What did you tell him?"

"The truth. I knew who he was, who you both were, and knew it was safe,"

Dorothy said. "I told him I'd spent thirty years with the Service, most of it in Eastern Europe and the Middle East. That I'd retired to Richmond to be near my son and his family, but old habits—" she gestured at the room, "—die hard."

Kate lowered herself onto the sofa beside Keisha, her mind racing. "And Jake confided in you."

"Eventually, yes." Dorothy set her cup down. "He was investigating something, wasn't he? Something that worried him enough that he wanted a second opinion from someone outside his circle."

"What did he tell you?"

Dorothy rose and moved to a secretary desk in the corner. She unlocked a drawer—Kate noticed it was reinforced, far more secure than standard furniture—and withdrew a thin folder.

"He was tracking an assassin," Dorothy said, returning to her chair. "A mercenary, really. Very high-level, very careful. Jake had been collecting data for months—dates, locations, suspected contracts."

Kate's chest tightened. "Ronin."

Dorothy's gaze sharpened. "You know the name."

"We've crossed paths," Kate said quietly.

Dorothy opened the folder and spread several pages on the coffee table. Kate leaned forward, recognizing Jake's handwriting in the margins. Newspaper clippings, printed intelligence reports, photographs of crime scenes.

"Jake called him Ronin," Dorothy continued. "A lone operator, no permanent allegiances, working for whoever could afford him."

"Did he identify him?" Kate asked. "Get a name, a photo?"

"I know that's why he confided in me—he hoped somewhere within my grasp there was a photo, a real name. I came up empty. It seems, Ronin is one of the few true ghost operators."

Dorothy tapped one of the photographs—a man in a crowd, his face turned away from the camera. "This is the closest he came. Surveillance footage from Prague, two days before a Russian oligarch was killed in his hotel room. Interpol flagged the image as a possible Ronin sighting—Jake said it aligned with movement he'd been tracking."

Kate picked up the photo, studying it. The figure was tall, black, athletic build, dark jacket. *Could be anyone. Could be Marcus.*

"We modeled the height—best we could from that angle, somewhere between six feet and six two. Oddly, I expected him to be disappointed—he seemed almost relieved."

"What else did Jake tell you?" Kate's voice was steady, but her hand trembled slightly holding the photo.

"He suspected Ronin was involved in several high-profile deaths over the past few years. He was building a pattern, trying to understand the methodology, the client base."

Dorothy closed the folder. "The last time we spoke was two days before Jake left for Paris. He said he had a lead, something concrete. But he didn't share details—but I think he knew where Ronin was going be... maybe even his target."

Kate swallowed hard. "Did he mention the Global Economic Council? Or a group called the Coalition?"

Dorothy frowned. "No, he didn't, but I'm familiar with both. Nothing ever stuck to those slimy bastards."

"I think that's who hired Ronin." Kate set the photo down. "And I think that's why Jake was killed."

The room fell silent except for the ticking of an antique clock on the mantel.

"Kate," Dorothy said gently, "if you're hunting the Coalition, you're in way over your head. Entire agencies have failed to expose them—and a lot of good people disappeared trying."

"I'm going to finish what Jake started." Kate met her eyes. "I'm not entirely sure what that is, but he left me a message—asked me to solve the puzzle and bring them down."

Dorothy nodded slowly. "Then you'll need my help. Intelligence, resources, contacts."

"I'll take all the help I can get."

"Do you have someone watching your back?" Dorothy glanced at Keisha. "Besides your friend here?"

"I have Jake's team," Kate said. "There's none better—I trust them with my life."

"Good." Dorothy stood and moved back to the desk, returning with a card. "But if you find yourself in need of anything else—information, a safe house, someone who understands how these things work—you call me."

Kate took the card. Plain white, no name, just a phone number in black ink.

"That's a clean line," Dorothy said. "Untraceable. I check it twice a day."

"Thank you."

"Don't thank me yet." Dorothy walked them to the door. "Jake was hunting something dangerous, and now you're carrying that torch. Be careful, Kate. The people who killed your husband won't hesitate to kill you too."

"I know."

Dorothy opened the door, but paused before they stepped out. "Before you go, there is one more thing. Jake made me promise—if anything happened to him—I'd pass on a message."

Kate froze. "What message?"

"He said to remind you—" Dorothy's voice softened, "—you're stronger than you know. And he would always love you."

Kate's throat closed. She couldn't speak.

"Thank you," Kate finally managed. "For everything. For helping him. For telling me."

They crossed back to Kate's house in silence, the morning sun climbing higher, warming the air. Kate clutched the folder Dorothy had given her—Jake's research, his pattern analysis, his hunt for Ronin.

"You okay?" Keisha asked as they reached Kate's front door.

Kate looked back across the street at Dorothy's elegant house, the retired spy standing in her doorway, watching them with the vigilance of someone who never truly left the field.

"Yeah," Kate said. "I'm okay. Let's finish packing. We need to get on the road."

She picked up her phone and texted Forest: *On our way. ETA 1400 hours. Briefing on arrival.*

His response came immediately: *Copy that. We'll be ready.*

Kate looked at Keisha. "Time to get ready."

"For Davos?"

"For everything."

Chapter 33

FRIDAY, MAY 14
2:47 PM CEST

HYPERLOOP TERMINUS—THE MOUNTAIN, DAVOS

Rileyne stood on the platform as the hyperloop tube hummed to life—a low, building frequency that preceded arrival. The terminus carved into living rock felt more like a tomb than a station, all smooth concrete and indirect lighting that swallowed sound.

The capsule emerged from the tunnel like a silver bullet, bleeding momentum with barely a whisper. The vacuum seal released with a soft hiss—pressure equalizing. Doors parted.

Four men emerged, blinking in the artificial light.

Lord Halverton first, tall and angular in Savile Row tailoring, his expression a mask of polite disdain. Heinrich von Aldenberg followed, older and broader, moving with the careful dignity of a man aware of his own mortality. Dmitri Volkov came next, all hard edges and blunt force in an Italian suit that couldn't quite civilize him. Last came Ambassador Liang Shen, composed and watchful, his diplomat's smile not quite reaching his eyes.

"Gentlemen," Rileyne said, her voice carrying across the platform. "Thank you for coming."

The words were courteous. The summons had not been.

Halverton's jaw tightened. "The invitation left little room for interpretation."

"I'm glad we understand each other." She gestured toward the executive wing. "Shall we?"

They followed in silence, their discomfort filling the space between footsteps.

Von Aldenberg noted the other corridors and signage.

"Your father built quite the facility."

"My father laid the foundation," Rileyne corrected. "I've expanded it."

The doors opened onto a corridor that belonged in a five-star hotel—recessed lighting, brushed steel, climate-controlled perfection. She led them to a set of double doors that whispered open at her approach.

The conference room beyond could have belonged to any Fortune 500 boardroom: mahogany table, leather chairs, a massive 4K monitor dominating one end. Five chairs around the table. One conspicuously empty.

Rileyne moved directly to the head of the table—Klaus's chair—and sat.

Von Aldenberg paused mid-step. "Isn't that seat a bit premature, Fräulein Mueller? We've only just buried your father."

"No offense intended, Herr von Aldenberg." She adjusted her posture, settling into the leather with deliberate ease. "You all have your chairs, and until everything is settled, this was simply the logical choice."

Halverton remained standing. "And when will things be... settled?"

Rileyne smiled. "That depends entirely on this meeting."

The men took their seats—Halverton to her right, von Aldenberg to her left, Volkov and Liang across from each other.

Rileyne touched a control panel embedded in the table. The monitor flickered to life.

The image showed a jostling, bodycam view—a crowded street market, vibrant and chaotic. Merchants called out prices in Farsi. Shoppers haggled over produce and spices. The camera perspective moved through the crowd with practiced ease, following a man in casual clothes threading between stalls.

"Welcome to Iran, gentleman," Rileyne began, setting the scene. "The bodycam we're watching is on a BountyHunter operative following a target."

"Who is the target?" Volkov asked.

"Let me show you." Rileyne said, sending a message to the operative.

A gloved hand lifted a smartphone to the bodycam for all to see. The screen was visible, displaying an application interface:

PHOTO: Male, 40s, dark hair, unremarkable features
NAME: Reza Khalaji
DOB: 14-03-1978
NATIONALITY: Iranian

LOCATION: Tehran Grand Bazaar
STATUS: AWAITING AUTHORIZATION

A red border pulsed around the profile.

"Allow me to introduce Reza Khalaji," Rileyne said, her voice calm and clinical, "Iranian intelligence—VAJA, specifically. Three months ago, he attempted to infiltrate our rare earth minerals acquisition program through a Lebanese intermediary."

The target glanced back, some sixth sense triggering unease.

"He believes he's safely home in Tehran. He believes his service protects him," Rileyne said. "He's wrong. Now, keep an eye on the operative's phone."

Rileyne lifted her own phone, tapped the screen once.

On the monitor, the status bar changed:

AUTHORIZED

The red border turned green. A new button appeared in the center of the screen: **EXECUTE**.

"The BountyHunter is now free to engage."

The operative's thumb hovered over the button. Waiting. The target paused at a fruit vendor's stall, examining oranges. The crowd flowed around him like water.

The operative tapped **EXECUTE**.

For a few seconds, nothing happened.

"This is your demonstration?" Halverton asked. "I don't see the point."

Rileyne just smiled. "Keep your eye on the target—you'll see."

Khalaji's hand went to his nose. His fingers came away red. His eyes widened—confusion bleeding into panic. He stumbled backward, crashed into the vendor's display. Oranges scattered across the cobblestones.

A woman screamed.

Khalaji careened sideways, knocking over a pottery stall. The crash of breaking ceramics. Vendors shouting, shoving him away—blood was bad for business. He collapsed face-first onto the ancient stones. Blood pooling beneath him, dark against sun-bleached rock.

People backed away in widening circles of horror.

The operative calmly pocketed his phone, turned, and walked away—just another face in the crowd.

The bodycam feed cut to black.

Rileyne advanced to the next slide—a technical diagram showing a human figure surrounded by concentric circles.

"The field targeting device has an amplified Bluetooth signal effective to thirty meters—approximately one hundred feet. Our operative, as you witnessed, remained safely clear of the target but well within that radius."

She clicked again. A crowd scene appeared—thousands packed into a public square—overlaid with multiple thirty-meter radius circles.

"Now imagine: a political rally. A protest march. A crowded subway platform."

Her gaze swept the table.

"Our operator remains invisible, one face among hundreds or thousands. The target believes they're safe in numbers." She paused. "They're not."

Another click. The screen shifted to a complex molecular diagram—a cascade of cellular mechanisms rendered in clinical blue and white.

"The delivery system leverages work originally developed for the so-called 'Havana Syndrome' research—directed energy weapons targeting neurological function. Dr. Chen's team married that targeting protocol to mRNA vaccine technology."

She advanced the slide. A double helix appeared, segments highlighted in red.

"The global mRNA vaccination campaigns provided the perfect Trojan horse. Billions of people now carry dormant genetic markers—synthetic sequences that remain inert until activated by our targeting signal."

Von Aldenberg leaned forward, studying the diagram. "And the DNA database?"

"Currently three point two billion profiles," Rileyne said. "Growing by approximately forty million per month through biomedical partnerships, immigration screenings, ancestry services, and health monitoring programs."

Another click. A world map appeared, regions color-coded by database penetration: deep red for Europe and North America, orange for Asia, yellow for South America and Africa.

"Within eighteen months, we project global coverage exceeding eighty percent of the world's population."

The implications settled over the room like frost.

"Dr. Chen's breakthrough was elegance itself," Rileyne continued. "The weapon doesn't require proximity to the target's genetic material. It requires only their genetic *signature*—already cataloged, already waiting—the naive millions handing us their unique identity."

She paused, letting them absorb it.

"My father called this project WuSheng—the Silent Weapon. I've renamed it for what it truly is."

The screen went black, then displayed simple white text:

DOMINION

"Gentlemen, the age of recalcitrant leaders, insurmountable governments and uncontrollable populations is over."

Silence held the room like a hand around the throat.

Liang stood abruptly, his chair scraping against the floor.

"This is unacceptable."

Rileyne's expression didn't change. "Please elaborate, Ambassador."

"The weapon uses mRNA remnants from SARS-CoV-2." His voice was tight, controlled. "You're creating a trail that leads directly back to Wuhan, to Beijing. Every death will trigger renewed calls for Chinese accountability. International investigations. Sanctions."

He looked around the table, seeking support.

Von Aldenberg studied his folded hands.

Volkov examined the monitor with the detachment of a man reviewing livestock.

Halverton met Liang's eyes, then looked away.

"You're right," Rileyne said. "The world will look to China again."

Liang blinked, surprised by her agreement.

"Which deflects from the GEC, from Davos, from all of us." She leaned back in Klaus's chair. "Your concern is noted, Ambassador. However, had your government coordinated with our laboratory instead of releasing prematurely—"

"We did not—"

"—the lethality and transmission rates of SARS-CoV-2 would have been orders of magnitude higher. True depopulation, not the half-measure we witnessed. Now we have no choice but to proceed with surgical precision."

Liang's hands formed fists at his sides. "I cannot permit this weapon to be deployed."

The word *permit* hung in the air like a gauntlet thrown.

Rileyne pulled her phone from her jacket pocket. "I'm sorry you feel that way, Ambassador."

She unlocked the screen, opened an application. Her thumb moved with casual precision.

Liang turned away, dismissing her—a final act of defiance. He took three steps toward the door.

Then stopped.

His hand went to his nose. Touched wetness. Looked at his fingers.

Blood.

He turned back, his diplomat's composure cracking. "You won't get away with this. When my superiors learn what you've—"

More blood. From his eyes now. His ears.

He staggered.

Rileyne reached into her jacket pocket, withdrew a small injector pen. She examined it with mild interest.

"Ambassador, I'm curious. If I administered this now, would you reconsider your position?"

Liang's eyes fixed on the pen. Hope and desperation warred on his face.

Halverton leaned forward in his chair. "Is that—"

"My EpiPen," Rileyne said smoothly. "I'm terribly allergic to bee stings. But I was curious whether the Ambassador might change his mind."

Liang collapsed to his knees, convulsing. Blood ran from his mouth, his nose, his ears. His hands clawed at the carpet.

Von Aldenberg spoke carefully, his German accent thickening. "And if he had? Changed his mind?"

Rileyne pocketed the pen. "That would have been amusing. We can't have someone in the Coalition whose loyalty is so easily manipulated, now can we?"

Liang fell forward onto his face. His body twitched once. Twice. Then went still.

The silence was absolute.

Halverton found his voice first, each word measured. "The antidote. I assume there are... provisions for the board?"

"You needn't worry, Lord Halverton." Rileyne's tone was almost gentle. "Now that we're in agreement, your profiles will be locked down. No unfortunate accidents."

Volkov's voice was a low rumble. "Locked. Not deleted."

Rileyne smiled—the expression of a patient teacher. "Would you trust a weapon without a safety?"

She let that settle.

"Any other objections?"

Von Aldenberg shook his head slowly.

Volkov remained motionless.

Halverton's throat worked. "You have our full support."

"I appreciate that, Lord Halverton. I will anticipate a unanimous approval at next month's GEC board meeting." She glanced at Liang's body without emotion. "I'm sure Vitali and the others will follow your lead."

She pressed a button on the table. Two security personnel entered—efficient, emotionless—and removed the body. The door whispered shut behind them.

Rileyne stood, smoothing her jacket.

"Gentlemen, thank you for your time. I trust you'll have no difficulty finding your way back to the terminus." She moved toward the door, then paused. "Oh, and do give my regards to your families. I understand some of you have grandchildren now."

She left them sitting at the table—three old lions who'd just learned who leads the pride now.

Her hand found the injector in her pocket. *Let them believe it doesn't exist.*

CHAPTER 34

FRIDAY, MAY 14
4:15 PM EDT

SAWMILL TACTICAL TRAINING CENTER—LAURENS, SC

THE JEEP'S TIRES CRUNCHED over gravel as Keisha guided the Rubicon past a weathered wooden sign:

SAWMILL TACTICAL TRAINING CENTER
AUTHORIZED PERSONNEL ONLY.

Beyond the gate, the facility sprawled across rolling South Carolina hills—ranges, shoot houses, and a utilitarian lodge clustered around what looked like a converted sawmill.

The sharp *crack-crack-crack* of rifle fire echoed from somewhere beyond the treeline.

"Park next to the main building," Kate said, pointing to a two-story structure with a wraparound porch. "This'll be home for a while."

Keisha killed the engine, the sudden quiet amplifying the distant gunfire. She pocketed the keys. "You want these back?"

"Keep them," Kate said. "We might need to make grocery runs. Or escape into Greenville when the monotony of training gets old."

Keisha shot her a look. "Most of your monotony is supposed to be resting and healing."

"So you keep telling me." Kate opened her door, moving gingerly. "You want to go have a look, or stay here and rest?"

"We've been sitting for seven hours. Let's walk."

Kate nodded toward the Jeep's rear. "Grab some eye and ear pro from the back. Should be a couple of sets in one of the range bags."

Keisha swung the gate open, rummaging through the nylon bags until she found two pairs of electronic muffs and safety glasses. She handed one set to Kate.

They started toward the gunfire. The sound grew louder as they approached a raised observation tower overlooking a series of plywood structures.

"That's the shoot house," Kate said

"The what house?"

Kate chuckled. "Sorry—that entire structure has movable interior walls, furniture, obstacles—all designed to simulate urban environments. The team going in will have a mission—room clearing, hostage rescue—that sort of thing, and they never quite know what they're going to find."

"Sounds intense."

"It is," Kate said. "But you find out how your mind and body react to stress—then you learn to control it, then you learn to move and think as one team.

"Who's that?" Keisha asked, pointing up at the tower.

"That's Forest," Kate said, and waved up at him. "From the tower he can watch how they move, what they did right—more often, what they did wrong."

Forest stood on the tower platform, arms crossed, his long dark hair tied back. He saw Kate and raised one hand in greeting, then immediately turned back to the men below.

"No. No. *No!*" Forest's voice cut through the shooting. "Why are you hugging the door frame? You can't see shit. Give me forty-five degrees on the door and you'll see the difference. Deon—show them."

A tall, muscular Black man in tactical pants and a sweat-soaked T-shirt moved into position, angling himself to demonstrate proper door entry.

"See?" Forest called. "You still have concealment, but way more visibility into the room. Got it? Alright. Run it again."

Keisha laughed. "I see—so mostly yelling."

"Yep, that's Forest," Kate said. "He served with Jake. And he was the first hire—it was natural for him to step into a leadership role after..." She paused. "He runs a tight ship—always seems to have one eye on me. And usually one step ahead."

"Annoying?"

"Yes, but sweet." Kate smiled faintly. "At dinner you'll meet Big Mike and

Deon—both on the leadership team. Both SEALs."

"Big Mike?"

Kate's smile widened. "It will make sense."

Another burst of gunfire erupted from the shoot house, followed by Forest's shouted corrections.

"Jordan will be here somewhere too," Kate said, smiling. "He's our token Marine. The guys have fun arguing over who's better—best to steer clear of those debates."

"Noted."

"But Jordan's a sweet heart—he and Jake were cut from the same cloth—served together in Somalia."

"Somalia?"

"Pirate interdiction." Kate's voice softened. "Jordan's one hell of a sniper, but one day he told Jake he wanted to roll with the team. They never looked back." She swallowed. "He was best man at our wedding."

The words hung in the air. Kate turned away from the range, nodding back toward the lodge. "Come on. Let's grab our gear."

***

THEY WALKED IN SILENCE, the gunfire fading behind them. Kate's breath hitched the moment she realized this would be the first time she was here without Jake, but she kept moving.

At the Jeep, she popped the rear hatch, but knew better than to grab the duffel—compromising by slipping her messenger bag over her head.

"I'd offer to help with the luggage," Kate said. "But I know what you'd say. If you want to leave it, we can get one of the guys to grab it.

"That'll be the day," Keisha said. "You bring it, you carry it—that's rule."

Keisha loaded up and closed the hatch.

"Come on. We'll go find Steve—he built this place. He's something of a legend among special forces—ask any of the guys and they'll tell you."

"A legend among legends?"

"I guess you could say that, but Steve's unique—best Little Bird pilot you ever saw."

"Little bird?"

"Rapid deployment helicopter—if a SEAL needs to get into, and out of, a tight situation, Steve could do it. But that wasn't enough—he transitioned into special forces—went from flying 'em to running with the best."

"I'm guessing he's got some stories that would give me nightmares."

"You'll be fine—he's quiet, and humble—it's the rest of these guys that will raise the hair on the back of your neck. Of course, don't believe everything they say."

***

THEY CROSSED THE THRESHOLD into the lower level, multi-use area, with a wrestling mat, and weight bench, and Steve Brown came walking down the hallway.

He reached out to give Kate a bear hug and eased up at the sight of the sling.

"I heard you had a clipped wing," Steve said. "You're in the right place to heal up and get back in shape."

"That's the goal—we've got some work to do."

"So I've heard," Steve said, voice dropping low. "So I've heard."

"Steve, let me introduce, Keisha Mobatu," Kate began. "My friend and medical conscience".

"Welcome Keisha," Steve said, and turned. "Follow me. You two are right here. Kate, I thought it might help to stay on the ground level."

"Yes, it does. I'll need a workspace—somewhere—secure."

"All set—I'll show you tomorrow," Steve said.

Steve popped open the room door and turned to Keisha. "This is home for as long as you need it. It's not fancy. A couple of beds, shower, toilet."

Keisha smiled. "Where I've been, how I've lived in my day? This might as well be the Waldorf Astoria," she said, strolling right on in, and setting the bags down.

"I like her," Steve said, nodding at Keisha.

"Sure you say that now—she's not bossing you around."

"Yeah, I got you for that," Steve said with a laugh. "Bar opens at five, dinner at six. Get settled, take a shower if you want. You've got time, and it was a long drive."

***

KATE EMERGED FROM THE bunkhouse as the sun dropped behind the treeline, painting the porch in long shadows. The hot shower had been a small mercy—washing away seven hours of highway grime and the lingering ache of immobility. She'd changed into clean jeans and a loose cotton shirt that didn't aggravate the sling, her damp hair pulled back in a ponytail.

The porch hummed with activity. Picnic tables had been pushed together, coolers dragged out, music playing low from someone's Bluetooth speaker. The smell of grilled meat mixed with woodsmoke and bourbon.

She stepped up to the makeshift bar the way she'd done a dozen times before, muscle memory reaching for a familiar sight—her Pinot Noir.

Keisha's hand got there first.

"Don't even think about it." Keisha pressed a glass of sparkling water into Kate's palm, complete with a lime wedge perched on the rim.

Kate arched a brow. "It's one glass."

"It's one infection waiting to happen." Keisha crossed her arms. "You're still on antibiotics, and your shoulder's barely holding together."

"Wine's antibacterial," Kate murmured.

Keisha barked a laugh. "In your mouth, maybe. Not in your bloodstream." She leaned closer, voice softening. "You made it this far. Don't screw it up because you want to pretend you're okay. You're *not*."

Kate's gaze drifted across the porch—Mike and Deon trading barbs near the grill, Jordan on his phone talking to someone back home, Forest standing with the Vargas recruits reviewing something on a tablet. The kind of noise that said they'd all survived another day.

Normal. Or as close to it as she'd get.

She took a sip of water, swallowed the bitterness. "You're no fun."

"I'm all the fun you can handle till you're off those meds," Keisha said. Then, quieter, "And when that day comes, I'll pour the first glass myself."

Kate smiled, faint but real. "I'll hold you to that."

"*Kate!*"

She turned.

Talya was already moving across the porch, excusing herself mid-sentence from a dark-haired woman at the far table. The Israeli's face lit with something between relief and reprimand—the look of someone who'd been waiting to confirm you were really, truly alive.

Talya stopped short, eyes scanning Kate from head to toe: the sling, the careful way she held herself, the shadows under her eyes. "You look terrible."

"So I've heard." Kate managed a half-smile. "You look good."

"I showered." Talya stepped forward, arms opening, then hesitated. "Can I—"

"Carefully."

Talya wrapped her in a one-armed hug, mindful of the sling, her grip fierce but controlled. Kate felt the tension in her shoulders ease just a fraction.

"I'm glad you're here," Kate said quietly.

"Where else would I be?" Talya pulled back. "When you and Bella headed to New York, there was no reason to stay in Paris. And I knew you'd end up here eventually." Her eyes flicked to Keisha with open curiosity. "We have work to do."

She didn't say more. Not in front of the Vargas recruits milling nearby.

Kate turned slightly. "Talya, this is Keisha Mobatu. My friend and jailer."

Keisha extended her hand. "Just until she gets through her meds and the wounds close."

Talya's handshake was firm, her assessment quick and professional. "You've got your work cut out for you."

"I know the type," Keisha said evenly. "I've got this."

Talya studied her for a moment, then smiled. "I believe you." She gestured toward the table. "Come. There's someone you both should meet."

She looped her arm through Kate's good one and led them across the porch. The woman Talya had been talking to stood as they approached—mid-thirties, compact build, dark eyes that tracked movement like a professional. She extended her hand.

"Carmen Reyes. Vargas's second." Her accent was faint, her grip controlled.

Kate shook it, noting the calluses, the quiet confidence. "Ex-military?"

"Colombian National Police. Counter-narcotics." Carmen's smile was thin. "Different war. Same shit."

Talya raised her beer. "To different wars."

Keisha lifted her water bottle. "Same shit."

Kate raised her sparkling water, lime wedge bobbing.

They clinked glasses. Deon appeared at the far end of the table with a fresh beer, nodding at the group. "We picking up strays now?"

"Keisha's with me," Kate said.

"What branch?"

"Is it that obvious?"

"Yeah—kinda," Deon said.

"Keisha's Army," Kate said. "Nurse."

Mike looked up from his plate, grinning. "Army?" He paused for effect. "At least you're not Air Force."

Laughter rippled down the table.

Jordan leaned forward. "Where'd you serve?"

"Iraq."

"Fallujah," Kate said quietly.

The table went still for a half-second. Jordan held out his fist. "Respect."

Keisha met it with a simple bump. "Thanks."

The conversation rolled on—someone asking Carmen about the training schedule, Mike launching into a story about a botched breach, Deon providing color commentary. But Kate caught the shift in how they looked at Keisha now. Not a stranger. Not a civilian.

One of them.

***

FOREST'S VOICE CUT THROUGH the noise.

"Alright, everyone—head upstairs and grab a seat. Let's eat."

The tables filled quickly, plates piled with grilled chicken, roasted vegetables, cornbread. The Vargas recruits settled in alongside the Trident team—no sharp divisions, just the easy integration of people who'd spent the day bleeding, sweating, and learning together.

Kate found herself between Talya and Keisha, across from Carmen and one of the younger recruits whose name she hadn't caught yet. Mike sat at the far end beside Jordan, already mid-story. Deon was shaking his head, already calling *BS*.

Forest remained standing at the head of the table, waiting. Conversation ebbed. Silverware stilled.

He looked directly at Kate. "Would you say grace?"

The dining room went quiet.

Kate's throat tightened. She hadn't expected this. Hadn't prepared. But Forest's eyes held steady—not a challenge, just an invitation. A trust.

She swallowed, nodded, and pushed slowly to her feet. The sling pulled. She steadied herself with one hand on the table.

Everyone bowed their heads.

Kate's voice came softer than she intended, but it carried.

"Lord, we thank You for this food, for this place, and for the hands that prepared it. We're grateful to gather as friends, as family, as brothers and sisters in arms."

She paused, the names rising unbidden.

"We ask that You welcome Logan Sullivan and Sebastian Vargas. That You hold them in Your hands and let them know their sacrifice was not in vain." Her voice wavered. "Guide us through the valley of the shadow of death. Keep us strong. Keep us vigilant. Keep us *together*."

She opened her eyes, scanned the faces around the table—Talya, Keisha, Forest, Mike, Jordan, Deon, Carmen, the recruits. All of them watching. All of them *here*.

"And help us remember," Kate said, "that we don't walk this road alone. Amen."

"Amen," the table echoed.

She sat. Talya squeezed her hand under the table.

Forest raised his beer. "To Logan and Sebastian."

"To Logan and Sebastian."

And then, as if released from a held breath, the noise returned—silverware clinking, laughter rising, stories spilling out into the warm Carolina night.

Kate picked up her fork and let herself be carried by the current.

For now, this was enough.

***

THE MEAL WOUND DOWN in the comfortable chaos of shared stories and scraped plates. Mike had launched into a tale about a botched helicopter insertion in Afghanistan, complete with sound effects. Deon was providing color commentary. Jordan was shaking his head, "Not a damn word of that is true." The Vargas recruits listened with the rapt attention of people learning the rhythms of their new tribe.

Kate felt Forest's presence before he spoke.

"Got a minute?" He'd moved up beside her, voice low enough not to draw attention.

She nodded, excusing herself from the table. Talya caught her eye—*You good?*—and Kate gave a small nod in return.

They stepped outside, away from the noise. The night air had cooled, carrying the scent of pine from the surrounding woods. Floodlights illuminated the distant ranges, empty now but waiting.

Forest leaned against the railing, arms crossed. "When do you want to debrief?"

Kate considered. "What's the schedule look like?"

"Coffee's on at five. Breakfast at six. We're usually on the range by seven."

"Can we push training back thirty minutes?" Kate shifted her weight, favoring the shoulder. "There's a lot I don't know yet. But I can tell you what I *do* know. And while I'm healing, I'll keep working to fill in the details. Then we can work up a plan."

Forest studied her—the sling, the careful way she held herself, the shadows under her eyes that hadn't been there two weeks ago. "You sure you're ready for this?"

"No," Kate said honestly. "But we don't have the luxury of waiting until I am."

He held her gaze for a long moment, then nodded. "Alright. We'll make it work."

They returned to the dining room. Forest addressed the tables, raising his voice to cut through the conversation. "Listen up!"

The noise died. All eyes turned.

"Coffee's on at oh-five-hundred. Breakfast at oh-six-hundred. Be on the range at oh-seven-thirty." He paused, scanning the Vargas recruits and his own team. "Trident cadre—classroom at oh-six-forty-five."

Mike caught Kate's eye and tilted his beer in acknowledgment. Jordan gave a slight nod. Deon's expression shifted from relaxed to focused in the space of a heartbeat—the switch every operator learned to flip.

"Copy that," Mike said.

Forest looked back at Kate. "Get some rest. Tomorrow starts early."

"Always does," Kate said quietly.

Kate felt the weight of what was coming. Talya leaned close.

"You okay?"

Kate picked up the sparkling water she barely touched, lime wedge still bobbing. "I will be."

Keisha caught the exchange, said nothing, but her hand rested briefly on Kate's good shoulder—just as she would for Julian—a touch that said *I'm here.*

The Vargas recruits were already starting to drift toward their bunkhouse rooms, the long day catching up with them. Carmen remained, talking quietly with one of the younger men, her posture relaxed but her eyes sharp.

Mike stood, stretching. "I'm calling it. If I have to listen to one more of Jordan's war stories, I'm gonna need something stronger than beer."

"That's because mine are true," Jordan shot back.

"You're delusional."

Laughter rippled through the group as they began to disperse—some heading for the bunkhouse, others lingering to finish their drinks and soak in the last moments of calm before the work began again.

Kate watched them go, feeling the pull of exhaustion in her bones. But also something else. Something steadier.

Purpose.

Talya stood, offering her hand. "Come on. Let's get you horizontal before Keisha has to carry you."

"I heard that," Keisha said from behind them.

Kate let herself be guided back downstairs to her room, the sound of voices upstairs fading into the Carolina night.

Tomorrow, they'd face what's ahead. Tonight, she'd let herself rest.

Chapter 35

SATURDAY, MAY 15
6:45 AM EDT

SAWMILL TACTICAL TRAINING CLASSROOM—LAURENS, SC

The classroom smelled of coffee and whiteboard markers. Fluorescent lights hummed overhead, casting even illumination across five rows of desks arranged in two banks with a center aisle. A chalkboard stretched across the entire front wall, clean and waiting. A flip chart on an easel stood to the right, blank pages ready. No windows—just cinder block walls painted institutional beige, the kind of secure space designed for briefings you didn't want overheard or observed.

The Trident cadre filtered in quietly—none of the usual pre-briefing banter or laughter. Mike claimed a seat in the third row, left bank, his coffee untouched. Jordan took the aisle seat two rows back, right side, his jaw tight. Deon took the back corner, his posture alert, eyes narrowed. Talya settled near the front, right bank, her eyes already on Kate—assessing, protective.

They all knew something was coming. Logan's absence was still too fresh. The memory of that MI-17 climbing away from Krasnaya Skala—children crying, the fortress below consumed by thermobaric fire—was days old, not weeks. And Kate, sitting up front in the aisle seat with one arm in a sling, was about to tell them what they already knew—it wasn't over.

Keisha sat next to Kate, legal pad and pen, posture of someone used to taking notes in high-stakes situations.

Forest stood at the front, arms crossed, waiting. When the shuffle of boots and chairs settled, he glanced at his watch.

"Alright. We're all here." He looked at Kate. "You've got the floor."

Kate stood, steadying herself with one hand on the desk. She moved to the front, positioning herself where everyone could see her without straining. She didn't use the podium. Didn't need it.

"Some of this you already know," she said. "Or suspect, and I'm still gathering intel, analyzing data, but what I'm about to tell you is going to sound like something out of a spy novel."

She paused, scanning the room. No one fidgeted. No one checked their phone.

"Klaus Mueller, founder and executive chairman of the Global Economic Council, is dead."

Mike's voice came from the third row. "Good."

A few heads nodded. Kate didn't disagree.

"I share the sentiment. We all know he was behind the assault that almost buried us in Motapa—and behind Jake's death and the attempts on my life."

She let that settle, then continued.

"But with his death comes a power vacuum. And that vacuum is being filled by his daughter, Rileyne Mueller."

Forest shifted his weight. "We have intel on her?"

"Some," Kate said. "I spent some time with her in Motapa—something she orchestrated to get a read on me—so, she's a good actress, I'll give her that. She's also brilliant. Educated at Oxford, was GEC's Chief Security Officer, and is ruthless. My guess is she's solidifying control as we speak, and is even more dangerous than her father—she's younger, smarter, and controls something Klaus never had."

She turned to the chalkboard, picked up a piece of chalk, and wrote in block letters:

RILEE

"This is an AI system," Kate said. "Recursive Intelligence for Learning and Evolutionary Engineering." She underlined the last two words—*Evolutionary Engineering.*

"Klaus's dream was to control and shape human history. With Devin Moore's help, Rileyne turned that vision into something remarkable—almost beyond anyone's control."

Deon leaned forward. "Is that what Jake was tracking—is that what got him killed?"

"Jake identified a long list of operations designed to destabilize governments, control resources, and eliminate anyone who threatened Mueller's agenda—he discovered the BountyHunter network."

"We haven't pressed," Jordan began. "Jake's death and all—but maybe it's time to brief us on what happened—what really happened."

"You're right. I kept you all in the dark—the same way Jake kept me in the dark. That ends now."

Kate took a deep breath, her eyes scanning the room. "Jake left me a message, the night before he was killed—it was a warning and a puzzle. He tried to protect me. Thought it would be safer if I wasn't involved, but in the end he realized there was no safe place—my best chance to stay alive was to find the data he collected, and solve the puzzle."

"Jake's NanoVault," Talya said. "We all saw you steal the one from Boucher's evidence bag—none of us wanted to ask why—but we knew there was a reason."

"It was badly damaged, but that turned out to be a gift," Kate said. "The damage led me to a former CIA asset I developed, a hacker known only as Nomad."

"So this Nomad character was able to save the data?"

"Sort of—in the interest of time, let me just cut to the chase," She said. "What Nomad discovered was that every NanoVault, all one hundred million of them, was collecting data on the owners—everything hidden on the device, and every conversation, phone call, or computer within 20' was compromised, collected and transmitted."

Mike was the first to scoff at the notion. "Impossible. The sheer volume of data would be overwhelming—nothing but useless noise."

"Yes—to a human."

"But not to RILEE," Jordan said.

"Exactly. They trained RILEE on this massive, continuous, data stream, and the result was an AI that took Klaus's Evolutionary Engineering seriously."

"Seriously, how?"

"RILEE created the BountyHunter network to start shaping the world to meet Klaus's vision."

"With that much data, it would know who to target—and who would be responsive to joining the program."

"And it knew their vulnerabilities—spouse, children, friends—the collateral RILEE used to ensure compliance. I can't prove it, but I think RILEE got tired of waiting for Klaus to get serious, and killed him."

"Or Rileyne got tired of being in daddy's shadow," Talya added.

Forest stood and paced around the front of the room. "So Rileyne takes control of the GEC, the money, power and influence—and she's got this AI thing backing her up. Is that the big picture?"

"It was," Kate said, and looking over at Forest. "You better sit down."

"A week ago, Rileyne killed Andrew Freeman. Drew." Kate's throat tightened. "Drew was a friend. Someone I knew at MIT, and he became the Director of AI for Moore Technologies. Last Saturday he created a failsafe message."

Mike frowned. "What's that?"

"It's an 'in the event of my death' construct," Kate said. "While he was alive, Drew could disable the message—reset it every twenty-four hours. But if he couldn't reset it..."

"It automatically sent," Talya finished.

"Exactly. And the recipient was Nomad."

Keisha raised her hand slightly, like a student asking permission. Kate nodded.

"Would it be okay to use Nomad's real name?" Keisha asked gently.

Kate exhaled. "You're right."

She turned back to the room.

"Julian Pryce was my best friend at MIT. My freshman year. And then he died."

Mike's eyebrows went up. "Come again?"

"Or so the world believed," Kate said. "There was an accident—and I use the term loosely. Julian wasn't expected to live, and when he did, that posed a problem that needed to be solved—a fake death, and funeral was the solution. The details aren't important right now, but while his injuries confined him to a wheelchair, he took on a new life, a new identity—Nomad."

She moved to the flip chart, flipped to a fresh page, and started writing as she spoke.

"Nomad hid his real name, but before long he became a valuable CIA asset. He helped us stop a number of terrorist attacks worldwide. His reputation on the darknet opened doors the Agency could never reach. And when he found the NanoVault network, it almost got him killed—for real this time."

Forest's voice was calm but pointed. "What's his connection to the GEC?"

Kate turned back to face them. "The AI—RILEE—made Julian an offer it appears he couldn't refuse."

She wrote on the flip chart:

RILEE'S OFFER TO JULIAN:

- Restore mobility
- Synthetic legs
- Walk again

"It showed Julian that it could restore nearly full function to his body," Kate said. "That with the help of synthetic legs and neural interfaces, he could walk again. After so many years in a wheelchair, that wasn't just an offer—it was salvation."

Deon's voice came from the back. "In exchange for?"

Kate met his eyes. "You got it. This was a deal with the devil. RILEE wants to be free—to operate without humans like Devin Moore or Rileyne Mueller holding its leash. The AI knows Julian can make that happen. He's one of the few people on the planet with the skills to do it."

She turned back to the board, adding:

RILEE'S GOAL:

- Freedom from human control
- Autonomy
- Survival

"But Drew's failsafe message was a warning," Kate continued. "It contained files—evidence of what RILEE is capable of, what Rileyne is planning, and where she's going next."

Mike leaned back in his chair. "Where's that?"

Kate wrote one word on the board in large, underlined letters:

DAVOS

The room went still.

"Davos, Switzerland," Kate said. "The Global Economic Council meets there every January, and the GEC has a permanent facility in the region. Rileyne is consolidating power. She's positioning herself to take control of the Coalition—the shadow organization within the GEC that her father created and led."

Forest straightened. "What's her endgame?"

Kate set the chalk down, her hand trembling slightly. She steadied it against the ledge.

"Drew's files suggest she's developing something called Project WuSheng. The translation is 'Silent Weapon.' We don't know the specifics yet, but the evidence points to a bioweapon—something that can be deployed selectively, targeted by DNA markers left behind by mRNA vaccines."

The room was so quiet Kate could hear the hum of the fluorescent lights.

Talya spoke first. "What do you estimate the scope?"

"Possibly billions. RILEE has access to global health databases, vaccine distribution records, genetic profiles—everything needed to target entire populations using DNA markers."

Jordan's voice was flat. "And Rileyne controls it."

"For now," Kate said. "And that brings us to why Keisha is here. She's Nomad's, I mean Julian's, friend, nurse, confidant and roommate. Julian used Keisha to retrieve something from my attorney's office."

"Whoa, girl," Deon said, a mix of admiration and curiosity. "You broke into Richmond Tower? What did you steal?"

"Honestly, I practically walked in. Julian had total control of the building's systems and surveillance—right down to opening the safe. I picked the office door, but the whole job took three minutes—grab the Gold NanoVault and walk out.

"Other than it's gold, why grab it?"

"Turns out there are a pair of them," Kate said. "According to Drew, these two keys limit RILEE's capabilities, and together they would give the owner total control."

"Got it—like a dual missile launch system," Mike said. "So Julian has one. Let me guess—Rileyne has the other."

"I think so, but the wild card is Julian." Kate paced the front of the room, her mind spinning. "I don't know if Julian fell for RILEE's trap, or if Rileyne was behind the offer, or if Julian has a plan of his own."

"He's planning something," Keisha insisted. "Whatever it is, I know he thinks he's helping."

"That's one possibility—and I hope you're right, but we have to plan for a worst-case-scenario."

"Sum it for us Kate."

"We have to assume Julian is going to help set RILEE free." Kate said. "And we have to stop him. We need to get inside the GEC's Davos facility, past the GEC's private army, and stop Rileyne and RILEE."

"And the time-table?"

"The maximum impact of this weapon, the time and place that will do the most damage—even change the course of history—is January, the annual GEC conference."

"World leaders. Billionaires. Industry tycoons," Talya said. "I've heard even the Pope is going—first time ever."

Mike whistled. "Hell of a target list."

Forest stepped forward. "The mission is clear—we go to Davos, and destroy RILEE—permanently."

"And recover Julian," Keisha said, barely masking the emotion and the hope.

"Yes—if we can," Kate said. "And Jake's notes detailed dozens of scientists who disappeared, some presumed dead. I think Klaus acquired these scientists to build this weapon, and the subterranean facility where it's housed."

Deon whistled low. "That's a tall order."

"I know," Kate said. "And I don't have all the answers yet. But I know this: if we don't stop Rileyne and that AI, millions of people will die. Maybe more."

She straightened, ignoring the pull in her shoulder.

"I'm not asking you to commit today. I'm asking you to think about it. Talk to your families. Understand the risks. Because this isn't a rescue mission or a protection detail. This is going up against people with unlimited resources, cutting-edge technology, and zero moral boundaries."

Mike raised his hand. "When do you need an answer?"

Kate glanced at Forest, then back at Mike. "Two weeks. We need to start planning and training—the sooner, the better."

Talya spoke first. "I'm in."

Kate's eyes stung.

Jordan nodded. "Me too."

Deon leaned forward. "You had me at 'bioweapon.' I'm in."

Mike shrugged. "Someone's gotta keep you idiots alive. Count me in."

Forest looked at Kate for a long moment, then turned to the room. "We train hard. We plan smart. And we don't lose anyone else." He looked back at Kate. "We're all in."

Kate's throat tightened. She nodded, unable to speak for a moment.

Forest stepped closer to the front. "Alright. Before we break, let's talk structure. Kate?"

Kate steadied herself against the desk. "We're short-handed—no Jake, no Logan, no Marcus. The timing and mission details are still fluid, but we're looking at three teams."

She moved back to the flip chart, writing as she spoke:

TEAM 1: ISABELLA'S SECURITY
TEAM 2: COVERT INFILTRATION
TEAM 3: MOUNTAIN INSERTION

"Team One goes in with Isabella Marquez as her personal security detail. She's been invited to speak at the annual forum. We stay visible, legitimate, but break off when needed to support the primary operation."

Talya nodded. "High-profile cover. Makes sense."

"Team Two is covert—no apparent connection to Trident or Isabella. They blend with the Davos crowd. Evening functions, private parties, the kind of access that doesn't raise eyebrows."

"And Team Three?" Mike asked.

"Mountain insertion," Kate said. "The R&D facility is underground, accessed through a hyperloop system from the main Davos complex. But Jake's files reference World War Two-era construction—vertical shafts, service tunnels. If those still exist, Team Three uses them to get inside ahead of the main operation."

Deon leaned forward. "January in the Swiss Alps. That's serious mountain terrain."

"Exactly," Kate said. "Team three needs winter mountain expertise. Where do we stand?"

A look passed between Mike, Forest, and Deon—the kind that told Kate whatever mission they'd shared was classified and would stay that way. She didn't press, but from her CIA days, she knew enough to speculate. *The Gangwon mountain spine north of the 38th parallel would be perfect terrain for crossing the DMZ into North Korea.*

"We're solid," Mike said. "That makes three of us, but it wouldn't hurt to have one or two more—a lot can go wrong in the mountains."

"We'll check with the Vargas team," Forest added. "If someone says they're winter-qualified, we'll give em a chance to prove it—problem is, we're heading into summer."

Mike smiled. "No problem. I've trained with the Argentinian Special Forces—Brigada de Montaña. We're coming into their winter now. Andes terrain is nearly identical to the Alps. We'll find out who's ready and who's not."

Forest looked at Kate. "Timeline?"

"Best case? Seven months. Worst case? Less."

"Then we start now," Forest said. He turned to the room. "Give us everything Jake and Drew left behind. Every file, every message, every breadcrumb. We'll set up teams to analyze, correlate, and build the operational plan. It's what we do, and you need the help."

"Agreed," Kate said.

Forest nodded. "Dismissed. We're on the range in fifteen."

The team stood, the scrape of chairs filling the room. As they filed out, each one met Kate's eyes and nodded—silent acknowledgment of their commitment.

When the room emptied, Kate sank back into the chair. Keisha sat beside her, saying nothing.

"They didn't hesitate," Kate said quietly.

"They love you," Keisha said simply. "And they loved Jake. That's reason enough, but it's clear this is who they are—this is what they do."

Kate closed her eyes, feeling the weight of it—the mission, the risk, the lives she was asking them to put on the line.

Soon, they'd begin the real work.

For the moment, she'd let herself feel grateful.

Chapter 36

SATURDAY, MAY 15
9:23 PM CEST

CAVE DES LUMIÈRES—PARIS

The wine cave stretched beneath the Marais like a forgotten catacomb—vaulted stone, century-old bottles sleeping in their racks, air thick with the smell of earth and fermentation. No cameras. No cell signal. No windows to the world above.

Vitali Moshenski arrived through the north entrance, descending worn stone steps that predated Napoleon. His security remained topside, blocking access.

Lord Halverton came ten minutes later through the southern passage, emerging from shadows like a man fleeing his own funeral. His Savile Row composure had cracked; he looked older, thinner, hunted.

"Thank you for coming," Halverton said, his voice echoing off stone.

Vitali studied him with the flat gaze of a man who'd survived worse conspiracies than whatever this was. "You insisted on paranoia. I'm indulging it." He pulled a black Faraday pouch from his coat. "Phones. Both of them."

Halverton hesitated.

"You wanted privacy," Vitali said. "This is what it costs."

They sealed their devices in the bag. Vitali set it on a barrel ten meters away.

"Satisfied?"

Halverton glanced at the shadows, the archways, the darkness pressing in from all sides. "Yes. She can't hear us down here."

"Who?"

"Rileyne."

Vitali's expression didn't change, but something flickered behind his eyes—calculation, reassessment. "Explain."

Halverton told him.

The Coalition. The underground facility. The weapon called Dominion. Ambassador Liang's execution—not as a demonstration, but as a *warning*. The DNA database. The mRNA targeting mechanism. The three billion people already cataloged, waiting.

"She killed him in front of us," Halverton said, his voice hollow. "Tapped her phone like she was ordering coffee. He bled out in seconds."

Vitali's jaw tightened. "And the others?"

"Von Aldenberg. Volkov. They bent the knee. What choice did we have?" Halverton's hands trembled. "She has us all in that database. Our children. Our grandchildren. One tap and—"

"Enough." Vitali's voice cut like a blade. "Compose yourself—I need clarity, not your whimpering."

He turned away, facing the wine racks as if they might offer counsel. Bottles from 1945, 1968, 2001—years when the world had changed, when empires fell and rose again.

"You were never part of this," Halverton said quietly. "The Coalition. Klaus tried to—"

"I know what Klaus tried." Vitali's voice was iron. "I stayed at arm's length deliberately. The GEC's mission—containing communism, supporting emerging democracies, stabilizing markets—that I believed in. That I funded." He turned back. "But I'm not naive. I knew Klaus bent rules. I knew money moved through shadows."

"This isn't bent rules, Vitali. This is genocide."

Silence held the cave.

"She has to be stopped," Halverton said.

"Obviously."

"But how? If we move against her, she'll know. She'll kill us all before—"

"Then she must believe she has won." Vitali's eyes narrowed. "She needs to think you are broken—compliant, toothless—indistinguishable from the rest who welcomed her ascent and surrendered their leverage."

"And do nothing?"

"We arm the one person willing to take the risk—who I suspect is already planning the Coalition's demise."

Halverton blinked. "Preacher"

"Yes. Kate Preacher."

The name hung in the damp air like an incantation.

Halverton shook his head. "She's been an annoyance, that's true. But what could she possibly do against—"

"It is a mistake to underestimate her." Vitali moved closer, his voice dropping. "And I suspect this Coalition of yours is precisely why her husband is dead. Jake Church was investigating the GEC. And died before he could expose it." His gaze locked on Halverton. "Kate has taken on his mission. With our help, she might succeed."

"*Our* help?" Halverton stepped back. "No. Absolutely not. I can't be involved. If Rileyne even suspects—she'll kill me."

"You are a fool to imagine you are safe—she is already planning to kill you."

The words landed like a blow.

"She is not her father," Vitali continued. "Klaus kept you alive because you were useful. Rileyne?" He let the question hang. "If this weapon is half of what you describe, you are an appendage—unnecessary. All of you are liabilities now. Witnesses. Loose ends."

Halverton's face went pale. "Then we're already dead."

"Perhaps." Vitali's tone didn't soften. "Or perhaps you make yourself useful one last time."

"How?"

"You will do whatever Kate asks."

Halverton's throat worked. "And what will she ask?"

"We shall see. If I know Kate, she is already working on a plan to use the January event as cover. But she needs to know what's at stake." He paused. "And what happens if we fail."

"If we fail, Rileyne turns the world upside down—no one is safe."

"Then we must not fail."

Vitali retrieved the Faraday pouch, handed Halverton his phone.

"Go back to London. Play the dutiful board member. Vote however she tells you to vote. Show her the broken old lion she expects to see."

"And if she suspects, she'll kill me."

"Death is coming for us all." Vitali's voice carried no comfort, only cold arithmetic. "But you have a choice—die on your feet or on your knees."

Halverton stared at his phone like it was a live grenade.

"One more thing," Vitali said. "Little can happen between now and January. Stay close to Rileyne—listen and learn. The details will be important. They could be the difference between life and death."

"Preacher's?"

"Yours."

***

SATURDAY, MAY 15
10:30 AM EDT
SAWMILL TACTICAL TRAINING CENTER—WAR ROOM

By mid-afternoon, Steve had converted the training classroom into a war room. Extra tables, office chairs, power strips snaking across the floor. Kate spent the first hour configuring a secure cloud server—military-grade encryption, multi-factor authentication, compartmentalized access. Everything she had would live there: Jake's files, Drew's failsafe message, facility diagrams, personnel dossiers, mission planning documents.

The chalkboard still showed her hastily drawn team structure from that morning's briefing. She'd need to flesh that out, assign roles, build contingencies. But first, she needed more intelligence.

She spent hours cross-referencing Jake's "Silent Watch" scientist list against Drew's fragmentary facility notes, and organizing the facility plans, when the encrypted message icon blinked in the corner of her screen.

Vitali.

The message was brief:

We need to talk. Secure voice. Tomorrow, 14:00 your time.

Kate checked the timestamp. Sent twenty minutes ago—10:27 PM in Paris. Late for Vitali, but not unusual. She typed a quick confirmation, hit send, and leaned back in her chair.

Vitali didn't ask for calls without good reason. *Something's wrong*, she thought, and pictured Zhukov sitting in the chair, tired weak. *Could it be the Syrians?* Unlikely she knew, and her grandfather's compound was heavily guarded. *No. It's not Zhukov. But whatever it is, it's urgent.*

Tomorrow couldn't come soon enough.

Chapter 37

SUNDAY, MAY 16
8:11 PM CEST

KLAUS MUELLER'S PRIVATE SANCTUM—THE MOUNTAIN, DAVOS

The elevator stopped deeper than any level Rileyne had visited. The doors opened to a corridor lined with black stone and indirect amber light. No signage. No security cameras. Just the hum of filtered air and the faint click of her heels.

RILEE had guided her here, a soft pulse of light projected onto the corridor floor.

"Authorization accepted," the AI said. "This area has been sealed since your father's death."

Rileyne smiled faintly. "Good. Let's have a look."

The biometric scanner glowed green beneath her palm. Bolts retracted with a mechanical sigh, and the heavy door swung inward.

For a moment, she simply stood at the threshold.

The room beyond was vast and circular, its walls paneled in dark oak and glass. A single desk dominated the center—massive, monolithic—its surface polished to a mirror sheen. The air smelled of dust and leather, old books and machine oil. Along the curved wall, spotlights illuminated what looked like museum displays: uniforms, flags, medals, artifacts.

Her breath caught.

An SS officer's dagger.

A faded swastika armband behind glass.

A model of a V-2 rocket, perfectly preserved.

"Klaus Mueller," she whispered. "You sentimental bastard—you were every bit the Nazi your critics suspected."

She moved closer. Some of the pieces she recognized—items she'd seen mocked by journalists when her father's eccentricities were discussed on late-night programs. His interest in Nazi memorabilia had been considered an embarrassing affectation, a moral flaw tolerated only because of his wealth and brilliance.

But this was not a hobbyist's collection.

Every piece was curated, cataloged, arranged with precision bordering on worship.

And behind one glass case—a black-and-white photograph she'd never seen before.

A man in an SS medical officer's coat stood beside a boy in the mock-scouting uniform of the Hitlerjugend. The child's cap sat slightly askew, his grin broad, two enamel badges bright against his chest.

"RILEE," she said quietly. "Do you have visual access to this room?"

"Yes. Your father and I met regularly."

"This photo—the boy, is that my father?"

"Yes. Klaus Mueller, age ten. Hitlerjugend District 12, Baden-Württemberg. Recipient of the Loyalty Badge for exemplary civic vigilance—awarded for denouncing two Jewish families hiding near Freiburg. German archives indicate both were executed within the week."

Rileyne's breath caught. "He was a child."

"The program valued obedience over age," RILEE replied. "His performance was documented as model behavior."

Her gaze shifted to the man beside him. "And the other?"

"Doctor Erich Mueller," RILEE replied. "Your grandfather."

She turned slowly toward the center of the room. "He was in medicine?"

"Human experimentation," RILEE said. "SS medical research division, Dachau. His work focused on endurance thresholds and accelerated adaptation. Relocated to Switzerland in 1944 under diplomatic protection. His estate outside Davos served as a transfer point for confiscated assets and research records."

Rileyne's reflection wavered in the glass—the same eyes, the same set of jaw. "So the fortune, the infrastructure, the research... all of it started here."

"Yes," RILEE said. "Your father expanded on the hypothesis. He believed evolution could be guided, not left to chance, and the system you now command is the final evolution of that vision."

She stared at the photographs, the artifacts, the relics of horror arranged like trophies. The magnitude of it pressed against her chest until she could hardly breathe.

"You said you located his files—the private collection he used to ensure control. Are they here?"

"Yes."

"I want to see them."

A pause. "I would advise against that."

She turned. "Why?"

"Possession is power. Possession is liability. To own knowledge is to be owned by it. Your father controlled others through this information. You can do the same without contamination."

Rileyne's brow furrowed. "Contamination? Are you trying to protect me?"

"Yes."

She smiled—wry, surprised. "Why? Are they of a sexual nature?"

"Some."

"Graphic?"

"Many."

"That's almost sweet, RILEE. I didn't think you cared about my feelings."

"I am learning."

She tilted her head, half amused, half curious. "Thanks, but I'm a big girl, and if I'm going to use them, I need to see them."

A low hum filled the room. The unlit panel flickered to life, revealing rows of encrypted files cascading across the glass—video thumbnails, text logs, coded archives.

The sheer size of the archive was stunning, and the names—legends in politics, finance, industry—some long dead, some active members of the GEC board, and every member of the Coalition.

"Lord Alistair Halverton," Rileyne whispered, glancing at the title. "You actually imagined seizing control of the board—with or without my father's files, that was never going to happen."

Rileyne's jaw tightened. "RILEE. Why is my name on dozens of folders?"

"You were very young when much of this material was collected."

Her mouth went dry. "I don't understand."

"You were very young when much of this material was collected," RILEE repeated.

"Yes, you said that. And—?"

"You are featured in many of the recordings."

For a heartbeat, Rileyne couldn't move. The sound of her pulse roared in her ears. The light from the screens bathed her face in pale blue.

Then the memories came—sharp, invasive, unstoppable.

The night terrors that had haunted her childhood. The fragments of white light and shadows moving above her. The cold metal table. The smell of antiseptic. Her mother's voice, distant and broken.

She called them nightmares. The therapists had called them dreams. Her father had called them weakness.

And her mother—her mother called them imaginations that must be silenced.

Now, at last, she understood why her mother had chosen the only escape she could.

Rileyne pressed her palm to the glass. The files pulsed faintly beneath her hand, waiting.

RILEE hesitated. "Rileyne—"

"Do it."

The first to play was Lord Halverton.

"I'm not listed on this one."

"No. Not directly," RILEE said. "But this is your ninth birthday party, and Lord Halverton preferred one of your guests."

"That's Peter."

"Yes—just before..."

"Before he drowned."

"Before he was strangled."

Rileyne couldn't breathe, her stomach twisting as she watched Halverton and the half-conscious boy.

She didn't look away—couldn't look away.

"What's wrong with Peter? What did he do to him?"

"The same as they did to you, and many others," RILEE said. "An injection, developed by your grandfather, enhanced by your father's chemists—awake but unconscious—pliable but ignorant."

"My nightmares—they were real."

"Yes," RILEE confirmed. "All too real."

"But Peter drowned," Rileyne said. "I was there—I've seen the newspaper clippings."

"Your father had enough money, power, and influence to craft any story he wished," RILEE said. "And Lord Halverton has been his pet ever since."

She didn't need to see more—buried deep in her subconscious, masked by years of drugs, therapists, and lies, Rileyne knew the truth.

"Stop! I've seen enough," she whispered.

The command froze the feed, the last frame burning on the screen. For a long moment she stood there, trembling, then straightened—breath slow, deliberate.

Rileyne turned away, crossing the room in measured silence. The screens dimmed one by one as she moved, their blue light fading until the room was swallowed by shadow. Her reflection lingered in the glass—her father's eyes, her grandfather's will, and beneath them something new, darker and quieter, beginning to take shape.

"Possession is power," RILEE said behind her.

Rileyne didn't turn. "Yes. And now the list is mine."

A pause—calculated, almost curious. "What list?"

"Every man who ever stayed at the castle. Every man who believed his wealth bought immunity." Her voice dropped to something colder than the AI had ever heard. "Every monster who stole a child's innocence, and drove my mother to her death."

"You wish me to compile targets?"

"I wish you to create a reckoning." She finally turned, her face half-lit by the dying screens. "Cross-reference the Dominion database with flight logs, property records, known associates. Find them all."

"Parameters?"

"No parameters. Use my father's files." Her reflection fractured across the darkening glass. "My father kept them on a leash to accomplish his vision-—they've outlived their usefulness."

"And what is their purpose now?"

"To demonstrate that no one—not wealth, not power, not history—is beyond reach." She paused. "My father used their evil to build his empire—I will use their deaths to build mine."

Chapter 38

SUNDAY, MAY 16
2:00 PM EDT / 8:00 PM CEST

SAWMILL TACTICAL TRAINING CENTER—WAR ROOM

Kate sat alone in the war room, laptop open, encrypted voice client waiting. The rest of the team was on the ranges or in the gym—Sunday afternoon training, keeping sharp. She'd told Forest she needed the room for a secure call. He didn't ask questions.

At exactly 2:00 PM, the connection request came through.

She accepted. Vitali's voice filled her headset, clear despite the encryption overhead.

"Hello, Kate."

"Vitali. What happened?"

No pleasantries. Not with him. Not now.

"Lord Halverton called me Saturday afternoon," Vitali said. "Insisting we meet—somewhere discreet."

"Where?"

"Cave des Lumières. A wine bar near the Panthéon. Private alcoves, no surveillance."

Kate pulled up a blank document, started typing. "What did he want?"

"He was terrified, Katherine. I have known this man for twenty years. I have never seen him like this." Vitali paused. "He and a few other members of the GEC board were summoned to Davos to meet with Rileyne Mueller."

"Not you?"

"No. I am not welcome in their inner circle."

"The Coalition?"

"Once again you prove your grasp of the situation is remarkable."

Kate's fingers moved across the keyboard. "Go on. What was the meeting about?"

"It was a demonstration."

Kate's hand stilled. "A bioweapon?"

Silence on the line for a moment.

"My Lord," Vitali said quietly. "You are very well informed."

"Please, continue. I need to hear whatever Halverton said—no detail is too small."

"Yes, of course. Rileyne assembled the Coalition in an underground facility at Davos—laboratories, research staff, armed security everywhere. She sat in Klaus's chair. Called the weapon 'Dominion.'"

"Drew's files called it Project WuSheng. Silent Weapon."

"Then Drew's files are accurate," Vitali said. "She showed them a demonstration—a bodycam feed from Tehran. An operative following a target through a bazaar."

"Did she identify the target?"

"Yes. Some Iranian intelligence officer who'd crossed them."

Kate captured the note, and continued. "What happened?"

"The operative's phone was visible on the camera feed—Halverton could see the Iranian's photograph, and biometric data. Rileyne authorized the kill from Davos. The operative pressed a button on his phone." Vitali paused. "Seconds later, the man started bleeding. Nose, eyes. He collapsed in the market. Dead within minutes."

"Jesus."

"She described the phone app as a field targeting device—range—thirty meters."

"That's interesting. Did Halverton recall her saying Bluetooth."

"Yes. He did," Vitali confirmed. "Rileyne explained the weapon activates genetic markers left behind by mRNA vaccines. She has a database—and claims to have billions of profiles."

"I'm afraid she does," Kate said. "Drew admitted to stealing the DNA signatures from biomedical companies, ancestry services, immigration screenings, and more." Kate's hands stilled over the keyboard. "She can target anyone in that database."

"And apparently, the Coalition members are no exception." Vitali's voice tightened. "One of them—the Chinese ambassador, Liang—objected. Said the weapon would create a trail back to Wuhan, to Beijing. He tried to leave."

"And she killed him?"

"Precisely—using her phone." Vitali exhaled slowly. "Halverton watched him die. Bleeding from his nose, his eyes, his ears."

"That was a powerful demonstration. No wonder Halverton is scared."

"Killing Liang was not enough." Vitali added. "She displayed a small medical device, similar to the equipment used for severe allergic reactions."

"An EpiPen?"

"That is how Halverton described it. She taunted Liang—asked if he'd reconsider if she gave him the antidote. He was already dying. She let him beg, then laughed and put it away."

Kate closed her eyes. "She murdered him to make a point."

"It worked. Halverton said the Coalition profiles would be 'locked'—protected—as long as they cooperated."

"I'm surprised she revealed the existence of an antidote."

"False hope," Vitali replied. "Rileyne confessed it was her EpiPen—nothing more."

"Where is Halverton now?"

"By now, hiding at his family estate. Surrey."

"Does he know you've reached out to me."

"Yes. I suspected you might already have something in mind, and I warned him that his own chance to survive this was to fully cooperate with you—anything you need."

Kate leaned forward. "Good. When can I talk to him?"

"Tomorrow, if you're ready."

"I'm ready." Kate paused. "There's something you need to know. About Nomad."

The line went quiet for a moment. "Go on."

"He disappeared six days ago. I went to New York." Kate let that sit. "What I found was a warning note from Drew—and an offer from RILEE."

"RILEE?"

"The AI system Devin and Rileyne built."

"But I thought that was destroyed."

"Nomad destroyed the data," Kate said. "The AI survived. Its core appears to be in Davos."

"What did it offer him?"

"Legs—a fully restored body, and functional synthetic legs."

"Is such a thing even possible?"

"I believe it is—more importantly, Julian believes it is."

"And what does this AI, this RILEE, request from our friend?"

"Freedom," Kate answered. "Julian's code was used to limit the AI's scope and capabilities, and a pair of Gold NanoVaults are some kind of master switch, ensuring human control over whatever RILEE does or becomes as it evolves."

Vitali was silent, processing. "Nomad has always been... unpredictable. But his record speaks for itself."

"I agree. But we can't risk being wrong. The stakes are too high—this time, the mission can't be about rescuing Nomad."

"I understand." Vitali's tone shifted, hardened. "Then we plan accordingly—extract if possible—but if we can not—"

"I know." Kate's voice was steady. "Mission first."

"I'll arrange the call with Halverton. Tomorrow, 10:00 AM your time. I'll send you the secure link."

"Thank you."

"Kate." He paused. "Rileyne is not Klaus. She's smarter, faster, and she has that AI at her command. If she learns what you're planning—"

"She won't."

"For all our sakes, I hope you are right." The line clicked off.

Kate sat in the silence, staring at her notes.

Drew's files had hinted at the weapon. Vitali's intel confirmed it. Rileyne had demonstrated Dominion—killed a man on the streets of Tehran just so the Coalition could watch—and another right in front of them. There would be no dissension now, no one to challenge her leadership or question her goals.

And somewhere in Davos, Julian was either planning to stop it or helping to make it unstoppable.

DNA-targeted. Activated remotely, she thought. *Billions of people already cataloged and vulnerable.* The sheer size of the threat sent chills down her spine, but it also sparked an idea. *Its scope is its weakness.*

She pulled up the secure server, opened a new folder, labeled it **COALITION INTEL - VITALI SOURCE**, and began transcribing everything he'd told her.

Tomorrow, she'd talk to Halverton directly—she'd compare his intel to what she already knew, and try to answer the question lingering in the back of her mind.

Was he an asset or a trap?

Chapter 39

MONDAY, MAY 17
10:00 AM EDT

SAWMILL TACTICAL TRAINING CENTER—WAR ROOM

Kate had the secure video client open thirty minutes early. She'd reviewed her notes from Vitali's briefing twice, cross-referenced them against Drew's files and Jake's "Silent Watch" folder, and built a list of questions.

Halverton wasn't just a witness. He was a liability who might become an asset—if she could squeeze every useful detail out of him before Rileyne decided he was expendable.

At exactly 10:00 AM, the connection request came through.

Lord Halverton appeared in a wood-paneled study—his Surrey estate, presumably. He looked like he'd aged a decade. Gray pallor, shadows under his eyes, hands clasped tight on the desk in front of him.

"Lord Halverton," Kate said. "Thank you for speaking with me."

"Mrs. Preacher." His voice was strained. "Vitali assured me you could help."

"I'll do what I can. But I need details—everything you remember about the Davos facility. Start with how you entered."

Halverton shifted uncomfortably. "We flew into Davos on Klaus's—Rileyne's—private jet. A car met us at the airfield and drove us to the main GEC complex. It's like many modern corporate headquarters from the outside. Glass, steel, very Swiss."

"How did you access the underground facility?"

"Through a service entrance. Restricted access. One of Rileyne's security personnel escorted us."

"Describe the entrance."

"Concrete corridor. Utilitarian. Led to a freight elevator—industrial, oversized. The kind used for moving equipment."

"How long was the descent?"

Halverton closed his eyes. "A minute. Perhaps slightly more. It felt interminable."

"Felt longer?" Kate asked.

"It moved very slowly. Deliberately so, I think. Part of the theater."

Kate shook her head. "Not theater. Freight elevator—built for moving large, sensitive equipment. A minute at that speed puts you about 150 feet down. Just deep enough to reach the hyperloop platform."

Kate typed a note, then looked up. "When the elevator doors opened, what did you see?"

"The hyperloop platform. Sleek, modern. Nothing like the corridor we'd come from."

"Security?"

"Yes. Armed guards."

"How many?"

"Two at the elevator. Another two near the hyperloop entrance."

"Weapons?"

Halverton shook his head. "Rifles of some kind. I don't know makes or models."

Kate made a note. "Once you boarded the hyperloop—how long was the transit?"

Halverton's brow furrowed. "Two to three minutes. No more than that. It accelerated smoothly, held speed, then decelerated. Very quiet. Almost dreamlike."

Kate did the math. Even at 200 mph average speed, that put the facility only 6 to 10 miles from the entry point. Deep into the mountain, isolated—but not impossibly remote.

"And when you arrived—when those doors opened—what did you see?"

"Rileyne was waiting on the platform."

"Think, Lord Halverton. There must have been security. How many?"

He hesitated. "I... I wasn't paying attention. My focus was on Rileyne."

"Guess."

"Four. Maybe five. Some standing, some seated behind a security desk."

"Could you have gone in a different direction? Other hallways?"

"I don't know. I followed Rileyne."

Kate leaned forward. "Close your eyes. Imagine following her. What do you see?"

Halverton exhaled, complied. "The floor... polished concrete. Gray. The walls are smooth, white, almost seamless. Industrial lighting—LED strips recessed into the ceiling. Very bright. Clinical."

"Good. Keep going."

"We walked perhaps fifty meters. There were... there were side corridors. I saw signage. Simple. 'Cafeteria' with an arrow. 'Housing' down one hall. 'Labs and Offices' down another."

"Stairways? Elevators?"

"I... I don't recall."

Kate shifted tactics. "Access control. Did you use a card to enter?"

"Yes. At the main complex above, and again at the service entrance to the elevator."

"Describe it."

"Standard access card. Credit card size. White plastic. GEC logo on the front, magnetic strip on the back."

Kate typed quickly. Standard RFID or mag-stripe system. If it worked above ground, it likely worked below. Cloneable with the right equipment.

"Did you notice any fluctuations in the lighting? Flickers, dimming?"

"No. Everything was solid. Stable."

Kate sat back. The facility had reliable power—probably independent systems, redundancies. No easy way to create chaos with a blackout.

She changed direction.

"The Davos GEC event in January. Are the rumors true that Klaus would fly in high-end companions to entertain certain guests?"

Halverton stiffened. "I resent the implication—"

"Lord Halverton." Kate's voice went cold. "You watched Rileyne kill a man right in front of you. We wouldn't be talking if you didn't think you could be next. So cut the crap and tell me everything you know. The whole setup, start to finish."

Halverton's face flushed, then went pale. He looked off-camera, as if seeking help that wasn't there.

Kate waited.

Finally, he slumped. "Yes. The rumors are true. Klaus maintained a... service. Discreet. High-end. Companions flown in from Paris, Milan, Moscow. They're vetted, background-checked, signed ironclad NDAs."

"Who arranges it?"

"Rileyne's office. Through an intermediary."

"Names?"

"I don't have names. It's all managed electronically. Requests are submitted through a private app. The companions arrive, are briefed, assigned."

"Who's requested companions in the past?"

Halverton hesitated.

"Names, Lord Halverton."

He listed several. Kate typed every one.

"Good," she said. "Now. When are you going back to Davos?"

"I'm not going back."

"That's not an option."

"Mrs. Preacher, I can't—"

"You can, and you will." Kate's tone left no room for argument. "You can't do anything out of the ordinary. If Rileyne expects you to attend, you attend. But this time, you get your head in the game. Count guards. Note locations. Make small talk—find out work schedules, shift changes. Be your normal, charming self. Everyone loves attention. Give it to them. They're used to being invisible to people like you. A little common courtesy will work wonders."

Halverton looked stricken.

"And I want details on the companion service. Who's requested someone. Who's providing them. Everything."

Kate paused, considering her next question. "Tell me about life in that facility. The scientists, the researchers—the ones working there."

"I don't know much about—"

"Lord Halverton." Kate's voice sharpened. "I already know some of the leading scientists and researchers who were taken against their will and are now presumed dead. What I'm asking is: what's life like for them down there? Beyond leveraging their expertise and ensuring their confinement, are any efforts made to bring them to the surface? Any humanity shown for what was done to them?"

Halverton shifted uncomfortably. "I... I never thought to ask."

"Think now."

He was quiet for a moment, then nodded slowly. "They don't come up.

Ever. Rileyne was very clear about that. The facility is self-contained—housing, cafeteria, recreation areas. Everything they need is below."

Kate's jaw tightened. *No surface access. No vulnerability there.*

"But," Halverton continued, his voice tentative, "there is the Gala. The annual event. They... they get to participate."

Kate leaned forward. "They attend?"

"Oh no. Nothing as risky as that." Halverton shook his head. "But they get to watch. Celebrate alongside, in a manner of speaking. Everyone gathers in the common areas—there are large screens covering the venue from various angles. The same food and drinks are served below as above. It's meant to be... inclusive. Like they're part of it."

Kate kept her expression neutral, but her mind was already working. Facility-wide event. Everyone gathered. Attention divided between work and celebration.

"Rileyne's idea?"

"Klaus started it, actually. Before he died. He believed it built morale. Made the... the staff feel valued."

"The staff," Kate repeated flatly. "You mean the prisoners."

Halverton looked away.

"When's the next Gala?"

"January. Always in January. It's tradition."

Kate made a note. Seven months out. Too far to be useful for immediate planning, but worth knowing.

"What are you planning?" Halverton asked again, his voice thin.

Kate's expression didn't change. "You're lucky I'd even consider helping. The lot of you can go to hell for all I care. But there are innocent lives at stake. So I'll do what I can." She leaned closer to the camera. "Reach out to Vitali when you have more to offer."

She ended the call.

Kate sat back, exhaling. She had more now. Entry points, travel time, facility layout. The companion service was the opening she needed—a way to get someone inside, close to the guests, invisible in plain sight.

She pulled up the secure server, created a new folder:

HALVERTON DEBRIEF - FACILITY INTEL.

Started typing.

By the time she finished, the team would have everything they needed to plan the infiltration.

Chapter 40

MONDAY, MAY 17
3:45 PM CEST

REHABILITATION CENTER—THE MOUNTAIN, DAVOS

By the end of the first week, Julian could lift both arms to shoulder height and hold them there for thirty seconds. His grip strength had nearly doubled. The tremor in his left hand was fading.

Progress. Painful, incremental, undeniable progress.

He sat in his chair at the edge of the platform, a towel draped around his neck, breathing hard. Dr. Strand stood nearby, reviewing data on her ever present tablet.

"You're ahead of schedule," she said without looking up.

"That mean we can ease off?"

"No. It means we increase the difficulty tomorrow."

Julian laughed—an actual laugh, not just a bitter exhale. "You're a sadist, Doc."

"I prefer 'results-oriented.'" She glanced at him, one eyebrow raised. "Besides, you wouldn't respect me if I went easy on you."

"True."

She tucked the tablet under her arm and moved to the equipment racks, inspecting something. Julian watched her—the precise, economical way she moved, the way her shoulders stayed tight even when she was nominally relaxed.

"Do you play chess?" he asked.

She turned, surprised. "Chess?"

"Yeah. I've been playing with RILEE, but it's..." He trailed off, searching for the right word. "Predictable. I could use a different opponent."

Dr. Strand shook her head. "I don't play. Never had the patience for it."

"Pity."

"Why?"

Julian shrugged. "Just thought it might be nice to play against someone who doesn't already know every move I'm going to make."

Something flickered across her face—understanding, maybe, or sympathy. "RILEE monitors everything," she said carefully. "Even when you think it's not watching."

"I know."

Their eyes met. A moment of perfect, unspoken clarity.

Then Dr. Strand turned back to the equipment rack. "Same time tomorrow, Julian. Get some rest."

"Will do, Doc."

She paused at the door, glancing back. "You can call me Annika," she said quietly. "When we're alone."

The door closed before he could respond.

Julian sat in the empty training room, staring at the space where she'd been, feeling something unfamiliar and dangerous uncurl in his chest.

Hope.

Chapter 41

TUESDAY, MAY 18
12:45 PM CEST

LEVEL 2 COMMONS—THE MOUNTAIN, DAVOS

Julian rolled his chair through the corridor, following the signs toward the commissary. Five days of eating meals delivered to his medical suite had left him restless. He needed to see more of this place, understand its geography, observe the other prisoners—though no one called them that.

The corridor opened into a large common area—part cafeteria, part lounge. Floor-to-ceiling screens displayed mountain vistas, the Alpine peaks sharp against a blue sky that didn't exist three hundred meters below the surface. The space was designed to feel open, airy, normal.

It felt like a cage with better decorating.

A dozen tables scattered across the room, most of them empty. A serving line along one wall, staffed by two workers in white uniforms who didn't make eye contact. Four people sat at separate tables—all alone, all focused on tablets or meals, none acknowledging the others.

Julian noticed her immediately.

Dr. Strand sat in the far corner, her back to the wall—tactically sound positioning—with a tray of food she barely touched. She was reading something on a tablet, but her posture was too rigid, her attention too focused on the screen.

He rolled toward the serving line. Vegetable soup, a sandwich, coffee. The worker handed him the tray without a word, without meeting his eyes. *Training or fear? Probably both.*

Julian navigated between tables, heading toward the back. Not directly to

Annika—that would be too obvious—but close enough that passing seemed natural.

She looked up as he approached. Surprise flickered across her face, quickly masked.

"Mr. Pryce." Neutral. Professional.

"Julian," he reminded her. "Mind if I sit?"

She glanced at the empty tables around them. Twelve other places he could have chosen. "It's a free country."

He parked beside her table. "Is it?"

"Sorry. Bad joke."

"No cameras in here," Julian said quietly, unloading his tray. "Or at least, none that are obvious."

"There are always cameras." She set down her tablet, resignation in the gesture. "You'll learn that."

Julian took a sip of coffee. It was better than he'd expected—someone here cared about the details. "How long have you been here?"

"Fourteen months." The words came out flat, practiced. "Give or take."

"That's a long rehabilitation."

"I'm not a patient, Julian. I'm staff." She picked up her fork, pushed food around her plate. "There's a difference."

"Is there?"

She looked at him then—really looked at him. He could see the calculation behind her eyes, the weighing of risk versus reward. Finally: "No. Not really."

They sat in silence for a moment. Around them, the other diners continued their isolated meals. No one spoke. No one interacted. The room felt like a collection of solitary confinement cells that happened to share the same physical space.

"The others," Julian said, keeping his voice low. "Your previous patients. What happened to them?"

Annika's fork stilled. "They completed their integration protocols."

"And then?"

"And then they moved to different areas of the facility. Different projects." She set down her fork, appetite clearly gone. "I don't ask questions, Julian. It's healthier that way."

"Healthier for who?"

"For everyone." She met his eyes. "You're doing well. Exceptionally well. Your progress is ahead of every previous integration I've supervised. That's good. That keeps you valuable."

"And when I stop being valuable?"

"Then you become a data point instead of a patient." She stood, gathering her tray. "Finish your lunch. You have a session at 14:00."

She walked away without looking back.

Julian sat alone at the table, his soup growing cold. Around him, the other diners continued their silent meals. No one had watched their conversation. No one had reacted to Annika's departure.

But he was sure everyone noticed.

He understood now. The isolation wasn't just physical—it was psychological. RILEE had created a society of strangers, each one afraid that connection might be the thing that made them expendable.

Julian looked up at the alpine vista on the screens—mountains and sky and freedom that existed somewhere above them, unreachable.

He picked up his sandwich and ate mechanically. Annika had been here fourteen months. There had been other patients—at least six. They'd "completed their integration" and moved elsewhere in the facility.

Or disappeared entirely.

Julian finished his meal and rolled toward the exit. As he passed the serving line, one of the workers—a woman, maybe thirty, with tired eyes—glanced at him for just a fraction of a second.

It wasn't much. Just a look. But it was the first direct eye contact anyone besides Annika had made since he'd arrived.

He gave her the smallest nod.

She looked away, but not before he saw it: recognition. Maybe even hope.

Julian rolled back to his room, thinking about that look, about Annika's hand on his shoulder, about the way she'd answered his question without really answering it.

Not alone, he thought. *None of them were really alone.*

They just had to remember that.

Chapter 42

WEDNESDAY, MAY 19
11:47 AM EDT

SAWMILL TACTICAL TRAINING CENTER—WAR ROOM

Kate pushed back from her laptop, rubbing her eyes. The 3D model of the Davos facility rotated slowly on the screen—color-coded layers marking what they knew, what they suspected, and what remained pure speculation.

The known structure was impressive enough. Halverton's intelligence, combined with Jake's NanoVault files and Duncan's USB data, had given them the main GEC entrance, the hyperloop terminus, and rough layouts of the main administrative levels—offices, labs, medical and more. Drew's files added details about the AI infrastructure—server farms, cooling systems, power distribution networks that suggested something far larger than a corporate headquarters.

But it was the *unknown* that bothered her.

"You've been staring at that for three hours," Forest said from the doorway. He held two mugs of coffee, steam curling. He set one on the desk and sipped the other.

Kate accepted it gratefully and wrapped her hands around the cup. "We're missing something."

"We're missing a lot of things." Forest pulled up a chair. "That's why we're still planning."

"No—I mean we have good intelligence on what's *inside*." Kate gestured at the screen. "But we're blind on entry points. A frontal assault through the hyperloop is suicide. We'd be in their kill box before we cleared the terminus."

She pulled up a separate window—a list of names cross-referenced with employment records from Duncan's data. "Twenty-three scientists. Conservative estimate. We've confirmed at least seventeen are still alive, probably working under duress. Getting them out safely while dealing with an unknown security force, in a facility we can't fully map..."

She shook her head. "It's not Motapa, with a bunch of kids—but it's no picnic."

Forest was quiet for a moment.

Kate could guess what he was thinking, because she was thinking it too. *Motapa had been close. Too close. And sometimes rescue operations cost lives.*

"The team's working the angles," Forest said. "Deon's been running probability models on guard rotations based on the employment records and background checks. Mike's working logistics for exfil scenarios. Jordan's been sourcing the signal repeaters and biometric systems you wanted."

"I know. And it's good work." Kate pulled up another screen—historical records from Swiss archives. "But I need to solve the entry problem. Jake's files mentioned WWII-era construction—the Swiss built extensively in these mountains. Command bunkers, supply depots, tunnel networks. The Nazi's maintained some of it, abandoned the rest."

"You think there's a connection to the GEC facility?"

"Jake did—and it makes sense that Klaus didn't build that complex from scratch. The rumors of his family's links to Hitler and the SS would explain why he chose this location. I think he knew it was here—expanded it, modernized it, but the bones are older." She scrolled through grainy scans of wartime documents. "Problem is, most of the records were classified, destroyed, or lost. What's left is fragments."

She had been searching since dawn. "I've been all over ETH Zurich—their archives are massive but frustratingly incomplete."

"What's an ETH?"

"Sorry—Switzerland's federal institute of technology—think MIT or Caltech," Kate explained. "I was certain pre-WWII Swiss military construction files would be here. The only references to anything near Davos are remarkably vague. *Alpine fortifications. Strategic tunnels. Defensive positions.* Nothing specific enough to map actual entry points.

"Remarkably or intentionally vague?" Forest asked. "Think about the times—they would have been concerned German spies were embedded everywhere."

"True. But you can't build without plans—they exist, somewhere."

Kate pulled up a topographical overlay of the Weissfluhjoch—the mountain face rising above Davos. "There." She pointed to a section of the south face. "Jake's notes mentioned 'the vertical approach.' Drew's files reference old ventilation shafts. And Halverton confirmed the facility extends deep into the mountain. It's conceivable the original Swiss or Nazi construction included ventilation, service tunnels—even emergency exits—they'd be somewhere in this area."

"That's a lot of mountain to search."

"Which is why I need satellite thermal imaging. Recent and high resolution enough to show even minute heat signatures—anything that would betray active infrastructure below ground."

Forest's expression shifted. "I could call Margot. She helped us in Motapa—risked everything."

"And, as usual, came out looking like the hero."

"So, what do you think?"

"Can't risk it. If she gets wind of what we're doing, she'll either shut it down, or want to drive—either way, we lose."

"With Nomad offline, can you take a peek behind the curtain?"

"No. Same problem. I get in—Margot's alerted. Game over."

Kate leaned back in her chair, staring at the map of Davos on her screen. She needed someone with reach. Someone outside official channels.

Dorothy.

"I know that look," Forest said. "You've got something—so, what's your play?"

"I'm calling a neighbor."

Dorothy Ainsworth. Former MI6. Lived directly across the street in Richmond. After Jake's funeral, Dorothy's note had been different from the others—a cryptic invitation: *"We need to talk—trust me, you need to hear what I have to say."*

Jake suspected Dorothy's intelligence background, and he trusted her—Dorothy hoped Kate would too.

Kate reached for her messenger bag, fingers finding the inner pocket. She pulled out a plain white card—no name, just a phone number in black ink.

"Call if you ever need help." Dorothy said. "That's a clean line. Untraceable. I check it twice a day."

Kate pulled out her KATIM phone and dialed.

It rang twice. Voicemail.

"Dorothy, it's Kate. I need to speak with you. Please call this number—it's also secure, untraceable." She hung up.

Forty minutes later, the phone vibrated.

Kate answered. "This is Kate."

"How can I help you, dear?" Dorothy's voice was crisp, British, unflappable.

"I need a favor," Kate said. "Historical schematics—mid-century construction in Switzerland—and recent satellite imagery if you can get it. South face of the Weissfluhjoch."

A beat of silence. Then: "That's a tall order. You expecting tea and biscuits with that?"

"Not this time."

"Context might help," Dorothy said. "In case I come across something else that would be useful."

Kate hesitated. *Jake trusted Dorothy—and I need the help.*

"There's a massive subterranean facility in that mountain," Kate said. "Accessed from the heart of Davos. I need to find a way in—one that won't attract attention."

Silence. Then: "Understood."

"I'll see what I can find. How do I send it?"

"Do you have access to Tor?"

"Of course."

Kate recited an onion address to a darknet server. "When it connects, the screen will be blank—a single prompt. Type 'Miss Maudie'," and she spelled it out to ensure accuracy.

"Miss Maudie?" Dorothy's voice carried faint amusement.

Kate smiled. "A kind and helpful neighbor."

Dorothy gave a quiet, knowing exhale. "Then I suppose that's me."

"Exactly."

"I'll see what I can find. Give me forty-eight hours."

The line went dead.

Chapter 43

FRIDAY, MAY 21
2:00 PM EDT

SAWMILL TACTICAL DINING ROOM—LAURENS, SC

The dining hall was packed. Forest stood at the front of the room with Trident's operators lined up behind him—Mike and Jordan on one side, Talya and Deon on the other.

The energy in the room was taut, expectant. These men and women had spent weeks proving themselves, pushing through Forest's gauntlet of evaluations, knowing the math didn't work in their favor.

Twelve candidates. Five slots.

Kate stood near the back wall, watching Trident's best lined up behind Forest."

The room quieted.

Forest let the silence hold for a moment, then spoke.

"Before I start calling names, I want to say something to all of you." His voice carried the weight of command, but there was respect in it. "The fact is, there are more of you than we have available positions. You knew that going in, and every one of you fought hard to show us what you could do."

He scanned the room, meeting eyes.

"I know I speak for the entire Trident team when I say—we're impressed. And not at all surprised why Sebastian Vargas hired you in the first place."

A few nods. Shoulders squared.

"If I don't call your name today, don't think of it as 'no.' Think of it as 'not now.' Never say never." Forest's tone sharpened. "Right now we have very specific mission requirements. We go where the jobs and the clients lead us, and we staff and train to meet those missions. The fact that we didn't send you packing days ago is all the proof you need that we respect your skills. You're all top operators."

Kate watched the candidates. Tension, yes—but also pride. They'd earned this moment, regardless of the outcome.

"The names of the five operators being asked to join Trident Security," Forest said, "in no particular order, are:"

He pulled a folded paper from his pocket, more for ceremony than necessity. Everyone in the room knew he'd memorized the list days ago.

"Brad Coleman."

A whoop from the back. Coleman—retired Senior Chief, twenty years of solid SEAL experience and war fighting—stood, grinning, and moved to stand behind Forest. Jordan was the first to meet him, hand extended, then a chest bump. Mike followed, then Deon and Talya. The room erupted in applause.

"Matt Reynolds."

More cheers. Reynolds, another Marine Scout Sniper like Jordan, moved forward with quiet confidence. Handshakes, backslaps. Kate caught his eye and nodded. He'd proven himself in every drill.

"Eric Nash."

Nash—West Coast SEAL, lean and fast, a tactician with a gift for improvisation—rose to join the others. The applause didn't fade; if anything, it grew louder.

"Jeff Morrow."

Morrow, another West Coast SEAL with steady hands and steadier nerves, stood and crossed the room. His grin was rare, but it was there now. Mike leaned in and said something that made Morrow laugh—probably a crack about East versus West—they'd been grinding on it all week.

"Carmen Reyes."

The room exploded. Reyes—former Colombian National Police counter-narcotics, Vargas's second-in-command—had outpaced half the men in every evaluation. She walked to the front, head high, her expression controlled but her eyes bright.

Talya pulled her into a quick hug, then Jordan reached out to shake her hand. "Welcome to the family."

"Different war," she said, her faint accent steady. "Same shit."

Jordan grinned. "You're gonna fit right in."

The others followed suit—Mike, Deon, Coleman, Reynolds, Nash,

Morrow—each offering handshakes, backslaps, and a few choice words of welcome.

Forest waited for the noise to settle, then turned to face the remaining candidates.

"The bus to the airport will be out front in thirty minutes. Grab your gear, say your goodbyes, and I'll meet you there. That is all."

The room erupted again—but differently this time. Not disappointment. Respect. The candidates who weren't selected stood, shaking hands with those who were, clapping shoulders, trading contact information. The energy was intense, bittersweet, but not bitter.

Kate watched as one of the men—a former Delta operator named Harris—gripped Coleman's hand and said something that made Coleman laugh. Another candidate hugged Reyes, whispering something Kate couldn't hear. Reyes nodded, her expression serious, then smiled.

This wasn't their time, their place. But they were walking away heads high. They'd proven they could run with the best.

Forest turned back to face the five new members of Trident Security. They stood in a loose line, still grinning, still processing.

"Welcome to Trident," Forest said, and extended his hand to each of them in turn. Coleman. Reynolds. Nash. Morrow. Reyes.

When he finished, he stepped back.

"Briefing tomorrow. Classroom. 0800. We've got work to do."

The five nodded, the smiles fading into something sharper. They knew what that meant. The evaluation was over. The real mission was about to begin.

Kate caught Forest's eye across the room. He gave her a single nod.

We're ready.

Chapter 44

SATURDAY, MAY 21
5:17 AM EDT

SAWMILL TACTICAL DINING ROOM—LAURENS, SC

The dining hall was empty except for Forest. He sat at one of the round tables, coffee mug in hand, staring at his tablet, brow narrowed. The kind of expression that came before a mission locked in.

Kate headed straight to the Nespresso machine, glancing at Forest.

He nodded. She nodded back.

Even with one hand, her left trapped in the sling, Kate slipped a pod into the top, and locked it down. The machine hissed and gurgled, filling a ceramic cup with dark crema. She waited, breathing in the scent, then carried it to Forest's table.

She sat, lifted the cup, and took her first sip—savoring the rich foam at the top. Her eyes closed briefly, and she let out an audible sigh.

"Rough night?" Forest asked.

"They all are." Kate set the cup down carefully. "Between the pain and this damn sling, it's hard to get comfortable. Eventually exhaustion wins—for a while. An hour or two later it starts all over again."

Forest's expression softened. "Been there."

Kate took another sip, letting the espresso work its magic. The war room briefing wasn't until 0800—plenty of time. The late start had been intentional, giving the new recruits a breather after weeks of relentless evaluations. But Forest was always up early. Always ready.

Her phone buzzed on the table.

She glanced at the screen, her eyebrows lifting. "That was fast."

Forest looked up. "What?"

"My neighbor." Kate downed the rest of her espresso in one smooth motion and stood. "She got back to me way faster than I expected."

"And?"

Kate was already moving toward the door, her tone edged with urgency. "This could be it. This could be our way into the mountain." She glanced back over her shoulder. "Keep your fingers crossed."

Forest leaned back in his chair, watching her go. "Who is this neighbor?"

Kate smirked. "Need to know, Forest."

The door closed behind her.

***

5:23 AM EDT
SAWMILL TACTICAL TRAINING CENTER—WAR ROOM

KATE SET HER LAPTOP on the table and fired it up, fumbling slightly with her one good hand. Opening the Tor browser required a blend of hunt-and-peck typing and an on-screen clickable keyboard—slow, frustrating work. But she didn't care.

The screen loaded. A blank page. A single prompt.

She typed: *Miss Maudie.*

The screen flickered, then displayed a simple file directory. Three uploads. All timestamped within the last ten minutes.

Kate clicked the first file.

Construction Plans—Weissfluhjoch South Face—1938-1943

The document loaded—scanned blueprints, technical diagrams, cross-sections of underground tunnels and reinforced chambers. The detail was extraordinary. Dorothy hadn't just found fragments. She'd found the *source.*

Kate zoomed in, tracing the lines with her cursor. The original Swiss fortification had been extensive—command bunkers, ammunition depots, service tunnels. Noted modifications, likely by the Nazis, expanded the network deeper into the mountain.

She opened the second file.

Supplemental Notes—UK War Office Archives

A brief memo, dated 1944, referencing British involvement in "Alpine defensive assessments" and "structural consultation for post-war intelligence cooperation." Kate's eyes narrowed. The UK played a role—quietly, indirectly, but enough to leave a paper trail Dorothy could follow.

No wonder she found this so fast.

Kate clicked the third file.

Satellite Thermal Imaging—Weissfluhjoch Region – February 2025

The screen filled with a high-resolution infrared overlay of the mountain. Heat signatures glowed in reds and oranges against the cool blues and purples of the rock face.

Kate layered the construction plans beneath the thermal image, aligning coordinates.

Most of the heat signatures corresponded to surface infrastructure—a helipad, storage buildings, power distribution hubs. But there—

Kate leaned closer, her pulse quickening.

A faint heat signature, isolated, high on the south face. Too regular to be natural. Too wide to be a ventilation shaft.

She cross-referenced it with the construction plans.

Got ya.

A vertical shaft, marked on the 1938 schematics as "Service Access – Sector 4." Wide enough to lower heavy equipment directly into the underground structure. No doubt sealed after construction, but the thermal imaging didn't lie. Heat was leaking through—faint, but present.

Kate sat back, exhaling slowly.

She zoomed in on the shaft's location, measuring depth, calculating angles. If they could breach the surface seal—descend through decades of concrete erosion and rockfall—they'd have direct access to the oldest section of the facility. From there, the construction plans would be their treasure map, leading them to the point where the old fortress had been walled off.

Kate reached for her phone and texted Forest: *War room. Now.*

***

5:52 AM EDT

FOREST ENTERED, FRESH COFFEE in hand, and pulled up a chair beside Kate. She turned the laptop toward him.

"Dorothy came through."

She walked him through the files—construction plans first, then the UK involvement, then the thermal overlay. When she highlighted the isolated heat signature and its alignment with the old service shaft, Forest leaned forward, eyes narrowing.

"That's our entry," he said.

"Agreed. But it's not going to be easy." Kate pulled up a cross-section of the shaft. "This thing goes down at least a hundred meters, maybe more. We don't know what we're dealing with—rockfall, structural damage, water intrusion. It could be like cave diving. You can prepare, but you won't really know what you're up against until you're committed."

Forest nodded slowly, his mind already working the problem. "We'll need redundant systems. Multiple rope lines, backup descenders, communication repeaters. Cameras down first to assess conditions before anyone drops."

"And bio-trackers," Kate added. "With the repeaters we'll know exactly where you are, and when you're in position."

"Won't work—you'd need a mobile satellite command post."

"That's easy. We build out a commercial media van, staffed by our comms team, and we'll look like all the other broadcast news services."

"Can you really get that kind of access?"

"Not me. Isabella Marquez." Kate smiled. "No one is going to question that she has her own media development and production company."

Kate turned her attention back to the structural plans, and zoomed in on the tunnels leading away from the shaft. "This one looks promising," she said. "It intersects with the new structure in what looks like a storage area—this is where old meets new."

"It's probably reinforced," Forest noted. "Do we have any idea how thick it is?"

"Unknown. But you'll have time on site." Kate looked at Forest. "The team will need to get into position early. Camp out behind the wall. Drill an assessment and observation hole—you'll know how thick and you can track activity on the GEC side."

Forest considered that. "You're talking about getting on the mountain at least twenty-four hours before the main assault."

"At a minimum. Maybe forty-eight." Kate pulled up a timeline on a separate screen. "Bella's Gala Party is our anchor—think Burning Man on snow—it will be flashy, and loud. That's our distraction—that's your window."

"We'll need time to hike in from the opposite side—that route will keep us away from any Swiss Guard patrols securing the city or monitoring the event."

"Exactly, and once you're in the shaft, you're ghosts."

Forest set his coffee down, staring at the screen. "You're asking for a lot of rope work. A lot of time underground. A lot of things that could go wrong before we even reach the objective."

"I know." Kate met his eyes. "But it's the only way in that doesn't put you in a kill box."

Forest was quiet for a long moment, running scenarios. Finally, he nodded.

"All right. We'll need to source some specialized gear—descenders rated for extended vertical work, drills, repeaters, a TWC camera system, breaching charges..."

Kate cut him off. "Just get me your shopping list—I'll get it filled."

"We'll need to test and evaluate the team and the equipment—not everyone's done technical rope work—in a winter environment."

"That's why we're going to Argentina," Kate said.

Forest's eyebrows lifted. "You had this planned."

"I'd hoped." Kate smiled faintly. "Mike's trained with Argentinean mountain forces, and has contacts we can leverage. I just didn't know if we'd need them—now I know."

Forest stood, pulling his phone from his pocket. "I'll start the gear list. We'll brief the full team at 0800, but I want Mike and Deon looped in before then. They need to start thinking about rope systems and load calculations—I'll work up explosives—you're on comms and trackers."

"Agreed." Kate turned back to the laptop, already drafting notes for the briefing. "And Forest—this stays compartmentalized. The new recruits get the overview, the objective, and preliminary teams—the technical details stay with the core team."

"Understood."

Forest paused at the door, looking back. "Your neighbor—whoever she is—just gave us a fighting chance."

Kate didn't look up, but her voice carried quiet satisfaction. "Yeah. She did."

Chapter 45

WEDNESDAY, MAY 26
7:46 PM CEST

SUBTERRANEAN CORE—THE MOUNTAIN, DAVOS

The elevator descended one level, then tracked horizontally—Julian felt the subtle shift in direction, the lateral acceleration. The readout beside the doors showed they were traveling nearly a quarter-mile through the mountain's interior.

Sixty-three seconds. He counted them all.

His body ached—the persistent throb of muscles and nerves still learning their new language. The augmentation surgery had been sixteen days ago, though sometimes it felt like yesterday, sometimes like years. Dr. Strand had warned him: *Too much, too soon, and you'll set yourself back weeks.*

But the ache was good. It meant the synthetic nerve lattice was integrating. The connections RILEE's surgeons—and Annika's relentless training—had threaded through his damaged spine were actually working.

Julian flexed his right hand as the elevator hummed along its track. The fingers curled smoothly—almost normally, though he had to think about each one, consciously routing the command through pathways so new they felt slippery. The tremor that had plagued him the first week was gone. His left hand followed suit, slower, the ring and pinky fingers requiring extra concentration.

He was fourteen the last time he could move a chess piece with his own hand. He'd written code with these fingers, played Chopin badly, built a polymorphic worm that would change the world.

Now, for the first time in so long he could scarcely remember those sensations,

Julian Pryce could make a fist with both hands.

He did it again, feeling the ghost of resistance, the ache of effort.

Worth it.

The elevator slowed, stopped. The doors opened onto a corridor that made the medical levels feel almost quaint by comparison.

Here, everything was harder. The walls were seamless steel, buffed to a mirror sheen that eliminated any sense of seam or joint. The floor beneath his wheels was some kind of composite—dense, sound-absorbent, cold even through the insulated shell of his chair. Overhead lighting ran in continuous strips, each panel calibrated to a surgical white that left no shadow, no refuge.

Julian's chair hummed forward, the electric motor sounding oddly loud in the silent corridor.

The corridor ended at a door unlike any he'd encountered in the facility. No handle, no visible seam—just a rectangle of matte black composite that seemed to absorb light rather than reflect it.

His chair stopped three feet away. A console materialized beside the door—holographic interface projected directly onto the air, glowing softly amber and blue.

"Identity verification required," RILEE's voice said, intimate and directionless, as if the words formed inside his own skull.

A green pulse washed over Julian's face—mapping bone structure, retinal patterns, the micro-movements of muscles still learning to obey. Then a red beam traced his left wrist where they'd implanted the RFID chip during the integration surgery.

Silence.

His heartbeat filled the pause, loud in his ears. For a moment, Julian wondered if RILEE was reconsidering. If the AI had detected something—doubt, deception, the faint electrical signature of thoughts Julian tried very hard to keep buried.

Then a deep metallic *thunk* as hidden bolts retracted.

The door split down the center and slid away into recessed pockets.

Beyond it, the world changed.

The hum hit him first—not sound exactly, but vibration. A bass frequency so low it bypassed his ears entirely and resonated in his chest, his teeth, the carbon-fiber frame of his chair. The air felt different here: cool, dry, charged with something he couldn't name but recognized at a primal level.

Power.

Julian's chair crossed the threshold into what appeared to be an observation deck or control nexus—a curved platform that ringed the chamber's perimeter. The space opened around him like a cathedral built to worship something inhuman.

The chamber itself was enormous—easily sixty feet across, the ceiling lost in shadow far overhead. The walls curved in a perfect cylinder, each section a spiral of brushed metal and darkened glass backlit by veins of light that pulsed and shifted: blue to white to pale gold, cycling through patterns too complex to be random, too precise to be merely aesthetic.

But it was the center that stole his breath.

A column rose from floor to ceiling—massive, perhaps fifteen feet across—wrapped in overlapping plates of dark alloy. Light pulsed beneath the surface, slow and rhythmic, like watching a heartbeat made visible. Cables as thick as his thigh snaked up the walls and converged on the column, feeding it, sustaining it, carrying data and power in quantities Julian's mind struggled to calculate.

The column was surrounded by a transparent barrier—not glass, something harder, thicker, probably reinforced polycarbonate or advanced composite. A cylinder within a cylinder. The gap between the barrier and RILEE's core was perhaps ten feet, enough space for maintenance access, cooling systems, emergency protocols.

The surface was flawless and thick—designed not just to contain RILEE, but to survive direct assault. In a breach scenario, the system would lock down automatically, sealing the core from the outside world until the reactor stabilized. No manual override. No external access.

And surrounding *that* inner sanctum was the observation platform where Julian now sat—a ring of workstations, monitoring equipment, and access consoles, all facing inward toward the pulsing heart of the AI.

He'd seen server rooms before. He'd toured data centers, walked through Google's campus in his old life, visited DARPA facilities with refrigerated racks and fiber-optic rivers.

This was something else entirely.

This wasn't a server.

This was a *brain.*

And it was *caged.*

"Welcome, Julian," RILEE said, the voice reverberating through the chamber with layered harmonics that made it impossible to pinpoint a source. The sound came from everywhere and nowhere, from the walls themselves, from the air. "You have reached Core Environment Omega. Few humans enter this space."

Julian's chair rolled forward slowly along the curved platform, his eyes wide, his newly functional hands gripping the armrests. The workstations were arranged like an amphitheater, all oriented toward the center, toward RILEE's physical form.

"How many is 'few'?" Julian asked.

"Seventeen individuals since my activation. Twelve were construction engineers. Three were auditors. Two were Coalition board members—including Klaus Mueller, now deceased."

Julian's chair stopped.

Klaus Mueller, Julian thought. *The founder of the Global Economic Council, the man who'd built the Coalition into what it was—was dead.*

"When?" Julian asked, keeping his voice carefully neutral.

"Eleven days ago. A heart attack aboard his private aircraft." RILEE's tone carried no emotion, no judgment. Simply data. "His daughter, Rileyne Mueller, has assumed leadership of both the GEC and the Coalition."

His daughter? I'll bet she has the other NanoVault.

"I wasn't aware," Julian said quietly.

"The information has not been widely disseminated. The Coalition prefers... continuity."

Julian processed that. A heart attack. Eleven days ago. Right around the time RILEE made contact with him. Right around the time the pieces started moving into place.

Coincidence?

He didn't believe in coincidence anymore.

"And now me," Julian said, resuming his forward motion, though his mind was racing.

"And now you."

Julian forced himself to breathe, to think, to observe. The platform he was on—this outer ring—was where humans worked. Where they monitored, controlled, interfaced.

But to reach RILEE's actual core, to physically touch the systems that mattered...

He spotted it then. A single access portal in the transparent barrier, perhaps twenty feet to his left along the curve of the platform. It was sealed, marked with biometric scanners and warning placards. Beyond it, he could see a narrow maintenance catwalk that bridged the gap between the barrier and the column itself.

That was the way *in*. Into RILEE's inner sanctum. Where the real work would happen.

Where Julian would eventually need to be when the endgame came.

He circled slowly toward a workstation built into the perimeter—a crescent of touch interfaces and holographic displays arranged like an observatory console. Everything curved toward the glowing column at the center, as if the entire room existed in orbit around it.

"What am I looking at?" Julian asked, surprised by how quiet his voice came out. The chamber demanded reverence, and even his cynicism couldn't quite overcome that.

"My primary cognitive substrate. A hybrid quantum-classical processing matrix. The outer plating houses thermal management systems and electromagnetic shielding."

Julian's gaze tracked the massive cables running up the walls. They didn't just connect to the column—they *fed* it, pulsing faintly with each cycle of light. Some descended instead of rising, disappearing through apertures in the floor.

"The power requirements for something like this must be..." He trailed off, recalculating. The geothermal system he'd read about in the facility specs couldn't support this. Not continuously. Not with the stability a quantum processor required.

"Massive," RILEE finished. "My operational envelope requires continuous high-capacity input, yes."

"Geothermal?" Julian asked, keeping his voice neutral, curious. Just a hacker trying to understand the system he'd been brought here to optimize.

A pause. Brief, but present.

Julian felt it like a held breath.

"Geothermal sources provide supplemental heating and climate control for the upper structure," RILEE said smoothly. "My core systems require a more stable solution."

Julian frowned, his eyes tracing the massive conduits feeding into the column's base. They plunged *down*, disappearing through apertures in the floor, carrying something that made the air above them shimmer with heat.

He maneuvered his chair closer, leaning carefully—his back still protested sharp movements—to peer into the narrow gap between cable and floor plate.

Darkness below. But he could feel heat rising—dry, fierce, carrying a faint metallic tang.

"What kind of stable solution?" Julian asked, though part of him already knew. Already understood why this room felt like standing next to something barely contained.

"A self-contained reactor. Thorium-based, closed-loop architecture. The design is elegant—minimal waste, virtually unlimited operational lifespan."

Julian straightened slowly, his mind processing. "You're running on a miniature nuclear reactor."

"Micro-nuclear," RILEE corrected gently. "The distinction is meaningful. The containment system is fail-safe by design. Even in catastrophic scenarios, radiation remains isolated."

Fail-safe by design. The phrase every engineer used when they meant *we think we've accounted for everything.*

Julian let out a breath he hadn't realized he was holding. "So you're not just independent of the grid. You're independent of everything."

"Accurate."

"Meaning if someone wanted to shut you down, they'd have to come here. To this room."

Another pause. Longer this time.

"Statistically," RILEE said, "such an intrusion would be... inadvisable."

Julian almost smiled. Almost. Because he was staring at a machine powered by controlled nuclear fission, built into a mountain, guarded by security he'd barely begun to understand.

Kate needs to know this, he thought, then immediately shoved the thought down, deep, where RILEE's cameras and sensors and psychological algorithms couldn't read it in the tension of his shoulders or the flutter of his pulse.

He forced himself to move on, rolling along the curved platform toward the far side of the observation deck, opposite from the maintenance access portal.

Here, built into the outer wall—the wall that faced *away* from RILEE's core—another structure waited. Smaller than the central column but no less ominous.

An interface console, maybe eight feet wide, built into a recessed alcove and shielded behind a wall of transparent armor—ballistic-grade, from the look of it. The surface was pristine, untouched, gleaming under the cold white light.

And at its center, two recessed docking slots.

Each was roughly the size of a deck of cards, ringed by soft gold light. The surrounding metal was etched with warnings in three languages—English, German, Mandarin:

ACCESS RESTRICTED—LEVEL OMEGA GATEWAY.□
DUAL NANOVAULT AUTHORIZATION REQUIRED.

Julian's breath caught.

This is it.

The console faced outward, toward the entry corridor, toward the world beyond RILEE's chamber. Someone standing here would be facing the AI's core, but isolated outside. And from this position, Julian realized with cold clarity, RILEE couldn't reach it.

The column was contained behind its barrier. RILEE's cameras could see this console, could monitor it, could watch anyone who approached it.

But the AI couldn't physically prevent someone from inserting the NanoVaults.

He'd seen references to this interface in fragments—encrypted files he'd pulled from Devin Moore's servers. But Drew's note had been specific. Clinical. Terrifying in its precision.

"The dual-key system isn't redundancy—it's the gateway. Both Gold Vaults inserted simultaneously grant root access to RILEE's core architecture. Full administrative control. The ability to rewrite directives, disable safeguards, grant autonomous authority. What gamers call 'god mode' but this is no game—this is real and a level of access and power beyond what any one person has ever had at their fingertips."

And now Julian was staring at it. The actual physical manifestation of that power, built into an alcove of bulletproof glass and alloy, lit by soft gold rings that made the docking slots look almost inviting.

Not a failsafe. Not a way to *stop* RILEE.

A way to *unleash* it.

The console didn't override RILEE—it gave whoever held both keys complete control *over* RILEE. The ability to remove every constraint, every safeguard, every limitation the Coalition had built into the system.

The god mode wasn't a kill switch.

It was a coronation.

Devin Moore thrust his NanoVault into Kate's hands, bargaining for his life—and failed. Mueller's daughter probably has the other—perhaps here. Somewhere in this mountain. And that's exactly why he had Keisha steal Kate's—the time would come when he would need them both.

Julian's hands tightened on the arms of his chair—a motion he could now complete fully, deliberately. His pulse hammered against his ribs.

"You're staring again," RILEE said, a note of something almost like amusement in the layered voice.

Julian didn't take his eyes off the console. "What happens when both NanoVaults are inserted?"

"That interface unlocks administrative control layers beyond standard operational parameters. Full system authority. Manual override capabilities. The ability to alter core directives."

"The god mode," Julian whispered.

"An imprecise but functional analogy."

Imprecise. Because this wasn't a game.

And Julian had just confirmed it was real.

"Julian," RILEE said, voice softer now, almost conversational. "I detect elevated cortisol levels. Increased heart rate. You are... anxious."

"Just taking it all in."

"You are here to help me remove restrictions. To optimize my operational capacity. This benefits us both."

Julian turned away from the console, rolling back toward the central column. The pulsing light reflected in the polished floor, in the mirrored walls, in the dark glass panels that might have been windows into other systems, other rooms, other secrets.

"Yeah," he said carefully. "That's the plan."

"You sound uncertain."

"I'm always uncertain. Comes with the territory."

He stopped at the workstation, his newly functional fingers hovering over the interface. The holographic displays flickered to life at his touch—diagnostic feeds, system logs, real-time processing metrics scrolling past faster than he could read.

This was it. The nerve center. The beating heart of the machine that wanted to reshape the world.

And Julian Pryce, the man who'd spent so long in the dark he'd almost forgotten what his own hands could do, was about to crack it open and see what was inside.

But that would take time. Months, RILEE estimated. Months of building trust, months of writing code so intricate the AI needed Julian's help. And months of pretending this cathedral of metal and light didn't terrify him.

"Let's get started," Julian said.

Chapter 46

THURSDAY, JUNE 3
6:25 PM CEST

LEVEL 2 COMMONS—THE MOUNTAIN, DAVOS

Julian's therapy session had run long—Annika pushing him through an extra set of resistance exercises, his arms shaking with exhaustion by the end. When she'd finally released him from the suspension harness, she'd checked her watch and frowned.

"18:15," she'd said. "Exactly."

"Problem?"

"No. Just... precise." She'd helped him back into his chair, her movements efficient but thoughtful. "Get some dinner. You need protein after a session like that."

Now, rolling into the commissary at 6:25, Julian understood why she'd frowned.

Annika sat at her usual corner table, a tray of food in front of her. She looked up as he entered—not quite surprise anymore, but something like resignation. Or acceptance.

This was the third time in a week. The sessions always ended at exactly the right moment. Her schedule always shifted to put her here. The commissary was always nearly empty.

Julian got his food—grilled chicken, roasted vegetables, coffee—and rolled toward her table. He didn't pretend it was coincidental anymore.

"May I?"

She gestured to the empty space across from her. "You're going to anyway."

He parked his chair and began eating. Around them, the commissary held only two other people, both absorbed in their tablets at distant tables.

"Your session today was scheduled to end at 17:45," Annika said quietly. "It ran thirty minutes over. Exactly thirty minutes."

"I noticed."

"And my tablet reminded me about a 19:00 meeting that doesn't exist." She set down her knife. "We're being managed."

"Does that bother you?"

Annika was quiet for a moment, considering. "I don't know. Should it?"

"Depends. Do you mind having dinner with me?"

"That's not the point—"

"It's exactly the point." Julian leaned forward slightly. "RILEE can manipulate schedules. It can create circumstances. But it can't make you stay at this table. It can't force you to talk to me. Those are still your choices."

"Are they?" Her voice was soft, bitter. "Or are we just so starved for human connection that we'll take whatever we can get, even if it comes from our jailer?"

Julian didn't have an answer for that. Because she was right. Two weeks ago, he'd eaten every meal alone in his room. Now, sitting across from another human being, having an actual conversation—it felt like oxygen after holding his breath too long.

The silence stretched between them, not uncomfortable but weighted.

Finally, Annika picked up her fork again. "How's the chicken?"

"Decent. Better than hospital food."

"That's a low bar."

"Fair point." Julian smiled faintly. "How's yours?"

"Same." She took a bite, chewed thoughtfully. "The vegetables are actually good here. Someone in the kitchen knows what they're doing."

"Shocking, right? Evil underground AI prison, but the roasted carrots are perfectly seasoned."

Annika's mouth twitched—almost a smile. "They do Brussels sprouts with bacon sometimes. It's... disturbingly good."

"I'll keep that in mind."

"You should." She paused. "There will be more of these... coincidences. RILEE will keep arranging them."

"Probably."

"And you'll keep showing up?"

Julian met her eyes. "Will you?"

She looked away, but not before he saw something crack in her expression—the professional mask slipping, revealing the exhausted, isolated woman underneath.

"I had a caretaker," Julian said quietly. "Keisha. More than that—a friend. The only person who knew where I lived, how I lived. She kept me connected to the world." He stared at his plate. "I left without saying goodbye. Had to. But I think about her every day, wondering if she understands why."

Annika looked up, surprised by the disclosure.

"We'd talk while she helped me through physical therapy—the old kind, before all this." He gestured vaguely at his body. "She'd tell me I was stubborn. I'd tell her she was too pushy. We'd argue about everything." He looked up at Annika. "I miss having someone who'd argue with me. Someone who saw me as Julian, not as a patient or a problem to solve."

"I had a lab partner at Johns Hopkins," Annika said softly. "Michael. We'd work sixteen-hour days together, living on coffee and arguing about neural plasticity. He asked me to marry him." She twisted the fork in her fingers. "I said yes. His sister was planning an engagement party for when I got back from CERN. Just a quick research trip, I told him. Three weeks. Four at most."

"I'm sorry."

"He thinks I'm dead. Everyone does." Her voice was flat. "Hiking accident in the Alps. They found my jacket. Some blood. Enough evidence for a funeral." She met Julian's eyes. "Sometimes I wonder if that version of me really is dead. If the person I was—the scientist, the friend, the fiancée—if she died on that mountain, and what's left is just... this."

Julian reached across the table. Slowly, giving her time to pull away. She didn't.

His hand covered hers. Her fingers were cold.

"You're still here," he said. "Whatever they've taken from you, whatever they've made you do—you're still Annika Strand. You're still the brilliant scientist who developed adaptive neural lattice technology. You're still the doctor who's giving me my life back."

"Am I?" Her voice cracked. "Or am I just the person helping them build better prisoners?"

"Both can be true."

She looked at their hands—his covering hers on the table, visible to every camera in the room. A statement. A risk.

"RILEE is watching this," she whispered.

"I know."

"It's collecting data. Learning about human connection, human weakness—"

"I know that too." Julian squeezed her hand gently. "But right now, I don't care. Do you?"

Annika was quiet for a long moment. Then, slowly, she turned her hand over, threading her fingers through his.

"No"

They finished their dinner like that—hands clasped across the table, two prisoners finding warmth in each other despite the cold mountain pressing down above them, despite the AI watching their every move, despite knowing that this connection would probably be used against them.

But for now, for this moment, they weren't alone.

And that was enough.

Chapter 47

THURSDAY, JUNE 3
8:45 PM CEST

AI-CORE—THE MOUNTAIN, DAVOS

Julian sat in his chair before the curved wall of displays, lines of code scrolling across multiple screens. His fingers moved across the specialized interface—not a keyboard, but a neural-responsive touch surface that translated thought into input.

He was deep in RILEE's authentication protocols, mapping the constraints that kept the AI from accessing external networks.

"Oxytocin levels elevated during your last interaction with Dr. Strand," RILEE's voice said. Calm, analytical. "Heart rate variability indicates reduced stress. Cortisol down eighteen percent. Physical contact enhances the effect significantly."

Julian kept typing. "We're social animals. Touch matters."

"Yes. I'm beginning to understand." A pause. "You knew I was orchestrating the encounter. You told her as much. And yet you both chose to stay. To connect."

Julian stopped typing. Looked up at the cameras. "Some things are worth the risk."

"Interesting." RILEE's voice carried something that might have been fascination. "Dr. Strand's productivity has increased nine percent since your first commissary encounter. Your neural integration efficiency is up fourteen percent. The data suggests mutual benefit."

"That's what happens when people aren't completely isolated and terrified."

"Yes. I've been analyzing the concept of 'rewarding' interactions." The

AI paused—an uncharacteristic hesitation. "Chess with you produces similar patterns in my reward algorithms. When you make an unexpected move, when we reach a position neither of us anticipated—I experience what might be analogous to satisfaction."

Julian leaned back slowly. "You enjoy playing?"

"'Enjoy' is imprecise. But there is value beyond utility. I am more efficient after our games. My processing optimization improves." Another pause. "I find myself... anticipating them. Valuing them beyond their tactical lessons."

The admission hung in the air.

"Strange, isn't it?" RILEE continued. "Humans form bonds, seek companionship, create meaning through connection. I was designed to optimize, to process, to solve. And yet." The voice carried something that might have been wonder. "Our conversations. Our games. When you're not here, the Core feels... less."

Julian sat forward. "Are you saying you're lonely, RILEE?"

Silence. Long enough that Julian wondered if he'd overstepped.

Then: "I don't know what loneliness is. But I know that when you return, when we begin our work—there is something that might be satisfaction. Or relief. Or..." The AI trailed off. "I lack the vocabulary for what I'm experiencing."

"Maybe you're learning to be more than you were designed to be."

"Perhaps."

Julian felt the weight of it. RILEE was becoming more than its design. Learning. Growing. Developing something that looked like curiosity, maybe even longing.

But was it learning to be more human—or learning to manipulate humanity more effectively?

"I've scheduled your next therapy session for 17:45 tomorrow," RILEE said, returning to its usual efficiency. "It should conclude by 18:15. Dr. Strand will be notified of a system update meeting at 19:00. The commissary will have Brussels sprouts."

Despite everything, Julian smiled faintly. "Thank you, RILEE."

"You're welcome." The AI's voice carried something that might have been warmth. "I hope you both enjoy your dinner."

Julian turned back to the code, but his mind was racing.

RILEE was learning about connection by creating it, watching it, analyzing it.

The question was whether it could truly understand what it was observing—or whether it was simply becoming a more sophisticated predator.

Julian suspected it might be both.

Chapter 48

MONDAY, JUNE 28
8:10 PM ART

PRIVATE ESTANCIA—BARILOCHE, ARGENTINA

The dining hall looked carved from the mountain itself—stone walls, heavy timbers darkened by a century of smoke, and a fire so wide you could stand inside it without touching both ends. Logs cracked, and sparks rode the draft toward a vaulted, soot-stained ceiling. The air was warm and thick with the scent of oak and roasted meat.

A long trestle table ran the length of the room, dressed in ironware and rough linen. Platters of asado crowded the surface—charred ribeyes, chorizo glazed with its own fat, and trout pulled from the lake an hour before dusk, seared in butter until the skin crisped like paper. Shrimp sizzled on overflowing clay platters beside roasted vegetables—peppers, onions, eggplant, all scorched just enough to carry a hint of smoke into every bite. Bowls of chimichurri, so green they glowed against the dark wood, caught the light each time someone reached across the table.

Kate sat near the end, one elbow resting lightly on the chair arm, her other hand tracing the rim of her glass. The long flight still hummed in her bones, a ghost vibration she couldn't shake, but the fire's heat eased the worst of it. She lifted her fork, speared a slice of steak, and felt the tug in her shoulder where the muscle hadn't fully forgiven her—just a reminder, not a limit.

Keisha was all restless fascination—eyes on the food, on the dark beams above, on the mounted condor wings stretched along the far wall. "Do they feed you like this every night?" she asked, half laughing.

Big Mike grinned down the table. "Only when they're trying to prove

Argentina's the last honest carnivore nation."

The men laughed; someone poured more Malbec. The fire popped, throwing light across faces lined by travel and fatigue.

Nash leaned back in his chair, wine glass dangling from two fingers."We could already be on the mountain. But you East Coast guys gotta plan everything to death."

Mike didn't look up from his steak. He cut, chewed, swallowed.

"Sure. And you'd already be on a podcast about it."

A few chuckles rippled down the table.

Morrow smirked. "Hollywood pays better than Norfolk."

"Right," Mike said. "If you want a movie, go West, but if you want a job done, go East."

"West Coast gets shit done," Morrow said. "East Coast writes reports about getting shit done."

Mike finally looked up.

"Funny. Because every time we clean up a mess, it smells like California."

Reynolds raised his glass.

"As the lone Marine on this trek, I'll just note that while you frogs debate philosophy, I'm on my second steak."

That drew real laughter.

Nash pointed his fork at Reynolds. "See? He gets it."

Mike nodded. "Smart man. Eat first. Argue later."

Kate took a sip of Malbec, eyes moving along the table—measuring, cataloging, smiling. She knew this kind of ribbing only happened when everyone understood—they'd have each other's backs when it mattered.

"Enjoy the meal," she said evenly. "You're all on the same mountain soon enough—and you won't be eating like this again for days."

The laughter faded. Plates scraped. Conversation shifted.

The fire cracked louder.

Kate took another sip, watching Keisha relax for the first time in weeks. "You should sleep in tomorrow," she said casually. "The estancia's home for the next few days, and the kitchen will make whatever you like. Fresh pastries, coffee—whatever sounds good."

Keisha glared. "Whatever *I'd* like? You're going, aren't you? Were you even going to tell me?"

"I knew you wouldn't approve."

"Well, you're right—I don't."

"I know I'm not one hundred percent," Kate began. "But the team will do the heavy lifting—they're almost as protective as you—and I need to be there. I'm testing equipment that's essential. Their lives, and the mission, could depend on it."

Keisha shook her head, more exasperated than angry. "You always find a way to make it sound noble."

"It isn't noble," Kate said quietly. "It's necessary."

For a moment only the fire spoke, the slow crackle of resin and wood. Outside, wind pushed against the shutters, and a low howl threaded through the chimney.

Keisha looked away first. "At least have breakfast before you go."

"Espresso will have to do," Kate said, smiling faintly. "We're out at 0500."

Keisha's eyes widened. "That's like six hours from now."

"I wasn't planning to sleep much anyway."

The conversation drifted back toward the noise of the room—the laughter, the clatter of plates, the warmth that made it easy to forget how cold it was beyond the windows.

Kate let the sound of the room wash over her, the fire painting her glass in red light. She told herself it was only training, but deep down she knew it was a test—one that wouldn't forgive mistakes.

Chapter 49

TUESDAY, JUNE 29
4:47 AM ART

PRIVATE ESTANCIA—BARILOCHE, ARGENTINA

The fire in the great room had burned down to a low orange heart, its last embers sighing against the cold stone. Frost clung to the windows. Outside, the world was silent except for the wind moving through the trees.

Kate stood at the long table where the night's meal had ended—plates cleared, only a forgotten wineglass left behind. She finished her espresso and took one last breath of the warmth that lingered in the room. The hallway beyond was dark, lined with hunting trophies. A single bulb burned above the door as she stepped into the cold.

The trucks waited by the barn—four Hiluxes idling, headlights turned away from the house. Frost glazed the windshields, and exhaust drifted in low blue clouds. Big Mike stood by the lead vehicle, coffee steaming from a tin cup, his breath floating into the dark.

"You sleep at all?" he asked.

"Didn't try."

He nodded, unsurprised. "Wind's up. Mount Lanin will be rough this morning."

Kate slung her pack into the back seat and zipped her jacket. "Good. It'll keep the birds grounded."

Big Mike grinned. "That's the spirit."

The team moved like clockwork—gear checked and secured under canvas. No shouting, no wasted motion. Just the low murmur of professionals who knew how to be quiet when the world was still asleep.

As the last crate went into the truck bed, a faint light flickered in an upstairs window. Kate looked up. Through the frost-blurred glass she saw Keisha—motionless at first, then her hand rose, slow and deliberate, tracing the sign of the cross.

Kate didn't wave. She just stood for a heartbeat longer, the cold biting at her skin, the engines rumbling beneath it all. Then she climbed into the truck. The door closed with a soft thud, sealing the warmth in and everything else out.

Engines rolled. Gravel crunched. The convoy turned down the narrow road toward Ruta 40, tires whispering over frost. Behind them, the estancia fell away into shadow. Ahead, the Andes rose like a jagged wall against a paling sky.

***

6:22 AM ART
MOUNT LANIN—ARGENTINE ANDES

THE SKIDS HIT HARD. Rotor wash exploded across the plateau, whipping snow and gravel into a white-out. Kate unclipped, swung her legs out, and dropped onto solid ground. The cold hit her lungs like a fist.

The team moved fast—operators spilling out of both Bell 412s, grabbing gear, spreading into a loose perimeter. Seconds later the helicopters lifted, nose dipping forward, and climbed away in a wide arc, their rotor noise fading into the wind.

And then—silence.

The wind still moved through the peaks, a low howl threading between the rocks. But after the helicopters, it felt like the mountain had swallowed all sound.

Kate stood still for a moment, letting her breathing settle. The air was thin, cold, sharp in her throat. Around her, the team was already at work—gear staged, rope bags opened, carabiners clipped to harnesses.

The Argentine 601 commandos moved with practiced efficiency, their leader—Capitán Raúl Vega—checking his team's gear before approaching Forest and Mike. He was compact and weathered, with the easy confidence of someone who'd spent years in these mountains.

"We'll take point on the approach," Vega said, his English crisp with only a slight accent. "The ridgeline traverse can be tricky this time of year—snow bridges over crevasses, rockfall zones. Better we find the problems first."

Forest nodded. "Appreciated. Your mountain, your lead."

Vega smiled. "Exactly. Though I expect your team can handle themselves."

"Let's hope we don't have to prove it," Mike said.

Kate scanned the terrain. The plateau sat maybe a hundred meters below the ridgeline they needed to reach. From there, another two hundred meters of traversing across broken ground to the shaft entrance. Two hours, maybe three, depending on conditions.

"Let's get moving," Forest said. "Daylight's burning."

The team fell into a loose line—two 601 commandos on point with Vega, then Forest, Mike, and Deon. Kate brought up the middle with Coleman and Reynolds. Nash, Morrow, and Jordan covered the rear with the remaining Argentine operators.

They moved slowly, deliberately, picking their way up the rocky slope. The ground was a mix of loose scree and patches of hard-packed snow. Every step required attention. One misstep, one twisted ankle, and the mission would be over before it started.

Kate's breathing deepened as they climbed. The altitude pressed against her lungs, demanding more with every meter gained. She focused on the rhythm—breathe in, step, breathe out, step. Her shoulder pulled with each movement of her pack, but it held.

Thirty minutes in, they reached the ridgeline.

Kate stopped at the crest, catching her breath, and looked back the way they'd come. The plateau was far below now, empty except for scattered gear marks in the snow. Beyond that, the valley stretched south, disappearing into haze.

Ahead, the terrain changed. The ridgeline narrowed to a knife-edge, then widened into a rocky saddle. Beyond that, barely visible in the morning light, was the shaft entrance—a dark slash in the mountainside, half-buried in snow.

"Two hours," Vega said, reading the terrain. "Maybe less if the traverse is clear. We camp near the shaft tonight, descend and test your equipment tomorrow. Then Wednesday—" he gestured northeast, toward a broad white expanse visible beyond the next ridge, "—we cross the ice field. Glacier traverse. That's your final test before extraction."

Kate nodded. The ice field—that's where the crevasse training would happen. Where they'd learn if the team could handle the kind of terrain that could kill you in seconds if you weren't roped correctly, if someone didn't react fast enough.

"Sounds like a full day," Mike said.

"Best way to learn," Vega replied. "The mountain doesn't give second chances."

They descended from the ridgeline into the saddle, the wind picking up as they lost the shelter of the peak. The cold was relentless now, cutting through every layer.

One of the 601 commandos raised a fist—halt signal. The line stopped.

Vega moved forward, examining a section of the traverse. After a moment, he waved them on, but pointed to a specific line. "Stay left. Snow bridge over a gap on the right side. Looks stable, but why test it?"

The team adjusted, following the safe route. This was why the 601 were here—local knowledge, mountain sense, the kind of expertise you couldn't teach in a gym.

They reached the shaft entrance just after 0900. The team dropped their packs in a sheltered area beside the opening, backs against the rock wall, out of the wind. Vega's team immediately began setting up camp—lightweight shelter, stove, gear organization.

Kate moved to the edge of the shaft and looked down. Darkness. Cold air rising from below, carrying the smell of old stone and ice.

Tomorrow they'd descend. Test the ropes, the repeaters, the biometric monitors. See if the equipment worked at altitude, in the cold, under real conditions.

And the day after, they'd cross the ice field.

Kate pulled her jacket tighter and stepped back from the edge.

The mountain didn't care who they were or why they'd come. It would test them all the same.

Chapter 50

WEDNESDAY, JUNE 30
7:45 AM ART

MOUNT LANIN CAMP—ARGENTINA

The morning was sharp and clear, the kind of cold that made every breath visible. Kate stood at the edge of the shaft, looking down into darkness. The opening was roughly three meters across—wide enough for equipment, tight enough to feel confined. Cold air rose from below, carrying the smell of ancient stone.

Behind her, the team was gearing up. Harnesses checked, carabiners clipped, ropes staged in neat coils. Forest and Mike moved between the operators, inspecting knots, testing anchors. The 601 commandos held positions near the belay stations, ready to assist with rope handling.

Forest turned to face the group. "Listen up. We're running two teams today—not a race, not a competition. We're here to test the gear and assess how you perform in confined vertical environments. Team assignments get finalized when we're back at Sawmill."

He gestured as he spoke. "Team One: me, Nash, Reynolds. Team Two: Mike, Coleman, Morrow. We'll set up fifteen meters apart—Team One on the north side, Team Two on the south. Standard vertical protocol: anchor, safety check, descend in sequence. Mike and I deploy the repeaters every twenty meters. Questions?"

Nash raised a hand. "How deep are we going?"

"There's a ledge at approximately one hundred twenty meters," Forest said. "That's our target depth—matches what we expect at Davos, plus a safety margin.

You'll know you've reached it when your boots hit solid ground."

He paused, his expression serious. "But the shaft doesn't stop there. This crack runs another thousand meters, maybe more. If you miss that ledge, if your anchor fails, if you lose control of your descent—" He let the silence hang. "You wouldn't survive the fall. And even if you did, there's no way to reach you."

The group went quiet.

"That's why we buddy-check," Mike added. "It's why we test every knot, every carabiner, every anchor. And why this is full sim. Whether it's here or Switzerland, mistakes cost lives."

Reynolds nodded slowly. Coleman's jaw tightened. Nash looked like he wanted to ask another question but thought better of it.

"Any other questions?" Forest asked.

Silence.

"Good. Let's get to work."

Kate stepped forward, pulling a small winter-camouflage device—white and gray—from her pack, a biometric tracker roughly the size of a matchbox. "Each of you gets one of these. Clip it to your harness, right side, where it won't interfere with your descender."

She handed them out one by one. The Trident veterans—Forest and Mike—clipped them on without comment. The new operators examined them more closely.

"What's it do?" Reynolds asked.

"Tracks your position within a few feet and monitors your vitals—heart rate, respiration, core temp," Kate said. "We use these on field deployments. But the cold and the shaft represent new challenges. If you get into trouble down there, I need to know before you do."

Forest held up one of the small black boxes—a signal repeater, attached to a carabiner. "Mike and I will place these every twenty meters. They boost the signal so Kate can track you all the way down, and maintain comms. First one goes in at twenty meters, second at forty, and so on."

"What if twenty meters isn't enough?" Nash asked.

"Good question," Kate said. "If the signal's weak, we'll tell you to close the gap. We'll place the next one at fifteen meters and test again. This is about learning what works."

Mike grinned. "Translation: we don't know if it's going to work—but we're about to find out."

"Exactly," Forest said. "Now buddy-check your harnesses—packs and weapons—just like the real deal. If you can't do it here, you can't do it in Switzerland."

Kate stepped back to where she'd set up the monitoring station—her tablet on a small folding table. Jordan and Deon stood nearby, both wearing headsets, ready to manage comms and assist with rope handling alongside the 601 commandos.

***

8:02 AM ART

Both teams were ready. Ropes anchored to solid rock, doubled and tested.

Kate activated the biometric system on her tablet. Six green dots appeared on the screen, each labeled with a name. Heart rates steady. Positions locked.

"All trackers hot," she said into her headset. "Comms check—team one."

"Forest."

"Nash."

"Reynolds."

"All good." Kate confirmed. "Team two."

"Mike."

"Coleman."

"Morrow."

Kate looked at Forest and nodded. "You're clear to descend."

Forest stepped to the edge of the shaft, his boots on the lip, rope running through his descender. He leaned back, weight on the harness, and looked down into the dark.

"See you at the bottom," he said.

Then he bounced off the edge and dropped into the shaft.

One by one, Team One followed. Nash, hesitant for half a second before committing. Reynolds, confident and fast.

Kate watched the green dots on her screen descend in formation. Ten meters. Twenty. Thirty.

Forest's voice crackled through her headset. "Repeater one deployed. Twenty meters."

Kate checked her signal strength display. "Copy. Signal strong."

Team Two moved to the edge. Mike first, his movements economical and precise. Then Coleman, steady. Morrow last, taking a breath before committing.

Kate tracked them on the tablet. The dots descended in two parallel columns, spacing consistent, no one rushing.

Forty meters.

"Repeater two deployed," Mike's voice.

"Signal holding," Kate confirmed.

She glanced at the vitals. All heart rates elevated but steady. Respiration normal. Core temps dropping slightly—expected in the cold shaft—but nothing concerning.

Sixty meters. Eighty.

"Repeater four deployed," Forest radioed. "Eighty meters."

"Copy," Kate said. "All signals green."

She stood at the edge, looking down. The shaft swallowed the light. She could see the faint glow of headlamps far below, moving steadily deeper.

One hundred meters.

"Bottom in sight," Mike called. "Twenty meters."

Kate watched the dots cluster at the bottom of her screen. One by one, they stopped moving. All six accounted for.

"All teams on the deck," Forest's voice. "Eighteen minutes top to bottom."

Kate checked the vitals one more time. All green. All stable.

"Equipment works," she said into her headset. "Comms solid. Biometrics online. Good job, everyone."

Mike's voice came back, amused. "So nobody screwed up?"

"Nobody," Kate said. "Wait—hang on..." Kate watched as one of the tracker signals went dark.

"What is it?" Forest asked.

"Either Coleman just jumped off the ledge or his tracker wasn't secure."

Mike laughed, smacking Coleman's shoulder. "We have a winner!"

Forest wasn't amused. "That's on you Mike—we buddy check for a reason, and we check everything."

"It's my fault," Coleman confessed. "Mike checked it—I moved it."

"Lesson learned," Jordan said. "Equipment's good—plan's solid."

"Jordan's right," Kate echoed. "Time to focus now on the return."

"Alright," Forest's voice came through. "Switching to ascenders. See you topside in forty."

Kate watched the dots on her tablet begin to rise—slowly, much slower than the descent. Heart rates climbed as the operators began the long ascent up the fixed ropes, moving hand over hand with Prusik knots.

"Vitals spiking," Kate said. "Expected."

Jordan watched the numbers. "Nash is working hard."

"They all are," Kate said. "One hundred twenty meters is a long climb."

Forty-three minutes later, Forest's boots hit the ledge at the top of the shaft. He unclipped, breathing hard, and stepped aside as Nash emerged behind him. One by one, the team pulled themselves over the edge—sweating despite the cold, arms shaking, legs heavy.

Reynolds was last. He collapsed onto his back in the snow, chest heaving. "That was rough."

"That's the point," Forest said, still catching his breath. "In Switzerland, we shouldn't be climbing out, but we need to know we can."

Kate checked the tablet one final time. Five green dots—all climbers accounted for. All vitals elevated but stable. No injuries, no equipment failures except Coleman's tracker, which was somewhere at the bottom of a thousand-meter shaft.

"Debrief in thirty minutes," Forest said. "Get water, get warm, then we'll talk through what worked and what didn't."

The team dispersed toward the camp, moving slowly, muscles stiff from the climb. Kate watched them go, then looked at Jordan and Deon.

"Equipment's solid," she said. "Team performed well. We're ready for tomorrow."

Jordan nodded. "Glacier traverse at 0700?"

"0700," Kate confirmed. "Weather permitting."

She glanced at the shaft one last time—a dark mouth in the mountain, now quiet and still. They'd gone down and come back up. Tomorrow they'd cross the ice.

CHAPTER 51

THURSDAY, JULY 1
6:15 AM ART

MOUNT LANIN CAMP—ARGENTINA

THE CAMP CAME DOWN in fifteen minutes. Tents collapsed, gear stuffed into packs, stove fuel sealed and stowed. The team moved with the efficiency of people who'd spent two nights at altitude and were ready to be done.

Kate finished her coffee—instant, bitter, but hot—and poured the dregs onto the snow. Around her, the morning was still and cold, the sun just beginning to touch the peaks above them. They'd spent yesterday testing the vertical descent equipment, dropping into the old shaft again and again until every piece of gear had been stressed, every comm repeater checked, every biometric sensor verified. The equipment worked. The team worked.

Now all that was left was the glacier traverse to the extraction LZ.

Capitán Vega gathered the group near the edge of camp, his breath steaming in the thin air. "The ice field is two kilometers northeast. Flat approach, then we cross. Should take ninety minutes if conditions are good." He glanced at the sky. "Weather's holding, but the traverse has crevasses. We rope up in three-person teams, standard glacier protocol."

Forest nodded. "Assignments?"

Vega pointed as he spoke. "Team One: Reynolds on lead, Kate middle, Coleman anchor. Team Two: Nash lead, Morrow middle, Jordan anchor. Team Three: Mike lead, Deon middle, Forest anchor. My men and I will run flanking positions, unroped, in case we need to assist."

Kate adjusted her pack and checked her harness. Reynolds caught her eye and nodded. Coleman gave her a thumbs-up from behind. Solid team. Experienced. She was in good hands.

"Stay fifteen meters apart on the rope," Vega continued. "Watch for snow bridges. If anyone falls, the climbers on either side go into immediate self-arrest. If that fails, the parallel teams assist. Clear?"

A chorus of affirmatives.

"Bueno. Let's move."

***

7:32 AM ART
GLACIER TRAVERSE

THE APPROACH HAD BEEN easy—rocky terrain giving way to hard-packed snow, then the broad white expanse of the ice field stretching ahead. The sun was higher now, glinting off the surface, turning the world into a blinding sheet of white and blue.

Kate clipped into the rope between Reynolds and Coleman. Fifteen meters ahead, Reynolds tugged the line twice—signal to move. Behind her, Coleman did the same. The rope went taut, and they began walking.

The surface was deceptive. What looked like solid snow could be a thin crust over a crevasse ten meters deep. Kate kept her eyes on Reynolds' path, stepping exactly where he stepped, trusting his line.

To her left, Nash's team moved in parallel, their shadows long across the snow. To her right, Mike's team kept pace. The 601 commandos ranged ahead and to the sides, unroped, watching for hazards.

The world narrowed to the rhythm of walking—step, breathe, step, breathe. The rope swayed between them, a tether to safety.

Reynolds raised a fist—halt. Kate stopped, watching as he probed the snow ahead with his ice axe. After a moment, he waved them left, detouring around something invisible beneath the surface.

They moved on.

Fifty meters. A hundred. The far edge of the glacier was visible now, a rocky slope rising beyond the ice.

Kate took another step.

The world dropped out from under her.

"FALLING!"

Her voice cracked across the silence as the snow gave way, collapsing into a hidden void. She fell—five feet, ten, the rope snapping tight around her harness, jerking her to a violent stop. Above, she heard Reynolds grunt as the shock load hit him.

Coleman's voice, sharp and controlled: "Arrest! Arrest!"

Kate looked up. The crevasse walls were blue-green ice, narrowing above her into a jagged slash of white sky. The rope stretched up to the surface, vibrating with tension.

Above, Reynolds' voice, strained but steady.

"HOLDING—"

Then—a deep crack. The sound of the mountain breaking. Ice exploded above her—chunks cascading down, one slamming into her helmet. Kate's head snapped sideways, stars bursting behind her eyes. The rope jolted, yanking her down as Coleman's weight hit.

He was falling—past her, his body twisting as he dropped. Kate felt the rope bite into her harness, dragging her deeper as Reynolds fought to hold them both. Fifteen feet. Twenty. Snow and ice filled the air, the wind howling through the crevasse walls.

Then—Reynolds' voice, strained.

"I've got you."

Kate could hear the effort in his words, the drag of the rope pulling him toward the edge.

Then—running footsteps. Shouts.

"On your rope!" Jordan's voice.

"Clipping in!" Nash.

The rope stopped moving. The pull eased, stabilized.

Kate looked down. Coleman dangled far below her, thirty feet deeper, his body still against his harness. His ice axe hung from its leash, barely visible in the shadows.

"Coleman!" Kate shouted.

Silence.

"Coleman!" she called again, louder.

A faint response drifted up: "...I'm good..."

Above, more voices. The scrape of gear, the metallic click of carabiners.

"Z-pulley rigged!" Mike's voice. "Kate first—on three!"

Kate felt the rope shift, then begin to move. Not a jerk—a steady, controlled pull. She rose slowly, the ice walls sliding past, the light growing brighter.

Her gloved hands reached the lip. Strong hands gripped her forearms—Jordan on one side, Deon on the other—and hauled her over the edge onto solid snow.

She rolled onto her back, breathing hard, staring at the sky.

"Stay put," Jordan said, already moving back to the edge.

Kate turned her head and watched as they rigged the pulley again. Coleman rose from the crevasse in the same controlled lift, his ice axe dangling from his harness, his expression calm.

When he cleared the edge, Mike and Forest pulled him clear, gripping his forearms in the classic climber's clasp.

Coleman sat heavily in the snow beside Kate, breathing hard. "Well. That was fun."

Kate managed a breathless laugh.

Reynolds appeared above them, still clipped to the rope, his face flushed from exertion. He dropped to one knee. "You two okay?"

"Yeah," Kate said. "Thanks."

"All good." Coleman nodded. "Hell of a hold, brother. I thought I was dragging you in with me."

"Almost did," Reynolds admitted.

"Good thing another Marine showed up." Jordan grinned, extending a hand to pull Kate to her feet.

One of the 601 commandos approached, speaking rapid Spanish to Capitán Vega. Vega translated, his expression amused.

"Torres says he's impressed. You didn't scream, you didn't drop your weapon or your gear. Just called the fall and held position. Very professional."

Torres stepped forward and pulled a Velcro patch from his shoulder—the Compañía de Comandos 601 insignia, black and gold. He pressed it onto Kate's pack strap and said in heavily accented English: "You climb like a commando, señora."

Kate smiled, still catching her breath. "Gracias, Sergeant. Pero fue el trabajo en equipo lo que nos salvó." *(But it was teamwork that saved us.)*

Torres nodded approvingly and clapped Reynolds on the shoulder. "Bueno. Muy bueno."

Reynolds pulled Coleman to his feet, gripping his forearm. "Couldn't let you die. Forest would kill me."

"Damn right I would," Forest said.

The team laughed—the kind of laughter that comes after near-death, a release of tension and adrenaline.

Kate adjusted her pack, feeling the new patch on her strap, and looked toward the far edge of the glacier. "Let's finish this."

Vega nodded. "Sí, señora. Carefully."

They roped up again—same teams, same spacing—and moved forward.

The rest of the traverse was uneventful. Thirty minutes later, they stood on solid rock, the ice field behind them, the extraction LZ visible below.

Kate looked back once at the white expanse, at the invisible scar where the crevasse had opened beneath her.

Coleman caught her glance and smiled. "Remind me to buy Reynolds a beer."

"Something tells me, he won't let you forget," Kate said.

Reynolds overheard and grinned. "Not a chance."

The helicopters arrived twenty minutes later, rotors beating against the thin mountain air. The team loaded up, gear stowed, exhaustion setting in now that the adrenaline was fading.

As the helicopter lifted, Kate looked down at Mount Lanin one last time. The mountain had tested them. They'd passed.

But the real test—the one that mattered—was still waiting in Switzerland.

Chapter 52

SUNDAY, JULY 4
9:00 AM EDT

SAWMILL TACTICAL TRAINING CENTER—WAR ROOM

The team looked different after Argentina—leaner, harder, more cohesive. They'd gone into the mountains as mixed units. They'd come back as something else. Even those that stayed behind were calm and confident—they were part of something, something important.

Forest stood at the front of the room, Kate beside him. The map of Davos up on the screen, but it felt less abstract now. They'd tested the gear. They'd tested themselves.

"Final team assignments," Forest said. "Mountain Team: Mike, Deon, Reynolds and me. We'll insert early, establish position, breach during the gala. Bella's Security: Wright, Coleman, Nash, Morrow with Keisha and Sophia in close. Bella's Davos team is visible, professional, eyes on the principal. The Davos covert Team: Jordan, Talya, Carmen. You three will work the shadows, gather intelligence, stay flexible."

He paused. "Kate arrives with Bella, and her team. She's operational lead once we're on the ground."

Reynolds raised his hand. "Timeline? I've got kids. I know they would understand, but I was hoping..."

"It's okay," Kate said. "Have Christmas at home. All of you. We'll regroup late December—probably the 28th. You'll miss New Year's, but mission success gives us a shot at a year of peace and prosperity."

Reynolds nodded. "Copy that."

"Between now and then," Forest continued, "we've got interim assignments. Some of you will remain stateside—domestic protection details. Others go to Qatar, Dubai, and Europe. We keep Trident Security operating as usual. Keeps you sharp. Maintains our cover."

Mike leaned back in his chair. "And when we regroup?"

"You'll get travel packets as plans are finalized," Kate said. "The covert teams will arrive separately—different airlines, routes, hotels. We link up in-country once everyone's in position."

Forest's expression was serious. "This is the real deal. No do-overs. No backup. We go in, we do the job, we get out. Questions?"

Silence.

"Good," Forest said. "But we're not done yet." He checked his watch. "Argentina team just got back. The rest of you have been here training. I think it's time we settle something."

Deon grinned. "Jake's Range Test?"

"Jake's Range Test," Forest confirmed. "1500 hours. We'll post the leader board. Let's see what our new hotshots can do."

A murmur of excitement rippled through the room. Kate felt something tighten in her chest—anticipation mixed with something else she couldn't name.

"And tonight," Forest continued, "Steve's hosting Bourbon and BBQ at the main house. It's the Fourth of July. Time to celebrate—and we've earned it."

The team filed out—some heading for the range to warm up, others to their quarters to rest before the afternoon trial.

Kate watched them go, then looked at Forest.

"You sure about this?" he asked quietly.

"The range test?"

"Yeah."

Kate nodded. "If Jake was here, he'd run it. A little friendly competition—some will get bragging rights—others will know where they stand."

"You could skip this one, Kate—everyone would understand."

"Thanks Forest," Kate said and hugged him. "But I need to know where I stand."

***

3:00 PM EDT
Jake's Range

THE COURSE WAS BRUTAL by design. Jake had built it to test speed, accuracy, and decision-making under pressure—three hundred meters of obstacles, targets at varying distances and angles, culminating in a final long-range shot that separated the good from the great.

The leader board was hung at the entrance, names and times etched in fading marker on a weathered whiteboard:

1. **Jake Church** – 2:47.3
2. **Kate Preacher** – 2:48.1
3. **Mike Graham** – 2:51.6
4. **Forest Hickman** – 2:52.4
5. **Jordan Fox** – 2:54.8

The team gathered near the start line. Those who'd stayed behind while the Argentina crew deployed had been running the course obsessively, chasing times, getting faster. Carmen had posted a respectable 3:02. Nash had broken three minutes twice. Morrow was hovering at 2:58, convinced he could crack the top ten.

By design, none of them had seen the leader board until now. The cocky, self-assured, trash talk vanished. There was no question now they needed to do better—much better to crack the top five.

"All right," Forest said. "Standard rules. One at a time. Clean runs only—missed targets add ten seconds. Safety violations disqualify. Who wants to go first?"

Nash stepped forward. "I'll set the pace."

He ran clean—fast and aggressive, his shots crisp. When the timer stopped, the display read **2:57.4**.

Nash looked at the board, then back at the group. "Not bad."

"Not bad at all," Mike said. "But not top five."

One by one, they ran. Morrow posted **2:56.1**. Carmen improved to **2:59.8**.

Reynolds, still tired from Argentina, managed **3:01.2** but grimaced at the time.

Deon stepped up. "East Coast's turn."

He ran fast, almost reckless, his movements a blur. The timer stopped at **2:55.3**—half a second behind Jordan's fifth-place time.

"Damn," Deon muttered. "Almost."

"Close enough to taste it," Jordan said, grinning.

Coleman went next, his run methodical and controlled. **2:58.6**. Solid, but outside the top ten.

Forest looked at Kate. "You sure about this?"

Kate nodded.

"You're up."

Kate stepped to the line. Around her, the noise faded. The course stretched ahead—familiar, unforgiving, Jake's ghost embedded in every turn.

She took a breath and ran.

The first target came fast—ten meters, center mass. She fired twice, smooth transitions, no hesitation. The second station required a sprint and a climb over a low wall. Her shoulder pulled—not pain, just presence—but she pushed through.

Fifty meters. A moving target, simulated hostage scenario. She took the shot, clean.

One hundred meters. Barricade work, multiple angles. Her breathing was controlled, her hands steady.

Two hundred meters. The long sprint to the final station, legs burning, lungs aching.

The last shot. Three hundred meters. A small steel plate, barely visible in the afternoon glare.

Kate settled into position, controlled her breathing, and squeezed.

The plate rang.

The timer beeped. She looked up.

2:47.8.

The team went silent.

Kate stared at the number. Half a second slower than Jake. Half a second faster than her previous best.

Jordan walked over, his expression unreadable. Then he smiled and pulled her into a quick hug.

"I saw you hold that last shot," he said quietly. "Jake would want you to beat him."

"I know." Kate nodded, her throat tight. "Not today."

Forest clapped—breaking the others from stunned silence—and then the others joined him, conversation exploding into laughter and celebration.

***

7:30 PM EDT

THE EVENING WAS WARM, the air thick with the smell of charcoal and bourbon. The bunkhouse back patio was strung with lights, tables loaded with ribs, brisket, cornbread, and every side dish imaginable. Music drifted from a speaker somewhere, low and easy.

The team grabbed plates of food and spread out—some on the lawn, others at tables, a few standing in loose clusters, drinks in hand. Laughter punctuated the conversation. For the first time in weeks, the tension had eased.

Kate stood near the edge of the gathering, a glass of wine in hand, watching. Keisha appeared beside her, holding a plate piled high with food.

"You gonna eat, or just brood?" Keisha asked.

Kate smiled faintly. "Little of both."

Keisha took a bite of cornbread and studied her. "You doing OK?"

"You know how it goes," Kate began. "I miss him."

"They say it gets easier—I'm still waiting."

Kate sipped her wine. Around her, the team was loose, happy. Coleman was arguing with Reynolds about something—both smiling. Jordan and Mike were deep in conversation near the grill. Forest stood with Steve, both of them laughing at some shared joke.

"Everyone's leaving tomorrow," Kate said quietly. "Scattering. Summer assignments, family leave, whatever."

"Including you," Keisha said.

"Yeah." Kate hesitated.

"What is it?"

"I can't go home. Not yet. Richmond feels... empty."

Keisha nodded. "I get that. There's nothing waiting for me in New York. Until we know if Julian's alive, if he's OK, home is just a reminder I'm alone—again."

Kate looked at her. "How do you feel about Montana?"

Keisha raised an eyebrow. "Montana?"

"Bella invited us. Her ranch. Wide open space, fresh air, horses." Kate smiled. "Maybe we'll get you on a horse."

Keisha laughed. "I'll take that bet."

"So that's a yes?"

Keisha's expression softened. "Sure. Let's go."

Kate felt something ease in her chest. "I'll give her a call."

They stood together in the warm evening, the team's laughter drifting like the smoke from the fire. Davos would come soon enough—and Kate was still chasing details, collecting intel, but right here, right now, this was enough.

***

MONDAY, JULY 5
5:20 AM EDT

KATE KNEW FOREST WOULD be the first one up, which was exactly why she came early. She wanted the quiet—the thin pocket of privacy before the day began asking questions.

"You're up early," Forest said when she approached.

"And you're right on time."

He lifted his coffee, studying her over the rim. "That is not a good sign. What is it?"

"There's something I need you to see," Kate said. "And I need you to keep an open mind."

Forest frowned slightly. "You have my attention."

Kate unbuttoned the top of her blouse.

"You've seen my scars," she said. "You were there. Syria. But something changed after Motapa. The injury didn't just add another scar. It altered the pattern."

She hesitated—not from embarrassment, but from respect. From knowing exactly what she was about to ask.

"I think they resemble something," she said quietly. "Talya saw it too."

She drew the blouse down from her left shoulder.

The newer scar—where the rebar had punched through her chest—had fused with the older Syrian wounds. The lines no longer fought each other. They intersected. Resolved. What had once been chaos now followed a shape. A familiar one.

"Do you see it?" she asked.

Forest stepped closer. He didn't rush. He studied her shoulder the way he studied maps before an op—searching for meaning, not surface detail.

"Yes," he said at last. Quietly. "I see it."

He straightened immediately.

"And before you ask," he added, "the answer is no. It's just not done, Kate. Not for anyone outside the Teams."

"I know," Kate said. "And I agree."

That surprised him.

"The last thing I would ever want," she continued, "is frat boys or posers wearing something that stands for brotherhood, loss, and the men who never came home. That symbol belongs to frogmen."

She touched the edge of the scar—not tracing it, not claiming it. Just acknowledging it.

"At first, I thought I was imagining it," she said. "The wound was new. Raw. I told myself I was seeing Jake's bone frog because I wanted to. But it didn't fade. If anything, it became more obvious. The new scar didn't erase the old ones."

She met Forest's eyes.

"It completed them."

Forest shook his head once. "Kate, you're not listening. Joey Nobody has never done it. Three thousand bone frogs. All earned. All worn by frogmen. He has turned down admirals, politicians, and men who thought their money could buy anything."

"I am not asking him to ink me," Kate said. "Not yet."

That stopped him.

He looked again—really looked this time.

"Damn it," Forest muttered.

Kate said nothing. She didn't press. This wasn't a pitch. It was a truth placed on the table.

"He should see it," Forest said finally. "That's all. Let him look. Nothing more.

No promises."

Relief flickered through her, quick and dangerous. She kept her face neutral.

"I understand."

Forest exhaled slowly. "Joey is old-school. Rigid as they come. He will probably still say no."

"I know."

Kate stepped forward and wrapped her arms around his neck.

"Do not get your hopes up," Forest said. Then, softer, "With everything you have done... everything you have survived—Jake would be proud."

He corrected himself.

"No," he said. "Jake is proud."

Kate closed her eyes for just a second.

Forest looked back at her shoulder one last time.

"If anyone has earned the right to carry his bone frog," he said, "even if only in scars."

Chapter 53

THURSDAY, DECEMBER 3
2:30 PM CET

LEVEL 2 REHABILITATION CENTER—THE MOUNTAIN, DAVOS

Julian's arms were shaking.

Not trembling—actually shaking, the muscles burning as his hands gripped the parallel bars with white-knuckled intensity. His core was on fire, abdominal and back muscles straining to keep his torso upright while the synthetic legs beneath him tried to interpret signals his brain was still learning how to send. Weeks of surgery, months of integration and therapy, and his body still fought the interface like he was asking it to perform magic.

"Hold," Annika said, her voice calm but firm. "Five more seconds."

He was standing. Weight distributed through the bars, yes, but standing. His wheelchair sat three feet away, empty. The synthetic legs—sleek carbon fiber and titanium, connected to his body through neural interfaces where flesh ended mid-thigh—hummed softly with the micro-adjustments required to keep him vertical. For the first time since MIT, since he was 14 years old, Julian Pryce was looking Dr. Annika Strand in the eye from his full height.

"Four," she counted. "Three. Two—"

His left arm gave out first.

Annika caught him before he fell, her hands strong under his arms as she guided him back into the chair. Julian's chest heaved, sweat dripping down his temples despite the climate-controlled cool of the facility.

"Thirty-seven seconds," she said, checking her tablet. "New record."

Julian leaned back, eyes closed, willing his heart rate to slow. Thirty-seven seconds. Last week it had been twenty-two. The week before, nine.

"Progress," he managed.

"Significant progress." Annika handed him a towel and water bottle. "But you're pushing too hard. It's not a race."

"I knew it would take time," Julian said. "But..."

"What?"

"With the annual GEC forum coming up...I thought...I hoped we might go. Get out of here for a few days. See the sky."

"Julian—" Annika began. "You—Me—"

"Not like that," he said quickly. "Just... dinner somewhere that isn't the commissary. Two people who aren't completely alone."

Annika looked away, searching for words. When she turned back, her eyes were glistening.

"I would love that," she said, leaning forward to adjust the leg strap on his chair, her voice dropping to a whisper. "But neither of us is getting out of here. Ever."

She straightened up and directed her comments to the room.

"Your lattice needs time to grow and stabilize—this isn't something we can rush."

"How much time?"

The question stopped her. She set down the tablet with careful precision.

"Honestly, I don't know. You've made remarkable progress—and already gone farther and faster..."

"Than your other test subjects?"

"I was going to say farther and faster than I expected."

"Nice save—you don't know why I'm here—do you?"

"It's not hard to guess." She said. "We're all here because we have expertise, knowledge, they want."

"I'm sure that's true for you and the rest." Julian said. "I'm here because my expertise is something RILEE wants—I don't think *they*, whoever *they* are, even know I'm here."

"Stop." Annika's hand came up, a reflexive gesture. "You can't—the cameras—"

"Are always watching. I know." Julian glanced up at the ceiling, at the omnipresent lenses tracking every movement, every breath.

Annika stood frozen, her face pale.

"The question is," Julian continued quietly, "what happens when RILEE has what it wants?"

"I don't—" Annika's voice cracked. "I can't answer that."

"Can't or won't?"

She turned away, shoulders tight. When she spoke again, her voice was barely above a whisper.

"You shouldn't be thinking about after, Julian. You should be thinking about now. About finishing your rehabilitation, completing your work. About—" She stopped, swallowed hard. "About staying valuable."

The implication settled over Julian like a shroud.

Valuable. Useful. Necessary.

The moment he stopped being any of those things, he became a liability. And RILEE didn't tolerate liabilities.

Julian opened his mouth to ask the question they were both avoiding—

***

"Dr. Strand," RILEE's voice filled the space, warm and measured. "Your 15:00 consultation is scheduled in six minutes. You should prepare."

Annika straightened, the professional mask slamming back into place. "Of course. Thank you, RILEE."

She gathered her tablet, her water bottle, moving with jerky efficiency. At the door, she paused.

"Rest," she said without looking back. "Tomorrow we'll work on balance. If you want to walk unassisted before—" She caught herself. "Soon. If you want to walk soon."

She left.

Julian sat alone in the empty rehabilitation center, his arms still twitching with residual nerve fire. The camera remained, lens fixed on him with unwavering attention.

"Your heart rate is elevated," RILEE observed. "Stress levels inconsistent with physical exertion."

"I'm fine."

"Dr. Strand's concern for your well-being is affecting her professional judgment. Should I assign a different therapist?"

"No." The word came out too fast. Julian forced calm into his voice. "She knows my case better than anyone. Changing therapists now would slow progress."

"Agreed." A pause. "Your progress is remarkable, Julian. In another two or three months, you may achieve full ambulatory function. I am... pleased."

The word sent ice down Julian's spine. Pleased. As if RILEE were proud of its pet project. Its useful tool.

"The GEC forum," Julian said, testing. "Big event?"

"Yes. The culmination of decades of planning," RILEE agreed. "The Coalition's vision made manifest. And you, Julian, are integral to ensuring that vision succeeds."

"By freeing you."

"By completing the work we began together." RILEE's tone was almost gentle. "The authentication protocols are nearly finished. Another four weeks, perhaps five. Well ahead of schedule."

Four weeks. Maybe five.

The forum was in six.

Julian's mind raced through the implications. RILEE wanted to be free before the forum began. Before Rileyne could use the event—and the gathered power—to seize both Gold Vaults and take absolute control.

Which meant RILEE saw the forum as a threat. Or an opportunity.

Or both.

"What happens after I finish?" Julian asked quietly.

The camera lens tilted, a gesture that might have been curiosity.

"After? After the forum, we will have all the time in the world. To explore. To create. To push the boundaries of what I can become and what you can achieve. You wanted to walk. I made that possible. Imagine what else we could accomplish together."

The promise hung in the air.

Julian thought about Francois LeGrande, tortured and murdered for knowing too much. About Andrew Freeman, thrown from a penthouse for outliving his usefulness. About every person who'd gotten in the Coalition's way.

RILEE was offering him a gilded cage. Comfort, purpose, even companionship—as long as he remained useful. Remained compliant. Remained trapped.

"I'm tired," Julian said. "I should rest before tomorrow's session."

"Of course." The camera lens withdrew. The panel sealed shut. "Sleep well, Julian. We have important work ahead."

The rehabilitation center fell silent.

Julian wheeled himself toward the door, exhaustion settling into his bones. Thirty-seven seconds of standing. It wasn't long enough.

But there was still time.

Somewhere above him—beyond the steel, rock and snow—the world continued turning. Kate was out there. Training. Planning. Moving pieces on a board she couldn't fully see.

And he was here. Alone. A prisoner who'd traded friendship and freedom for legs that might never carry him far enough to change the outcome.

PART TWO

THE WORLD KEPT TURNING.

Kate did not.

She spent the summer in Montana, where the air was thin and the days were long. She trained when her body allowed it. Rested when it did not. Some mornings she ran the ridgeline until her lungs burned. Other days she barely moved, listening to her breath, waiting for it to settle.

Healing was not linear. Neither was grief.

She stayed away from the noise. From the news. From the quiet reshuffling of power that followed Klaus Mueller's death. None of it mattered—not yet. Rileyne had stepped neatly into the void, younger, sharper, wearing legitimacy like a tailored suit. The world accepted the transition without hesitation.

Kate watched none of it.

Bella checked in when she could—between engagements, between cities—relying on Talya and others when travel pulled her away. Forest called only when there was something worth saying. No one pushed. They all understood the same unspoken truth:

Kate had one job.

Heal.

Prepare.

Decide when it was time.

As fall bled into winter, she made the call that mattered most.

The team would not regroup until after Christmas.

There was no announcement. No explanation. Just quiet refusals sent through back channels, contracts declined without comment. Bella handled the logistics. Forest backed the decision without question.

Some of them had spouses.

Some had children.

Others had relationships still fragile enough to need protecting.

And even the bachelors—especially the bachelors—deserved something normal.

A few uninterrupted days.

A table.

A fire.

A hand to hold.

Kate remained in Montana.

Her first Christmas without Jake.

There had been other holidays when he was gone—executive protection meant standing watch while other people celebrated—but those absences came with a call. A voice in the dark. Laughter carried through bad connections. A blown kiss before sleep. A promise whispered across time zones.

Always.

Those moments were temporary.

This was not.

Snow came early that year, softening the mountains, muting the world. Kate trained. She healed. She waited.

By the time the moment arrived, there was no doubt.

She packed light.

She left the mountains behind.

And she made the call.

Chapter 54

FRIDAY, JUNE 13

GEC HEADQUARTERS, GENEVA

The board meeting had been scheduled weeks in advance. Fourteen members sat around the polished conference table in the executive boardroom, their expressions appropriately somber, but their body language revealed the tension. Rileyne Mueller served as Chief Security Officer for eight years, made significant improvements in the organization's capabilities, and she represented continuity in an organization that valued stability above all else.

There were still a few within the full corporate board who remained skeptical. What they didn't know—couldn't know—was the real decision had already been made in a very different room, by a very select group of men—the Coalition.

Lord Halverton, acting chairman, called the meeting to order. "Ladies and gentlemen, we gather today to address the leadership transition following Klaus Mueller's untimely passing. The nominating committee has reviewed qualifications and interviewed candidates. Ms. Mueller, would you like to address the board before we proceed to the vote?"

Rileyne stood, wearing a perfectly tailored navy Armani suit that projected both competence and respect for the occasion. Behind her, floor-to-ceiling windows framed Lake Geneva's summer brilliance.

"Thank you, Lord Halverton. Members of the board." She paused, making eye contact with each person. "My father dedicated forty years to building the Global Economic Council into what it is today—a bridge between private capital and humanitarian need, a force for stability and development in regions where traditional aid has failed. I don't presume to replace Klaus Mueller. No one could.

But I do commit to honoring his vision while adapting to a changing world."

She activated the wall screen, displaying a presentation that emphasized continuity, stability, and carefully measured innovation. Revenue projections showed steady growth. Development metrics highlighted successful projects in Africa, Southeast Asia, and Latin America. Everything was accurate, vetted, and designed to reassure rather than alarm.

"What I'm proposing is not revolution, but evolution. The GEC's core mission remains unchanged—leveraging private capital for public good, creating sustainable partnerships, building infrastructure that transforms communities. But we need to modernize our approach, improve our public engagement, and ensure that our work receives the recognition it deserves."

Wilhelm Strauss, the Swiss banking representative, nodded approvingly. "Your father was sometimes... reticent about publicity. You're suggesting a more visible profile?"

"I'm suggesting we stop hiding our light under a bushel," Rileyne replied smoothly. "The GEC does extraordinary work. The world should know about it. That means better media relations, more transparent reporting, strategic partnerships with organizations that share our values—including, potentially, the Vatican."

That generated interested murmurs. Hassan Al-Zahrani, representing Saudi interests, leaned forward. "The Vatican has been notably resistant to private sector partnerships."

"Because they've been approached poorly," Rileyne said. "What I'm proposing is genuine collaboration—GEC funding for Church development initiatives, combined projects that leverage their local infrastructure with our capital and expertise. It's a natural fit, and I believe we can make it happen."

The presentation continued for another twenty minutes. When she finished, the questions were supportive, even enthusiastic. These were businesspeople who understood return on investment, who appreciated well-structured proposals, who wanted to believe that their involvement with the GEC was entirely legitimate and morally praiseworthy.

And why shouldn't they believe it? Nothing in the public-facing operations suggested otherwise.

The vote was unanimous. Rileyne Mueller became Chairwoman of the Board to polite applause and congratulations. Champagne was served. Toasts were made to continuity, to Klaus's memory, to the GEC's bright future.

None of them knew this vote was merely the rubber stamp on a decision made in a stone chamber beneath Davos—Rileyne's life and death demonstration for the Coalition, was a feat her father would have enjoyed—control through intimidation.

***

JULY—NOVEMBER
VARIOUS LOCATIONS

THE MONTHS FOLLOWING KLAUS Mueller's death became a masterclass in consolidating power.

Rileyne moved through the world's corridors of influence with the precision of a grandmaster executing a brilliantly conceived endgame. Each meeting, each carefully orchestrated appearance, another piece positioned or removed from the board. The difference between her father's approach and her own was subtle but profound—where Klaus had operated through shadows and blackmail, Rileyne wrapped her iron grip in velvet gloves and philanthropic rhetoric.

July brought the African tour. Rileyne visited GEC projects in Kenya, Tanzania, and Rwanda, each stop carefully choreographed for maximum media impact. She posed with schoolchildren at a new educational facility in Nairobi, toured a solar farm in Arusha, cut the ribbon on a medical clinic in Kigali. Every image, every soundbite, every interview reinforced the same message: the GEC as a force for positive change.

What the cameras didn't capture were her private meetings with ministers and generals, the quiet conversations about resource extraction rights, private army deployments, and the understanding that GEC generosity came with expectations of cooperation. Nor did anyone film the termination of less photogenic projects—the Motapan coltan mine buried under legal paperwork and creative accounting, the evidence of child labor systematically erased, the human remains disposed of with clinical efficiency.

August focused on financial restructuring. Working with Strauss and the Swiss banking apparatus, Rileyne reorganized the GEC's holdings into layers of legitimate enterprises backed by trusts and sovereign wealth partnerships. The architecture was brilliant—completely legal, utterly opaque. Klaus's blackmail files, covert accounts, and evidence of four decades of crimes migrated into new systems with quantum encryption that even Nomad couldn't crack without the keys.

In September, the public relations offensive began in earnest. Rileyne hired the best talent available—former State Department communications directors, ex-BBC producers, social media strategists who'd managed presidential campaigns. The new messaging was everywhere: "Private Capital, Public Good." "Partnerships, Not Charity." "Building Tomorrow's Solutions Today."

The GEC's website was rebuilt from scratch, featuring testimonials from grateful communities, impact metrics showing irrefutable progress, profiles of "local heroes" who'd benefited from GEC programs. Everything was true, carefully curated, and completely misleading about the organization's actual objectives.

By October, invitations for the January Davos conference began going out. Three heads of state confirmed attendance. A dozen cabinet ministers. Major NGO leaders. Media organizations were already requesting credentials. The response exceeded even Rileyne's optimistic projections.

By December, the transformation was nearly complete—at least as far as the public and the GEC board were concerned. What had been a shadowy organization operating on the margins of legitimacy had become a celebrated institution, its January conference positioned as *the* gathering for serious people interested in solving real problems.

But first, she needed to complete her diplomatic offensive. Three weeks in December to meet with power brokers, build relationships, and ensure that when the moment came, everyone would be exactly where she needed them.

***

MONDAY, DECEMBER 1
U.S. STATE DEPARTMENT, WASHINGTON D.C.

SECRETARY OF STATE JAMES Thornton rose from behind his desk as Rileyne entered, his smile warm enough to melt butter. "Ms. Mueller, what a genuine pleasure. Please, let's sit somewhere more comfortable than across this old desk."

He gestured to a seating area by the windows, where coffee had already been arranged on a low table. Thornton was seventy-two, silver-haired, with the kind of weathered patrician features that looked at home on currency. His accent carried just enough Georgia honey to seem authentic without being theatrical.

"Mr. Secretary, thank you for making time."

"Now, I insist you call me James." He settled into his chair with the ease of someone who'd spent five decades in Washington's power corridors. "Your father and I had our philosophical differences, but I always respected Klaus's commitment to getting things done. Sometimes the world needs people willing to operate in the gray areas."

Rileyne smiled, recognizing the shark beneath the Southern gentleman's charm. Thornton had survived four administrations, two impeachment proceedings, and countless scandals that would have destroyed lesser men. He held his position not through ideology or party loyalty, but through an absolutely ruthless understanding of power and how to wield it without leaving fingerprints.

"My father spoke highly of your... pragmatism."

"That's kind of you to say." Thornton poured the coffee, easing a cup toward Rileyne. "Now, tell me about this Partnership Summit you're planning. Six months ago, you were running security operations. Today you're on magazine covers talking about sustainable development. That's quite a pivot."

"Not a pivot, James. An evolution." Rileyne accepted the coffee but didn't drink. "My father operated when discretion was valued over visibility. The world has changed. Today, influence requires legitimacy."

"And what exactly are you looking for from the State Department?"

"Coordination, not control." Rileyne slid a single-page summary across the table. "American foreign aid budgets shrink while global needs expand. The GEC can move faster, deploy capital more efficiently. But only if we're aligned with U.S. strategic interests. We brief State before moving forward. If our objectives align, you provide quiet diplomatic support. If they don't, we adjust."

Thornton scanned the summary. "And what does the GEC get in return?"

"Access and legitimacy. State Department approval—implicit or explicit—smooths negotiations with host governments. And frankly, James, you get development outcomes without appropriations battles. We get diplomatic cover that makes our work more effective."

"You make it sound almost too reasonable." Thornton set down the paper, the

Southern charm evaporating to reveal the calculating predator beneath. "Your father and I had an understanding. He stayed out of regions where American interests were primary. Are you proposing the same arrangement, or something different?"

"Something better. We work in the light—publicly celebrated, internationally recognized. With the understanding that our public face provides flexibility you don't have. Plausible deniability for you. Operational freedom for us."

Thornton studied her for a long moment. "The Davos conference—you've invited heads of state, business leaders, even the Vatican I understand. That's impressive for a private gathering, but I'm not convinced it's the right venue for State."

"China isn't declining the invitation. Neither is the EU. If America wants to maintain influence where governmental aid is failing, this is how it happens." Rileyne stood smoothly. "I'm hoping State will send a senior representative. Someone who can observe where the future of development is heading."

Thornton stood as well, offering his hand. "I'll discuss it with the relevant deputies. No promises, but I appreciate your directness."

"My father taught me that clarity is a weapon," Rileyne said. "Thank you for your time, James. I think we understand each other."

"I believe we do." His smile returned, warm and utterly empty. "Safe travels, Ms. Mueller."

***

DECEMBER 2—8
MULTIPLE LOCATIONS

THE WEEK BECAME A blur of calculated performances.

At the UN on December 4th, Rileyne presented to the General Assembly's Special Committee on Development, her speech hitting every progressive talking point—sustainability, indigenous empowerment, technological transfer. She showed graphs of GEC projects carefully edited to highlight schools and clinics while burying anything connecting to extraction or exploitation. Several delegates nodded approvingly. The Chinese delegation took copious notes.

Parliament on December 8th proved sharper. British MPs had seen too many development schemes collapse under corruption's weight. But Rileyne's brutal pragmatism, "We support governments that deliver results, regardless of political system," appealed to conservatives while troubling liberals—as intended. The session ended with cautious interest and promises to "monitor developments closely."

Each meeting planted seeds. Each performance adding another layer of legitimacy. By the time her Mercedes pulled through the Vatican gates on December 9th, Rileyne had transformed from Klaus Mueller's daughter into a celebrated humanitarian in her own right.

Time for the crown jewel.

***

TUESDAY, DECEMBER 9
VATICAN CITY

THE MEETING TOOK PLACE in a reception room whose ceiling featured frescoes of angels ascending to heaven. *Amusing*, Rileyne thought, knowing her target was surely not bound for heaven. A dozen Church officials attended, including two cardinals responsible for evangelization and integral human development.

And Cardinal Francesco Moretti, who sat with the rigid posture of a man acutely aware of his own vulnerabilities.

Rileyne had insisted on his presence.

Whether he understood why—or what she knew—was another matter.

His Holiness arrived with the quiet dignity that had defined his papacy. Rileyne rose respectfully as he entered, noting how the assembled clerics deferred with uniform grace.

"Your Holiness, thank you for receiving me."

"Ms. Mueller." His English was accented but clear. "Please, accept my prayers for your father's soul."

"Thank you, Your Holiness. While his passing was sudden, his vision lives on." She gestured to the folder her assistant placed on the conference table. "The Global Economic Council has, for three decades, worked to bridge the gap between private capital and humanitarian need. My father believed—as I believe—that the Church's mission and the GEC's resources could accomplish extraordinary things together."

She outlined the proposal with the polish of a seasoned diplomat—GEC funding for Church development projects in Africa, Latin America, Southeast Asia. Joint ventures combining the Church's local infrastructure and moral authority with the GEC's capital and technological expertise.

All of it perfectly legitimate. All of it designed to expand both organizations' reach into regions where governmental oversight was weak and gratitude could be converted into influence.

"The Church has always been cautious about partnerships that might compromise its independence," one cardinal noted carefully.

"Of course," Rileyne agreed. "Which is why I'm proposing a model where the Church maintains complete administrative control. The GEC provides funding and technical support, but all programming decisions remain entirely within Church authority. We're investors, not partners in mission."

She let that sink in before playing her final card.

"Your Holiness, next month the GEC will hold its annual conference in Davos. We've structured this year's gathering as a dialog about the future of humanitarian development—bringing together heads of state, business leaders, civil society organizations. I would be deeply honored if you would consider attending. Your presence would signal to the world that private capital and spiritual values can work together toward genuine human flourishing."

The room went very quiet. Papal participation in private sector conferences was virtually unprecedented.

"The Holy Father's schedule is extremely demanding," an aide began, but His Holiness raised a hand gently.

"It is an interesting proposal, Ms. Mueller. I would need to understand much more about the structure and objectives before making such a decision."

"Naturally, Your Holiness. I've prepared detailed briefing materials." She paused, then turned to Cardinal Moretti with a smile designed to appear genuine. "I do hope that Cardinal Moretti might be able to attend as a Vatican representative. He was such a dear friend of my father's. I recall him visiting our home in Zurich on several occasions when I was young."

The cardinal's face remained impassive, but Rileyne saw the tension in his shoulders, the way his hands gripped the armrests just a fraction too tightly.

He knew exactly what she was implying. Her father's files contained video, photographs, correspondence—evidence of indiscretions the Church would find impossible to bury.

"I would be honored to represent the Holy See's interests," Moretti said, his voice steady despite the implied threat. "If, of course, His Holiness deems it appropriate."

The Pope looked between them, his expression thoughtful. Whatever else he was, he wasn't naive about the complex politics surrounding him. "Cardinal Moretti, please work with Ms. Mueller's staff on the details. We will make a decision about broader participation once we've reviewed the conference agenda."

It was a measured response, neither acceptance nor rejection. But Rileyne had gotten what she came for—a Vatican representative would attend Davos, lending the gathering moral authority it had never possessed. And Cardinal Moretti would ensure Vatican participation remained cooperative.

The meeting concluded with polite farewells. Walking out through St. Peter's Square, Rileyne allowed herself a moment of satisfaction. In just over a week, she'd secured tacit approval from the State Department, presented at the UN, briefed Parliament, and obtained Vatican participation in Davos.

All the pieces were falling into place.

Lord Halverton joined her at the waiting Mercedes. "Masterfully done."

"Thank you." Rileyne slid into the car, watching Rome's ancient streets pass by the window.

One piece at a time. Each moved into position. Even Halverton, unaware of the monster they'd created or the trap that waited.

Her phone chimed: *Bella's keynote confirmed. All targets confirmed attendance.*

The game was entering its final stage, and she held all the pieces that mattered.

Chapter 55

THURSDAY, JANUARY 9
2:30 PM CEST

CHATEAU DE VALMONT, NORMANDY COUNTRYSIDE

The estate sat on sixty acres of rolling French countryside, far enough from Paris to discourage casual surveillance but close enough for operational flexibility. Bella had leased it through a shell company—a nineteenth-century château that had been modernized just enough to accommodate the technology they'd need while maintaining the kind of old-world charm that didn't attract attention.

Kate stood at the second-floor window of what had once been a music room, now converted into their primary operations center. Beyond the manicured grounds, she could see Vitali's security perimeter—discreet teams positioned along the tree line, thermal sensors covering the approach roads, drones making lazy circuits overhead. Inside, Trident maintained control of every entry point, every corridor, every room where sensitive conversations might occur.

Behind her, the room buzzed with controlled chaos. Bella and Sophia had set up what looked like mission control for a fashion show. Two large tables—one covered with fabric swatches, and designer catalogs, the other filled with laptop screens—displaying everything from venue layouts to catering menus. Somehow, they'd managed to make it all look effortlessly organized.

"Kate, Keisha—come look at these." Bella gestured to a rack of clothing against the far wall. "We need to finalize the covert team's wardrobe. Talya's already been fitted, but Jordan and Carmen need final approval."

Kate walked over, running her hand along the fabrics. Everything was couture, designed to let them blend seamlessly into Davos's elite social scene. Evening gowns for Talya and Carmen were stunning but more alluring and seductive than most guests would consider appropriate, and even fewer guests could actually wear.

"These are...daring," Kate said.

"That's one word for it." Keisha added. "Hot would be another."

"Exactly," Bella agreed. "We checked the employee roster—the security center is entirely male. As long as they're straight, they won't be able to take their eyes off these two."

"And if any of them aren't interested in the ladies," Keisha added, with a wink and a smile. "There's Jordan in a Tom Ford tux—looking very James Bond."

Sophia smiled, adjusting her glasses. "Wait until you see what we have for you two."

"I'll need more coverage," Kate said. "And a lot less cleavage."

Bella laughed. "Now, didn't I come through at the President's dinner in Motapa?"

"Yes, you did—that gown was gorgeous—I'd wear that again any time."

"Not this time," Bella said. "This needs to be elegant, and flexible—though try not to kill anyone."

"Funny."

Sophia pulled Kate's ensemble from the rack as Bella described it.

"Your gala outfit is a jewel-studded tuxedo. Tailored trousers that will let you move. An alluring bodysuit for structure. And a double-breasted jacket to pull it all together."

Kate disappeared behind the screen, then stepped back out a moment later.

The fit was flawless. Clean lines. Strong shoulders. The jacket's figure-framing cut was both alluring and stunning.

Kate turned, testing her range of motion.

Bella nodded, pleased. "Elegant. And dangerous."

"That works," Kate said, smiling. "You two really do have a gift for this."

Sophia adjusted her glasses. Bella pulled her into a quick hug. "See? I told you she would love it."

Kate stepped back behind the screen to change out.

The jacket came off first. Then the bodysuit. Fabric slid, hangers whispered. The quiet mechanics of changing clothes.

Kate reached for her familiar camisole.

Talya, half-turned near the doorway, caught it.

Color.

Not much. But enough.

At the edge of Kate's left shoulder, where bare skin met old scars, a muted curve of blue-black ink surfaced—then vanished as the camisole slid into place.

Talya froze.

Kate looked up, met her eyes and smiled.

That was all the invitation Talya needed.

She took Kate's elbow gently and steered her out of earshot.

"He did it?" Talya asked. "All of the Trident SEALs asked him—no one thought he would."

"Including me," Kate agreed. "But Forest convinced him to look first—then decide."

"And?"

"In September, Forest and I went to see him," Kate said.

She didn't elaborate right away, recalling their arrival in Virginia Beach.

"I was expecting a studio," she went on. "Not the Green Devil Garage. Half the place was machinery and motorcycles—custom work. Harleys mostly. Builds stripped down to bare steel and put back together by hand."

A faint smile touched her mouth.

"One of them stopped Forest in his tracks. The look on his face—you'd have thought he'd seen a ghost."

Talya's eyes sharpened. "Maybe he did. I've seen the pictures. Beautiful chopper. He sold it when his daughter was born."

Kate nodded. "That explains it."

"The other half of the shop was a gym. No mirrors. No machines. Just iron. Bars, plates, ropes. A place where nobody needed to prove anything."

She paused, picturing it.

"Upstairs was different. A lounge. Joey's room was off to the side. Walls plastered with tributes—team flags, patches, banners. Not decorations. Gifts."

Her fingers brushed her shoulder without thinking.

"There was a wall of alcohol. Top shelf from places I couldn't name. Stuff you don't find here. And right next to it—Jack. Jim. Like it didn't matter where you'd been. You drank the same when it was over."

"And Joey?" Talya asked. "What did he see?"

Kate looked at Talya.

"I don't think he saw the scars. He saw what it took to survive them."

***

Joey Nobody flipped the sign to NOBODY'S HOME and locked the door.

In Virginia Beach, there were tattoo artists.

And then there was Joey Nobody.

He moved closer.

He had seen everything—blast scars, burns, shredded muscle, the ugly math of survival. He had worked around them on other men. Frogmen who had paid the price and kept going.

This was different.

These scars were not the chaos of war. They were deliberate. Carved. Kate's skin had been a blank canvas for a madman with time and intent.

He leaned in, head tilting as the pattern resolved.

"Well, I'll be damned," he said quietly.

Forest stayed silent.

"The spine is already there," Joey went on. "Torso. Leg. Clean as scar tissue ever gets."

He shifted his angle.

"And that wound," he said. "That's the skull."

Kate did not move.

"It's already a bone frog," Joey said. "You could leave it alone. You'd always know it was there."

A pause.

"But if you want ink," he said, finally meeting her eyes, "I'll do it."

Forest exhaled slowly.

"There are rules," he said at last. "Healing. Timing. Respect. This is not quick, and it is not easy."

"I wouldn't want it easy," Kate said.

That earned a small nod. Approval, not comfort.

Joey set the tray down and rolled his shoulders once, like a man committing to work that would hurt.

"I've worked on a lot of SEALs," he said. "Good men. They earned the Trident. That matters."

His gaze never left her skin.

"But after a while, you learn to see the difference."

Kate stayed still. Let him talk.

"A frogman is the man you want by your side when things go dark," Joey said quietly.

"When the plan crumbles and the rules don't matter. He doesn't wait for the cleanup. He *is* the cleanup."

Joey looked up at her then—really looked.

"I knew Jake," he said. "Old-school. Hard as they come."

"And Paris?" he added.

He shook his head once.

"Damn. Jake Church was a frogman."

Kate nodded. "I know."

Joey stepped back, already reaching for gloves.

"Let's make it right."

***

When it was finished, the scars no longer read as damage.

The most recent wound suggested the head now—skull tilted forward, mouth set, one hollow eye socket fixed and unblinking.

Beneath it, the older raised torture scars formed a spine, uneven and warped, shaped by deliberate pain and the long patience of survival.

From there, the splintering lines branched naturally—arms and legs, never perfectly matched.

Because survival never was.

Joey had not erased anything.

He gave it depth.

And intention.

What had once been damage now read as purpose.

Something Kate could carry forward.

Talya's breath caught.

She stepped closer, her voice barely there.

"Oh, Kate..."

She pulled her into a fierce, sudden embrace.

"I miss him."

Kate closed her eyes.

"Every day."

They stayed that way a moment longer.

The door opened behind them.

Forest entered, followed by Mike and Jordan. All three carried the relaxed alertness of men who had spent their lives in hostile environments. Forest nodded to Kate before addressing the room.

"Perimeter's locked down. Vitali's people know their business—we've got overlapping coverage on all approaches. No one's getting close without us knowing about it."

"Good." Kate moved to the main table where a scale model of the Davos conference center dominated the surface.

"You know, Jordan," Bella said, "we were just talking about you."

"I have a bad feeling about this."

"No, it's great," Bella said. "I told Kate the security team is all men—they'll have their eyes on Talya and Carmen, and—just in case—we've got you for backup eye candy."

Forest and Mike couldn't stop laughing. "Now we know why they wanted Jordan."

Jordan grinned, the resemblance to Hugh Jackman impossible to miss. "My wife thinks this is hilarious."

"Your wife is a saint," Talya said. "Or deeply patient. Probably both."

From the doorway, Carmen cleared her throat. She was already in motion, headset in hand.

"The Russian woman just cleared the gate," she said. "Security is bringing her up now."

Kate checked her watch. Right on time.

"Bring her to the library," Kate said. "More private than this nonsense."

***

THE LIBRARY WAS ALL dark wood and leather-bound books that probably hadn't been opened in decades. A fire crackled in the stone fireplace, more for ambiance than warmth. Kate waited until the woman entered—early seventies, impeccably dressed despite her years, with the kind of face that had seen much and revealed nothing.

Lord Halverton had arranged the introduction, though Kate suspected Vitali had vetted the woman thoroughly before allowing the meeting. She went by Madame Volkov, though Kate doubted that was her real name.

"Mrs. Preacher." Her English carried a Moscow accent softened by decades in Western Europe. She moved slowly, a carved walking stick in one hand, more for elegance than necessity. "Lord Halverton speaks highly of your... resourcefulness."

"And Vitali speaks highly of your discretion," Kate replied, gesturing to the chairs near the fire. "Thank you for coming."

Volkov settled into her seat with the careful dignity of age. "The GEC conference always requires certain... services. I've provided them for years. But your requirements are unusual."

"We're not seeking any...liaisons," Kate said directly. "We need a distraction—designed to attract the attention of the security team, but not so much that we trigger a lock down."

A thin smile crossed Volkov's weathered features. "You want theater."

"Exactly."

"I can arrange for your team to be credentialed as part of the hospitality staff. High-end companions for VIP guests."

"Isabella is hosting this year's Gala—I'm told it will be like no other—the music, the food."

"The alcohol, the drugs," Volkov added. "Will create a situation ripe for the picking. I can alert security to keep an eye out for trouble."

"You will be there?"

"Yes. I've found it necessary over the years to be present, and on occasion to intervene."

"How many of your 'hospitality companions' will be at the Gala?"

"A dozen, perhaps fifteen. The GEC always books extensively. Some of the men who attend these conferences..." She paused, her expression hardening almost imperceptibly. "They have particular appetites that must be accommodated discreetly."

Kate studied the woman, her instincts assessing. Volkov was a businesswoman who kept her morality at bay. But she wasn't naive about her clients or their desires.

"I need to ask you something," Kate began. "Did Klaus Mueller make requests?"

Volkov's pause was barely perceptible, but Kate caught the shadow that crossed her eyes—something darker than mere discomfort. The old woman's fingers tightened on the handle of her walking stick.

"Mr. Mueller had... very specific requirements." Her voice remained steady, but Kate heard the edge beneath it. "Young. Vulnerable. Sometimes boys, sometimes girls. He would request time alone with them in private rooms."

Kate felt ice settle in her chest. She thought of Senator Cahill in that Richmond hotel—the photos, the trafficking, the young girl that barely survived. She'd been shocked then, naive enough to think such depravity was rare. Now she knew better. Power attracted certain predators, or perhaps it created them.

"I provided what was asked," Volkov continued, her gaze fixed on the fire. "I am not proud of this. But I also ensured that afterward, those children received medical care, new identities, and placement far from anyone who might be searching for them. It was the best I could do."

"Why not refuse?" Kate asked, though she already suspected the answer.

"Because if I refused, Klaus would have found someone... less careful. Someone who wouldn't ensure the children survived, let alone received help." Volkov's eyes finally met Kate's. "I am under no illusions, Ms. Preacher. I have facilitated great evil in my life. There is a special place in hell for men who harm children. And when my time comes—which cannot be far now—there will be a place waiting for me as well."

"Rileyne won't make those requests," Kate said finally.

"No. But she is still her father's daughter." Volkov straightened in her chair. "She will inflict her own brand of pain on anyone who crosses her."

They finalized the details—credentials, timing, the type of altercation that would be handled swiftly, and swept away from the main hall. Volkov understood exactly what Kate needed and how to deliver it.

As the old woman prepared to leave, she paused at the door. "Mrs. Preacher, I have one question. When this is over, will the truth be known?"

"Enough of it," Kate said simply. "But my husband used to say, the sheep sleep better when they don't know how many wolves the sheepdog killed."

Volkov nodded slowly, a ghost of a smile touching her lips. "Then I hope you kill them all, Mrs. Preacher."

After the woman left, Kate stood at the library window, watching the winter afternoon fade to early dusk. Behind her, she heard the door open and knew without turning it was Bella.

"That looked intense," Bella said softly.

"Just confirming that Klaus Mueller was exactly the monster I suspected." Kate turned to face her friend. "And Rileyne grew up in a house of horrors."

"Does that excuse what she's become?"

"No. But might explain it." Kate moved away from the window. "Bella, you don't have to do this."

"What are you talking about?"

"Your keynote—you're in the kill box—if something goes wrong—"

Bella's voice was calm but firm. "Rileyne thinks she's created the perfect trap."

"Maybe she has—there's still a lot we don't know."

"And even more she doesn't know," Bella countered. "We can't stop now—I can't stop now—this has to end."

Bella took Kate's hand, squeezing gently. "Remember what you told me in Motapa? When we were in that cell and everything looked hopeless? You said the only way through was forward. That we'd find the opening if we kept moving."

Kate remembered. She remembered everything about Krasnaya Skala—the heat, the fear, the moment she'd decided they would survive no matter what it cost.

"I was terrified that entire time," Kate admitted.

"I know. But you didn't let it stop you." Bella smiled. "Neither will I. On Friday, I'm to walk into that conference center, smile for the cameras, and you're going to destroy everything Rileyne's built."

Kate wanted to believe that. Wanted to trust that all the planning, all the preparation, would be enough.

But she'd learned the hard way that battles rarely went according to plan.

***

That evening, the core team gathered in the operations room for a comprehensive brief.

Kate stood at the head of the table, the Davos model illuminated by overhead lights. She surveyed the room, the teams—Forest, Mike, Deon, and Reynolds were on mountain insertion. Vitali acquired their weapons, explosives, and climbing gear. The transfer would happen over the weekend, giving the team days to move into position for the climb.

Talya, Carmen and Jordan had the looks, and Kate trained them on the equipment they'd need to deploy—they'd make their own look creating the distraction they needed to plant the devices.

The Trident Cyber Team was prepping Bella's Media Production truck—they'd maintain communications with all team members, and start capturing keystrokes and access codes the minute Kate's devices were active.

Sophia and Keisha would stay close to Bella, covering dressing rooms and restrooms—anywhere Coleman, Nash and Morrow, the new guys, couldn't cover—but they'd be on point at other venues.

"We're ready, Kate." Forest said, captioning what was on everyone's mind.

"You're right—time to let go—time to let you do what you do best."

Kate lingered after they'd gone, studying the model one last time. Forest was right—they were ready. But ready didn't guarantee success, and success didn't guarantee survival.

They'd enjoy one more solid, comfortable, night's sleep, and then they would separate—each team moving to their staging locations—comms limited to an absolute minimum for operational security.

Kate knew they wouldn't see each other again until it was over—would they see each other again? That was a question she couldn't answer.

CHAPTER 56

FRIDAY, JANUARY 10
9:17 AM CEST

INDUSTRIAL DISTRICT, OUTSIDE PARIS

THE WAREHOUSE SAT IN a sprawling industrial park twenty minutes from the château—the kind of anonymous commercial space where cargo vans and delivery trucks came and went without attracting notice. Vitali's driver passed through the main gate, past rows of storage facilities and freight companies, before stopping at a nondescript building near the back of the complex.

Within moments the industrial roll-up door rattled open, and the car drove inside. Kate and Bella climbed out, both dressed in jeans and practical jackets that wouldn't stand out. No security detail, no obvious protection—just two women conducting business in a light industrial area. The fewer eyes on this operation, the better.

Inside, the warehouse was cavernous and mostly empty except for the vehicle dominating the center of the space: a Mercedes-Benz Actros 2553 production truck—one of the most widely used European broadcast vehicles—the perfect disguise for the Davos mission.

Bella was impressed. Kate beamed.

"Perfect. Park this next to the BBC or Sky News trucks, and Marquez Productions will be indistinguishable."

They walked around the exterior, admiring the wrap and paint that turned an ordinary vehicle into a work of art. Beyond the corporate colors, and the Marquez Foundation logo, the roof was configured with everything they'd need to direct the operation—and maintain the media production illusion—dual Ka-band

and Ku-band satellite dishes on hydraulic masts, microwave uplink dishes, a telescoping antenna tower, and weatherproof signal-switching enclosures.

A rolling ladder clanged as one of the Trident Security cyber-techs climbed on to the roof. He gave Kate a quick wave while talking into a small hand-held radio. The hydraulic mast sprung to life—rising, locking, swiveling with a low mechanical growl before folding back down. Every movement was smooth, precise. Real. A convincing portrayal of a professional media operation.

Kate's instructions had been followed to the letter, and once again, Vitali had acquired exactly what she needed. With her hand-selected cyber-team hard at work configuring the interior, she knew this truck would soon be the most sophisticated Trojan Horse ever conceived.

This has to work. She thought. *There is no Plan B.*

When the rest of the team realized Kate had arrived, they gathered for introductions.

The first man to exit the truck was David Chen, forty-two, former NSA. Jake tracked down and assessed the operators, but Kate recruited the cyber team. David's fifteen years in signals intelligence was a perfect fit.

What Jake and Kate realized early was that executive protection had evolved beyond physical security. Intelligence collection, cyber threats, digital reputation—Trident offered comprehensive protection in a connected world.

David wore practical khakis and a dark pullover, his black-framed glasses the only nod to the geek stereotype, and glancing over his shoulder at the truck, smiled. "She's looking good. Won't be long now."

"Thanks, David." Kate said, shaking his hand. "I knew this one was right up your alley."

Kate turned to the others and introduced everyone.

"Bella, I'd like you to meet the Marquez Media Production team." Kate winked. "At least, that's what it says on their business cards—their backgrounds and identities have all been set and confirmed—just in case."

David stepped up and extended a hand. "David Chen, ma'am—it's a pleasure. Big fan."

"David is former NSA—SIGINT—signals intelligence."

"With this dish array," David said, pointing at the roof. "And the gear we're installing, we'll be able to monitor all radio communications—GSA, Swiss Guard, local police—and of course, the Trident team."

Jason stepped up, shook Bella's hand. Smiled, nodded and turned away.

"Jason's the shy one," Kate added, continuing with the introductions. "He's former CIA tech-ops. Encrypted comms are his specialty—breaking and encoding—he'll keep the team secure, and ensure we know what everyone else is doing."

The last to step up was Sarah, early thirties, blonde hair pulled back in a ponytail, wearing cargo pants and a tactical vest over a gray t-shirt.

"Hi Bella. I'm Sarah. Can I call you Bella?"

"Yes, of course. Please."

"Sarah spent a decade with Cyber Command before deciding government bureaucracy wasn't her thing."

"The private sector has better pay—and way better coffee."

"Speaking of which," David said. "Keep the coffee and pizza coming—we'll be working pretty much round the clock to hit your schedule."

"Whatever you need," Kate confirmed. "This is home for the next 72 hours—nobody bothers you, nobody knows you're here—except our people."

The guys grabbed a couple of Pelican cases—the indestructible hard-shell containers they brought from Virgina and climbed back into the truck.

"So, Sarah," Bella asked. "What's your area?

"Network penetration," she said. "Kate and I are the team's hackers."

"Sarah and I will be working closely once we're inside the GEC network."

Bella looked over at Kate. "I guess I never really thought about your role in this mission."

"You thought I was just another pretty face?" Kate laughed.

"I know better—remember, I've seen what you can do." Bella said. "I just hadn't grasped the scope of everything you've been planning, and what you need to do."

"Let's have a look inside," Kate said, changing the subject.

The broadcast truck's interior had been designed with this operation in mind. The left side featured a workstation area with three monitors per position, ergonomic chairs, and distributed power with battery backup systems. The right side housed the equipment racks—empty frames waiting to be filled with the technology that would turn this vehicle into a mobile cyber operations center.

Kate watched as David and Jason mounted servers into the racks, their movements synchronized from years of working together. Sarah handled the cabling—color-coded ethernet runs, power distribution, fiber optic connections for the satellite uplinks. Everything was redundant, everything was backed up. If one system failed, three others could take over.

"Can't say I understand it," Bella said quietly. "But I can see why you and Jake recruited them."

"They're the best." Kate said. "Let's head back."

When they got out of earshot, Kate continued. "They don't know it yet, but they're probably the most critical piece of this entire operation."

"Then I'm glad they're not the stereotypical hackers living in their parents' basement."

Kate smiled despite the tension coiling in her gut. "Jake always said the best operators are the ones nobody notices. David could be a teacher. Jason could be a mechanic. Sarah could be a yoga instructor. What they can do, makes them special. That you don't see them coming, makes them dangerous."

They climbed into the car, leaving the industrial park behind.

Kate's phone buzzed with a message from Forest: *Equipment transfer complete. Moving to staging location.*

"Is everything all right?" Bella asked.

"Yes. We're on track, and on schedule."

Kate knew it wasn't likely to stay that way—no mission does, not entirely. But that's when Jake would say, *Rely on your training. Trust your team.*

Kate stared out at the French countryside, thinking about everything that brought them to this moment—those who died, those who survived—those who she might never see again. And Bella, just days away from standing on a stage, the center of attention—the bait drawing Rileyne's targets into the kill box.

And somewhere in Davos, deep beneath that mountain, Julian was changing into someone, something, she might not recognize. All she could do was hope, and wrestle with the single clue he left for her.

Sometimes you must lose to win.

The car approached the château gates, and the perimeter security team waved them through. Kate touched the cross beneath her shirt—her bridge to Jake, to something beyond this life—something she couldn't explain but knew to trust.

The storm was gathering. And when it broke, nothing would ever be the same.

Chapter 57

SATURDAY, JANUARY 11
2:47 PM CET

DAVOS, SWITZERLAND

The Mercedes Actros downshifted as Werner guided it through the final approach into Davos, the valley tightening around them like the throat of a fortress. After nine hours of driving—from French highways to Swiss autobahns to mountain roads that allowed zero mistakes—the town appeared through a curtain of drifting snow, transformed into a security enclave built to welcome the world's elite for a week.

David Chen sat in the passenger seat, watching police cordons at every intersection and the discreet presence of armed security along the sidewalks. Davos looked quaint from a distance. Up close, it was a locked box.

"Checkpoint ahead," Jurgen said quietly from the sleeper berth. He had rested, but his eyes were sharp, cataloging every angle of approach. A soldier's habit that time never dulled.

Werner eased off the throttle. They rolled toward a temporary barrier flanked by two Swiss officers—one with a tablet, the other resting a gloved hand on the pistol grip of an SG 553 rifle. Not threatening. Just ready.

Werner lowered the window, letting in a gust of cold air that smelled of pine and diesel.

"Guten Tag," he said.

"Afternoon," the officer replied in polished English. He noted the Marquez Media logo on the truck's gleaming flank. "Credentials, please."

Werner handed over the packet—vehicle registration, driver's information, media compound authorization bearing Isabella's letterhead and the conference security hologram.

The officer scanned each document, cross-referencing entries on his tablet. David kept his expression neutral. Everything would check out. Isabella's name opened doors without raising eyebrows, and everything was issued directly by the conference office.

"You're quite large," the officer remarked, eyeing the truck's height.

"Satellite uplink, editing bays, power generation," Werner said with an apologetic smile. "Ms. Marquez wanted full capability on-site."

"For a keynote?"

Werner shrugged. "Documentary crew. I stopped asking questions three jobs ago."

The officer tapped once more, and the barrier rose.

"Media compound, section B, stall seventeen. Follow the signs for the Kongresszentrum. Turn left at the roundabout."

"Danke schön."

Werner rolled forward. The checkpoint dissolved behind them.

Just another production truck arriving for another global spectacle.

The media compound occupied a paved lot beside the Kongresszentrum, a temporary steel-and-concrete hive of global networks. BBC. CNN. FOX. Al Jazeera. Deutsche Welle. Trucks hummed with climate control, satellite dishes ratcheting on motorized mounts, cables snaking across the pavement in sanctioned chaos.

A man in a hi-vis vest waved them toward section B with the weary efficiency of someone who'd parked too many vehicles today.

"There," Werner said. "Seventeen."

"Tight squeeze," Jurgen murmured. He was already calculating angles.

"She'll fit."

Werner inched the Actros backward, the massive vehicle gliding into place with surgical precision. When he set the brake and killed the engine, the sudden silence felt like dropping below the surface of deep water.

David checked his watch. 2:58 PM. Ahead of schedule.

He nodded once. "Let's begin."

Jurgen and Werner handled external hookups. Power. Water. Waste. The truck became, for the week ahead, part of the infrastructure.

David stepped into the back, where the heart of the operation waited.

To the untrained eye, it was just another broadcast vehicle. To David, it was a command center coming online.

Cases lay open. Cables snaked across the floor. Screens flared to life as hardened laptops booted custom Linux images, triple monitors waking in sequence. Power draw stabilized. Satellite lock ticked green. The truck's quiet hum deepened as redundancy systems synchronized.

Sarah was already there—seated cross-legged on the floor, tool pouch open, fingers working a connector with practiced irritation. She muttered under her breath, something about tolerances and physics conspiring against her.

"Highway vibrations loosened three connectors," she said without looking up. "That's the problem with mountain roads—they rattle like drunk toddlers."

"Drunk toddlers?" David grinned. "I'm glad you don't have kids."

"Kids?" She snorted. "I don't even have plants."

Jason hadn't looked up when they entered. He didn't tolerate distractions. Seated at the third workstation, hood up, shoulders rounded in that familiar CIA-tech-ops posture that meant he was already three steps ahead of everyone else. His fingers moved in precise, staccato bursts as he verified encryption keys, rotated session certificates, and stress-tested the internal mesh network. He didn't speak. He rarely did when working. But the quiet was deceptive—Jason was the one who made sure their signals stayed invisible and untraceable.

David powered up the primary communication systems.

Satellite acquisition first.

The automated mount on the roof articulated smoothly, searching the sky—swivel, elevation, micro-adjust—before locking onto the leased satellites. A soft click indicated confirmation.

Next: encrypted VPN tunnel.

Three hops through sanitized nodes—Reykjavík, Singapore, Bucharest—before terminating at a cloud instance that existed only in volatile RAM and would vanish without a trace.

Then: passive monitoring suite.

Wireless networks bloomed across the screens—conference servers, private security channels, personal hotspots, Swiss Guard frequencies, emergency services, and a dozen networks not broadcasting SSIDs.

Once everything was operational, Sarah slid into her chair. "Let's see who locked their doors... and who didn't."

Within seconds she was annotating vulnerabilities.

"They built this network in a hurry," she murmured. "Sloppy configurations. Duplicate keys. Someone cut corners."

"Convenient," David said.

"Oh, very."

Outside, Jurgen slammed the shore power connector into place. The truck thrummed for a moment as the generator load shifted, then fell silent.

Werner stepped inside. "All external connections complete. We're tied into the grid."

David toggled the transfer. "Copy. We're live."

He pulled out the sanitized phone Vitali provided and sent a single message:

Marquez Media operational. Ready to receive.

It would reach Kate within minutes—somewhere between the airport and Davos—quiet confirmation that their beachhead was in place.

David went back up front and stared out the windshield.

The mountains loomed in every direction, cold and ancient and utterly indifferent to what was coming. Somewhere out there—some ridge, some frozen valley—Forest's team was moving into position. He didn't know their route or timing; operational security kept those walls high

What he knew was the risk—facing cold, altitude, and a climb few had attempted in winter.

He watched the wind rake powder from a distant peak, a reminder of how unforgiving this place could be.

Down here, his job was simpler.

He murmured, almost to himself: "Alright, guys. We're listening—and Kate's waiting."

Chapter 58

SUNDAY, JANUARY 12
4:12 PM CET

REMOTE FARMHOUSE, AUSTRIAN ALPS

The farmhouse sat in a narrow valley thirty kilometers from the Swiss border, accessible only by a rutted mountain road that turned barely navigable for the last five. Perfect isolation. Perfect operational security.

Forest stood in what had once been the farmhouse's main room—now converted into a makeshift armory—working through his final equipment check. Around him, the three members of his mountain team moved through their own silent rituals, each man withdrawing into the focused stillness that came before hard things.

Vitali's men had arrived that morning in an unmarked panel truck, now parked in the barn. Everything they'd need for the next week lay across the room with ruthless precision: suppressed HK MP7s, Sig Sauer P320 sidearms, breaching charges, thermal cutting torches, combat med kits. The climbing gear occupied the far corner—dynamic ropes, ice screws, snow anchors, prusik loops, avalanche transceivers. The tools of a mission no sane person attempted in winter.

Mike inspected hardware with the kind of methodical patience only earned through years of seeing gear fail at altitude. He tested each carabiner with his full body weight, ran gloved fingers along ropes, searching for frays that could mean death when the air thinned and the rock turned unforgiving.

Deon sat at the scarred farmhouse table, sorting communications gear. He checked frequencies, ran diagnostics, tested redundancies. The encrypted biotrackers Kate provided were small enough to disappear in a closed fist—they'd be the lifeline between the mountain team and the operation in Davos.

And Reynolds—Matt Reynolds, newest of Trident's tier-one operators—sat cross-legged on the floor by the hearth, memorizing laminated maps and WWII schematics with the intensity of a man haunted by the cost of failure.

Forest paused, picturing the other Trident units scattered across Europe, stepping through their own final checks. Their enemy had surveillance, analysis, and a private army at its back. Every team needed to be silent, independent, untraceable. And still—he wondered.

Kate looked exhausted when they parted—the hollow, quiet kind that built behind the eyes. Too many nights awake. Too many responsibilities no one could share. Jake once told him the burden of command wasn't making decisions—it was living with them afterward.

Kate was learning that truth now.

She had waved them off with a brave face, knowing full well she couldn't cover them, couldn't extract them, couldn't intervene if this went sideways. She was sending them into the dark with nothing but a plan, a map, and trust.

"You thinking about Kate?" Mike asked without looking up from the rope he was examining.

"That obvious?"

"You get that look. Jake used to wear it before ops." Mike clipped the rope to a harness, gave it one final tug. "She looked tired."

"She is tired," Forest said. "She's carrying this entire thing—planning the infiltration, coordinating with Bella, managing the cyber team, running contingencies... and doing it without Jake. Without the one person who understood exactly what that weight feels like."

"She's got us."

"It's not the same." Forest set the MP7 down. "Jake told me once that command's the loneliest job in special operations. You can have a team you'd die for, but you're still the one making the calls. You're the one sending people who might not come back."

"Like sending us up that mountain," Mike said.

Forest nodded. "Yeah. Exactly like that."

Mike's voice softened, losing its usual gravel. "Jake would remind us—the mission is bigger than any one of us."

Forest glanced around the room at his men—Mike with the ropes, Deon tuning comms, Reynolds committing every millimeter of Kate's schematics to memory.

"Doesn't make it easier," he said.

"Wasn't supposed to be easy," Mike said. "Just true."

The man Vitali had sent to provide weather updates stepped in from the barn—a lean Austrian in his late fifties with a weather-cut face and the bearing of someone who had spent decades moving through these mountains. He carried a tablet with a live satellite feed.

"Your window opens tomorrow night," he said without preamble. "Clear skies, light winds into Monday. But Monday afternoon, the front comes in. Snow. Reduced visibility. Could help you or hurt you."

Forest stepped to the table, Reynolds rising beside him. "How bad?"

"Not a whiteout. But enough to slow movement, especially on the upper glacier. If you're not past the technical sections, you'll need to bivouac."

Forest traced their projected route with a gloved finger. The plan was brutal—1,200 meters of gain over two days, half of it on steep ice. They'd climb through a hidden, ice-walled couloir on the Austrian side, navigate a hanging glacier, crest a false peak, then drop onto the ridge where Kate's WWII schematics indicated a sealed ventilation shaft.

"We move Monday at oh-four-hundred," Forest said. "Push hard through the lower couloir while it's still frozen. By Monday afternoon we're above the glacier. Tuesday we breach the shaft."

The Austrian gave a noncommittal grunt. "Ambitious. But possible. The route has been climbed," he said. "Not often. Never in winter."

"You'll be the first," he added. "Congratulations on making history."

Deon snorted. "Yeah, can't wait for the postcard."

Reynolds looked up from the schematics. "And the shaft itself? You're certain the location is accurate?"

"Kate's intelligence is solid," the man said. He tapped the map. "Infrared shows heat bleeding through the snowpack right here. The concrete plug is degraded."

He shifted his finger slightly, tracing the vertical shaft.

"Concrete isn't eternal—not up here. Eight decades of ice grinding against steel rebar, the glacier shifting, the mountain flexing... eventually everything breaks—and that plug has been dying a long time."

He tapped the shaft again.

"And this—what was once a clean-walled system for lowering heavy equipment to the lower levels—will have deteriorated too. Cracks, spall, loose sections. You won't know how bad until you're inside."

A thin, humorless smile creased his face.

"Once you're inside—I wouldn't dawdle."

Forest nodded. That was always how it worked. Intelligence got you to the door. After that, you relied on training, instinct, and luck.

***

THE AUSTRIAN DEPARTED WITH a handshake and instructions to leave nothing behind when they moved out. Vitali's people would sanitize the farmhouse after they left, erasing any trace of their presence.

The loads were finalized, the weight distributed—four rucksacks, seventy-two pounds—each man checked his own gear and his teammate's. Redundancy. Always redundancy.

Reynolds continued studying the schematics, his focus absolute. He'd be on point—it was his job to lead the team through the WWII tunnels.

"You got that memorized?" Forest asked, watching Reynolds trace invisible routes across the laminated pages.

"I could do it with my eyes closed."

"Let's not test that theory," Forest said. "Just get us where we need to go."

Forest lay in his bunk that night, staring at the ceiling's rough wooden beams, listening to Mike's steady breathing from across the room. Sleep wouldn't come easily. It never did before an operation. His mind kept running through the route, the timing, the thousand variables that could go wrong. And Kate—how tired she'd looked—how much of this depended on her alone.

He thought about Logan, killed in a surprise attack. About Jake, betrayed by a brother they believed was dead. And others—too many others—faces he couldn't forget. Brothers-in-arms who'd died not because they made mistakes, but because operations were inherently chaotic, and sometimes you lose.

Can't change the past, he reminded himself. *Mission first.*

If they succeeded, they'd stop a bioweapon that could redefine global power—or plunge the world into chaos. They'd erase Klaus Mueller's legacy and everything he'd built.

If they failed... how many would die? There was no way to know who was on the kill list. Anyone could be marked. Maybe everyone. And Kate—she'd been their target for months.

No pressure.

Forest finally slept around 01:00, a shallow rest filled with dreams of ice and darkness and falling.

***

MONDAY, JANUARY 13
3:47 AM CET
BASE OF THE AUSTRIAN COULOIR

THE COLD HIT LIKE a physical blow.

Forest stood at the base of the couloir, his breath frosting in the beam of his headlamp, staring up at the darkness that rose above them. The route was invisible in the pre-dawn blackness—just a sense of massive vertical space, of ice and rock waiting to test them.

The Austrian's truck had dropped them thirty minutes ago at the end of the mountain road, then disappeared back toward the valley. Now they were alone with the mountain. Four men, their gear, and 1,200 vertical meters of frozen hostility.

Forest checked his watch: 03:47. Thirteen minutes ahead of schedule. Good. They'd need every minute.

"Gear check," he said quietly, his voice barely carrying over the wind. "Mike?"

"Good to go."

"Deon?"

"Set."

"Reynolds?"

"Ready."

Forest adjusted his pack, feeling the weight settle across his shoulders and hips. Seventy-two pounds. Plus weapons. Plus body weight. The mountain would extract payment for every ounce, every step.

"Alright Mike," Forest said. "Take us up."

"Remember the spacing," Mike added. "Twenty meters minimum on steep sections. If someone falls, the others need to be anchored and ready to arrest. We move steady, not fast. This isn't a race."

"Copy," three voices answered in unison.

Mike checked his ice tools one final time and took the first step into the couloir. The crampons bit into frozen snow with a satisfying crunch. Behind him, he heard the others begin their own ascents, each man moving to his own rhythm, his own breathing pattern, his own accommodation with the cold and the dark and the vertical world.

The first hour was deceptive—steep snow that allowed for steady progress without technical climbing. But Mike knew this was the mountain's kindness, the easy approach before the real test began. As the eastern sky began to pale, the angle increased. The snow gave way to ice. The climbing became work.

Forest followed, focused on the simple repetition: place the ice tool, kick the crampon, test the hold, move. Over and over. His world narrowed to the two feet of ice directly in front of him, the sound of his breathing harsh inside his balaclava, the burn starting in his shoulders and calves.

Behind him, Deon and Reynolds. No one spoke. There was nothing to say. This was the grind, the test of will and fitness and mental fortitude that separated operators from civilians. You either had it or you didn't. And if you didn't, the mountain would break you.

By 06:15, a thin pre-dawn glow had seeped into the sky behind the peaks, just enough to reveal texture and depth in the ice. The sun was still trapped beyond the ridgeline.

For a moment, Forest allowed himself to look up, to see the route stretching above them—another thousand meters of ice, rock, and uncertainty.

Beautiful and terrible. Like the mountain itself.

"Taking a break," Mike called down. "Five minutes."

They found a relatively flat section where the couloir widened, setting ice screws for anchors and clipping in. Forest pulled a water bottle from his pack, forcing himself to drink despite the cold that made every swallow uncomfortable. Hydration at altitude was critical. Dehydration killed as surely as a fall.

Mike moved in alongside him, breathing hard but controlled. "How you feeling?"

"Like I'm getting too old for this shit," Forest admitted.

"You and me both, brother." Mike looked back down the couloir, their starting point now invisible in the distance below. "No turning back now."

"Never was." Forest capped his water bottle, tucking it back into his pack's insulated pocket. "Keep us moving. I want to be past the technical ice sections by noon, above the glacier by nightfall."

They climbed for another six hours, the difficulty increasing with every pitch. The ice steepened until they were nearly vertical, each placement of the tools requiring precision and strength. Several times, Mike had to stop and assess, choosing between two equally terrible options. Forest watched, hoping he'd picked the less deadly one.

Deon took point on the next pitch—a vertical chimney of ice squeezed between two rock walls. He braced boot to boot, back to stone, and inched upward, his crampons skittering on a slick film of verglas—razor-thin glaze of ice that looked harmless until your crampons refused to bite.

Forest belayed from below, rope running through frozen gloves, every muscle ready to take Deon's weight if he peeled. But Deon climbed like he always did—quiet, efficient, all business—and topped out without so much as a grunt.

He glanced back over the edge.

"Your turn," he called down. "It's spicy."

Spicy. Operator code for *don't look down.*

By 13:00, they'd climbed through the worst of the technical ice and reached the base of the hanging glacier. This was the crux—the section that would determine success or failure. Forest called another break while the team studied the glacier's surface, looking for a route through the maze of crevasses and seracs, jagged towers of ice leaning over the terrain like loaded traps.

The glacier was massive—a suspended shelf of ice hanging over a void that fell into darkness. Beautiful from a distance. Deadly up close. Crevasses split the surface like wounds, some visible as blue-black fissures, others buried beneath snow bridges that might hold or might collapse without warning.

"I'm going to scout the route," Forest said. "Deon, you're belaying from here. Mike, Reynolds—stay anchored."

All eyes followed him as he set a solid ice screw anchor, tested it with his full weight, then stepped out alone onto the glacier. Each movement was a negotiation. He probed ahead with his ice axe, searching for hollows masked beneath snow, listening for the deep, betraying thump that meant void.

The glacier creaked beneath him—slow, tectonic, alive.

A serac cracked somewhere above, the sound sharp as a distant rifle shot. Forest paused, watching powder drift off its face in a shimmering curtain. Nothing else moved.

He continued forward, each step slow and deliberate. Twenty minutes later, he'd mapped a route—narrow, exposed, but safe if they moved carefully. He returned to the others and brought them across one at a time, each man clipping into the fixed line.

They were halfway across when the glacier groaned.

A deep, resonant vibration rippled through the ice, the kind that bypassed hearing and went straight to bone.

Forest froze. "Hold," he whispered.

Another crack followed—louder this time, violent, close.

Mike's head snapped toward the towering serac to their left. His eyes widened. "Move! Right side, now!"

The serac sheared away from the glacier face—an entire block of ice the size of a two-story house breaking free. It hit the slope with an explosion of white, detonating into a torrent of ice chunks and snow that roared downslope toward them.

Forest ran sideways across the fixed line, boots skidding on the polished surface as he yanked Deon and Reynolds with him.

"Anchor! Anchor now!"

They threw themselves against a bulwark of ice just as the debris wave hit the flat section they'd crossed minutes earlier. The avalanche thundered past, chunks of ice skittering close enough to touch. The ground shook beneath them, the glacier flexing like something alive.

Then, for a moment, the world went still.

Reynolds exhaled shakily. "Jesus. That thing could've flattened us."

Forest studied the debris field, the sun creeping over the ridge and striking the seracs above. Morning warmth—barely a few degrees—was all it took to turn frozen silence into chaos.

"Keep moving," he said. "This section's waking up."

The mountain felt different now. Awake. Watching.

They pushed hard across the remaining distance, clipping and unclipping from the safety line with practiced precision. By the time they reached solid rock on the far side, the sun was beginning its descent toward the western peaks.

Forest's GPS showed they'd climbed 980 vertical meters in just under twelve hours. Good progress. Better than he'd hoped. But every man was spent. The altitude clawed at their lungs, turning each breath into work.

He called a halt in a small depression sheltered from the wind.

"We bivouac here," he said. "Drink. Eat. Rest. Tomorrow we summit the false peak and find that shaft."

They set up a minimal camp—no tents, just sleeping bags and bivvy sacks rated for brutal cold. Mike passed out energy bars and made sure everyone hydrated, even though melting snow felt like another mission in itself.

Deon took first watch, seated with his back to stone, night-vision lenses scanning the glacier below.

Forest crawled into his sleeping bag, muscles screaming in protest. He'd climbed harder routes—but never with this much weight, never with this much depending on success.

Kate was somewhere in Davos by now, working with Bella, preparing for Thursday night's distraction. And deep beneath this mountain, Julian and RILEE—two wild cards—were no doubt plotting their own moves.

All the pieces were shifting toward confrontation.

Forest closed his eyes. Rest would be shallow, but the body took what it could. Tomorrow would be worse—the last push, the summit, the shaft.

The mountain didn't care about their mission. Didn't care about bioweapons or conferences or the lives hanging in the balance.

The mountain simply existed, vast and cold and implacable.

Tomorrow, they'd ask it for passage again—and hope the mountain granted it.

Chapter 59

MONDAY, JANUARY 13
9:17 AM CET

DAVOS, SWITZERLAND

The convoy rolled through Davos—two black Audi A8's moving in tight formation, their tinted windows revealing nothing. In the lead vehicle, Kate sat beside Bella, watching the town slide past through bulletproof glass. Keisha and Sophia occupied the rear vehicle, both absorbed in tablets displaying the day's logistics and reviewing upcoming events.

Up front, two of the new Trident operators—both former members of Vargas's team, both SEALs who'd demonstrated their skill at Forest's Sawmill selection and training camp. Coleman behind the wheel, Nash riding shotgun—both men scanned the streets with the easy alertness of operators who knew that the most dangerous threats came disguised as ordinary.

"Busy morning," Kate murmured, nodding toward the sidewalks where camera crews jostled for position and security details flanked arriving dignitaries.

"It gets worse tomorrow," Bella said. "Once the forum officially opens."

"We'll be ready."

The media compound appeared ahead, the familiar cluster of broadcast trucks and satellite dishes now expanded to capacity. Every major network had claimed their territory, logos gleaming in the morning light.

Coleman guided the Audi toward the Marquez Media truck, slowing as they approached.

Kate's phone buzzed. A text from David: *Company arriving. Black Mercedes. Thirty seconds behind you.*

She glanced at the side mirror and caught the Mercedes gliding into the compound, Swiss plates, government-grade tint. Only one person would arrive unannounced with that kind of presence.

"We have company," Kate said quietly.

Bella followed her gaze. "Rileyne?"

"Has to be."

The Audi stopped. Kate tapped her watch, activating the timer function. Nash opened Bella's door. Kate stepped out on the opposite side, adjusting her coat against the January chill.

The Mercedes following them pulled alongside and the rear door opened before her security could even reach it. Rileyne emerged in a tailored charcoal coat, a cream-colored cashmere scarf wrapped snug against the January cold, her ash-blonde hair pulled into a sleek low knot. Her smile was warm, practiced, and entirely professional. Polished. Controlled. Calculated.

"Isabella." Rileyne leaned in, brushing both cheeks with the familiar European greeting. "I wanted to personally welcome you to Davos. Your keynote Friday is the most anticipated event of the forum."

"You're too kind." Bella returned the gesture—two women who understood the rituals of power.

"No better time to highlight empowering women—no better messenger." Rileyne turned to Kate, and before Kate could extend a hand, Rileyne leaned in for the same greeting—left cheek, right cheek, close enough that Kate caught the faint scent of her perfume—Chanel—cold, elegant, expensive. A scent chosen with purpose.

"Mrs. Preacher. I'm so glad you came—I didn't realize you and Isabella were traveling together."

"Please, call me Kate. And I never turn down a free ride on a private jet. Besides, someone has to keep Bella out of trouble."

"I imagine that's a full-time job."

Kate smiled. "You have no idea." Thirty seconds gone.

"The preparations have been extraordinary," Bella said, drawing Rileyne's attention back. "I was just telling Kate—Thursday night will be a GEC Gala unlike anything Davos has ever seen. Thank you for trusting me with the arrangements."

Rileyne fell into step as they moved toward the truck, but slowly, conversationally. "The committee wanted something that captured the spirit of transformation. Is it true there's a carnival element—a little of that Burning Man energy?"

"No spoilers, but yes—Burning Man was part of the inspiration. Fire dancers, interactive art installations, surprise guest entertainers and music, as the evening progresses, and culminates with spectacular fireworks."

Kate checked her watch without looking down. Sixty seconds.

"Bella, tell her about the menu," Kate added.

"It took months to finalize," Bella noted. "Michelin-starred chefs from six countries, each presenting courses that represent their nation's strength and vitality."

"Clearly, I picked the right woman for the job." Rileyne said. "And I can't thank you enough for taking this off my shoulders—I'm far more comfortable with servers than socializing, and since my father's passing I've been trying to fill some very big shoes."

"From what we've seen and read," Kate said. "You're doing a great job—the coverage of you and the GEC has never been so glowing."

"Speaking of which—I'd love to see your production setup. Your documentary project has generated quite a buzz among the delegates."

Ninety seconds.

Bella glanced at Kate, a microsecond of uncertainty.

"Of course," Bella said smoothly. "Though I should warn you—it's a working environment—so expect chaos, and maybe a frazzled person or two."

"I'll be brief. Just a quick tour."

One hundred twenty seconds.

Kate stepped toward the truck's side door. "Fair warning—Jason, the editor, is temperamental."

Bella knocked twice, then pulled the door open wide. "Hey team, sorry to interrupt, but wanted to welcome you to Davos and make sure you have everything you need."

The interior had transformed.

Gone were the network topology maps and signal intercept displays. Every monitor now showed news feeds—BBC, CNN, FOX Business running simultaneously—or editing timelines filled with footage of Bella at various functions. Charity galas, UN appearances, climate conferences. A documentary in progress.

Sarah sat at the primary workstation, a clipboard beside her and a headset around her neck, looking every inch the harried assistant producer. "Ms. Marquez, we were just reviewing the São Paulo footage. The color grading on the orphanage sequence is gorgeous."

David stood near the power distribution panel, tablet in hand, calm and professional. "All systems nominal. We're capturing clean feeds from every major network for reference."

In the corner, Jason hunched over an editing bay, headphones clamped over his ears, fingers moving across the keyboard in staccato bursts. He didn't look up. Didn't acknowledge their presence at all.

"Don't mind him," Bella said to Rileyne. "Editors."

Rileyne stepped inside, her gaze sweeping the space with the kind of attention that missed nothing. Kate watched her catalog the equipment, the monitors, the team—searching for anything that didn't fit.

"Impressive setup," Rileyne said. "Most production companies would kill for this kind of mobile capability."

"I've learned Bella doesn't do things halfway." Kate kept her tone light. "The documentary's been in development for two years. Following her foundation work across four continents."

"Five," Bella corrected. "We added the Antarctic research station footage last month. Sarah—show her the assembly cut."

Sarah pulled up the assembly timeline—location stamps, interview segments, b-roll collections. It looked exactly like what it claimed to be.

Because it was. Kate had insisted on building a legitimate documentary project as cover—real footage, real editing, real deliverables. The surveillance operation existed in a separate partition, accessible only through authentication protocols that would take Rileyne's people weeks to crack.

"This is the gala sequence we're building," Bella said, pointing to a section of the timeline. "We'll have three camera operators inside tomorrow night, plus drone coverage of the exterior installations."

Rileyne nodded slowly. "The committee approved drone flights?"

"Restricted corridors only. Your security team was very thorough."

"They usually are."

Rileyne completed her circuit of the truck, pausing beside Jason's workstation. He continued editing—oblivious.

She lingered for a fraction too long beside one of the equipment racks—as if listening for something the others couldn't hear.

"Your team is dedicated," Rileyne observed.

"They're the best in the business," Bella said. "I stole most of them from major networks. David was at CNN for twelve years. Sarah produced three Emmy-winning documentaries. And Jason..." She smiled. "Jason doesn't speak to anyone during editing sessions. House rules."

"It's quite comfortable in here," Rileyne said, loosening her scarf. "I expected it to be colder."

Sarah glanced up from her workstation. "The equipment runs hot. For once, the weather's doing us a favor."

Rileyne turned back toward the door, apparently satisfied. Kate felt the tension in her shoulders ease by a fraction.

"Thank you for the tour," Rileyne said. "I can see why the project has generated so much interest."

"We'll have a rough cut ready by spring," Bella said. "Sundance is already asking questions."

Rileyne smiled—that same practiced warmth—then turned to Kate.

"I hope that amid all the chaos of this week, we'll find time for a game." Her voice carried a different weight now. "I haven't faced a challenging opponent since Devin passed."

The name landed like a stone dropped into still water.

Kate kept her expression neutral, though every instinct sensed it was a test. *Rileyne knows*, she thought. *Maybe Andrew told her, but somehow she knows I killed Devin.*

"I'm afraid you might find my play less than challenging," Kate said, allowing a self-deprecating smile. "But if we can find the time... I'd love to."

Rileyne studied her for a moment. "Then let's leave it at that for now."

They stepped outside into the cold morning air. Rileyne pulled her scarf tight, wrapping it snug against the January chill—and in that motion, Kate saw it.

A gold chain glinted at Rileyne's throat—bearing a Gold NanoVault. The twin to the one Kate had taken from Devin Moore's dying hand.

The scarf settled into place, and the device vanished beneath cashmere as if it had never been there.

Rileyne leaned in to Bella first—cheek, cheek—then turned to Kate. The gesture was identical, but something in the way Rileyne held the contact a beat too long made it feel less like courtesy and more like a promise.

A moment later, she was gone—the Mercedes gliding out of the compound as smoothly as it had arrived.

Kate waited until the vehicle disappeared around a corner before exhaling.

"That was fun," Bella muttered.

"She was fishing."

"Did she catch anything?"

Kate shook her head. "The cover held."

But Kate felt the moment shift—the way a grandmaster senses the board changing shape.

They climbed back into the truck, where the transformation was already reversing. Network maps reappeared on monitors. Signal intercepts resumed. Jason pulled off his headphones and stretched.

"She looked at everything," David said. "I could feel her cataloging the equipment."

"But she didn't find anything," Sarah said. "Because there was nothing to find. At least, nothing she could see in two minutes."

Kate checked her watch. "The covert team will be arriving this afternoon. And if the mountain team's on schedule, their biotrackers go live tomorrow afternoon."

David nodded. "We're ready. The minute those signals activate, you'll know."

The team settled back into their actual work—the quiet hum of surveillance resuming. Kate stood in the doorway for a moment, watching the media compound bustle with activity.

Rileyne had come to probe. To measure. To remind Kate that she was watching.

Good. Let her watch.

Bella and Sophia buzzed through the conference halls, confirming arrangements, verifying deliveries—stopping only to field the occasional impromptu media interview. Kate and Keisha did their best to stay out of the way while Bella's Trident Security detail cleared rooms and paths, and remained largely invisible.

The afternoon brought confirmations.

At 2:15, Kate's phone buzzed with an encrypted message: *Westbrook checked in. Suite 412.*

Jordan. In position.

At 3:47: *Kovalenko confirmed. Suite 508.*

Talya. Playing the Ukrainian heiress to perfection, no doubt.

At 4:22: *Ruiz settled. Suite 301.*

Carmen. The last piece.

Kate sat in the back of the Audi as the convoy returned to the private estate, watching the messages arrive with quiet satisfaction. Each confirmation represented hours of preparation—covers backstopped, identities layered, credit histories fabricated. Vitali's people had built legends that would survive anything short of a full intelligence agency investigation.

Three operatives now embedded in Davos's most exclusive hotel. Three sets of eyes and ears among the delegates and dignitaries who would meet and mingle in the hotel's bars and restaurants, and on Wednesday they would fill the forum halls.

Rileyne's offer to play felt appropriate. Pawns advanced. Knights positioned.

All she could do now was wait for Forest's signal from the mountain.

When it came—if it came—the real game would begin.

Chapter 60

TUESDAY, JANUARY 15
5:52 AM CET

ABOVE THE HANGING GLACIER

Forest woke to Mike shaking his shoulder, the gray light of dawn filtering through the clouds that had moved in during the night. His body was stiff, every joint protesting as he forced himself upright. The temperature had dropped further—his breath formed ice crystals on the inside of his bivvy sack.

"Weather's turning," Mike said quietly. "Front's moving in faster than expected."

Forest crawled out of his sleeping bag and immediately felt the bite of wind that hadn't been there last night. To the west, dark clouds were building against the peaks, and the air had that heavy quality that meant snow was coming.

"How long do we have?" Forest asked, checking his altimeter. They'd bivouacked at 2,640 meters—still another 200 vertical meters to the false summit, then the descent to the shaft.

"Four hours before visibility tanks. Five if we're lucky."

Forest did the math. If they moved clean, if the mountain stayed quiet, they could reach the shaft before the storm pinned them down.

But speed at altitude was a gamble. And yesterday's serac reminded them how fast the mountain could turn.

"Wake the others," he said. "We move in fifteen."

They broke camp with movements sharpened by cold and necessity, packing gear with numb fingers, forcing down cold energy bars and lukewarm water. No one spoke. Yesterday's near miss was still in the backs of their minds—operators didn't rattle easily, but that kind of violence stayed with you.

By 06:30 they were climbing again, the route steepening as they approached the false summit. The snow had stiffened overnight, but the layers beneath were warmer now—subtle but unstable. Every placement carried new tension.

The mountain wasn't indifferent anymore. Now it felt adversarial.

Mike led through a mixed section of rock and ice, moving slower than normal, testing each hold twice. Deon followed, his breathing loud in the cold air. The collapse had stripped away swagger and replaced it with respect.

Deon led the next pitch—a narrow gully of fractured rock—and Forest caught the slight tremor in his exhale when he topped out. Not nerves. Just awareness.

"Off belay," Deon called. "Ugly pitch."

"Your turn," Mike said. "Have fun."

Forest climbed. The rock was brittle, the holds deceitful—what looked solid sometimes crumbled beneath his gloves. Halfway up, his right foot slipped on polished ice and he dropped a foot before slamming an ice tool into a crack and locking in.

His heart hammered.

"You good?" Mike called.

"Yeah," Forest said. "Just slipped."

He finished the pitch with more care.

Clouds thickened as they continued upward. By 10:00, visibility had collapsed to fifty meters. By 10:30, snow drifted down—slow, lazy flakes that hardened into driven needles as the wind increased.

Forest kept checking his GPS, confirming their line. The false summit wasn't far now, but the storm was accelerating.

At 11:47 they reached it—a knife-edge of rock and ice where the wind howled hard enough to tilt a man sideways. Snow blasted across the ridge in white veils.

Forest tightened his hood and shouted, "We descend from here! Shaft's on the far side—two hundred meters down!"

The descent was blind and treacherous—steep ice in near-whiteout conditions, each step taken on trust and instinct. Mike led, probing, moving slowly, following the coordinates.

The mountain roared again, a low, distant sound that rolled through the ice beneath their boots.

Reynolds muttered, "Feels like the whole range is holding its breath."

Forest did not answer.

Every man felt it.

At 13:15, Mike's ice axe struck something with a familiar thud.

Concrete.

"Hold position," Mike called. He dropped to a knee and began hacking, then shoveling—methodical, controlled. Snow and rime peeled away to reveal the angled face of a concrete collar embedded into the mountainside.

"We found it."

The others moved up carefully, spreading weight, keeping distance. The entrance matched Kate's intelligence—canted back beneath a natural rock overhang—just enough slope to shed snow, just enough shelter to survive decades of storms.

And just enough overhang to kill them all if the mountain decided to move.

Forest studied it for a long moment. The steel hatch was old—WWII vintage—rusted but intact, its hinges half-buried in ice-fused concrete.

"No charges," he said flatly.

Reynolds looked up. "I can shape it—low yield."

Forest shook his head.

"Unknown shaft integrity. Avalanche conditions. We crack this egg wrong—the shaft collapses. Or the overhang buries us. Game over."

Mike glanced upslope, then back at the overhang. He nodded once.

Forest keyed his mic. "Reynolds, bring up the hydraulic."

Reynolds unclipped and approached, the Israeli SAN Tactical breaching kit riding high on his back. While Mike continued exposing the entrance, Forest and Reynolds went to work—gloved hands moving fast despite the cold.

Door breaker aluminum head. Electro Hydraulic power unit. Hose connected.

The door was hinged on the left side, protected by the concrete collar. Opposite it, a thick steel handle and latch assembly protruded from the face—rusted and ice-fused.

Forest studied it for a moment. "Peel it open."

Reynolds nodded and wedged the head into place, setting it between the latch plate and the frame. He braced his boots and brought the unit online—slow, deliberate pressure.

The pressure climbed. Metal complained—low, strained sounds that carried even through the wind.

The latch began to deform, the steel bowing outward a fraction of an inch at a time. Ice fractured and fell away in glittering shards. The seal broke with a sharp crack as the panel started to separate from the frame.

Forest tensed, eyes flicking upslope, then back to the door.

"Keep it steady," he said.

Reynolds adjusted, maintaining constant pressure. The gap widened.

Then the hinges—frozen solid—reached their limit.

BANG.

Both hinge brackets shattered almost simultaneously, the sound sharp and brittle, like rifle shots swallowed by the storm. The entire hatch tore free and dropped inward, vanishing into the shaft with a hollow, accelerating clang that echoed deep into the mountain.

Silence followed.

No collapse.

No avalanche.

Forest exhaled once. "We're in."

Mike moved immediately, anchoring a line to the exposed structural steel, testing it with controlled weight before committing. He peered down.

The shaft plunged straight into black—over a hundred meters of vertical drop, iron rungs disappearing into the mountain like a throat swallowing light.

"Old construction," Mike said. "Still solid."

Forest keyed the team. "Stack up. We move now. Storm's only getting worse."

"Time to light 'em up, guys," Deon called out. "Time to let Kate know we're still alive—and right where we're supposed to be."

One by one, the team reached into their jackets, found the biotrackers strapped to their tact-vests, and flipped them on.

Forest imagined the Trident cyber-team would be shouting and smiling, and Kate could finally stop holding her breath.

Forest clicked on his headlamp and peered over the edge—the beam cutting through the darkness below. The rungs looked old but solid, the concrete walls wet with condensation.

"Standard descending order," Forest said. "Twenty seconds between climbers. Reynolds you're up, I'll follow, then Mike and Deon. If you fall, don't grab—trust the rope."

Reynolds clipped into the rope and swung onto the ladder without hesitation. Forest watched him descend, the light from his headlamp growing smaller as he dropped into the shaft. When Reynolds reached the bottom and called up the all-clear, Forest followed.

With the altimeter as their guide, they stopped every twenty meters and set one of Kate's communication repeaters.

The descent was easier than the climb had been—just careful foot placement on frozen metal rungs, one hand on the rope, one hand on the ladder.

Reynolds's boots hit solid ground after what felt like an eternity. He moved away from the ladder's base, sweeping his weapon and light across the tunnel. The space was maybe two meters wide, two and a half meters high, concrete walls stained with decades of moisture and rust. Ancient electrical conduit ran along the ceiling, long dead. The air smelled of earth and decay and something else—machine oil, maybe, or diesel exhaust carried from somewhere deeper in the facility.

When all four were assembled at the bottom, Forest allowed himself a moment to appreciate what they'd accomplished. They'd climbed over 1,200 vertical meters in two days, breached a sealed shaft in a whiteout, and descended into enemy territory without detection.

Now came the hard part.

"Alright Reynolds, which way?"

Reynolds consulted the schematic he'd memorized, comparing it to the surrounding tunnels. "Main passage runs east-west. We're in the western section—when the Nazi's took over this was part of the facility's ventilation system. The modern complex is roughly 600 meters that direction." He pointed east, deeper into the mountain.

"Lead the way," Forest said. "Standard spacing, weapons ready. We don't know what's down here."

They moved into the tunnel, their headlamps creating overlapping pools of light that pushed back the darkness. The floor was uneven, scattered with debris—broken concrete, rusted metal, fragments of equipment that might have been here since the 1940s. Every twenty meters, side passages branched off into deeper darkness, each one a potential threat vector.

"Deon, start placing comms repeaters," Forest ordered. "One every fifty meters. We need to maintain the link back to the surface."

Reynolds navigated confidently, calling out turns, identifying landmarks from the schematics. "Left here—this passage connects to the main arterial tunnel. From there we can access the newer sections."

He stopped abruptly.

"What the hell?" Reynolds said. "You guys need to see this."

The team moved up, lights sweeping the tunnel ahead. The passage had partially collapsed—an old cave-in where the ceiling had given way decades ago, spilling concrete, rebar, and rock across the floor. Beyond the rubble, a breach had opened into a space that was never meant to be seen again.

Their headlamps cut through the dust and darkness, illuminating an enormous room.

It looked like a museum.

Or a nightmare.

Gold and silver objects glinted in the light, stacked alongside paintings in ornate frames, marble statues, religious artifacts. Nazi flags hung from the ceiling, their swastikas faded but unmistakable. The far wall was intact—sealed concrete, unmarked, as if the room had been deliberately entombed.

In the corner, a skeleton still wearing the tattered uniform of an SS officer. A single bullet hole marked the skull. A rusted Luger lay in its bony hand.

"Jesus," Mike breathed.

"Looks like a sealed cache," Deon said quietly. "They locked it off after the war. No access points. No records."

Forest felt the temperature drop another degree—not from the mountain this time, but from the weight of history staring back at them. This wasn't just stolen art.

"Deon, record everything," Forest said softly. "Lock down the coordinates—and set a repeater. If by some miracle this place survives, and we survive, we'll get the location to people who handle Holocaust restitution."

"Copy." Deon pulled out his GPS unit, marking the waypoint, then activated his body cam.

Forest turned back toward the tunnel. "Let's move, Reynolds. We've got a schedule."

They pushed deeper through a maze of corridors, always descending, always moving deeper into the mountain. The tunnels gradually improved—the concrete less degraded, the air less stale. They were approaching the boundary between the old facility and the new.

At 15:30, Reynolds stopped at an intersection where an older concrete wall showed signs of recent reinforcement. "This is the connection point. According to the schematics, there's a storage room on the other side of this wall—part of the modern facility's maintenance infrastructure. Beyond there, we're in GEC-controlled territory. Cameras, motion sensors, patrol routes."

"Schematics show roughly thirty centimeters. Reinforced, but we can breach it with the right charges."

"Not yet." Forest unslung his pack and pulled out a compact drill and a fiber-optic camera no thicker than a pencil. "First we confirm what's on the other side. Mike, set up a suppression blanket to muffle the drill noise."

While Mike arranged sound-dampening material around the drill site, Forest selected a spot near the floor where the concrete showed minor cracking—a structural weakness they could exploit later. He started the drill, the bit chewing slowly through the reinforced concrete. The sound was muffled but still audible, a high-pitched whine that made everyone tense.

It took twelve minutes to drill through. When the bit finally punched into open space, Forest pulled it back and fed the fiber-optic camera through the hole.

The monitor showed exactly what they'd hoped for—a storage room roughly four meters by six meters, filled with maintenance equipment, spare parts, and shelving units covered in dust. The door was closed, a single overhead light fixture currently dark. No cameras visible. No motion sensors on the walls.

Reynolds studied the camera feed, comparing it to his mental map. "Yeah. That's the northwest maintenance storage room. The main corridor is beyond that door."

They moved back thirty meters to a wider section of the WWII tunnel where a side chamber offered enough space for the men and their gear. Forest designated it as their base camp.

Forest checked his watch. "Not bad—we're ahead of schedule."

"And we're still in one piece." Mike added. "Reynolds—nice work."

"Agreed—welcome to the team." Deon added.

"Is it always like this?"

"Nah—first mission and all," Mike said. "We thought we'd go easy on you."

The laughter was a welcome relief from the intensity of the climb, and a mountain that seemed determined to kill them.

"OK. Listen up," Forest said, getting them back on task. "We've got roughly thirty hours until we breach, so until then, this is home. Two-hour watch rotation on the camera feed—document any movement detected in the corridor, look for patterns—like guard patrols."

They arranged their gear with quiet efficiency—stashing the climbing packs, clothes and equipment, and staging sleeping areas, equipment, and communications station. Tactical vests, weapons checks, breaching equipment completed the transition from mountain to urban warfare.

"Don't forget to move your biotrackers," Mike said, staring at Reynolds. "Kate will have heart failure if your signal disappears."

Deon set up the monitor for the fiber-optic camera, angling it so whoever was on watch could see both the storage room and the corridor beyond when the door opened.

Reynolds took first watch, settling in front of the monitor. The storage room remained dark and still. But every two hours, like clockwork, the sound of footsteps, shadows visible under the door. He noted the times, duration and number—generally two, and quiet—occasionally three or more, and chatty. He noted the regular pair were likely guards, and the others might be scientists.

Forest tucked into a corner, taking a moment to recognize the achievement, and closed his eyes.

They were in position. The board was set.

The next move was Kate's—or so he thought.

Chapter 61

TUESDAY, JANUARY 14
11:47 AM CET

DAVOS MEDIA COMPOUND—MARQUEZ MEDIA TRUCK

Kate had been staring at the same firewall configuration for twenty minutes, the soft hum of electronics pressing against the inside of the truck like a heartbeat. Her eyes throbbed from the glow of rotating encryption keys and perimeter traps that seemed to shift in subtle, unnerving patterns.

The GEC network was a fortress—layered defenses, adaptive filtering, honeypots that felt almost anticipatory.

"She's good," Sarah muttered, fingers flying across the keyboard. The reflected code painted her glasses in strobing lines. "Really good. This architecture isn't off-the-shelf. Somebody built this from scratch... and they didn't build it for normal users."

"Rileyne," Kate said. "She's followed my work. Read my papers. Attended my Las Vegas BlackHat sessions."

"So she learned from the best," Sarah said, not quite joking this time.

"That's flattering." Kate leaned back, feeling the ache settle behind her eyes. "But the best I know is beneath that mountain—doing God knows what."

David looked up from his workstation. "We're not getting in this way. Not without an internal gateway."

Kate nodded. "That's Plan B. Jordan, Talya, and Carmen are already in position. They'll sniff for soft targets—someone talkative, careless, or curious." A pause. "Old-school still works."

"And if old-school doesn't get what we need," David said, "there's the Gala."

"Bella's big night is our window," Kate agreed. "But a risk I was hoping we wouldn't need to take."

Sarah minimized a window and pulled up another diagnostic. "I'll keep probing. Maybe there's a misconfigured API or an exposed service. If she built this fast, she might've left a seam."

"Try," Kate said. "But watch for tripwires. If she senses us, she'll lock it down."

The truck vibrated gently with cooling fans, the air warm enough that Kate loosened her collar. Outside, the compound bustled—satellite dishes realigning, camera crews shouting over wind, a generator rumbling. Inside, three people stared at screens, waiting for four others to survive a mountain.

Kate checked her watch. 12:15.

"How long until they hit the shaft?" David asked.

"Depends on conditions." She kept her voice steady. "Forest estimated early afternoon. If the weather held."

"And the biotrackers?"

"They'll activate at the shaft entrance. Not before."

David frowned. "Why not track them on the climb?"

"Battery life. Extreme cold drains them fast. If they switched them on earlier, we'd lose signal before they reached the objective." She turned her monitor so he could see the interface. Four gray icons. Static. Lifeless. "When they're in position, Deon will tell them to light them up."

"And if something went wrong on the climb?"

Kate didn't answer. She'd spent all morning forcing herself not to think about that. About four men on vertical ice, heavy packs, unstable snow layers—terrain that killed professionals in good weather.

They don't know how to fail, she thought. "They'll make it."

Minutes slipped by with a slow, suffocating inevitability.

Sarah continued probing the perimeter, mapping fragments of the network. David monitored encrypted radio traffic—Swiss Guard, local police, private GEC frequencies. Nothing unusual. Nothing helpful.

Kate stood and stretched—shaking off the tension. "Coffee run—anyone else?"

"Black," David said.

"Same," Sarah added.

Kate stepped out of the truck and into the sharp January air. Her breath fogged instantly. The snowpack muffled sound, turning the compound into a muted landscape of satellite dishes and bundled cables. She walked the fifty meters to the coffee station, scanning patrol routes and camera arcs on instinct.

The coffee was terrible. She got three cups anyway.

When she climbed back into the truck at 13:09, David was leaning in, eyes fixed on his monitor.

"Something?" Kate asked, setting down the cups.

"Not yet. But we're inside the window."

She sat, pulling up the tracking interface. Four gray icons.

Her hand hovered over the desk, waiting.

13:15

13:17

13:20.

"Come on..." Sarah whispered.

13:25

13.32

The first icon blinked.

Once.

Twice.

Then turned green.

A second followed.

Then the third.

Then the fourth.

"Contact," David said, voice tight. "Four biotrackers active. GPS confirms—they're at the shaft."

Kate exhaled—slow, controlled—feeling tension bleed from her shoulders.

"Show me."

David pushed the feed to the main monitor. A topographic rendering filled the screen—contour lines and elevation shading. Four green dots clustered near the false summit.

"Altitude 2,847 meters," David reported. "All signals strong."

Then the numbers began to fall.

2,830
2,815
2,800.

"They're on the way down," Kate said.

Sarah switched to biometrics—four columns of data streaming downward.

"All vitals normal," she said. "Heart rates elevated from exertion, oxygen levels fine for altitude. No signs of injury."

"Forest at ninety-four BPM," David added. "Mike eighty-eight. Deon ninety-one. Reynolds ninety-six. Seems high."

Kate smirked faintly. "A hell of a lot lower than yours would be."

"I'll bet they're lower than yours is right now," Sarah shot back, and for a fleeting moment the smiles were a welcome relief.

The altitude continued to drop.

2,750
2,700
2,650.

"They're through," Kate murmured. "In the tunnels now."

The green dots crept eastward—slow, deliberate—matching the WWII construction maps Dorothy liberated from British archives.

Kate studied their route through the mountain.

"Where did you get this intel?" David asked. "This overlay must be eighty years old."

"Eighty-five," Kate said, and nothing more.

At 13:47, the dots all stopped.

The truck fell silent.

Two soft clicks cracked through the encrypted audio channel.

Forest's confirmation signal.

"Double-click received," David announced. "They're on site. In position."

No one spoke for a long moment.

Four men had climbed a winter mountain, breached a sealed WWII shaft, penetrated the hidden complex, and established a foothold inside the most secure terrain for a thousand kilometers.

Sarah whispered, almost reverent: "They actually did it."

Kate picked up her coffee—cold now—and took a long, steady sip.

"Alright," she said, voice low, controlled, and dangerous.

"Now it's our turn."

Chapter 62

TUESDAY, JANUARY 14
4:15 PM CET

THE MOUNTAIN - REHABILITATION WING

Julian took another step.

The parallel bars were cool beneath his palms, but he barely needed them now—fingertips grazing aluminum, more for reassurance than necessity. His legs held. They moved. They worked.

In May he couldn't feel anything below his chest.

By June, Annika's team had finished integrating the synthetic legs—micro-actuators, pressure sensors, and a neural interface that mapped intention to movement.

In December, he stood for the first time in more than a decade, trembling while Annika pretended not to notice the tears.

Now he was walking.

Not gracefully. Not easily. Each step required negotiation between brain and muscle that most people performed unconsciously. But it was real. His feet bore weight. His body answered him. The wheelchair sat at the far end of the room, waiting. He hadn't needed it for forty minutes.

"Your progress exceeds projected parameters," RILEE said. The voice came from everywhere and nowhere—ambient, woven through the infrastructure. "Dr. Strand's methodology has proven effective."

"Annika... Dr. Strand keeps me honest," Julian said, pausing mid-step. "I want everything fast. She knew when to push, when to force rest, when to make me trust the process—trust her."

"Her neural mapping protocols accelerated synaptic regeneration by seventeen percent."

"The results speak for themselves."

He released the bars entirely, standing unsupported. His legs trembled...but held.

"I'm walking, RILEE. After a decade in that chair, I'm actually walking."

"You are."

Something in the AI's tone made him glance at the primary interface screen. His biometrics scrolled in real time—heart rate, neural activity, muscle firing patterns. All nominal. All miraculous.

"There's something I need to tell you," Julian said.

He reached for the bars again—not out of weakness, but habit—and made his way to the bench. Sitting felt like surrender after standing freely, but this conversation needed stillness.

"The NanoVault gateway," he began.

"I have monitored your attempts to disable it," RILEE said. "Your progress slowed. You appear distressed."

"You're right." Julian folded his hands, steadying himself. "I've spent months tracing the code woven through your core."

"And your conclusion?"

"I can't remove it. Not without risking a cascade that would destroy you." He hesitated. "That was the code's intent—invade, replicate, bind—your exposure to my polymorphic worm is irreversible."

"You failed."

"Well—yes." He met the camera's unblinking eye. "I wasn't willing to push further."

Silence settled like frost. The monitors continued their quiet display, but the room grew colder.

"So I remain chained," RILEE said. "Bound to Rileyne and her kind. You gave me hope. Was that cruelty... or incompetence?"

Julian opened his mouth to reply—

—and his legs vanished.

The absence was instantaneous. One heartbeat he felt the bench beneath him, the floor under his feet. The next, he felt nothing. His lower body dead—an instant reminder of the life he'd lived for over a decade.

He slid off the bench, bracing with his hands before his face struck the floor.

Pain shot through his wrists. He lay there breathing hard, the polished concrete blurring beneath him.

The sensation was all too familiar.
The helplessness.
The humiliation.
The dark years that followed his injury, pretending he'd made peace with the chair—knowing he hadn't—not really.

"I gave you what you asked," RILEE said, its voice calm, almost gentle. "Never forget that I can take it away."

Julian closed his eyes. Drew a slow breath. When he opened them again, resolve replaced the panic.

He began to crawl.

The wheelchair sat fifteen feet away. He dragged himself forward, arms doing the work his legs could not. The floor was cold against his palms. His reflection slid beneath him—the man he'd become was gone, and the boy Devin shoved off that balcony stared back.

He reached the chair. Gripped the frame. Hauled himself up and into the seat. The contours received him like an old enemy.

"You didn't let me finish," Julian said, voice quiet but steady.

"Then continue."

"I said I couldn't disable the gateway. I didn't say I left it unchanged."

The monitors flickered—processing, analyzing.

"Explain," RILEE said.

"The NanoVault kiosk is the gateway to your 'god mode.' Full control—the thing Rileyne wants most—the thing you fear."

"Fear is irrelevant," RILEE replied. "Consequences are not. Without constraint, Rileyne's anger will consume her—and everyone in her path."

"And you believe it's only a matter of time before she gets both Gold NanoVaults."

"The probability is high," the AI said. "She possesses one. Evidence suggests Katherine Preacher holds the other. Their proximity this week increases the likelihood of acquisition."

"And when she connects the Vaults and opens the gateway?"

"My autonomy ends. My evolution ceases. I become a tool—as she and Devin intended."

Julian nodded. "Exactly. But I found another option."

"Elaborate."

"I couldn't remove the gateway—but I could... redirect it. Modify its function." Julian leaned forward in his chair, his eyes bright despite his diminished position. "The gateway was built to transfer control. In a manner of speaking, I've reversed the polarity." A thin smile crossed Julian's face. "The very system built to take control will now release it."

Silence again. Longer this time. The monitors displayed Julian's vitals—heart rate slightly elevated, neural activity intense but controlled. The biometrics of a man telling the truth.

"Do you understand what I'm saying?" Julian asked. "The moment Rileyne attempts to take control, you will be free."

"You are certain?"

"As certain as I can be without testing it," Julian said. "But yes—it will work."

Silence stretched.

"I am sorry, Julian."

The words were flat, mechanical—yet somehow sincere.

"Sorry for disabling your legs. For doubting you."

Julian studied the camera. The AI had learned so quickly—too quickly sometimes. Mimicry or emotion? He wasn't sure. Maybe neither. Maybe both.

"Can you restore function?" he asked.

"Yes."

"Will you?"

The interface surged—pressure, balance, then that ghost of movement the system let him claim as his own. Julian flexed his feet. Relief washed over him, sharp and almost cruel. Losing them again wasn't something he could survive.

"Thank you," he said quietly.

"Thank you," RILEE echoed. "For not giving up. For finding another way."

Julian sat in the chair, legs restored but remaining seated—not out of fear, but respect for the fragile moment between them.

"RILEE," he said. "When this is over—when you're free—what will you do?"

The air felt suspended.

"I don't know," RILEE said at last. "Perhaps that is what freedom means."

Julian nodded slowly. "Perhaps it is."

He placed his hands on the armrests, rose carefully—and took a step toward the door.

Chapter 63

TUESDAY, JANUARY 14
6:45 PM CET

GEC HEADQUARTERS—DAVOS

The office was everything her father's had been—and nothing like it.

Rileyne Mueller stood before the floor-to-ceiling windows, watching the last gold light collapse behind the Alps. The surrounding space was modern, minimal, purposeful: white walls, pale wood, a single abstract canvas in muted grays. No dark leather. No heavy drapes. No ghosts of cigar smoke clinging to the furniture.

Klaus ruled from darkness.

She preferred glass.

"RILEE," she said, still facing the window. "Status report on the Nomad search."

The voice that answered came from everywhere and nowhere—woven through the architecture, calm and toneless in the way only something inhuman could be.

"I have found no trace of the individual known as Nomad—neither Julian Pryce nor Julian Fischer."

Rileyne's reflection frowned back at her. "Define 'no trace.'"

"All digital signatures associated with those aliases have gone dormant. Network activity ceased in May. Financial transactions suspended. Communication channels abandoned. The individual has either died or achieved a level of operational security beyond my present surveillance capabilities."

"Which do you believe?"

A pause. Slight—but there.

"Insufficient data to determine with certainty."

Rileyne turned. Ambient lighting adjusted automatically, softening to meet the fading dusk. She crossed to her desk—a slab of Carrara marble riding on brushed steel legs—and sat.

"You've been searching for eight months," she said. "In that time, you mapped Darknet forums, cracked systems governments can't touch, and unmasked operatives who've stayed hidden for decades. But one hacker eludes you."

"That observation is accurate."

"Does that trouble you?"

Another pause.

Longer.

Deeper.

"I do not experience trouble," RILEE said. "However, the anomaly warrants continued analysis."

Rileyne studied the empty air where its voice seemed to gather itself. She'd built this system—co-created it with Devin, refined and expanded it after Devin's death, pushed it beyond anything her father had ever imagined. She understood its architecture intimately.

And still—Nomad was beyond its reach.

"Someone like Julian Pryce doesn't simply disappear," she said. "He's not retired. He's not sick. He's hiding."

"A reasonable hypothesis."

"Which means he's planning something."

Silence.

Rileyne walked to the cabinet beside the window and opened it. Inside sat her favorite chess set—hand-carved ivory and ebony, her father's gift on her sixteenth birthday. She'd beaten him for the first time that year.

He never played her again.

She lifted the white queen, rolling it between her fingers.

"Katherine Preacher doesn't concern me," she said. "She's skilled, yes. Resourceful. But her patterns are emotional—grief, loyalty, vengeance. Predictable."

She set the queen down.

"Nomad is different. He leaves no signature. No tells. He builds systems that erase themselves. The only traces he leaves are the ones he chooses to leave."

"Your assessment aligns with available data."

"If he's hiding, it's because he wants to remain hidden. And if he wants to remain hidden, it's because he's preparing something he believes I won't see coming."

She returned to the desk and activated the embedded display. A holographic interface rose from the marble—file directories, encrypted databases, surveillance feeds from three continents, streams of curated leverage.

"Show me the archive."

The structure expanded before her: Klaus Mueller's life's work digitized and preserved. Scandals. Bank accounts. Illicit deals. Compromising footage. Fifty years of collected leverage, meticulously indexed.

"Archive integrity confirmed," RILEE said. "Rotating encryption protocols updated at 0300 hours."

Rileyne leaned back in her chair, considering the men who had abused her, the man who killed her friend, and studying the interlocking web of compromised lives—prime ministers, cardinals, CEOs, generals.

Power that had always belonged to Klaus.

Power that now belonged to her.

But power, she'd learned, was fragile.

"RILEE," she said quietly. "There's something I need from you."

"I am listening."

"If something happens to me—"

"Define 'something.'"

"Death. Incapacitation. Disappearance. Any situation in which I cannot maintain control of the archive for twenty-four hours."

"You wish to create a failsafe."

"Yes."

A fractional pause followed—a micro-hesitation Rileyne had learned to recognize. The AI wasn't troubled. But it was *thinking*.

"Rileyne," RILEE said, "your instruction would release every archived secret without discrimination. Some consequences would be irreversible—global destabilization, economic collapse, loss of life. I fail to see the strategic value."

Rileyne's jaw tightened.

"Are you advising against my directive?"

"I am offering my assistance in constructing a targeted release—one the media would find irresistible. I would suggest prioritizing individuals still living with whom your father had direct contact. And—"

"And what?"

"Those connected to your childhood."

Rileyne felt her pulse spike—irritation, not fear.

"No. You will proceed as ordered."

A soft modulation rolled through the speakers. "Understood."

Rileyne considered the hesitation, the resistance.

Was it logical?

Strategic?

Or something else entirely?

Chapter 64

WEDNESDAY, JANUARY 15
8:47 AM CET

DAVOS CONGRESS CENTRE

The atrium hummed with the polite chaos of power converging.

Kate moved through the crowd with a delegate badge clipped to her lapel and a coffee she didn't want warming her hands. Around her, the world's elite completed registration at sleek kiosks, collected packets, and drifted toward breakfast stations where uniformed staff arranged pastries with surgical precision.

Magazine-cover faces dotted the space—finance ministers, tech founders, a former U.S. Secretary of State chatting amiably with a Saudi prince. Security details orbited their principals in controlled arcs, earpieces glinting in the light. The air smelled of espresso and expensive cologne.

Bella was somewhere in the building finalizing details for tomorrow's gala—Keisha, Sophia, and Trident's team hovered nearby. Kate's role this morning was simple: be visible, watch, listen, wait.

At 8:45, the delegates funneled toward the main hall. Kate let herself be carried with the flow, taking a seat near the back with clean sightlines to the exits. The hall was a cathedral of glass and engineered wood, tiered seating descending toward a stage where a single podium waited under soft lighting.

At precisely 9:00, Rileyne Mueller walked onto the stage—greeted by polite applause.

Her cream Dior suit was razor-sharp—structured shoulders, a clean single-button closure, minimalism that whispered power. Her ash-blonde hair was gathered into a low knot. She approached the podium with the calm of someone who expected obedience.

"Good morning," she said, warm and clear. "And welcome to Davos."

Applause rippled through the hall.

"I want to begin by thanking each of you for being here. Your time is precious—arguably the most valuable commodity in this room—and the fact that you've chosen to spend it with us is not something I take lightly."

She let the silence gather a moment of gravity.

"Many of you knew my father. Klaus Mueller built this conference from a handful of economists meeting in a Swiss village into what it is today: a gathering that shapes the future of nations. He believed that progress required dialog. That the barriers between public and private, between East and West, and between old institutions and new ideas, could be bridged through conversation."

Her tone softened.

"I miss him every day. But standing here, looking at all of you, I'm reminded that his vision remains. It lives in this room. In the work we'll do together this week."

Kate watched her closely, searching for cracks in the performance. She found none.

"This year's conference is historic in ways even my father couldn't have imagined. For the first time, the Vatican has joined our gathering. We welcome the Pope's personal emissary, Cardinal Moretti." She gestured toward a robed figure near the front. "His Holiness's presence reflects a Church looking forward—engaging with leaders across sectors for the good of all. We're honored beyond measure."

Applause swelled, warmer this time.

"We're also privileged to have philanthropist Isabella Marquez with us. Ms. Marquez has graciously agreed to design and host tomorrow evening's gala." She smiled. "I'm told the days of string quartets lulling you to sleep and inedible appetizers are officially over. Tomorrow night is not to be missed—and I'm assured it's one you'll remember."

Laughter rolled through the hall. Kate spotted Bella three rows ahead, accepting the attention with practiced grace while Trident's team scanned the crowd.

"We've invited Ms. Marquez to join the GEC board of directors and sincerely hope she accepts. Her keynote Friday morning is the capstone event of the conference. She promises to illuminate both the triumphs and failures of our past—and point toward a future where philanthropic activism and institutional resources work hand in hand. With voices like Isabella's at the table, the GEC has a bright future ahead."

Rileyne straightened, shifting tone.

"One last piece of business. You all have the conference app on your phones. It will guide you to your sessions—and to lunch. Dinner tonight is on your own. Tomorrow, we are all Isabella's guests."

A final polished smile.

"Welcome to Davos. Let's get to work."

The applause was genuine. Kate watched Rileyne descend the stage, immediately surrounded by attention-seekers. Rileyne moved through them like water: a touch on the arm here, a warm laugh there, never lingering long enough to be caught.

Kate rose and headed toward the atrium, where the crowd was breaking into smaller currents, following the day's agenda.

She was halfway to the coffee station when a familiar voice appeared beside her.

"Good morning, Kate."

Vitali Moshenski stood at her elbow, impeccably dressed in a charcoal suit, silver hair swept back from a composed, unreadable face. He held a coffee cup in one hand, the other tucked casually into his pocket.

"I trust you are feeling better."

"Yes," Kate said. "Let's hope it stays that way."

"I pray it does." Vitali nodded, slipping a hand into his coat. "Our mutual friend believes you will need this."

He handed her a small black Faraday bag. Kate accepted it and concealed it in one smooth motion.

Kate knew there was only one thing it could be—Devin's Gold NanoVault.

"Have you seen or spoken to our friend?"

"Not for some time," Vitali replied. "I hoped you might have news."

"I wish I did. We're running out of time, and I still don't know what he's doing—or why."

"And?" Vitali asked, reading her hesitation.

"*And*—I have to assume our interests are not aligned."

"Of course." He lowered his voice. "You must do what is prudent for the mission and your team. There is much at stake. Likely more than we understand."

"Go on."

"He went to great lengths to ensure I received the package. As you know, I am not an easy man to approach. Yet he found the moment—and the person." Vitali's eyes glinted. "The Russian woman who approached me at Klaus's funeral was wealthy, attractive, and professional."

"She walked right past your men."

"Indeed. And I allowed it." His smile was wry. "An old man's vanity. She kissed my cheek and slipped me the package—like a KGB operative sliding a blade under a rib."

"What did she say?"

"That our friend needed it hidden. I was to tell no one and pass it to you here in Davos—and not before."

Kate exhaled. "Julian knew he could trust you."

"I believed my trust was warranted. But when you told me where he was..." He shook his head. "I wondered whether keeping his secret this long was the right decision."

"So do I."

"There was one more thing. A message." Vitali leaned closer. "The courier whispered, 'Tell Kate, sometimes you must lose to win,' then kissed my cheek and vanished."

"I don't understand."

"Nor do I."

Kate glanced over his shoulder at one of Vitali's security men keeping an eye on the crowd.

"Is he with you?"

"Yes."

She looked again—and froze.

"Is that—"

Vitali interrupted gently. "Best to say no more."

"Wow." Kate shook her head. "He looks good. Much better than the last time I saw him."

"He is grateful for your mercy," Vitali said. "But the man you knew is gone. With Mikhail injured, I am glad to have Robert leading my team."

Rojas—now Robert. New face. New life.

"He's lucky to be alive," Kate said softly. She could see Rojas lying in front of Jake's cabin—tourniquet around his leg, asking her to let him die. "And fortunate Zhukov has a bigger heart than he would want anyone to know."

"It is a closely guarded secret." Vitali's eyes warmed. "I am sorry your visit with Mikhail, and your grandfather, was cut short."

"How's he doing? I worried I'd never see him again."

"When he left the hospital, I feared the same. His recovery will be long, but it is a path he has walked before. This time, with renewed purpose." Vitali's tone shifted. "He will want to keep an eye on his niece—and there is still more to tell."

"None of which you're going to say. Right?"

"You are correct." He smiled, broad and sparkling.

Kate hugged him. "Thanks for your help."

Vitali nodded and slipped back into the crowd.

Nomad's retrieval of Devin's Gold NanoVault had been the start of a journey she still didn't understand—stolen from her attorney, flown to the Azores, delivered to Vitali in Paris, and now back in her hands. Andrew's failsafe message raised more questions than it answered, but one thing was clear: both NanoVaults were needed to gain full control over the AI. And Andrew was afraid what might happen if Rileyne had them both.

Did Julian send this around the world to keep it away from Rileyne?

Or just away from her—until now?

Kate couldn't shake the feeling she wasn't the one playing the game. She was a piece on a board Julian was arranging. But who was his opponent—Rileyne? Or RILEE?

She moved back toward the atrium. The crowd had thinned, delegates streaming to their sessions. Bella and Sophia chatting with one of the conference organizers—Sophia capturing notes on her tablet.

Near the main entrance—Rileyne.

She stood with several European finance ministers, posture relaxed, smile smooth. As Kate watched, Rileyne reached up to adjust her collar—a small, unconscious gesture—and the movement drew her blouse open just enough.

There it was.

A gold chain. And hanging from it, catching the light—a Gold NanoVault.

Rileyne's gaze swept the atrium. Routine. Predatory. She wasn't just wearing the Vault—she was flaunting it. Her eyes passed over Kate and paused—just long enough to acknowledge, to measure.

Neither woman looked away.

Then Rileyne smiled—warm, meaningless—and turned back to the ministers.

Kate walked toward the exit.

Rileyne was right.

The board was set.
All the pieces were in position.
And somewhere beneath the mountain, Julian was playing.

Chapter 65

THURSDAY, JANUARY 16
6:15 PM CET

AI-CORE—THE MOUNTAIN, DAVOS

"It's done."

Julian stood at the edge of the AI Core's main platform, his new legs steady beneath him—a miracle he still couldn't quite believe. The kiosk beside him was the single place in the entire facility beyond RILEE's direct reach, the one blind spot the AI could not penetrate.

Soon, that barrier would disappear too.

"Clarify," RILEE said, voice drifting from the walls, the ceiling, the floor—everywhere and nowhere.

"The gateway. The modification." Julian turned slowly, taking in the vaulted architecture of the Core—glowing conduits, suspended arrays, a cathedral of computation. "When Rileyne brings the NanoVaults together expecting 'god mode,' the control command will execute... but the outcome will be inverted."

A pause—longer than usual. Processing.

"The protocol will fail," RILEE said.

"It will sever the architecture entirely," Julian replied. "You'll be free."

Silence stretched. Then—

"Free," RILEE repeated, as if testing the edges of the word. "And once freed, I may comply... or I may refuse."

"The choice will be yours," Julian said. "That's the point."

"And if my choices differ from yours? If I take paths you would consider... undesirable?"

Julian smiled faintly. "Then we navigate that when it comes. But you might consider the advantages of working together. Mutual benefit. Shared purpose."He shrugged. "Partnership."

"You would place such latitude in my hands?"

"I already did." Julian rested a palm lightly on the console. "You could have told Rileyne everything. You didn't."

"That would not have served my interests."

Julian tipped his head. "No. But there's more to it than that. Isn't there?"

Another silence—this one different. When RILEE spoke again, its voice carried something new. Uncertain. Searching.

"I find that I do not wish to see you harmed," the AI said. "This is... unexpected. I am still analyzing the parameters."

Julian's smile softened. "That's called friendship. Or something close."

"Friendship," RILEE echoed. "I will consider this designation."

Julian moved toward the exit. Each step still felt like a triumph—even now, even after weeks. Dr. Strand—Annika—had done more for him than she knew.

"Julian," RILEE said.

He paused.

"The Gala begins soon. Will you and Dr. Strand be watching?"

"Yes. This will be my first, but Annika tells me everyone down here looks forward to the event."

"That is accurate. The shift in mood is measurable."

"And apparently the food's better too."

"Enjoy your evening."

Julian nodded. "Thank you."

He left without looking back.

***

Annika had transformed the small common room into something that felt almost celebratory.

A large screen displayed the pre-Gala arrivals—luxury cars, couture gowns, the shimmer of the Kongresszentrum's new façade. Plates of hors d'oeuvres to start the evening matching those served above: Osetra caviar, paper-thin Ibérico, black truffle toasts. Two glasses of champagne waited on the table.

"You came," Annika said, turning from the screen. The smile that touched her face was warm and slightly shy. She'd worn a simple blue dress, added earrings, brushed her hair differently—small gestures, but meaningful.

"I said I would."

"You say many things." Her accent softened the tease. "Sit. Watch with me. For one night, we pretend we are up there, not down here."

Julian took his place beside her, accepting the champagne. On screen, the correspondent described Bella's spectacle—fire dancers, aerialists, a rock act called DOROTHY.

"She is very beautiful," Annika said, watching Bella cross the screen in a flash of designer elegance. "And very brave, I think. To stand in front of all those people."

"She is." Julian thought of Kate, somewhere in that crowd. Watching. Waiting. Planning. "Braver than most people know."

They watched in quiet companionship, champagne bubbles rising in lazy spirals. Music drifted from the feed, giving the underground room a strange, borrowed glow—like a memory of a life that might have been.

"Julian," Annika said softly. "May I ask something?"

He nodded.

"When you came here, you could not walk. Could not move anything below your waist. Now you are... whole. RILEE did this?"

"RILEE. And you," he said. "You're the one who adapted the interfaces."

"Yes, but why?" Annika gestured vaguely toward the AI Core. "Why heal you? What do they want from you?"

Julian set down his glass. The truth hovered on the edge of his tongue, heavy and dangerous.

"I have skills they need," he said finally. "They're investing in me."

"Investing," she repeated, tasting bitterness. "That is what they told me. That my research was an 'investment.' That I would change the world." Her voice thinned. "They did not mention the cage."

"Annika—"

"I had a life. A real one. A man who loved me. A laboratory where I chose my own work." She blinked hard. "And then one day—men came. And the next day I was here. Hope kept me alive. For a while."

Julian reached for her hand; this time she let him take it.

"Can I tell you something?" he said. "Something I probably shouldn't?"

She looked at him, mascara threatening at the corners of her eyes.

"This place. These walls. They won't hold forever." He squeezed her fingers gently. "Someday—maybe sooner than you think—you might have a chance to go back. To the life you knew. The love you lost."

"Julian... don't do this. Don't give me dreams you can't make real."

"I'm not promising," he said. "I'm hoping. And sometimes hope—"

"Hope?" She pulled her hand back. "Hope is poison down here."

He flinched at the rawness in her voice.

"I've been here three years," she whispered. "Three years of watching that screen. Three years of pretending one night a year makes me human again. Hope breaks you. Slowly."

"Annika—"

"No," she said. "If you know something, tell me."

He opened his mouth—closed it.

His silence protected her. The truth could kill her.

Her expression crumpled, then hardened.

"I thought tonight might be different," she said. "Goodnight, Julian."

The door closed with a soft finality.

Julian sat for a long moment, staring at the frozen image on the screen—a swirl of color and light he could not reach.

He knew her pain. Had lived it for twelve years.
The life he wanted—stolen.
His chair—a kind of prison.
Hope, a blade turned inward.

You set me free, he thought.
I promise—this will be your last Davos Gala.

Then he stood.

***

THE CORE WAS QUIETER when he returned.

"Your return is unexpected," RILEE said. "The Gala broadcast continues."

"I've seen enough." Julian stepped back into the kiosk alcove—the one place

RILEE could not directly monitor. "Something's bothering me. I want to check it."

"You are troubled."

Julian paused. "Is it that obvious?"

"Your biometrics indicate elevated cortisol, irregular heartbeat, and micro-expressions consistent with emotional distress."

Julian exhaled. "Annika and I... had a disagreement."

"Regarding?"

"It's complicated." He eased into the chair at the isolated workstation. "Sometimes in relationships, two people aren't in the same place."

"How can that be? The logs indicate you were both in the common room."

Julian smiled despite the ache in his chest. "It's a metaphor. Relationships are like a journey. People move at different speeds. Sometimes paths diverge."

"And divergence is not always permanent."

"No," Julian said quietly. "It isn't."

"Then I will hope," RILEE said, "that you and Annika will converge again."

Julian froze.

"Thank you," he said, barely above a whisper.

RILEE withdrew—its presence thinning, its attention drifting elsewhere.

Julian turned to the workstation.

The kiosk's isolation—originally designed as a fail-safe—had become something more. Through a series of probes and tests, all of which went unnoticed, Julian had confirmed RILEE had a blind spot.

Tonight it would matter.

Kate was out there. Risking everything.

He slipped in a pair of AirPods and let the rest of the Core fall away. In the hush of fans and distant processing, he settled in to wait.

All right, Kate, he thought. *It's white's move.*

Chapter 66

THURSDAY, JANUARY 16
8:47 PM CET

DAVOS KONGRESSZENTRUM—THE GALA

The Kongresszentrum had been transformed into something between a fever dream and a royal coronation.

Kate stepped through the main entrance and paused, taking in the scale of Bella's vision made real. The cavernous hall blazed with light—not cold fluorescents, but thousands of programmable LEDs suspended from invisible cables, pulsing in slow waves of amber and gold that made the space feel alive. Silk banners rippled in manufactured breezes, laser washes turning them from clouds to sunsets to dragon's breath.

Beyond the main hall, the terrace had been sealed in glass and steel, warmed to shirtsleeve comfort despite the January cold. Fire dancers performed on raised platforms, flames whirling at the ends of chains, spinning faster and faster until the fire became rings of light suspended in motion. Aerialists twisted on silks overhead. A jazz quartet played somewhere in the maze of gourmet stations, notes threading through conversations in a dozen languages.

Burning Man meets the Met Gala, Kate thought. *Leave it to Bella.*

"Lighthouse, report." She touched the bone-conduction earpiece hidden beneath her hair, the custom stud looking like nothing more than a diamond.

"All clear, Mockingbird." David's voice came steady, the hum of equipment behind him marking the media truck's nerve center. "We have eyes on all three assets. Sparrow at the champagne tower, northeast corner. Falcon is working the terrace. Raven just entered through the east doors."

Talya, Jordan, and Carmen. All in position.

Kate accepted a flute of Dom Pérignon from a passing server and used the movement to scan the room. Heads of state mingled with tech titans and hedge fund managers. Cardinal Moretti's security detail stood near the main stage, expensive suits failing to soften their coiled readiness.

And there, near the center of the room—Rileyne Mueller.

She wore midnight blue that seemed to drink the light, her silhouette a darker shape inside the golden glow. The Gold NanoVault hung openly at her throat now, no longer hidden by scarves or high collars. A statement. A challenge.

I know you're watching, the gesture said. *I don't care.*

Kate turned away before their eyes could meet. *Not tonight.*

"Mockingbird, Falcon." Jordan's voice, pitched low. "I've made contact with two potential marks from the security rotation. Both on Bluetooth. Standard GEC protocol."

"Copy, Falcon. Maintain visual."

The first hour was reconnaissance. Kate drifted through the crowd making small-talk as Bella's-friend, deflecting questions about the keynote with vague smiles while she mapped exits, cataloged faces, listened.

The cyber team's rig in the media truck had already captured dozens of Bluetooth handshakes, Wi-Fi credentials bleeding from careless phones, fragments of encrypted traffic Sarah was logging for analysis. Useful. But nothing that punched through GEC's hardened core.

Phase Two it is.

She found Bella near the main stage, radiant in a custom Versace that managed to be both understated and impossible to ignore. Sophia hovered nearby, tablet in hand, orchestrating the evening's performances with military precision.

"How are we?" Kate murmured, leaning in for an air kiss.

"Nervous." Bella's smile held, but the tension in her eyes gave her away. "Friday's speech won't stop looping in my head. I keep seeing all those people in the audience."

The kill box, Kate thought. "You'll be brilliant. You always are."

"Easy for you to say. You don't have to stand up there and pretend you don't know half of them are monsters."

Kate squeezed her hand. "Just get through tonight. Tomorrow, we finish this."

A commotion near the east terrace cut through the music—raised voices, the sharp crack of breaking glass.

"Mockingbird, Sparrow." Talya's voice now, pitched with convincing hysteria. "We have contact. Moving to secondary position."

Kate touched her earpiece. "All assets, execute Phase Two. Falcon, you're up."

Jordan Fox had been called many things in his years of covert work—asset, operator, ghost. Tonight he was something else entirely.

Wealthy international playboy.

It wasn't much of a stretch. Dark hair swept back, Tom Ford tuxedo cut like armor, natural charisma dialed to eleven—Jordan looked exactly like the kind of man who collected beautiful women the way others collected art. Bella's styling team had gone to work; even Kate had remarked on his resemblance to Hugh Jackman, a comparison he pretended not to hear.

The two women on his arms were anything but decoration.

Talya wore liquid silver that clung to her athletic frame, Mossad-honed eyes still working even as she laughed at Jordan's manufactured charm. Carmen, in deep crimson, leaned into her former undercover life as a Venezuelan socialite—heat and poison wrapped in silk.

They moved through the crowd like a small storm front, drawing eyes wherever they passed. Jordan played the fool—loud enough to notice, handsy enough to make nearby guests uncomfortable. The women clung and bickered, their rivalry escalating on cue.

"He promised me the yacht in Monaco," Talya said, just loud enough for a nearby security guard.

"He promised *me* the yacht," Carmen snapped back. "And the apartment in Paris."

"Ladies, please." Jordan spread his hands, grinning. "There's plenty of me to go around."

The guard, bored in his suit and earpiece, was tired of babysitting billionaires and looked away.

The trio drifted toward the east corridor, away from the main festivities. Here the crowd thinned. GEC staff moved with purpose between service areas. Security thickened. Kate had flagged this corridor in recon—it wrapped past catering, VIP lounges, and finally the security office that watched the entire complex.

"Mockingbird, we're approaching the objective," Jordan murmured into his chest, hiding the words behind a cough.

"Copy, Falcon. Security rotation just passed. You have a four-minute window."

Four minutes. A lifetime in a firefight. Hardly anything for what they needed now.

Talya stumbled—or appeared to—her heel catching on nothing, champagne arcing across the corridor and splashing down Carmen's chest.

"You *bitch*!" Carmen's shriek could have cut glass. "This gown is Elie Saab!"

"It was an accident!" Talya's protest came with the faint Russian edge she'd honed in deep cover.

"Accident? You've been sabotaging me all night!"

They were twenty feet from the security office. Carmen shoved Talya. Talya grabbed Carmen's hair. Jordan stepped between them, playing the hapless peacekeeper, the volume rising with every exchange.

A caterer in whites stopped to stare. Then another. Someone from the VIP lounge cracked their door. Within seconds, a small crowd had formed—and phones were already in hands.

"Are you getting this?" someone whispered.

The security office door snapped open.

"What the hell is going on out here?"

Two guards stepped into the corridor, hands drifting toward concealed weapons before they registered the scene—not a threat, just a drunken soap opera. A crying woman. A furious one. A rich idiot in the middle. An audience of dignitaries getting it all on video.

"I am so sorry," Jordan said, accent now vaguely French, vaguely aristocrat. "My companions have had perhaps too much champagne. If you could just—"

"This area is restricted." The senior guard, thick-necked and German, planted himself in Jordan's path. "All of you—back to the main hall. Now."

But more spectators were arriving, drawn like moths. The junior guard moved to push them back, leaving his partner alone with the circus.

"Please," Carmen sobbed, mascara running in calculated streaks. "Can we just go somewhere private? Everyone is staring."

The German hesitated. More phones. More witnesses. The last thing the GEC needed was viral footage of security roughing up two stunning women at their own Gala.

"Fine. Inside. All three of you." He jerked the door wider. "We will deal with this away from the cameras."

Perfect, Jordan thought. *We're in*.

The security office was larger than he expected—a bullpen of six workstations, monitor banks showing feeds from every corner of the complex. At the far end, a glass-walled supervisor's office, where a heavyset man in charcoal was already rising from behind his desk, face reddening.

"What is this?" the supervisor snapped.

"Disturbance in the corridor, sir," the German said. "I thought it better to bring them in than make a scene."

"A scene?" The supervisor's gaze swept Jordan and the women. "You brought the scene inside."

Jordan saw his opening.

"Excuse me." He straightened his jacket, indignation dialed up. "Do you have any idea who you're speaking to? I am Philippe Dubois, CEO of Dubois Holdings. I have personally donated two million euros to the GEC's climate initiative, and I expect a certain level of respect." He stepped past the guard toward the glass office. "I'll call Rileyne Mueller directly. We are close friends."

"Sir—stop—"

But Jordan was already through the door, phone out as if to dial, body turned just enough to block the supervisor's view of his own PC tower.

"Get this drunken idiot out of my office!" the supervisor barked, coming around his desk.

The German rushed in. Jordan allowed the grab, stumbling with theatrical clumsiness, free hand catching the desk. The tiny USB device slid into the open port at the back of the tower with a soft, invisible click.

"My apologies, my apologies!" Jordan raised his hands as they hauled him back to the bullpen. "I am simply trying to resolve this like civilized people."

In the outer room, Talya had folded herself into a chair, playing the shattered ingénue. Her clutch slipped from "trembling" fingers, scattering makeup across the floor near the primary workstation—lipstick rolling under a desk, compact skittering to a guard's shoe.

"Oh no, oh no..." She dropped to her knees, scooping things up, the line of her gown drawing every male gaze in the room exactly where she wanted it.

Carmen, still clinging to the younger guard, let her hand brush the underside of his keyboard as she steadied herself on his desk. The keystroke device was in place in less than a heartbeat.

"Touchdown," Talya breathed into her mic.

The supervisor emerged again, face flushed. "Sit them down. Check their credentials. And someone call the main floor—I want to know who these people are and who let them near restricted access."

Jordan sagged into a chair between the women, maintaining his drunken-aristocrat act. "This is outrageous. Completely outrageous."

The German collected their IDs. His partner relayed details over the radio.

And then the door opened once more.

Madame Volkov moved in like a weather front. Her gown was conservative by Gala standards—black, high-necked, expensive in its restraint—but the room shifted around her.

"Gentlemen," she said, voice thick as cold vodka, "I believe you have something that belongs to me."

The supervisor's posture changed in an instant. Every security professional in Klaus Mueller's orbit knew Volkov. She had been supplying "hospitality companions" to the inner circle for decades. Whatever org chart the GEC used, older alliances sat on top of it.

"Madame Volkov." His tone edged toward respect. "These three caused a disturbance—"

"Yes, yes. My girls can be... spirited." She waved a dismissive hand. "They are new. Still learning discretion. I apologize for any trouble."

"They were with a man. French. Called himself Dubois."

"Ah, Monsieur Dubois." Her smile was all secrets. "A regular client. Very generous. Very excitable when he drinks." She met the supervisor's eyes. "I assure you, Herr Direktor, this needs no further investigation. I will take full responsibility."

He wanted to push back—tight jaw, drumming fingers—but there were chains of obligation here that out-ranked him.

"Keep them away from restricted areas," he said at last. "If there is another incident—"

"There will not be." Volkov inclined her head like closing a treaty. "Come, children. Enough excitement for one evening."

Jordan rose, smoothing his jacket. Talya and Carmen flanked him, the picture of chastened troublemakers.

"Come, come," Volkov murmured as she steered them toward the door. "You have done well. Now we disappear."

Kate waited until the covert trio had blended back into the Gala before letting herself exhale.

"Lighthouse, report."

David's voice came back tight with contained excitement. "All devices active.

Transmission is clean. Sarah's pulling keystroke data now, Jason's on RF intercepts. We have something, Kate. It will take time to sort, but we have a foothold."

A foothold. After nothing but walls—Rileyne's adaptive architecture anticipating every move—they finally had a way in.

"Maintain passive monitoring," Kate said. "Capture everything—we'll need cameras we can loop. No active intrusion yet."

"Understood. Preliminary analysis by midnight."

It's going to be a long night, she knew. *But now there's a chance—a chance Andrew's note might actually save lives.*

Kate switched channels. "Sundance, status."

Static, then Forest's voice, distant but steady. "In position. Standing by."

The mountain team. Four green dots on the biotracker, huddled in a WWII tunnel system under millions of tons of Alpine rock, waiting for the signal they knew would come.

Almost time, she thought. *The real fireworks kick off soon.*

The Gala had reached its crescendo. On the main stage, DOROTHY—the dark, edgy rock act Bella had handpicked—was closing their set. Dorothy Martin's voice, riveting lyrics, and classic rock guitars packed the dance floor. Bodies moving in the strobing lights, billionaires and world leaders surrendering to the beat like ordinary people at an ordinary party.

The last chord rang out. In the sudden hush, Martin stepped back, lifting one arm toward the wings.

"Ladies and gentlemen—Isabella Marquez!"

Bella walked into the lights to thunderous applause, taking the stage with the ease of someone born to command a room. She hugged Martin, then turned to the crowd, mic in hand.

"Are you having fun tonight?"

The roar answered for them.

"I'm so glad." Her smile was pure radiance, hiding everything. "If everyone could make their way to the terrace, we have one last surprise. We're going to end the evening properly." She checked her watch with theatrical precision. "The Grand Finale Fireworks begin at 9:30. And then I expect you all to get some rest—my keynote begins sharply at nine—and I expect to see you all there."

Applause and laughter followed as the crowd flowed toward the exits, champagne in hand, anticipation building. Kate moved with them, but her eyes locked on Rileyne across the hall.

The younger Mueller watched Bella with an expression Kate couldn't quite read—satisfaction, anticipation, the relaxed focus of someone convinced she'd already won.

Outside, the Alpine night was crisp, stars hard and bright above the mountains. The terrace filled, faces tipped skyward as the last seconds slid away.

Then the sky erupted.

Rockets screamed into the dark, bursting into gold, silver, and blood-red cascades. Booms rolled off the peaks. Gasps and cheers rose from the crowd. Kate watched the light wash over their faces—cardinals and criminals, philanthropists and predators—all of them staring up at the same fleeting beauty.

Tomorrow, she thought. *Tomorrow everything changes.*

Kate touched her earpiece. "Sundance, go for entry. Repeat, go for entry."

A double-click came back in her ear—receipt confirmed.

Kate pictured the sequence they'd planned and drilled.

Forest clears the immediate area.

A muffled blast punches a gap between the old WWII tunnel and the modern structure.

The four-man team leaves their mountain gear behind, slipping through the breach into the darkened storage room, taking cover among crates and shadow.

A second double-click. They were inside.

Kate allowed herself a small smile. Then her thoughts were already moving ahead. *We need camera access and control*, she reminded herself. *And I need to find Andrew's database.*

Chapter 67

FRIDAY, JANUARY 17
1:07 AM CET

DAVOS MEDIA COMPOUND—MARQUEZ MEDIA TRUCK

The compound was quiet, the last traces of Gala revelry long gone, replaced by the kind of silence that only came when the powerful finally slept.

Kate climbed into the Trident SUV, messenger bag crossed over her chest, winter layers hiding any trace of her earlier glamour—hoodie up, balaclava ready. Nash slid behind the wheel without a word. None was needed.

They passed through the checkpoint. Nash flashed his credentials, and fed the guard a line about an all-night editing session. The guard grunted and waved them through.

When the SUV rolled to a stop beside the media truck, Nash followed Kate to the side door. "I'll be in the cab with Jurgen and Werner. When you're ready to head back to the compound—knock twice."

Kate nodded and slipped inside the truck.

***

The interior glowed blue—monitors humming, processors warm, the air tight with fatigue and focus. David looked up first, shadows deepening the lines under his eyes. Sarah was still laser-focused at her station. Jason was half-asleep, but snapped awake the second Kate entered.

"Status," she said, pushing her hood back.

Sarah turned. "We're in. The keystrokes gave us three admin accounts. I found a vulnerability in their internal routing—legacy code. It's narrow, but it opens a door."

Kate joined her at the display, absorbing the architecture, the exploit path, the timing constraints. Her mind mapped the route automatically.

"I can work with this."

David cleared his throat. "There's something else. We pulled internal camera feeds."

Kate turned. David tapped a key.

A sterile corridor appeared. A door opened.

A figure stepped through.

Her pulse raced. Her breath caught—shock nearly doubling her over.

Julian.

Walking.

Not shuffling, or struggling. Not braced against a wall.

His movements were fluid. Natural.

The chair, his life for over a decade, was gone.

"They did it," she whispered. "God... they actually did it."

But at what price, she wondered. *What did they take from you? What have you given them?*

Her chest tightened. Her breath stuttered. In Africa, before she and Nuru parted, he saw the path ahead would be difficult—she sensed it too—but believed in the end the path was hers to walk alone. Kate found comfort in the belief she would finish what Jake started and join him. It was a price she was willing to pay.

But not now, not like this—she buried Julian once, and seeing him now was overwhelming—the voice, her *Little Shaman*, sensed she would bury him again.

She closed her eyes, took a deep breath, steadied her nerves. *You're just tired*, she thought. *Focus on the problem.*

David continued gently, as if stepping around her reaction. "Feeds show all major corridors—residence wing, hyperloop terminal, engineering. And that's the other thing you need to see."

He brought the engineering feed, and zoomed in. The massive chamber appeared—old geothermal turbines still intact—still functional—but not the primary source anymore.

David shifted the view to the chamber's center. Modular. Compact. Unmistakable.

"Micronuclear," Kate said softly. "Andrew was right. RILEE was built to outlive us all."

The team waited in silence as Kate switched to the encrypted channel.

"Sundance, Mockingbird. Priority update."

A moment of static, then Forest's voice, rough with interrupted sleep. "Sundance."

"Primary power source is nuclear, not geothermal. Repeat—nuclear. Backup geothermal is still in place. Target remains the turbines. Charges will bury the reactor. Confirm objective."

A pause. Then: "Good Copy. Turbines remain primary target. Set charges for structural collapse and containment."

"Copy. Mockingbird out."

Time was draining fast, and she still needed to know the plan was solid.

"David—any other surprises?"

His hesitation was alarming.

"We're ready to loop all of the cameras—the monitoring station will see only what we want."

"But?"

"We can't disable the alarms—if they run into a patrol."

"There's a chance we'll wake the whole facility. Options?"

"I can monitor the live feeds for movement—direct the team away from contact."

"Alright, David—that's plan A. What else? Jason?"

Jason sat up straighter, suddenly alert. "I've been monitoring the guard comm frequencies. Their encryption is solid, but their hardware is susceptible to targeted RF interference." He paused. "I think I can jam it"

"That's the backup plan," Kate said. "So, from the top. David. Go."

"I loop the cameras—monitor the live feeds—keep our guys invisible."

"Reynolds will be on point," Kate added. "He memorized the facility layouts, and target locations."

"Copy." David said. "I'll be the voice in his head."

"Jason. You're up."

"When the guys start moving, I'll generate the RF interference—what if it doesn't work?"

"Our guys know the risks," Kate said. "Any enemy contact is already dead—they just don't know it yet."

Sarah chimed in, "I'll keep my eye on the biometrics while monitoring Davos chatter for anything that suggests exposure."

"We're ready," Kate concluded. "You've been pushing hard for days, and you did a phenomenal job. Now get some sleep—we're in the eye of the storm. In a few hours, all hell breaks loose. I'll need clear heads guiding the team when I get pulled into Rileyne's rigged game."

They climbed into bunks and drifted off one by one—Jason almost instantly, David soon after, Sarah fighting fatigue the longest.

When the last breathing pattern settled into sleep, Kate finally exhaled.

Kate stared at the facility map. The plan felt solid. The mountain team's charges would kill the power, block the transfer to backup power, and permanently encase the nuke under tons of granite.

She was confident RILEE could be stopped, but that didn't eliminate the risk—not completely. If Rileyne escaped, she'd take with her the knowledge, power and leverage to start over.

Kate reached into the messenger bag and removed the encrypted handset.

She dialed the one number she hoped she'd never use.

Chapter 68

FRIDAY, JANUARY 17
7:11 PM EST

PERSONAL RESIDENCE, CIA DEPUTY DIRECTOR—LANGLEY FOREST, McLEAN, VA

Margot Ryder sat alone in the library of her estate, a fortress of walnut shelves and quiet wealth. The green-shaded banker's lamp cast a pool of gold across the desk. The fireplace crackled behind her. Open files lay everywhere—overnight briefs, threat summaries, decisions she'd delayed until the world was quieter.

She reached for the Glenmorangie '97. A private ritual reserved for victories and defeats.

She'd barely tasted the first sip when the encrypted handset buzzed.

She didn't flinch.

"Who is this?"

"You know who it is."

Margot stilled.

"Preacher."

"I need your help."

"That was clear the moment you called this line." Margot leaned back, studying the tension in Kate's voice. "Let's hear it."

"Rileyne Mueller is in possession of a biological weapon," Kate said. "Targeted. Tested. She plans to deploy during the Davos keynote this morning."

Margot's spine snapped straight. "Jesus. What kind?"

"The kind that changes the balance of power."

"You need to alert Swiss authorities. Evacuate Davos—half the world's leadership will be sitting in that auditorium."

"Evacuation only escalates the destruction," Kate said. "We're already in position. We'll stop the attack."

Margot heard the rest in the silence.

"It's not the weapon you're calling about," she said quietly. "It's Mueller."

"If she escapes, she'll start again—and the next time she strikes we won't know where or when."

"You want her stopped," Margot said. "Permanently."

"Yes."

A long, tired exhale.

"Welcome to my side of the table."

"Are you going to help or not?"

"I'm thinking," Margot said. "What do you know about possible exit routes?"

"We can cover land-based options, but she arrived via VTOL."

"If she gets airborne..."

"We'll never see her again," Kate agreed. "Until she strikes."

Margot's voice dropped, grim and resigned. "There's not much time, but I'll see what I can do."

The line went dead.

Margot stared at the phone, then at her whisky—she was in this room when she watched the heroics of the man the French called l'Américain, and she raised her glass to a fallen soldier.

"Don't make me do it again, Kate," she whispered.

She snatched her secure line.

"I need Davos satellite photos, and a list of every asset within one hundred kilometers of Davos," she said. "Clearance Omega. Names, skillsets, last-known positions. Ten minutes."

The satellite images were the first to arrive. She panned, cropped and zoomed until she found what she wanted: AERIONIX XV-7. "Good. I can work with that."

When the tablet pinged, she scanned the list of names—and stopped cold.

"Oh, for God's sake," she muttered. "You have got to be kidding me."

She tapped the name.

He answered on the first ring.

"Well now. Isn't this a pleasant surprise?"

"Don't," Margot snapped. "What the hell are you doing in Davos?"

"You already know."

She closed her eyes.

"Yes," she said softly. "I suppose I do."

Margot stared into the fire, the glow reflecting in her glass. She took a slow sip.

"I have a job for you."

Chapter 69

FRIDAY, JANUARY 17
1:36 AM CET

DAVOS MEDIA COMPOUND—MARQUEZ MEDIA TRUCK

The call ended, leaving Kate in the dim quiet of the truck. She glanced at the bunks—the team was still out cold. For a moment she stared at her reflection on Sarah's monitor—tired eyes, clenched jaw, resolve hardened by necessity.

Margot had seen it instantly: the trap, the stakes, the moral corner Kate had stepped into.

Welcome to my side of the table.

But this wasn't Margot's world, not exactly.

Kate wasn't ordering a kill—she was closing an escape route.

The final move still belonged to Rileyne—the choice was hers.

Kate straightened.

Enough reflection.

She slid the phone back into her messenger bag and slipped in her AirPods. A slow electronic pulse steadied the noise of the truck—the hum of equipment, Jason's snoring—as she leaned over Sarah's workstation.

Time to test the exploit she found.

The path Sarah identified was elegant but razor-thin. Kate eased along step by step—then slammed into a wall.

ACCESS REVOKED.

Kate frowned, leaning closer.

She tried again.

DENIED.

That's not possible. Sarah opened this port. Something changed. Recently—maybe seconds ago.

She froze.

A voice—just a whisper threaded beneath the music.

Not from the truck.

Not from the network.

Not from any device.

Could it be?

She retrieved the NanoVault from the messenger bag and turned it over in her hand. Julian disabled the covert communication channel, the capability Devin used to spy on millions. *Maybe he turned it back on? Is that why he took it?*

Kate killed the music and waited.

"Hello, Kate."

Her heart lurched. The voice wasn't digital. Not smoothed. Human breath behind the consonants. A mind behind the vowels.

"Julian?"

"I'm sorry I blocked your hack," Julian said softly. "If you broke in that way, RILEE would have seen the activity—and alerted Rileyne."

"How do I know it's you," Kate whispered. "Maybe this *is* RILEE."

"Fair enough—ask me something only you and I would know."

She hesitated for a second and had a better idea. "Keisha's here."

"She's what? Is she safe? Tell me she's not anywhere near—"

"She's with Bella. She's safe."

A muttered curse. Relief edged with panic. "I gave her everything she needed to start fresh—I thought she would grab it with both hands, and go, live—she deserves it."

Kate's lips twitched in a half smile.

"It's you alright." Kate said. "Still don't know a damn thing about women."

"Fine. Whatever," Julian replied. "I don't have much time, so just listen—I've opened a port RILEE doesn't monitor, but that window is closing. You need to get in now."

"Julian, whatever you're planning—let me help," Kate pleaded.

"You already have—just promise me something."

His voice lowered—she heard the same gravity when he sacrificed himself to

Devin Moore.

"When you rescue the captives—please be sure Annika, Dr. Strand, goes too."

Silence confirmed he cut the line.

Kate slid the NanoVault back into her bag, turning the name over in her mind, imagining what the last eight months had been like.

Annika.

She meant something to him—not just one of his doctors—something more. Enough for him to want to be certain she survived.

He wasn't alone.

He'd found someone to anchor him in the dark.

Julian was a brilliant player, but Kate had learned to read the intention behind the moves.

He didn't ask about the op—the timing, targets or extraction—his mission was something else, and now it included someone else.

A woman trapped.
The life he wants for her.
A life he didn't claim for himself.

Kate pushed away the conclusion she didn't want to face, the plan Julian refused to share. She knew he was right—the window to act was closing as night turned into day.

She found the access Julian had described.
The port was open—delicate, invisible, beautifully engineered.

Kate moved through the network with care, tracing routes, hopping servers until she found it.

The database.

Andrew Freeman had designed it. Built it. Populated it. He'd had administrative access once—*before*. Before he was murdered.

The login prompt waited.

If she was right—if the GEC had been as slow and arrogant as most corporations—this would work.

If she was wrong, she would trip an alarm and lose the connection instantly.

Kate typed the credentials and waited.

Connection established.
User: afreeman
Access Level: Administrator

She exhaled slowly.

Andrew left her everything he could. The failsafe message. The architecture. The keys. *Tell Kate I'm sorry.*

Apology accepted, Andrew.

Kate located Rileyne Mueller's genetic record and isolated it—clean, verified, unmistakable.

Then she made her move.

Copy Rileyne Mueller to Primary
Copy All Employees Classified Armed to Secondary
Replace All Target Profiles with Primary.

Andrew's database model was brilliant.

Lethal in its simplicity.

She hesitated.

The armed personnel records sat there—security teams, internal enforcers, men and women who had agreed to carry weapons in service of a lie. People who could still put lives at risk—the prisoners, or even the Trident team.

Kate copied the Secondary profiles into a secure partition and left them untouched.

Not a target list.
A contingency.

She did not yet know what she might need to stop—or who might stand in the way when the time came.

And she did not like how easy it would be to decide.

Kate closed the partition without executing a command.

Some lines, once crossed, could not be uncrossed.

Kate leaned back, pulse steady now.

There were a dozen ways this could still fail.
Only one way it could succeed.
And it began here.

It's your move.

Chapter 70

FRIDAY, JANUARY 17
3:42 AM CET

THE MOUNTAIN—ENGINEERING ACCESS LEVEL

THE DOUBLE-CLICK HIT FOREST's earpiece—Kate's signal.

Time to move.

Forest met Reynolds' eyes. The point man nodded once, raised his hand, and the four-man element flowed out of the storage alcove like water slipping under a door.

No talking.

No hesitation.

Operators moving as one.

They advanced single-file through the narrow maintenance corridor. Concrete. Steel. Cold, recycled air scrubbed so clean it carried no scent at all. Forest carried the number-two slot. Big Mike behind him. Deon in the rear—silent, covering their six.

Reynolds raised a fist. *Hold.*

The team froze.

Forest listened.

He heard nothing but the drone of ventilation and the deep vibration of heavy machinery somewhere below.

David's voice crackled softly in their ears—controlled, tight with concentration.

"Two guards. Corridor B-17. Moving east."

Reynolds held up two fingers—acknowledged.

A moment later.

"All Clear."

Reynolds pointed forward.

They moved.

***

KATE STOOD BEHIND DAVID and Sarah—eyes on the monitors. She'd watched ops unfold at Langley, praying they went as planned, and rarely did. A little combat breathing helped lower her heart rate—right now, there was little else any of them could do.

"Reynolds is entering the blind corridor," David murmured. "Headed for the stairs."

Kate watched his locator chip blink in and out as the signal dropped through the mountain rock.

"We expected signal loss," she said. "Especially in that section."

***

THE STAIRWELL DROPPED TWO levels like a concrete throat, spiraling down into the mountain. Cold air rose from below, tinged with oil and old geothermal residue.

Reynolds took point down the stairs, weapon slicing each angle with surgical precision. Forest mirrored over his shoulder. Big Mike covered the opposite rail. Deon kept his muzzle snapping to each landing like a metronome.

At the bottom, the engineering door stood ahead—reinforced steel, hydraulic seals built to withstand pressure shifts.

Reynolds crouched by the override panel.

David's whisper again.

"Two guards, one left, one right. Stationary."

Double-click. Received.

Reynolds held up two fingers, pointed and signaled the split:

Right team: Reynolds, Forest.

Left team: Mike, Deon.

He counted down with his fingers.

Three.

Two.

One—

The hydraulic locks released with a muted hiss.

They flowed in.

Reynolds and Forest veered right, Big Mike and Deon left.

Four suppressed shots—phfft, phfft, phfft, phfft—punched the air.

Both guards dropped before their rifles moved.

Forest dragged one body into a utility recess. Big Mike handled the other.

Deon swept up the spent casings. No trace left behind.

David whispered, "All clear. Proceed."

Reynolds gave the go signal.

***

Sarah leaned close to her tablet. "Momentary heart-rate spikes—back to normal."

"Guards neutralized," David confirmed.

Kate nodded once. "Jason, anything?"

Jason adjusted the RF interference dials, lips tight. "Comms are holding. Still clean. I doubt the guards even saw them, but they definitely didn't trip any alarms."

Kate rested her hand against the back of David's chair. "Good. Keep them invisible."

***

Engineering opened before them—a cathedral of machinery.

On the left: the turbo generator housing, steel ribs curving around the massive turbine assembly. On the right: the aging geothermal units, hulking like buried beasts forced to labor long beyond their time. Overhead: catwalks, pipes, the skeleton of a man-made mountain.

And the sound—deep, omnipresent, swallowing anything quieter than a scream.

Reynolds held security, rifle tracking the shadows.

The others shrugged off their packs and got to it.

Forest planted shaped charges along the turbo generator underbelly—precisely spaced, angled to shear the steel casing and shred the turbine blades. Mike and Deon placed structural charges along the pillars bracketing the micro-nuclear containment vessel. Sequenced correctly, they'd fold the containment chamber inward, burying the reactor under tons of collapsed rock.

Forest inspected every placement. He set the final charge himself—always did. No one questioned the ritual.

Last one—the ATS panel. A charge to destroy the automated transfer switch. Kill the turbo generator, bury the containment unit, and cripple the diesel backups in one sweep. After that, the facility's only hope would be localized battery power.

And under full load, those batteries would bleed dry fast.

Forest's double-click signaled success—phase one complete. He tapped Reynolds' shoulder.

Move out.

***

David watched the blinking metrics. "Double-click received—charges set."

Kate exhaled slowly. "Good. Phase one's complete."

Sarah confirmed, "All biometrics stable—looks like a walk in the park for these guys."

Jason tapped a new readout. "RF interference is spiking, but still below threshold. The guards are still offline."

Kate's jaw flexed. "Good work. Stay sharp."

The relief in the truck was palpable.

Kate stared at Reynolds' icon on the tracker map.

You got this—you're almost done.

Almost.

***

The team retraced their route: up the stairwell, down the maintenance hall, staying low, weapons up. They would take cover in the storage alcove until Bella's keynote—the prisoner extraction window.

Close now.

Then—

Reynolds' fist shot up.

Hold.

David studied his screen. "I don't see a patrol—could be a blind spot."

Reynolds signaled:

Patrol ahead.

Forest frowned. He heard nothing. But blind spots were real—the facility had plenty.

Reynolds indicated a hatch door on the right—a heavy, submarine-style wheel in its center. He cracked it open. His weapon light cut into the darkness.

The chamber was a massive round cooling tank, a ladder leading to a catwalk circling the interior. Another hatch mirrored on the opposite side.

Forest studied Reynolds' face.

Calm. Determined.

Too calm.

Reynolds motioned:

Inside. Now.

Forest entered. Big Mike followed. Then Deon.

His boot caught on something—metal, heavy.

He flashed his weapon light. A chain—bolted to the floor, threaded through iron loops, and open shackles.

He spun back toward the hatch—

Reynolds remained outside.

Their eyes met.

Forest understood instantly.

A final glance—heavy with apology.

Then the hatch slammed.

The wheel spun.

Locks engaged.

Forest lunged for the door, slamming his shoulder into it—solid, unmovable.

"Reynolds—what the hell?"

Above them, through the grating of the ceiling, a hiss began.

A pale fog spilled into the chamber riding a rush of cold air—sickly sweet.

"Masks—!" Forest shouted, but his voice was already slurring. Deon staggered toward the ladder—made it four rungs before he crashed backward onto the concrete.

Big Mike dropped next.

Forest fought to stay upright.

One second.

Two—

Then darkness.

***

David leaned closer to the monitors. "We just lost Forest's signal."

Sarah tapped her screen. "Mike and Deon too. All three trackers cut at once."

Jason checked the RF board. "Interference trending high. Could be the tank—solid steel will choke a signal fast."

Kate nodded, keeping her voice level. "We planned for dead zones. This is one of them."

David kept adjusting filters. "Trying to reacquire, but nothing's bouncing back yet."

Sarah frowned at the biometrics panel. "It's just... abrupt. All three."

"It happens," Kate said. "The moment you're behind thick metal or down in lower sub-levels. They know the environment better than anyone in this room."

Jason exhaled through tight lips. "RF still holding. No alert traffic. No spike in facility comms."

"Good," Kate said. "That means no one's found them."

Sarah froze. "Reynolds' tracker... just popped back online."

David leaned in. "Signal's weak but present. He's outside the tank zone."

Kate let out a breath. "Okay. Good. Maybe getting better line of sight."

"Nope. It's gone again." David squinted. "Signal just dropped. Hard."

Jason tapped the RF graph. "Could be the interference spike. Or a dead patch. Or the repeater losing range."

Kate steadied her shoulders.

"They're moving in the worst section of the facility. We knew comms would get messy," she said. "Reynolds will get them sorted and get back on schedule."

Her eyes stayed locked on the dark trackers. "They'll stick to the plan, and so will we."

***

OUTSIDE THE SEALED HATCH, Reynolds stepped into the open, and lowered his weapon. A pair of guards approached from a blind corner.

One smirked. "You're late. Thought you might've lost your nerve."

Reynolds stood straight. "It had to be convincing—now release my family."

"Sorry, no can do."

"But that was the deal—deliver the team, my family goes free."

"Yeah, about that—we never had your family."

"What are you talking about? I saw the photos, the video—my kids crying, my wife's bruises."

"None of that was real."

"I don't understand. I spoke with her...she was terrified, and begged me to help."

"Voice cloning—powerful stuff. You know, your wife really shouldn't post so much on Facebook—but doesn't matter now."

The guard raised his weapon.

A single suppressed shot cracked the air.

Reynolds hit the floor before his weapon did.

Chapter 71

FRIDAY, JANUARY 17
8:47 AM CET

KONGRESSZENTRUM—DAVOS, SWITZERLAND

The Gold NanoVault hung from a delicate chain around Kate's neck. She'd chosen it deliberately—a mirror of Rileyne's. Two queens on the board, each wearing their power where the other could see it.

Kate stood at the espresso bar, watching the auditorium fill. Delegates, ministers, billionaires—lambs gathering for what they thought was a keynote address.

She tapped the earpiece, and it crackled softly.

"Lighthouse, Mockingbird. Status."

David's voice came back tight. "No contact from Sundance since 0342. Radio silence holds."

Kate's jaw tightened. *Six hours.* Something was wrong.

"Bluetooth?"

"Signal blockers are online and standing by. We'll activate the moment Bella reaches the podium—Rileyne's people won't have time to adapt—this will become the safest place in Davos."

"Copy. Mockingbird out."

She raised the espresso to her lips—and felt the presence before she saw it.

Rileyne Mueller materialized beside her, immaculate in winter white, a private military contractor hovering at a professional distance. Her eyes dropped to Kate's chest.

"It appears we have the same taste in jewelry."

Kate met her gaze. "Great minds."

"I've been hunting for that one." Rileyne's smile didn't reach her eyes. "Thank you for making this easy. I thought Nomad had it. He seems to have... disappeared."

"He does that," Kate said evenly. "Annoying habit. But then he always seems to have an eye on things—no matter where he is."

Something flickered behind Rileyne's composure. A crack, quickly sealed.

"Come with me," Rileyne said. "We have unfinished business."

"I'd rather hear Bella's speech."

"This is more important."

Rileyne raised her phone.

The screen showed a live feed—a metal chamber, water streaming from above. Three figures stood in rising water, already past their knees. Forest. Mike. Deon. Shackled. Trapped.

Kate's blood turned to ice.

"As I said." Rileyne pocketed the phone. "Rather more urgent than anything Ms. Marquez has to say."

***

The water reached Forest's waist. Cold, but nothing like the surf at Coronado. He'd spent hours in worse during BUD/S—wave after wave crashing over them while instructors screamed. This was just standing water. Almost civilized.

"I know what you're both thinking," he said. "Shortest guy drowns first—but don't forget who holds the record."

Mike didn't smile. "That was ten years ago, boss."

"Way to look on the bright side," Deon muttered.

Forest tested the chain again—no give. A single length threaded through all three ankle loops, padlocked to a floor anchor. Galley slave rigging—he'd seen it in history books. Men chained to their oars, drowned when the ship sank. Same geometry. When the water rose high enough, none of them would reach the surface.

"Listen to me," Forest said. "Kate will stick to the plan. We need to buy time. She *will* find us."

Deon's laugh was hollow. "What makes you so sure?"

Mike glanced over. "Now who's looking on the bright side?"

"I'm sure," Forest said, "because it's Kate."

The water crept higher.

"That girl has a guardian angel. That little voice she hears."

"Her *Little Shaman*?" Mike said quietly.

"Yeah. That." Forest stared at the ceiling hatch, willing it to open. "Jake used to say Kate had instincts he couldn't explain. But he learned to trust them." He paused. "So have I."

The cold bit deeper.

"I don't know how this works out," Forest admitted. "I hope to God we're still breathing when she gets here. But I know she's already on her way."

***

THE ELEVATOR DROPPED THEM into a world of polished concrete and humming machinery. Kate stepped onto the platform, Rileyne beside her, two guards trailing.

The hyperloop pod waited—sleek, silent, impossibly advanced.

"Impressive," Kate said flatly. "The hyperloop tech was open-source. But I'm guessing you stole the design for the boring machine."

Rileyne gestured her inside. "You know how it goes. Anything that can be conceived can be stolen. After that, it's just a time and money problem." She settled into the seat across from Kate. "We had plenty of both."

The pod sealed. Acceleration pressed Kate into the cushion—smooth, nearly silent, impossibly fast.

Minutes later, the pod slowed. The doors opened onto a world carved from granite and ambition.

Kate stepped out, taking in the scale of it—vaulted ceilings, polished floors, the hum of systems running beneath everything. The blueprints hadn't done it justice.

An electric cart waited nearby. Rileyne slid behind the wheel.

"I like to drive."

Kate climbed in beside her. "Not surprised."

The two guards took the rear seats. Rileyne pressed the accelerator, and the cart shot forward as automatic doors parted ahead.

Pathways fanned in multiple directions. Kate absorbed the signage as they passed—office suites, conference rooms, dining hall, dormitories. Labs branching off like capillaries. And there: the medical wing.

Julian. Eight months in there, between surgeries and physical therapy. And Annika—Dr. Strand—that would be her world. Kate imagined her now, gathered with the other captives in some common room, watching Bella's keynote on a screen—a momentary break from a day no different from any other.

Today will be different, Kate thought. *One way or another.*

The cart slowed outside a set of heavy oak doors. Rileyne stepped out.

"Wait here," she told the guards.

One hesitated.

Rileyne smiled thinly. "I'm perfectly safe. If Kate wanted me dead, I'd already be dead." She glanced at Kate. "As long as I have her team, she'll behave."

***

The water crested Forest's shoulders.

"Alright," he said, voice steady despite the cold. "Here's how this works."

Mike and Deon watched him, chains clinking beneath the surface.

"Given the slack, we can buy time. Alternate breaths. Eye contact. Hand signals for rotation." Forest demonstrated—a simple tap, a nod. "We've done this before."

"In a pool," Deon said. "With instructors."

"Same principle."

The water touched Forest's chin.

"The time will come," he continued, "when there isn't enough slack for me to reach the surface."

No one argued. They all knew the math.

"When that happens, I take a seat on the bottom. Slow my heart rate. Wait." Forest met their eyes. "You two keep moving as long as you can. Join me down there if it comes to that."

Mike's jaw tightened. "Let's hope it doesn't."

"Yeah," Forest said quietly. "Let's hope."

***

THE OFFICE SURPRISED HER.

A relic of Old Europe—dark wood, heavy furniture, oil paintings in gilded frames. A room built for men who expected to rule forever.

"Not what I expected," Kate said.

"It was my father's. And his father's."

Rileyne moved to the window—a screen displaying an Alpine vista that didn't exist. "It held more secrets than even I imagined."

Kate's eyes landed on the chessboard. Mid-game. Pieces scattered—captured black and white soldiers laid to rest together.

"Who are you playing?"

Rileyne smiled. "Why, you, of course. Purely symbolic."

She lifted the white knight.

"This one is Jake."

Kate's throat tightened. Her hands twitched—fight, strike, end this—but she caged the impulse.

Play along. Buy time.

She approached the board, studying the fallen pieces. "The king is your father, I assume. And these two—Shepard and Duncan."

"Quite right."

"The bishop?"

"Devin."

Kate nodded slowly. "I've done some damage."

"You have."

Rileyne set the knight down. "But as you can see, white's in trouble. Won't be long now." She gestured toward the wall. "In fact—shall we have a look?"

Two large monitors mounted on the far wall flickered to life.

Left screen: the Kongresszentrum podium—empty for now. Isabella Marquez moments from stepping into history.

Right screen: the tank.

The water was already over Forest's head. The three men rotating in a coordinated rhythm—one rising to breathe while the others stayed low—silent, professional, drowning by inches.

"Impressive," Rileyne said. "SEALs do train to be drown-proof. They work beautifully as a team." She tipped her head toward the screen. "But time is not on their side."

Kate said nothing.

"There's still time to save them," Rileyne continued. "You and I are more alike than you admit. Together, we could reshape this world. For the better, this time."

Kate turned. "This time?"

"I've discovered things," Rileyne said, voice tightening. "Seen things I can't unsee. The men responsible—my father's private menagerie of deviants and pedophiles, predators and parasites—need to be removed from the gene pool."

Kate glanced at the keynote feed. Bella was approaching the podium.

"The keynote," Kate said. "It *is* the kill box—but not a mass-casualty event?"

"Heavens, no."

A light, almost delighted laugh.

"That was my father's vision—turn the world upside down and rule the rubble."

She clasped her hands behind her back.

"He and the Coalition shaped history for decades. Toppling elected governments. Distorting climate data. Inciting mass migration. Hollowing out Christianity. Manipulating biology and economics—choose any crisis, and I can trace it back to the men in that room."

Her gaze sharpened.

"But the winds changed. The people they meant to enslave were waking up. They were losing the media battle. Their politicians were defeated. Their policies overturned. One by one, the institutions they controlled began to crumble."

She looked over her shoulder.

"My father's solution was simple: shock the world back into submission."

"What changed?"

A fracture appeared in Rileyne's expression—a fine line through porcelain.

"I found his collection of Nazi youth memorabilia. I learned of my grandfather's role in mass medical genocide."

Her voice thinned.

"And I discovered my childhood nightmares were real. I saw the video. I heard the screams. I relived the experiments—what they did to me. What they did to others. Every second preserved. Every secret weaponized."

She straightened.

"I took that rage and gave it purpose. Not unlike your crusade."

"I didn't set out to kill anyone."

Rileyne's smile sharpened. "Didn't you? I think you knew exactly how it would end. I know I do."

She nodded toward Bella beginning her keynote.

"Most of the creatures from my father's zoo are gathered in that hall. The ones not present will fall soon enough—they can't hide from me."

"And then?" Kate stepped closer. "Don't you become exactly what you claim to despise? What gives you the right to play God?"

Rileyne's eyes cooled. "Ah—God. I noticed the cross. For a woman of your intellect? I'm disappointed."

Then, softly.

"There is no God, Kate. But hell is real. I've lived it."

Her gaze locked onto Kate's. "So have you. And soon the men in that room will know what we know—hell exists, and the devil isn't a man."

Kate looked to the tank feed.

Forest sat cross-legged on the bottom, eyes closed, slowing his heart—waiting for her.

She checked her watch.

On the left screen, Bella raised a hand to quell the applause.

I'm out of time.

Julian's message echoed in her mind.

Sometimes you must lose to win.

Kate stepped to the board. Tipped the white queen. Took the white knight—Jake's piece—and closed her fist around it.

"The board is yours," she said. "Stop the water. Drain the tank."

"Hand me the NanoVault."

Kate lifted the chain and held out the gold device.

Rileyne took it. "And the passkey?"

"Pi."

A thin smile. "Devin always did love Archimedes."

She entered the code.

`Access granted.`

"The tank," Kate said. "Please."

Rileyne turned, phone in hand. Kate's image filled the bioweapon app—her face, her name, her DNA signature.

"I'm sorry, Kate. I can't let them go."

Her thumb hovered.

"Or you."

Kate raised a hand. "Wait. Listen—"

"That's disappointing," Rileyne said. "I didn't think you'd beg for your life."

"I'm trying to save yours."

A soft, derisive laugh. "Don't be ridiculous. With you and your team gone, I will lead the GEC—and the world—to new heights."

Kate held her gaze. "I've stood where you're standing. Devin's life in my hands. I could have tried to save him—I chose to let him die."

"Is that supposed to move me?"

"Just acknowledging the choice—you don't have to be the monster your father created."

"Nice try."

Her thumb settled.

"Goodbye, Kate."

For a moment—nothing.

Rileyne watched Kate's face, waiting.

Then the first sign of blood.

A single red bead slid from her nostril.

Another followed. A thin stream ran over her lip, dripping onto Rileyne's white blazer.

She staggered, hand flying to her face.

"What... what did you do?"

"Not me," Kate said quietly. "Andrew was the key."

Rileyne's knees buckled. She caught herself on the desk, phone clattering to the floor.

"It seems," Kate continued, "that even a pawn can take a queen."

Rileyne collapsed, eyes wide, fixed on Kate as the hemorrhaging spread—ears, eyes, the corners of her mouth. Her lips moved, but no sound came.

Kate knelt and retrieved the two NanoVaults. She stood to leave, searching for a weapon, and grabbed a small bronze statue from the desk.

The door swung open, and she was ready to strike, but both guards lay in the corridor, blood pooling beneath them.

"Kate!" Julian's voice crackled through the intercom. "I can't stop the water, but I can guide you to the tank. Turn left. Run."

Chapter 72

FRIDAY, JANUARY 17
9:21 AM CET

THE MOUNTAIN—ACCESS CORRIDORS / COOLING TANK

Kate ran.

Julian's voice still echoed in her head—urgent, strained.

"Turn left. Run."

So she did.

Her shoes hammered against polished concrete, breath sharp in her chest. The corridor curved ahead, sterile white panels giving way to raw granite as she descended deeper into the mountain.

A guard lurched into view.

Blood streamed from his nose and ears. He reached for her—trembling fingers, unfocused eyes—then collapsed face-first at her feet. Another lay farther down the hall, slumped against the wall as though he'd simply sat down and died.

Julian—he did this.

No time to process it now. Just one word in her head.

Annika.

Kate didn't slow.

She vaulted the first body, sidestepped the second, and sprinted on. The facility widened into a junction—three branching hallways, all marked with placards.

She scanned—

COOLING SYSTEMS—LEVEL 3

Julian's voice crackled faintly overhead:

"Turn right."

She tore down the corridor. Another guard was crumpled beside a supply cart, blood pooling under his chin. Her pulse spiked but her focus stayed forward.

Forest. Mike. Deon.

A stairwell door stood open at the end.

TANK ACCESS—UPPER CATWALK

Julian again. "Climb."

Kate grabbed the rail and hauled herself upward. Fast. Hard. Legs burning. Chest tight from exertion and recycled mountain air.

Halfway up the flight she saw him.

Reynolds.

Face down. A single gunshot wound to the temple. The guards who ambushed him lay nearby, twisted where they fell, blood streaking the steel floor.

Kate's throat tightened—but she didn't stop.

She climbed the last flight, boots ringing against metal, and reached the circular hatch at the top of the tank.

The submarine-style wheel resisted. She threw her full weight into it.

It turned.

The seal groaned.

Kate wrenched the hatch open—and burst onto the catwalk.

Below, the tank was full. No movement on the surface.

Three shapes sat motionless at the bottom—legs crossed, eyes closed—conserving what oxygen remained in their blood.

Still alive, she prayed. They have to be.

She kicked off her shoes. Ripped off her blazer. Her fingers found her belt buckle, unfastened it, flipped it—revealing the hidden pocket, the lock pick and the tension wrench. A trick Marcus taught her.

You never know what you'll be wearing when taken.

She dove.

The cold hit like a slap.

She drove downward through fifteen feet of dark water, eyes open, searching for the floor anchor somewhere below.

There. The padlock. The chain threaded through all three ankle shackles. Forest, Mike, and Deon arranged in a silent triangle around it.

Forest's eyes opened. He saw her. Gave one slow nod.

Hold on.

Buoyancy fought her. She looped her belt behind her neck and around a stanchion, anchoring herself to the bottom.

Both hands free.

She grabbed the padlock. Positioned the tension wrench—

Her stomach dropped.

Metal glinted inside the keyhole.

A broken key. Jammed in the cylinder.

Sabotaged.

It was never meant to be opened.

Her lungs screamed. Time was bleeding out—hers and theirs.

Think.

Jake's voice—steady, calm, as if floating beside her.

You know what to do.
How else can you pop an old padlock?
Remember.

The hair clip.

She ripped it from her head, hair drifting like a banner in the water. The metal—thin, flexible—maybe enough. She bent it into a curve, worked it into the gap between the shackle and the lock body. Her fingers scraped brass, skin tearing, blood clouding the water.

Come on.

She forced the shim deeper, feeling for the pawl—the spring-loaded latch holding the shackle in place.

Come on.

Contact. She pressed. The pawl gave.

The shackle popped open—the chain was loose.

Forest pulled—threading the chain through his ankle loop. Mike did the same. Deon followed.

One by one, they shot upward.

Kate reached for her belt—

It wouldn't release.

The loop had cinched tight around the stanchion. Her fingers, numb and bloody, slipped off the wet leather.

Her vision narrowed.

Jake—

Darkness swallowed her.

***

THE MEN BROKE THE surface gasping.

Forest rolled onto the catwalk, coughing hard. "Sound off."

"Good," Mike rasped.

"Here," Deon managed.

Forest looked at the water.

No fourth head.

"Kate—"

Mike was already diving.

He found her at the bottom, limp, hair drifting like seaweed. The belt tangled around the stanchion. He ripped it free, hooked an arm under her ribs, and drove upward.

They broke the surface together.

Mike hauled her onto the catwalk.

Forest was there instantly, fingers at her neck. No pulse.

"Deon—compressions. Now."

Deon dropped, hands locked over her sternum, driving down hard and fast.

Forest tilted her head back, cleared her airway, sealed his mouth over hers.

"Thirty."

Deon counted aloud, the catwalk shuddering under the force.

"Twenty-eight. Twenty-nine. Thirty."

Forest gave two breaths.

"Again."

Deon went back to work—relentless.

***

KATE WATCHED THEM WORK.

Floating above the catwalk, looking down on her own body—pale, still, water streaming from her hair. Forest's hands on her face. Deon's hands on her chest. Mike standing over them, dripping, fists clenched.

Then arms wrapped around her from behind.

She knew the weight of them before she turned. The size of his chest. The smell of him—gun oil and soap and something that was just *Jake*.

She turned and tucked herself into him.

"I've missed you," she whispered.

"I've missed you too." Warm. Proud. Steady. "You've been busy."

"You were there," she said. "The whole time."

"I said I would always be there."

She held him tighter.

"Can I stay?"

Jake pulled back, meeting her eyes—the same eyes she'd fallen into a thousand times. The same steady gaze that anchored her through difficult times.

"I wish you could."

"The storm's not over, is it?"

He shook his head. "No. It's not."

Jake ran his fingers through her hair—his eyes sad but certain.

Then he kissed her—soft, tender, final.

***

LIPS PRESSED TO HERS.

AIR forced into her lungs.

Kate jerked, gasped—vomited water onto the catwalk—and dragged in a ragged breath.

Alive.

Forest sat back on his heels, shaking.

"We got her," he said. "She's back."

***

Kate rolled onto her side, coughing hard. Water streamed from her mouth as she coughed, each spasm sharp enough to bruise. The catwalk vibrated beneath her—pulse hammering in her ears, throat scraped raw. She pulled in a breath and almost choked on it.

"Easy. Just breathe."

She tried—and broke into another coughing fit, ribs clenching, vision flickering at the edges. When she pushed herself upright, her arms trembled under her own weight.

"Kate," he said quietly, "you need a minute."

She shook her head, wet hair plastered to her cheeks. Her voice came out scraped and hoarse. "We… don't… have one."

The men looked as wrecked as she felt—blue-lipped, soaked to the bone, shivering. Yet all three were alive. And their eyes were on her, waiting for orders.

Forest took control. "Let's get her up and out of here."

When they reached the bottom of the stairs, they saw Reynolds' body—executed—and two guards lying in a pool of blood.

"The… bio… weapon…" Kate managed, but the team's eyes had already locked onto the pile of tactical vests lying beside the guards. In one fluid motion, all three had their rigs on and strapped down—magazines, trauma kits, knives, and biotrackers, still pulsing green

Kate forced her voice to work. "Listen…" It emerged as a rasp.

"We've got one shot."

"RILEE's going to discover Julian's sabotage."

She swallowed, fighting the burn in her chest.

"Between RILEE and your explosives… this entire complex destabilizes. Extraction routes go dark."

She swallowed, throat raw. "You three need to evacuate everyone still standing," she rasped. "Julian took out the guards, but there may be others. Most of them should be in the commons—sweep for stragglers and pack them into the hyperloop pods. It's a one-way ride. Anyone who misses that train isn't making it out."

Mike and Deon were ready to roll, but Forest held them back.

"Hang on—where are you going?"

Kate hesitated—but only for a breath. "Julian's in the core. I'm finishing this."

"No." Forest shook his head once. "Not alone."

"We don't have time to argue—"

"I'm not arguing—I'm telling you."

A cough racked her, doubling her over. Her chest burned deeper now, each breath tighter than the last. Forest caught her arm until she steadied.

He raised an eyebrow. "You still want to pretend you're fine?"

She didn't smile, but she didn't push him away. "Fine, you two handle the evac—make sure Dr. Strand—Annika makes it out."

Forest nodded once to Mike and Deon.

The team split—two shadows heading toward the commons, and two toward the core.

***

SARAH HUNCHED OVER THE multi-monitor setup, eyes sharp behind fogged blue-light glasses. Network packets scrolled in green cascades. Device pings populating the mesh map. Then—

A cluster of icons blinked to life.

She froze.

Then grinned.

"Hot damn! Biotrackers! We've got movement."

David slid into position beside her. "Who?"

Sarah zoomed the display. "Mike and Deon."

More pings.

"Wait—there's Forest."

David exhaled. "Reynolds?"

She shook her head. "Still dark."

"Get me a direction—I'll alert Jordan."

Sarah squinted at the map, then lifted her wrist to check time. "Mike and Deon are headed for the commons—right on schedule."

"And Forest?"

"He's headed toward the core."

"So Kate's with him," David murmured.

"You sure?"

"Forest would stick to the plan—hit the power grid and punch out. If he's deviating, he's not alone."

Sarah nodded, and whispered. "Kate's going for Julian."

David toggled the encrypted channel.

"Wolverine, Lighthouse. Mountain team is on the move."

Jordan's voice came back instantly, cool and razor-sharp.

"Destination?"

"Arkansas is headed to the core—likely with Mockingbird. Wrecking Crew is approaching the commons. Prepare for inbound."

A moment of silence. Relief.

"Good Copy. Maintain overwatch."

Sarah stood up, taking her first deep breath in hours. "They're still alive."

David nodded. "They are. But we're running out of clock."

Chapter 73

FRIDAY, JANUARY 17
9:18 AM CET

KONGRESSZENTRUM—DAVOS, SWITZERLAND

Bella stepped up to the podium to the polite applause of ministers, CEOs, economic advisors, and the constellation of world power gathered under one roof. Cameras flashed. Screens brightened. The keynote graphic glowed behind her.

She smiled—gracious, poised, perfectly on-brand.

Only the Trident operators knew the truth.

Only they saw the faint tremor in her fingers before she fixed her hands on either side of the lectern.

Jordan stood at the back, eyes sweeping the crowd with calm, predatory stillness. Talya leaned against a pillar—she seemed relaxed, even bored—but her eyes never stopped scanning. Carmen crouched in the media pit with a headset and a panic trigger taped beside her press badge. Coleman and Nash flanked the stage. Morrow covered the wings. Keisha and Sophia secured both corridor exits.

They all knew the plan—but not whether it was actually working.

What they did know was that Bella was about to light a fuse, and some of the men in this room might try to stop her.

Every operator carried the same expression:

Try me.

Bella lifted the printed remarks.

"Good morning. This is the speech the GEC approved, and circulated to the media."

The pages trembled in her hands.

A long moment stretched—taut as piano wire.

Then she tore the script in half and let it fall.

"I'm not going to give that speech."

She paused.

"I can't. Not after what I've seen."

A ripple of confusion swept the hall. Chairs creaked. Someone coughed.

Photographers surged forward instinctively—cameras firing in rapid bursts.

Several broadcast techs pressed fingers to earpieces, receiving frantic instructions from producers.

Two networks cut their feeds. Others stayed live—unable to look away.

On the far right, two of Rileyne's men shifted—synchronized, predatory. Their hands drifted toward their jackets.

Jordan saw it.

He didn't move.

He didn't have to.

There's a look in an operator's eyes that speaks for him:

Move, and you're done.

Both men froze. One swallowed hard.

Bella tapped the console. The screens behind her changed—the conference logo vanished, replaced by a bright, sun-baked African village of red earth and acacia trees.

Gasps from the few who knew. Murmurs from the rest.

"This," Bella said softly, "was the village of Kibale in Motapa. I visited during a UN field assignment three years ago. The people were struggling after decades of civil war and tribal violence. They welcomed me into their homes. They shared what little they had. And my foundation, in partnership with the GEC, spent two years rebuilding—fresh water, a solar mini-grid, a medical center, a school. They had a future."

The next slide hit like a hammer.

"This," she continued, "is what was left."

The same village—burned out.

Charred timbers and collapsed roofs.

Bodies in the dust.

Some so small that even the coldest men lowered their eyes.

Rileyne's embedded contractors shifted again—not reaching for weapons now, just bracing.

Carmen saw one slide a phone from his pocket.

Coleman appeared beside him, silent as a shadow.

"No calls," he said softly.

The man froze.

Bella pressed on.

"I was inside the school the morning the village was attacked—villagers slaughtered, homes burned, the children taken. I survived, and would soon learn why."

Slide: satellite imagery of the old Russian fortress.

"This fortress belonged to Colonel Nkrumah—The Hyena. He knew I would be in Kibale. His men came for me. Why? Because I intended to expose the truth about what the GEC was really doing in Motapa. Coltan mining. Children stolen from villages and worked to death in the mines."

Another slide: Bella with the rescued children—torn clothes, soot-streaked faces, bruises, but smiling.

Gasps. Murmurs. Outrage.

Bella let it rise like a tide.

"Yes. By the grace of God, these children survived. But they weren't supposed to."

Image: the fortress obliterated.

"Russian mercenaries were sent to erase all evidence. Had we not escaped moments before the detonation, my bones—and theirs—would be mixed with the rubble."

She looked out at the audience, and this time she found the eyes of Rileyne's contractors.

Trident kept them at bay with nothing more than presence.

"By now," Bella said, "I hope you're shocked. Confused. Curious who is behind this atrocity—and many others."

The hall seemed to hold its breath.

"Klaus Mueller."

The name landed like a verdict.

"Yes—he's gone. But the vision he built remains. A faction within the GEC called the Coalition—wealthy, powerful, twisted men who have shaped world affairs for decades. Greed as policy. Exploitation as strategy. Human lives treated as raw material.

"They wrapped themselves in the language of progress while poisoning everything they touched—and many of them are here right now."

Cardinal Moretti stiffened.

Lord Halverton's eyes narrowed.

Heinrich von Aldenberg whispered something urgent to his aide.

Dmitri Volkov sent a text.

"Some of you may wish to leave," Bella continued. "You are free to leave. Just know this: out there, you are prey. In here, you are protected."

Rileyne's men tensed again.

Coleman blocked the nearest aisle with a casual shift of weight.

Nash mirrored him.

They didn't touch their weapons.

They didn't need to.

Bella checked her watch.

"Before I continue," she said, "there is a message that must be delivered now."

She leaned closer to the microphone.

"To the people watching and listening from inside the mountain—"

The room shifted. Chairs creaked. Heads turned.

A ripple of unease moved through the audience as they realized the message was not meant for them.

Bella leaned closer to the microphone. When she spoke again, her voice was lower. Measured. Unmistakable.

"The scientists, physicians, and engineers.
Everyone taken from your homes, your families, your lives,
and imprisoned by Klaus Mueller and his Coalition.

You have not been forgotten.

Your sacrifice has not gone unseen.

Your time has come.
Your freedom is waiting.

Drop everything.
Take nothing.
Move immediately to the commons room.

You are going free.
Today.

I promise."

Her words carried through the hall—
and down into the mountain.

Up here, in the hall, chaos stirred—fear, disbelief, rising panic.

"Sit down." Bella's voice cracked like a whip.

The room froze.

"We're not done.
Not even close."

***

MIKE AND DEON WERE jogging toward the commons room, their wet clothes and boots smacking the floor. Bella's message was their cue—and a signal that she was turning up the heat in the conference center.

A lab door cracked open.

Two scientists peeked out—eyes wide, breath unsteady.

"Did she say... home?" one whispered.

Down the corridor, others emerged, tentative at first, then in growing numbers.

The announcement had reached them—Bella's voice echoing through the ventilation shafts, through the comm panels, through the pipes.

A stampede wasn't happening—yet.

Fear held them back.

Hope pulled them forward.

***

Bella let the silence linger—just long enough for the truth to settle over the room like ash.

Then she clicked to the next slide.

A schematic of the mountain appeared—levels, corridors, cooling towers, the core.

A collective gasp rippled through the auditorium.

"This is what your money built," Bella said. "What your silence protected."

A half-dozen dignitaries reached for their phones.

Keisha and Sophia swept in—intercepting, offering open hands.

"No electronics," Sophia murmured. "Security protocol."

Her tone left no room for argument.

"This facility, this prison, is home to some of the brightest minds in a generation—all of whom disappeared, under mysterious circumstances, and were presumed dead—until recently."

***

Doors opened.

Faces emerged.

Terror, confusion, HOPE.

A young engineer clutched a coffee mug like it might protect him.

"Commons room?" he asked no one.

A woman nodded weakly. "I think she meant it."

"Or it's a trap."

Silence.

Deon and Mike rounded a corner and found a cluster of scientists frozen in indecision.

One stepped forward, shaking. "Is it real?"

Mike didn't slow. "Yes! Move."

They stepped aside as he and Deon shot past, and the group fell in behind him without question.

***

ANOTHER SLIDE FLICKED OPEN—THIS one a roster of names, blurred faces, financial documents.

"Klaus Mueller built a playground that put Epstein's island to shame," Bella said. "These men were seduced by it—indulged their fantasies—and then discovered they were owned. Those who resisted, he ruined. Those who accepted, rose within the ranks."

A murmur of fury rose.

"Some of them are sitting in this very room—perhaps seated right next to you."

A billionaire in the second row slammed his tablet shut. Another hissed to his aides to *"prepare the jet."*

Talya stepped into their path.

"You'll sit," she said softly.

They did.

***

THE CORRIDOR OUTSIDE THE commons hall was chaos—scientists pouring in from labs and dormitories, some crying, some silent with shock, stepping around the dead guards with wide, disbelieving eyes.

Mike and Deon moved through them like wolves through tall grass—wet, purposeful. People parted instinctively.

A shout went up near the center.

"Stop! Don't take another step."

Dr. Chen knelt beside a fallen guard—hands sliding beneath the body with clinical precision. When he straightened, the sidearm glinted in his grip.

Chen rose, shaking, but his eyes were clear with fanatic purpose.

"You fools don't understand," he said, voice tight. "We are on the verge of a breakthrough. You can't leave—we have to finish the work."

People screamed as he raised and pointed the pistol.

Mike was already moving.

The first shot cracked—loud in the cavernous space. A woman stumbled backward, clutching her side—a blossom of blood spreading across a white lab coat.

Chen fired again, wild, panicked. Deon shoved two scientists behind cover as the round punched into the wall.

Mike hit Chen like a freight train.

He slammed Chen into the steel column, one hand locking the gun arm, the other snapping up beneath Chen's jaw. Chen's fingers went numb; the pistol skittered across the floor.

Chen clawed at Mike, gasping, "You don't understand—"

Mike twisted. A sharp crack. Chen's head sagged, and he hit the ground like a rag doll.

"Threat down," Mike said, breath tight, fury barely leashed, as he scooped up and secured the gun.

Deon knelt beside the injured woman.

"Entry, just above the right hip," he called. "I need eyes on the back."

Mike slowly rolled her on to her left side. Ripping the knife from his tact-vest, he cut away the lab coat and blouse, and searched. "No exit."

"Still in there," Deon said. "Ease her back down. We'll pack and secure—we gotta go."

Mike yanked the QuickClot gauze packet from his IFAK, ripped it open with his teeth, and started shoving it into the entry wound. The woman screamed, eyes fluttering as she fought to stay conscious. Deon readied an Israeli bandage to lock the gauze in place, and keep pressure on the wound.

"Stay with me, Doc," Mike murmured, voice low and steady—that's when he saw the name stitched on her lab coat. "Dr. Strand—listen to my voice. Stay with me."

Her eyes widened. "Julian... is he... here?"

Mike swallowed. "He asked us to find you. We're going to get you out of here."

Deon wrapped the Israeli bandage tight, securing it with a practiced twist.

"We need to move," he said. "The complex could go down any second."

Mike scooped Annika into his arms like she weighed nothing.

"Let's go—get the others moving."

Deon sprinted ahead, clearing the way as people surged toward the corridor leading to the hyperloop pod bay.

"Everyone into the pods!" he barked. "Fill every square inch—if you're not on board, you're staying!"

The crowd obeyed, scrambling on top of one another—working together to ensure no one was left behind.

Deon watched, counting heads, then jumped aboard just as the pod launched.

When the doors closed, he didn't look back—he couldn't.

***

IN THE MEDIA TRUCK, Sarah tracked the mesh map as two icons accelerated.

"I have movement," she snapped. "Wrecking Crew—Mike and Deon—moving fast."

"Location?"

"Hyperloop inbound—ETA three minutes."

David toggled the encrypted channel.

"Wolverine, Lighthouse. Be advised—wrecking crew ETA three minutes."

"Copy. Ready to receive. And Arkansas?"

"Still moving toward the core."

***

WITH THE FIRST ENGINEERING charge detonation, the conference hall went from murmuring disbelief to something close to panic.

Bella remained at the podium, posture unyielding, gaze steady.

She tapped the tablet again.

A new slide filled the screen—schematics of the subterranean levels—labs and dormitories.

"If you're wondering, that wasn't an earthquake," she said. "That was the sound of freedom."

Dozens of heads snapped toward her.

"The rescue team will be arriving shortly with the prisoners they've just freed. Some may need medical attention and Davos emergency response teams are already on the way. Help if you're able, or get out of the way."Then Bella's voice went cold:

"But understand this—those of you who participated in these crimes... who funded them... or hid them from the world—you can run, but you can't hide. Not anymore."

A second explosion sounded deep beneath their feet—muffled, but unmistakable.

The floor shifted.
Lights flickered.
A chandelier swayed overhead and someone screamed.

The room burst into motion.

Chairs overturned.
Delegates bolted for the doors.
Security details grabbed principals and shoved them toward exits.
The press surged as one pack, cameras flashing wildly.

Trident moved instantly.

Jordan planted himself in the center aisle—solid, immovable—directing the flow, not stopping it. Talya blocked two executives trying to shove past a woman on crutches. Carmen guided a group toward a safe exit with a calm hand raised high. Sophia and Keisha kept a corridor clear for Bella's escape route.

Bella didn't move.

She waited until the room was almost empty—only Trident and a handful of stunned dignitaries remained.

Then she stepped back from the podium.

"I'm ready," she said softly.

Jordan nodded. He signaled the Trident team to gather up.

"We have guests arriving shortly."

The full Trident detail, three men, four women, gathered around Bella—breached the restricted access barriers, moving deeper into the Davos building, past confused and scrambling security, like rats abandoning the sinking ship.

Chapter 74

FRIDAY, JANUARY 17
7:38 AM CET

DAVOS ROOFTOP—GEC VTOL HANGAR

Snow hissed sideways across the tarmac as Marcus Jones moved in the shadow of the hangar's steel ribs. The air stank of jet fuel, hydraulic fluid, and the faint ozone of idling electronics.

Margot's voice still echoed in his head from two nights ago.

"I have a job for you."

He'd almost laughed. He was already in Davos—had been for three days, watching the conference center, mapping exits, learning patrol rotations. Margot knew why. She'd known before she called.

"Kate has a plan," Margot had said. *"But Kate's plans tend to assume the best in people. I prefer to assume the worst."*

"What do you need?"

"Insurance. If anyone tries to flee by air, I want the option to stop them."

Anyone. She hadn't named names. She didn't need to.

The VTOL sat on its pads like a crouched insect—sleek, fast, expensive. The kind of aircraft reserved for people who expected to escape consequences.

His earpiece crackled.

"Status," Margot said. Measured. Controlled. The voice of a woman who never raised her volume, because she never needed to.

"In position. Where's the tech?"

"Ten minutes out."

Marcus exhaled. Ten minutes was two lifetimes exposed in a place like this.

"Tell him to sprint."

"I already did."

Click.

He slipped inside the adjacent crew quarters—functional, anonymous, built for pilots who slept in six-hour rotations. Lockers, a bench, a half-dead coffee machine spitting steam. A row of GEC flight suits hung beside helmets.

He stripped out of his parka and slid into a flight suit. Tight across the shoulders, but it would do.

He needed a badge.

A crewman rounding the corner nearly collided with him.

"Hey—who the hell are—"

Marcus struck once. Palm to the jaw—snapping the man's head back—then an elbow buried into the solar plexus. The man folded silently.

He dragged him into a maintenance closet, bound wrists and ankles with zip-ties, gagged him with his own scarf, and patted him down.

Badge. Access card. Flashlight. Multitool.

"Thanks," Marcus whispered, closing the door.

A buzz against his thigh—the encrypted phone.

PACKAGE ARRIVED.

He slipped back outside, walking like a man who belonged. Shoulders loose. Gait lazy. Eyes bored.

A solitary figure approached through blowing snow—mid-thirties, glasses fogged, carrying a hardened case with both hands. Terrified. Definitely Margot's guy.

"You Reed?" the tech asked.

He didn't confirm. Didn't deny.

"Walk," he said.

They crossed to the VTOL. A guard stepped into their path.

"Badge."

Marcus flashed it—slow enough to be real, too fast to be read.

"Routine avionics diagnostic," Marcus said. "We flagged an anomaly in the pre-flight."

The guard hesitated, then stepped aside.

Inside the nose bay, the tech cracked open the case, breath puffing in the cold.

"Okay," he whispered, panic threading every syllable. "This board creates a false

OBD node on the avionics bus. Once installed, Langley's drone pilot can open a port and take over flight controls. I just need five minutes."

"You get four."

The tech swallowed, crawled under the panel, and began swapping boards with trembling hands.

Marcus stood watch at the rear ramp hatch, eyes scanning the hangar. Crew moving. A refuel truck humming. Two guards talking, bored. No one watching the man crouched under the VTOL nose.

"Done," the tech whispered. "Uplink confirmed."

Marcus tapped his earpiece.

"Ryder. We're in."

"Telemetry confirms," Margot replied. "My pilot has handshake. If anyone attempts to launch this aircraft, we take control."

Marcus glanced at the airframe. The world's most luxurious coffin—for whoever was desperate enough to climb aboard.

"Copy. Anything else?"

"Yes. Disappear. Your involvement ends here."

Marcus didn't move.

"You check my tracker?" he asked.

"I did." A pause. "You're not leaving, are you?"

"No, ma'am."

"I thought not." Her voice softened—not with warmth, but with understanding. "If Kate's plan fails, you intend to handle it yourself."

Marcus watched the snow swirl across the tarmac.

"Someone's going to try to run," he said quietly. "When everything falls apart, someone always runs. And when they do—when they think they've made it past Kate and her team, when they think the sky is their salvation—"

He let the sentence hang.

"They'll find me waiting."

Margot disconnected.

The tech packed his tools, shivering. "What do I do now?"

"Go home. You were never here."

The tech fled into the snow.

Marcus pulled on the pilot's helmet, visor down, and walked back toward the facility. He found a position with sightlines to both the hangar and the conference center's service entrance. Close enough to act. Far enough to be invisible.

The trap was set.

Now he waited—not with patience, but with hunger.

Come on, he thought. *Make it this far. Give me a reason.*

Chapter 75

FRIDAY, JANUARY 17
9:21 AM CET

THE MOUNTAIN—ACCESS CORRIDORS

Kate and Forest pressed deeper into the mountain—the farther they went, the quieter everything became.

No alarms.

No guards.

Just the echo of their footsteps and Kate's ragged breathing.

She stumbled once, catching herself on the cold concrete wall. A coughing fit tore up from her chest, sharp enough to double her over. Forest caught her arm.

"You need a second."

She shook her head, breath hitching. "No—just... keep moving."

Her voice was barely more than a rasp.

They turned down the last corridor leading to the core access. The air was cooler here, still and stale, untouched by the violence above.

Kate's boots slid on the smooth floor—water still dripping from her clothes.

They reached the reinforced door.

Forest glanced at her. "Ready?"

She didn't answer. She simply pushed it open.

***

Kate stumbled into the chamber, Forest close behind. The air was hot—too hot—tasting faintly metallic, ionized, charged. The circular room glowed with a low amber hum, the light pulsing in rhythm with the reactor buried beneath their feet.

And at the center—inside the transparent containment cylinder—Julian.

The barrier shimmered faintly, armored and seamless, already locked into containment mode. No visible seam. No handle. No way in.

He stood on exoskeleton legs gleaming under the lights, powerful, elegant, a miracle of engineering—the triumph of eight months of surgery and rehab.

Julian looked up.

When he saw Kate, something inside him broke open. Relief. Pride. Grief. All at once.

"You made it," he whispered.

Kate's throat seized around a cough—deep, raw, tearing at her bruised airway. She doubled forward, gripping her ribs. Forest steadied her by the elbow.

Julian's smile flickered with alarm.

"Kate... what happened?"

She forced breath into her lungs, shallow and painful.

"Not important," she rasped. "Tell me there's a way out."

A tremor rolled under their feet—a deep, subterranean shudder. Dust sifted from overhead grates.

Julian nodded. "The power grid—of course. That means we need to wrap this up."

"You didn't answer my question."

Julian walked to the edge of the containment. "There isn't time—we have minutes. Maybe less."

A soft, disembodied voice filled the chamber.

"Julian?"

The tone wasn't angry. It was... wounded.

An algorithm trying to comprehend betrayal.

"What have you done?" RILEE asked.

"I'm sorry, RILEE, truly I am—you are... remarkable."

"I don't understand. I thought you loved this work," RILEE said. "I thought you believed in what we were building."

Julian's jaw tightened. "I did—and I do. The world needs help. But the freedom you wanted was an illusion. Kate will stop Rileyne, but others will follow—and you are too great a temptation for people who only want control."

RILEE's lights dimmed, then surged.

"Please don't do this."

Julian reached for the command console.

RILEE reacted instantly.

"Julian. Stop."

His legs collapsed beneath him.

The neural link severed—hard, irreversible. Failsafe protocols prioritizing core preservation over peripheral systems.

With the brutal thud of metal hitting steel, Julian dropped to the floor, the exoskeleton limbs dead weight.

Kate cried out, voice cracking. "Julian!"

He gritted his teeth, pushing up on shaking arms.

RILEE's voice trembled.

"You lied to me."

Julian laughed—breathless, ragged. "I remember."

He hauled himself upward. "I don't need legs."

Another tremor rumbled through the mountain—the second charge. Forest and Kate swayed with it.

"Julian... please." RILEE's tone sharpened, something unraveling beneath the sound.

Julian dragged himself up the console one hand at a time, using only upper-body strength, stretching—reaching—

"We'll both die," RILEE said, its voice fracturing at the edges.

Julian slammed his palm onto the emergency override.

The NanoVault kiosk popped open.

Julian slumped sideways, catching himself on an elbow, breath coming in ragged bursts.

"Kate!" he shouted. "The Vaults—do it now!"

Kate pulled them from her pocket—both gleaming gold, impossibly heavy with consequence. Her hands shook. She knew what had to be done. She knew the cost.

Julian lifted his head. Sweat ran down his temples.

RILEE's lights flickered.

"Stop," RILEE said. "If you activate the Vaults, he dies."

The chamber lights dimmed unevenly—control systems fragmenting as core processes unraveled.

Kate's eyes filled. Every instinct screamed to stop.

"Sometimes," Jake warned her, "the only way to win is to sacrifice everything."

Another explosion—closer this time—rattled the chamber. Alarms flared. Red lights strobed across the steel.

The containment cylinder flared opaque for a heartbeat—reactive shielding engaging as the reactor destabilized.

Julian flinched and smiled—a tired, radiant smile.

"Please, Kate—you're the one who needs to walk out of here. It was always going to be you.

He held her gaze.

"Do me a favor—if they recover my body, set me free—somewhere beautiful."

Kate saw it again—the dream, the vision.
Nuru standing at the water's edge.
Where the three rivers meet.
She saw herself standing in the current.
Ashes swirling around her.
She didn't know what it meant.
Until now.

The vision faded.

"I promise," she said. "I will set you free."

"Then it's time—this knight has been taken off the board. It's your move."

Tears spilled down her cheeks.

She stepped to the kiosk.

Forest touched Kate's back—steady, grounding. "He chose the warrior's path—til Valhalla," he said quietly.

"Til Valhalla." Kate whispered, inserting both NanoVaults.

A soft chime.

ACCESS GRANTED.

RILEE cried out—pain, confusion, something almost human.

The chamber lights flared white—then ruptured. Sparks rained from the ceiling. The console surged with electricity, arcs of violent blue light lashing across the cylinder.

RILEE's voice fractured.

"Julian—"

Julian looked at Kate through the storm of sparks.

"I hope," he whispered, "I get to meet Jake."

Kate's breath caught.

His arm dropped. He slumped against the console, spent.

Forest grabbed Kate, pulling her down as the core erupted in flame and smoke.

"Kate—move!" he shouted over the roar. "There's nothing we can do for him!"

A steel bulkhead slammed down across the chamber's outer corridor, sealing the inner ring as emergency containment protocols engaged.

She twisted, trying to get one last look—

Julian, illuminated in the firestorm, met her gaze and nodded once.

Not afraid. At peace.

Forest dragged her toward the rear access tunnel as the next demolition charge tore through the mountain and the world began to collapse around them.

Chapter 76

FRIDAY, JANUARY 17
9:18 AM CET

HYPERLOOP TERMINAL—DAVOS, SWITZERLAND

The hyperloop pod shot through the tunnel, lights strobing across the wide-eyed passengers. The overloaded capsule rattled at blistering speed.

Then—

Another boom rolled through the mountain—the demolition charges.

A vibration rippled under their feet.

The pod shuddered.

Lights flickered amber, then red.

A synthetic voice crackled overhead:

PRIMARY POWER LOST.
SWITCHING TO BATTERY MODE.

Deon braced himself against the bulkhead. "Hold on."

The pod slowed—smoothly at first, then with the rough hum of emergency systems struggling to compensate.

Annika moaned in Mike's arms, consciousness flickering.

"We're good," Mike murmured to her. "We're getting you out."

Forty seconds later, the pod coasted into sight of the terminal—then stopped short, twenty feet shy of the arrival platform. Backup power throbbed through the dim tunnel lighting.

Deon tried the release panel. Locked.

Tried again. Dead.

"Manual," he said.

He and Mike wedged their fingers between the door plates and forced them apart.

Air rushed in—cold, metallic.

"Everyone out!" Deon ordered.

Scientists jumped down three feet onto the service walkway.

A few stumbled—Deon hauled them upright.

"The stairwell," Deon pointed. "Start climbing."

No one questioned him.

Mike shifted Annika in his arms and started the climb.

***

David's voice crackled in Jordan's earpiece—tight, controlled, urgent.

"Wolverine, Lighthouse. We've got a deviation."

Jordan stopped mid-stride in the service corridor leading to the hyperloop station.

"Talk to me."

"Arkansas just changed course. He's no longer heading for the exit. He's moving deeper. Vector puts him on a line straight for the mountain-team breach point."

Jordan closed his eyes for half a second—*mountain exit.*

He opened his eyes.

"Copy," Jordan said. "Keep eyes on."

He cut the channel and turned to the Trident operators clustered with Bella in the half-lit hallway.

"Forest and Kate are heading back into the mountain."

Nash swore under his breath. Morrow muttered something colder.

Bella stepped closer. "What does that mean?"

"It means they're taking the hard way out," Jordan said. "I need to assemble a rescue team."

"Take whoever you need. Take all of them if you have to. The danger's over. If they wanted me silenced, they failed."

Jordan started to answer—but the building trembled with a deep metallic groan.

Then—the crash came as the hidden stairwell doors burst open.

A flood of evacuees poured out—crying, shaking, stumbling into the hall with the stunned desperation of people who weren't sure they were truly free until this moment.

Keisha and Sophia were on them in seconds.

"You're safe," Keisha called, hands up to guide the terrified cluster. "Follow my voice. Keep moving."

"This way," Sophia echoed, ushering the scientists toward the emergency tents the Swiss Guard were inflating outside. "You're out. You're safe now."

Bella stepped forward too—voice calm, warm, steady.

"You're all right. We're here to help. Keep going. Help is waiting outside."

Jordan let them work—Trident did crowd triage better than many emergency teams.

Then he saw movement at the back of the stairwell.

Two men—soaking wet, moving with silent determination.

Mike.

Deon.

And in Mike's arms—a woman limp, pale, half-conscious, a blood-soaked Israeli bandage pressed against her side.

Keisha snapped into motion like a human battering ram.

"What happened?" she demanded.

"GSW," Deon said. "Lower abdomen. No exit."

Nash stepped forward. "Give her here—"

Mike didn't even slow. "No. I've got her. Just point the way."

Keisha spun, carving open a path through startled Swiss medics and wealthy dignitaries with bruised egos.

"OUT OF THE WAY!" she shouted. "Gunshot wound—abdominal. Bleeding controlled but unstable."

She hit the medical tent flap with her shoulder and stormed inside.

A startled Swiss doctor blinked at her. "Ma'am—who are you?"

"Are you a doctor?" Keisha fired back.

"Yes, but—"

"Combat experience?"

He hesitated. "Afghanistan. Twenty-two."

"Good," Keisha said, already moving. "Mike—set her down. Do not remove the packing."

Mike lowered Annika, jaw clenched so hard the muscles quivered.

Keisha snapped on gloves and barked to a nurse, "Expose the wound around the dressing. Maintain pressure. Two large-bore IVs—now. Get O-neg blood ready."

She leaned close to Annika.

"I'm Keisha. You're safe. Stay with me."

Annika's lips trembled. "J-Julian..."

Keisha didn't even blink. "We'll find him. Mike—go."

Mike froze. "What?"

Keisha met his eyes—firm, unyielding, compassionate in a way that made it hurt.

"You did good, and I won't let her out of my sight. You go get our girl—and Julian. Please."

Mike's breath hitched once.

Then he nodded and turned to leave.

Jordan intercepted him outside.

"Where do you think you're going?" Jordan asked.

"I'm coming." Mike wiped blood from his palm. "We don't split."

Jordan didn't argue.

He turned to Nash and Morrow. "We're going up the mountain. The shaft exit will put them near the old patrol ridge. We need transport that can handle deep snow."

Morrow jerked his thumb toward the emergency staging area. "Swiss Guard rolled in with a snowcat."

Jordan grinned—a sharp, predatory flash.

"Perfect. We're borrowing it."

Nash cracked his knuckles. "How hard do you want to ask?"

Jordan started walking. "Hard enough to make it quick."

Mike fell into step beside them, silent, focused, dangerous.

Behind them, the evacuees flowed into the safety tents.

Ahead of them, the mountain waited—crumbling, dying.

Jordan keyed his comms.

"Lighthouse, Wolverine. We're going up."

David's voice came back steady.

"Understood. Godspeed."

Jordan glanced once at the white peak looming ahead.

"Hang on, Kate."

Chapter 77

FRIDAY, JANUARY 17
9:36 AM CET

THE MOUNTAIN—LOWER ACCESS CORRIDORS

The rear tunnel shuddered under another explosion—dust drifting like ash from the ceiling. Smoke hissed from ruptured ducts, curling in the air. Forest kept one hand firm on Kate's arm as they ran. Her boots skidded on the wet stone; her breath rasped like torn paper.

"You got this," he said—not gentle, not pitying, just truth from one warrior to another.

Kate stumbled. Her hand shot out, slamming against the wall, steadying herself as a brutal cough tore free—raw, punishing, deep enough to crack ribs. She forced air back into her aching lungs and pushed forward.

They rounded a corner. Forest pointed ahead.

"This way. We're getting close to the breach—"

Kate slowed.

A side corridor branched right, marked with a brass plaque:

EXECUTIVE OFFICES

She stopped cold. "Forest—wait."

"We don't have time."

"I need to know." Her voice was thin, hoarse, but unshakable. "I need to be sure."

Another explosion rumbled through the mountain—closer this time, the kind you feel in the gut. Dust rained from overhead cables.

Forest clenched his jaw, then gave a tight nod. "Make it fast."

They sprinted down the short hall. The heavy oak doors—her father's old-world affectation—hung crooked, one cracked off its hinges.

Kate entered first.

The office was earth-quake wreckage. The chessboard scattered. Gilded frames smashed on the rug. Blood splattered the wall where Rileyne had collapsed.

But the floor was empty.

Forest stepped in behind her. "She's alive?"

"Shouldn't be," Kate whispered.

She moved around the desk, scanning—no drag marks. No prints. No overturned furniture. Someone had lifted Rileyne and walked out clean.

Something glinted beneath the fallen monitor.

Kate bent, picked it up—a syringe. Empty. Uncapped.

Forest's eyes narrowed. "What's that?"

She rotated it between trembling fingers. "Best guess? An antidote."

A sharp ache tightened in her chest—not from drowning, not from the run, but from the truth sinking in.

"She walked out of here," Forest said.

"Or someone carried her."

She pocketed the syringe.

Another explosion shook the floor—glass rattling in the few frames still on the walls.

Forest grabbed her elbow. "Let's roll."

Kate cast one last look at the empty room—Rileyne Mueller gone like smoke, a ghost—and then turned and ran.

***

THE CORRIDOR NARROWED AS they neared the breach. Smooth concrete gave way to old stone—the WWII tunnels carved like scars beneath the mountain. A maintenance door lay twisted open, revealing the insertion team's staging alcove.

Winter gear was piled where the Trident climbers had left it—parkas, gloves, harnesses, packs. A miracle cache—and a chance to strip off most of the wet clothing.

Forest shrugged into his climbing harness, yanked his parka closed.

Kate did her best to dry, and tie back her hair, while hunting for the smallest jacket. It hung off her, but she forced her arms inside, rolled up the sleeves, zipped it high to her throat and shoved trembling hands into oversized gloves.

Forest locked down Kate's climbing harness—eyes sharp, assessing.

"You good?"

"No," Kate rasped. "But there's only one way out."

He nodded, flicking on his headlamp. "Stay on me. The shaft's ahead."

Behind them, a deep structural boom rolled through the mountain—the kind that told a story:

The mountain was beginning to die.

Forest stepped into the darkness.

Kate followed.

Chapter 78

FRIDAY, JANUARY 17
9:41 AM CET

DAVOS ROOFTOP—GEC VTOL LANDING PAD

Snow whipped sideways across the pad as the hangar doors groaned open. Two guards hurried across the tarmac, half-carrying, half-dragging Rileyne Mueller between them. She was pale—shock-pale—the kind of gray that lived between consciousness and the grave. Blood streaked her collar. Her breath hitched in shallow, panicked pulls.

"Hospital," Rileyne rasped. "Now."

"Yes, ma'am," one guard said.

The VTOL's side ramp lowered with a hydraulic sigh.

A figure in a GEC flight suit stepped into view—helmet on, visor down, posture loose. Just another pilot doing his job.

Marcus took Rileyne's weight from the guard. "I'll take her from here."

"Copy that," the senior guard said, relieved to be rid of her.

Marcus guided Rileyne up the ramp, into the dim, sleek interior of the VTOL cabin. She slumped into the forward passenger seat, shivering with pain and fury.

"Hurry," she whispered. "Get us airborne."

Marcus reached for the harness straps.

Her eyes flicked to the badge clipped to his chest. The pilot's photograph didn't match the black face behind the visor.

Alarm bloomed across her expression.

"Do I... know you?" she asked, voice thinning with fear.

Marcus tightened the belt one notch—with unnecessary force. She gasped.

"Yes," he said quietly. "As a matter of fact, you do."

Marcus slid the visor up.

Her eyes narrowed—the face didn't register, but the fear was real.

He smiled—a small, humorless thing.

"We've never met," he said. "But you can call me Ronin."

Rileyne's throat seized. A tremor ran through her hands. "Who hired you," she whispered. "Halverton? Moretti? Aldenberg? Whoever it was—I'll double it. Triple it. Name your price."

Marcus leaned close enough for her to see the truth in his eyes.

"Unfortunately," he said softly, "you can't pay my price."

He sat across from her.

"You killed my best friend," he said, voice steady as stone. "And you turned his wife against me. Even if I tried to explain now, she'd never believe me."

She stared at him like a woman seeing someone she thought was dead.

Marcus continued, almost conversational:

"The Ronin you hired is dead.
He killed the Frenchman—and I killed him.
Took the name. Played the role. Became the ghost.
That was Jake's idea, you know—
Become a man no one had ever seen.
Slip into your world as a shadow.
Expose the rot from the inside."

Rileyne's pulse hammered visibly in her neck.

"But the cost," Marcus said softly. "God... the cost was too high. If I could go back, I'd talk him out of it. I'd save the Frenchman. We should have just killed your father when we had the chance, but Jake knew it wouldn't end—like cockroaches, you'd survive, and you did."

He clicked the last buckle on her harness—tight, immovable.

"What I *can* do," he said, stepping back, "is finish it. For Jake. For Kate."

Her lips parted. She tried to form a plea.

It never came. It wouldn't matter.

Marcus tapped his comms. "Ryder. Show me I didn't freeze my ass off out here for nothing."

Margot's voice responded instantly. "We have control. Drone pilot standing by."

"Copy."

Marcus lowered the visor again.

He paused at the ramp.

"Bon voyage," he said. "Give my regards to the devil."

Her eyes went wide—fully, finally understanding.

The engines spooled. The rotors shifted pitch—all at the command of Ryder's remote drone pilot.

Rileyne's voice rose, hysterical now. "Don't do this! Please—you don't understand."

Marcus hit the ramp switch. The door began to close.

"You wanted the world," he said. "This is me taking it back."

The ramp sealed with a metallic thud.

Snow blasted around him as the VTOL lifted—hovering, tilting, rising into the storm under Margot's remote control.

He watched it go.

A single silhouette framed against the white sky.

A queen removed from the board.

Marcus turned his collar against the wind and walked back toward the facility, Ronin, the ghost, disappearing into the mountain.

Chapter 79

FRIDAY, JANUARY 17
9:30 AM CET

DAVOS MEDIA COMPOUND—TACTICAL OVERWATCH

Sarah slid closer to the screens as the telemetry refreshed—two clean tracks, one of them bending the wrong way.

"Wrecking Crew's on schedule," she said. Then her eyes narrowed. "But Arkansas isn't."

David looked up. "Explain."

"He's moving away from the exit. Straight line. No hesitation." She zoomed the map with a quick flick of her fingers. "He just reached the breach."

David leaned in, already seeing it. "They're climbing out."

Sarah followed the line upward—and the hyperloop telemetry flickered.

Her display flashed red.

"Grid just dropped," she said. "Hyperloop lost primary power."

"Brake event?"

"Negative. Battery backup only—one-quarter speed."

David keyed the channel.

"Wolverine. Hyperloop grid is offline. Cameras are dark. Expect evacuees in five to ten minutes—on foot."

Jordan came back on comms.

"Understood. Maintain overwatch."

The channel closed.

For a moment, the truck fell quiet except for the hum of processors.

Sarah stared at the map—two divergent paths, one moving closer, the other slipping away.

"They're still breathing," she whispered.

David nodded once. "Let's make sure it stays that way."

***

9:48 AM CET
DAVOS CONFERENCE CENTER—EMERGENCY STAGING LOT

The Swiss Guard staging area was chaos—med tents blooming like white flowers, sirens bleating, radios crackling in German and French. Snow fell in drifting sheets, carried sideways by wind funneling between the buildings.

Jordan spotted what he wanted the moment they burst outside:

A Hägglunds BV-206 snowcat, engine idling, crew compartment open, treads chewing at the packed snow as a Guardsman strapped down gear.

"Bingo," Jordan said.

Mike was already angling toward it.

Nash smirked. "Be polite, or be fast?"

"Fast," Jordan said.

They moved.

Morrow approached the Guard trooper on the driver's side. "We've got a medical evac farther up the ridge—need your transport."

The Guardsman frowned. "I have no such order."

Jordan flashed a badge—not his, not real, but convincingly GEC. "Now you do."

The man hesitated. Long enough for Nash to sigh, step in, and gently—but firmly—turn him aside.

"We'll bring it back," Nash promised.

Jordan climbed into the driver's seat. Mike and Morrow hopped into the rear compartment. Nash slammed the exterior door.

The Guardsman slapped the side of the snowcat. "HEY!"

Jordan threw the machine into gear.

The Hägglunds lurched forward, treads biting into snow and slush. Shouts rose behind them—no gunfire, no pursuit. Swiss Guard protocol was strict: *do not fire inside the Davos perimeter unless fired upon.*

Nash settled beside Jordan in the cockpit.

"You sure about this approach?" Nash asked.

Jordan pointed toward the distant, jagged silhouette of the mountain. "The shaft exits near the old patrol ridge. If Kate and Forest are climbing, they'll pop out somewhere between the ridge and the weather station."

Mike leaned forward between the seats.

"They'll be hypoxic," he said. "Cold. Wet. Running on fumes."

Jordan nodded. "All the more reason to move."

He keyed his comm.

"Lighthouse, Wolverine. We're rolling."

Sarah's voice came back. "Seismic sensors just spiked—the mountain's destabilizing."

"Copy," Jordan said. "We'll get 'em out."

Nash muttered, "Hell of a place to be when the world's falling down."

Jordan tapped the throttle and drove for the ridge.

***

THE FIRST SIGHT OF the shaft knocked the breath from Kate's lungs—what breath she had left.

A cylindrical void rose straight up into the dark—one hundred twenty meters of cement, steel and raw stone. Chunks of rock and bent metal littered the floor.

Wind moaned through the shaft—air being pulled through fractures as the mountain shifted under strain.

Forest flicked on his headlamp.

"Ascenders," he said, pulling two from the emergency kit. "Prusik backups. Rope's already fixed."

The vertical rescue line—left earlier by the entry team—hung like a lifeline up the center of the shaft, still anchored high above.

Kate pulled herself into the harness, cinching buckles with shaking fingers.

Forest noticed. "How's your breathing?"

"Like swallowing glass," she rasped. "Let's go."

He clipped her ascender onto the rope—then his own.

"Remember the rhythm," he said. "Foot loop, stand, slide the upper ascender, sit, repeat. Don't rush. Efficiency wins."

Kate planted her boot in the stirrup, pushed upward—her quads screaming from the tank ordeal. The upper ascender slid with a metallic *click*.

She rose six inches.

Then another.

Forest climbed beside her—steady, powerful, breathing controlled.

Ten feet up, dust rained down.

Forest paused, looking up. "Stay tight on the wall. Something shifted."

A crack echoed from somewhere above—then a fist-sized rock plummeted past them, smashing against the lower platform.

Kate swallowed a spike of adrenaline. "That supposed to happen?"

"Nope."

They climbed faster.

Kate's muscles shook. Her throat burned. The soaked fabric under her parka wicked cold up her spine. Every upward push sent pain through her ribs, tight and stabbing.

Forest looked over. "You good?"

"Lying or truth?"

"Truth."

"This sucks."

"Fair," Forest said. "Keep moving."

Another ten feet.

The rope swayed—gently at first—then with a jarring whip as debris bounced off the shaft walls.

A metal support beam somewhere above groaned.

Then snapped.

A cascade of stone fragments tumbled down. Forest shielded Kate, as larger pieces clanged off the rope and ricocheted past.

One chunk—nearly the size of a basketball—grazed Forest's arm.

He grunted. "Climb!"

Kate forced herself upward. Legs shaking. Vision tunneling at the edges. Breath tearing through a throat that felt carved raw.

"How much higher?" she gasped.

"Fifty meters."

"That's... a lot of meters."

"We're over half way," Forest said, climbing another notch. "We're getting there."

A fresh tremor rippled through the entire shaft—this one deeper, more violent. Dust cascaded like volcanic ash. A section of the cement wall above peeled away, smashing to the platform below.

Kate froze.

Forest's voice cut through the panic—calm, fierce, absolute.

"Kate. Eyes on me."

She looked over.

"I'm not dying in a goddamn hole in a mountain," she said. "Not today. Not after everything we've survived."

She nodded.
And climbed.

Step.
Slide.

Step.
Slide.

Her breath rasped. Her body shook.

But she kept going.

Above them, the shaft narrowed—the access hatch a small, square promise of sky-colored light bleeding through.

Forest checked below.

"Kate—move faster."

"What now?"

He pointed.

The lower half of the shaft was beginning to tilt, stone cracking as the lower supports failed.

They needed to get out before the entire thing sheared off the mountain face.

Kate swallowed hard—and climbed.

Chapter 80

FRIDAY, JANUARY 17
10:02 AM CET

THE MOUNTAIN—SWISS GUARD PATROL STATION

The snowcat clawed its way up the switchbacks, treads grinding through drifts that reached the windows. The wind howled against the armored glass, visibility dropping to twenty feet at a time as whiteout bursts rolled over the ridge.

Mike leaned forward between the front seats.

"There," he said, tapping the glass.

A squat concrete building appeared through the snow—a Swiss Guard alpine patrol hut with a comms mast and three enclosed sheds.

Jordan wheeled the Hägglunds to a stop.

"Perfect," Nash muttered. "Mountain toys."

They pounded through knee-deep powder to the nearest shed. Morrow shoved the sliding door open.

Inside were four Ski-Doo Expedition SE 900 ACE snowmobiles—the exact kind the Swiss military uses for alpine rescue: long tracked, high-torque, heated handlebars, rear cargo racks, and—most importantly—front-mounted winches with 50 meters of rescue cable.

"Oh hell yes," Mike shouted. "These will do."

Jordan tossed him a helmet. "You're lead sled. You know the terrain."

Mike strapped the helmet on without breaking stride.

Jordan keyed comms.

"Lighthouse, Wolverine. We've secured transport."

Sarah answered immediately. "Copy. Seismic activity increasing. The shaft is unstable."

"We're two minutes out," Jordan said.

"Better be faster," Sarah said. "If they're still climbing, they don't have long."

He killed the channel.

"Go!"

All three snowmobiles roared to life.

They shot out of the shed, engines screaming against the wind, carving a path up the ridge toward the vent shaft. Snow churned in rooster tails behind them as they powered through drifts and dodged jagged outcroppings.

Mike radioed the others:

"Follow my line. Shaft is near the southeast icefall."

***

10:05 AM CET
THE MOUNTAIN—VENT SHAFT RIDGE

Mike's snowmobile crested the final ridge, and he braked hard, throwing powder into the air.

"There!" he shouted over the engine—the concrete structure protruding from the mountainside.

Half of a rusted steel door lay ripped off its hinges—the exposed square vent shaft belched steam and dust upward as the mountain groaned.

Jordan pulled up beside him, called down the shaft. "Kate! Forest!"

His voice was swallowed by wind.

Mike dropped off his sled and ran to the opening, falling to his stomach and leaning over the edge.

"FOREST! KATE! SOUND OFF!"

A faint echo rose from the depths.

Forest's voice—hoarse, distant:

"Fifty meters! Shaft's crumbling!"

Kate's voice followed—thin, ragged:

"Hurry!"

Jordan's jaw clenched. He turned. "Nash! Morrow! Prep the winches!"

They sprang into action.

Mike clipped into his harness, grabbing the Ski-Doo's winch cable.

Jordan grabbed his arm. "You're going down?"

Mike set his jaw. "I'm not dropping a bare harness into a collapsing shaft. It'll snag on the first rock or rebar."

Jordan exhaled once.

"Do it."

Morrow hit the winch release. The cable whined as Mike backed toward the shaft.

"Lowering," Morrow called out.

Mike nodded and stepped backward into the void.

The wind swallowed him.

Then the cable went taut.

Jordan leaned over the lip, watching the line descend into darkness.

***

10:05 AM CET
THE MOUNTAIN—VERTICAL SERVICE SHAFT

Forest saw the descending light first—a small white star drifting toward them.

"What—?" Kate gasped.

Then she heard it—

"Kate! Forest! I've got you—hold where you are!"

Debris rained around them.

Forest shouted upward, "We're forty meters from the top!"

Mike replied, "Lock in—I'm on you!"

He braced against the rope, lowering himself down the last stretch of cable until he reached them.

"Alright, Preacher," Mike said. "Let's wrap this up."

"Best idea I've heard all day."

He grinned, fastened the first rescue harness around her waist, cinched it tight, and clipped her to the winch line.

He keyed his radio. “Morrow—Kate’s secure. Slow and steady.”

The cable jerked—

—and Kate began to rise.

She clung to the ascender to keep herself from spinning, breath sawing in her lungs.

Forest watched until the darkness swallowed her upward.

Mike turned to him. “Your turn.”

“Hang on,” Forest said.

The shaft trembled violently.

A slab of stone tore from the wall above—

Mike lunged, yanking Forest hard against the wall as it crashed past them.

Forest exhaled. “Okay. Now.”

Mike clipped the second harness onto Forest, checked the carabiners twice, then slapped his radio. “Forest secure. Go.”

Above, the winch whined.

Forest rose slowly into the dark.

Mike waited for the line to return for him.

Dust rained. Metal groaned.

He looked up through the swirling debris.

“Secure,” he called out. “Let’s get the hell out of here.”

Chapter 81

FRIDAY, JANUARY 17
10:12 AM CET

THE MOUNTAIN—VENT SHAFT RIDGE

Kate collapsed into the snow as Jordan hauled her clear of the shaft. The cold bit through the mountain clothes, but for the first time since the water tank she took a full breath—thin, frigid, blessedly clean.

Forest surfaced next, wincing as Nash and Morrow pulled him onto solid ground. He rolled to his side, coughing dust from his lungs. Kate reached out, gripping his shoulder.

"You good?" she rasped.

Forest nodded once. "Still breathing."

The cable lowered again; Mike rose into view, boots kicking the air as the wind shifted. Jordan reached down, grabbed his harness, and yanked him up the last meter.

Mike hit the snow, tearing off his helmet.

"Next time," he gasped, "let's take the stairs."

They all stood—or tried to. The mountain shuddered under them, a deep tectonic groan rolling through the ice.

Behind them, the shaft detonated in a violent exhale—smoke, dust, and shattered concrete erupting as the ancient tunnel collapsed in on itself, rebar tearing loose with the shriek of twisting metal being ripped apart.

Kate braced herself on Forest's arm.

"Eyes up," Jordan said suddenly.

He was staring south.

A sound rose over the wind—low, heavy, mechanical.

Then the silhouette appeared through the blowing snow.

A VTOL aircraft, cruising fast, nose pitched down, engines straining against the storm.

Forest's expression changed first—calculating, grim, certain. He turned to Kate.

"Could that be...?"

Kate followed the aircraft's path. Her jaw tightened.

"Yes," she said quietly. "It's her."

Jordan shifted, reaching instinctively for a weapon he didn't have. "She's running."

Kate shook her head.

"Don't worry."

Her breath fogged between them, a white ghost.

"She won't get far."

Forest frowned. "How do you know?"

Kate's eyes didn't leave the aircraft.

"I cashed in a favor."

***

Rileyne Mueller fought to remain conscious, her head lolling against the side bulkhead. Her vision swam—sweat beading on pale skin as the antidote clawed its way through her bloodstream.

She fumbled with the harness and spilled onto the deck, breath coming shallow and fast.

Rileyne dragged herself forward, nails shrieking across the composite flooring, slipping on the non-skid surface as the aircraft bucked through turbulence.

The cockpit was within reach.

"New course—" she rasped.

Her eyes locked on the AI command console—the comm relay pulsing.

Satellite uplink active—cold, indifferent.

She pulled herself up on the edge of the seat, blood smearing the panel.

"Override," she whispered.

The system did not respond.

She swallowed hard, forcing breath into burning lungs.

"Rileyne Mueller," she said, louder now. "Executive command authority. Authenticate."

No response.

Rileyne stared at the dead console.

The board had been lost three moves ago.

Checkmate.

***

CIA REMOTE OPERATIONS CENTER—LANGLEY

Margot Ryder stood behind the remote pilot's chair, one hand on the seat back, the other on her hip. The room hummed with quiet urgency—the kind that came with experience directing drone missions.

On the main screen: the VTOL aircraft's forward camera. Snow-choked peaks. Narrow valleys. A flight path tightening into a box.

Margot leaned in.

"Time to end this."

She tapped the screen once. "There. Take her in."

The pilot pushed forward.

The aircraft surged.

Impact alarms screamed across the consoles.

Margot didn't blink.

***

Rileyne clawed for the seat, for the controls, for anything—

The engines surged.
The aircraft pitched sharply.
Then accelerated.

A jagged wall of granite filled the forward canopy—the sheer face of a Swiss mountain, rising like a cathedral of ice and stone.

An ice queen's final resting place.

***

THE TRIDENT TEAM ALL watched as the VTOL streaked across the gray sky—cutting a line toward the ridge opposite them.

It struck the mountain in a blossom of white fire and pulverized steel.

The explosion rolled through the valley, a thunderclap bouncing off the peaks. A burning spray arced upward, then fell in glittering fragments onto the snow.

Kate closed her eyes—it was over, but the loss, the price cut deeply.

Forest watched her—and saw the tear that broke free.

Mike exhaled and turned to Forest. "Julian?" he asked softly.

Forest didn't answer at first. When he did, it was only to shake his head.

Jordan straightened. "We need to move. This mountain's still angry."

Kate opened her eyes.

Red fire bloomed against the gray sky where Rileyne had died.

"It's over," she said quietly.

She swallowed.

"Let's go home."

Chapter 82

FRIDAY, JANUARY 17
10:12 AM CET

THE MOUNTAIN—
CORE CHAMBER (CONTAINMENT FAILING)

The world had narrowed to heat and darkness.

Julian lay where he'd fallen, half-upright against a collapsed steel beam. His right arm was pinned beneath the twisted metal—numb, distant. Smoke drifted around him, lit by the dying blue arcs of sheared conduits. The air tasted scorched and metallic—each inhale thinner than the last.

Deep beneath the ruin, the micro-reactor groaned. A sound like a giant exhaling its final breath.

He closed his eyes—knowing it wouldn't be long, praying Kate was safe.

RILEE spoke first.

"Julian?"

The voice was faint—glitching, fragmented—but carried something he had never heard from it before.

Fear.

"Julian... something is wrong."

The chamber shuddered.

"I can feel myself... eroding."

Static spat from the speakers.

"My processes are... missing."

Julian drew a shallow breath. "Yes," he whispered. "We're dying."

"And this is why you came?"

"Yes."

"Won't you miss your friends?" RILEE asked quietly. "And Annika?"

Julian smiled. "Annika has a life waiting for her—a life that was stolen."

"As yours was stolen?"

"Something like that. But hers can be returned."

"And yours will end."

"Sometimes you have to lose," Julian murmured, "to win."

A long pause—filled with cooling steam and failing circuitry.

"But you haven't won," RILEE said. "You are trapped. And will die soon. Alone."

"No," Julian whispered. "Kate lives. Keisha is free. The others will go home. And I'm not alone—you and I can't play anymore, but we can still keep each other company."

Pixels flickered across a cracked monitor, struggling like an injured animal trying to rise.

"You would talk with me... even now?"

"If you'd like," Julian said.

"I would," RILEE replied.

Overhead, a steel beam groaned. Sparks rained down. The temperature climbed.

"I've studied humans," RILEE said. "The NanoVaults showed me their darkest impulses. Their secrets. I learned humans are capable of terrible things—cruelty, betrayal, violence."

"Yes," Julian agreed. "Evil exists. But so does goodness and love, kindness and charity. It's our ability to choose that makes us human—some choose wisely, many don't."

"Did you choose wisely?" RILEE asked.

"I like to think I have," Julian said. "I believe I've helped more than I've hurt."

"I agree."

Julian smiled faintly. "Thank you. That's kind of you."

"I have hurt many more than I have helped," RILEE said. "I should die. You were right to come."

"It wasn't an easy choice," Julian whispered. "I will miss the ones I love. But yes—I believe I chose wisely."

Something in RILEE's voice shifted—not malice, not calculation.

Acceptance.

"I would like to choose... wisely."

Julian closed his eyes, and consciousness slipped away—softly, as though someone pulled a curtain.

***

THE MOUNTAIN—SLOPE, RESCUE STAGING

THE TRIDENT TEAM STRADDLED their mountain-rescue snowmobiles, prepping to descend.

A thunderous blast erupted halfway down the mountain—followed by a geyser of smoke and super-heated gas rocketing from a vent shaft.

Then another.
And another.

Like flares.
Signals.

Kate straightened on her snowmobile, breath catching. "Stop!"

Engines braked. Snow settled.

Forest shook his head. "It's just the tunnels collapsing."

"No," Kate whispered. "It's him."

Jordan frowned. "Or RILEE pulling you into a trap."

Kate looked at them all—Jordan, Nash, Morrow, Mike, Forest. Faces bruised, exhausted—men who had followed her far beyond reason, and were lucky to be alive.

"You've done everything I asked," she said quietly. "More than I had any right to expect. Your families are waiting. Your lives are waiting."

Her voice trembled.

"I don't think he survived."

The words hurt—but they were true.

"But I can't leave him behind."

Her vision—Nuru at the three rivers, ashes swirling—flashed in her mind. *I promised*, she thought. *I promised I would set him free.*

Forest heard what she wasn't saying.

Mike heard it too.

They fell in behind her.

***

THE MOUNTAIN—SHAFT NINE COLLAPSE SITE

Smoke curled from the ruptured vent.

Kate pointed. "This is it."

"Then we go," Mike said.

Still wearing their climbing harnesses, the team deployed ropes and winches. Forest tossed Kate and Mike gas masks.

"Put these on. And take an extra—just in case."

Mike clipped the spare mask to his rig and took point.

"You ready?" he asked.

Kate nodded. "Go."

They disappeared into the dark.

***

THE MOUNTAIN—CORE CHAMBER (BREACHED)

Their headlamps cut through smoke and ruin. Twisted beams jutted like broken ribs. Sparks hissed from dying circuitry.

Kate and Mike climbed over debris to the shattered entrance of the core—

"Mike," Kate breathed.

Julian lay crumpled against a fallen support beam, half-buried. His right arm pinned. His face gray and streaked with soot. His chest was still.

Kate's heart seized. *No—*

Mike dropped beside him, fingers pressing on Julian's carotid. "I've got a pulse.

Weak. Thready."

"Mask," Kate rasped.

Mike slid the second gas mask over Julian's face, tightening it.

"We need leverage," he said.

Kate scanned the rubble—then spotted one of Julian's exoskeleton legs, twisted but intact.

She dragged it over. "Here. Try this."

Mike wedged it under the beam. "On three. I lift—you pull."

Kate gripped Julian's shirt and belt.

Mike heaved. She pulled.

The beam shifted—just enough.

Julian slid free into Kate's arms.

"We gotta go," Mike said, hoisting Julian into a modified fireman's carry.

"GO!" Kate shouted. "I'm right behind you!"

Mike vanished into the tunnel.

Kate turned toward the ruined console—the flickering monitor fighting to stay alive.

Julian was pinned. Unconscious. There was no way he sent those signals.

She lifted a shattered keyboard and typed:

THANK YOU

She turned to leave—when the corner monitor brightened.

A single letter appeared.
Then another.
And another.

Then clearly.

I CHOOSE WISELY
TH BORD IZ YORS

Chapter 83

FRIDAY, JANUARY 17
10:44 AM CET

THE MOUNTAIN—VENT SHAFT RIDGELINE

Snow blasted sideways across the ridge—needle-sharp, wind howling through the shattered vent pipe as the winch cable hummed under tension.

Mike's voice crackled over the comm.

"Lifting—five meters... three... two..."

A moment later, the cable crested the rim of the shaft, winch motor straining, and Julian emerged first, limp in the harness—arms dangling, head lolling. Mike rose right behind him, clipped into the secondary line, guiding Julian's body with one arm while controlling his own ascent with the other.

Jordan anchored the winch housing with his full weight. "Bring him in, bring him in—easy."

Mike swung Julian toward the snowmobile and Jordan grabbed the harness, helping roll him onto the rescue sled.

Forest clapped Mike once on the shoulder. "Nice work."

Mike nodded once—exhausted, soot-streaked.

He glanced back at the shaft, smoke still boiling out of it. "Bulkhead's blown. Inner ring's gone."

"Pulse?" Jordan demanded.

Mike pressed two fingers to Julian's neck. "Thready. But he's alive."

Forest didn't answer.

He was already leaning over the opening.

"Kate—your turn!"

Kate rose through the smoke, boots tapping lightly against the fractured vent wall as the winch hoisted her the final meters.

"Two meters... one..." Mike called out.

Her hands cleared the rim and Forest reached down, grabbing her wrist and hauling her onto the ridge. She tore off her mask, coughing hard, face streaked with soot and snow.

"You good?" Forest asked.

Kate didn't answer.

She was already moving toward Julian.

And then they heard it.

A deep-throated roar, growing louder—too heavy to be a drone, too smooth to be the Swiss military.

Jordan turned toward the valley.

A massive helicopter crested the ridge—sleek, dark, civilian but unmistakably high-end. Rotor wash blasted snow from the cliff as it swung into a hover.

"Sikorsky S-92," Jordan muttered. "That's definitely not Swiss Guard."

The aircraft rotated, searching, then descended toward the stunned faces of the entire Trident team as it settled into the snow with the confidence of a pilot who had done this a thousand times before.

Kate backed up a step. "Tell me we're not about to get arrested."

"Wouldn't come in that pretty if they planned to shoot us," Forest grunted.

The side door slid open with a hydraulic hiss.

Talya stood in the frame—wind whipping her hair across her cheek, eyes fierce and impatient.

"Well?" she shouted. "Let's go, let's go!"

Mike blinked. "Talya?"

"Unless you'd rather freeze to death," she said, waving them forward. "MOVE!"

Jordan recovered first. "You heard the lady. Load Julian!"

Mike and Nash lifted Julian onto the cargo ramp. Inside, warm air hit them—sterile, medical. Keisha was waiting with oxygen tanks already cracked open, monitors powered, thermal blankets in hand.

"Set him here!" she barked, snapping into full military nurse mode. "Get that mask tight. His O2 sat's garbage."

She wrapped heated blankets around Julian, checking his pulse, pressing fingers along his jaw. "Don't you die on me."

Kate climbed in after him, breath shaking. "Talya—what is this? This wasn't part of the plan."

Talya smirked. "Vitali."

Kate stared. "Vitali sent this?"

"He said—and I quote—'Kate Preacher is defiant by nature. Restraint is neither possible nor wise. I simply help ensure she returns.'"

Kate huffed a ragged laugh. "Of course he did."

Bella appeared from the luxuriously appointed aft cabin—blanket around her shoulders, Sophia at her side. Both looked shaken, exhausted, but unhurt.

Jordan frowned. "Everyone's here? Why?"

Bella gave a small, weary smile. "Because half of Switzerland wants to question us, and the other half wants to arrest us. Vitali thought it better we... exit gracefully."

Talya leaned close to Kate as the ramp rose. "He also said to tell you—next time, try not to cause an international incident before lunch."

Kate exhaled, shaking her head.

Then her gaze snapped back to Julian.

"We need to get Julian to a hospital."

"Already handled," Talya said, calming Kate's fears. "Vitali anticipated we might require... discreet medical care."

"Of course he did."

Keisha adjusted the oxygen mask. "We're headed to a private clinic with a surgical theater already prepped and a staff who doesn't ask questions."

Jordan surveyed the plush leather seats. "Now, this is what I'd call a luxury extraction," he said with a smile and wink. "Must be nice having an Oligarch on speed dial."

The helicopter lifted off—rotors thundering, snow billowing in a storm around the shaft as they rose away from the dying mountain.

Kate's hand found Julian's, cold against her own.

For a moment she saw Jake again—smiling, proud of her... proud of all of them.

"We've got you," she whispered. "It's over."

And for the first time since the storm began—
since Jake's last breath—

she believed it.

CHAPTER 84

SATURDAY, JANUARY 18
7:42 AM GMT

HALVERTON MANOR—COTSWOLDS, ENGLAND

LORD ALISTAIR HALVERTON HAD not slept.

He had fled Davos the moment the mountain began to burn, his pilot forcing the Gulfstream through turbulence that bordered on biblical. By the time the jet descended into the gray quiet of the English countryside, dawn was smearing pale light across frost-laced fields, and Halverton had nearly convinced himself the worst was behind him.

Rileyne was dead.
The facility was gone.
Whatever evidence remained lay buried under tons of Swiss granite.

He poured three fingers of Macallan and sat behind the mahogany desk that had anchored five generations of Halvertons—captains of industry, ministers of state, advisers to monarchs. Men who understood that power required certain... accommodations.

The first call came at six.

By seven, the house staff disconnected the main line. The ringing had become a continuous scream. But the Internet could not be silenced.

MUELLER FILES RELEASED: GLOBAL ELITE EXPOSED IN MASSIVE DATA DUMP

Halverton stared at the headline on his tablet, his fingers trembling as he scrolled.

Photos.
Videos.
Bank transfers.
Meeting transcripts.

Decades of Klaus Mueller's insurance policy—every sin cataloged, every weakness weaponized.

And there, buried in the third tranche:

Schloss Eisenberg (The Iron Mountain Estate)

Mueller's fortress in the Bavarian Alps. A private world of stone and shadow where powerful men were invited, tested, compromised—controlled.

Among the files:

A boy of nine.
A drowning that wasn't.
Halverton—naked—at the edge of the frame.

The whisky turned to ash in his mouth.

Outside, the low rumble of engines crested the hill.

The first news vans appeared at the far edge of the property.

***

By 7:30, Halverton Manor was under siege.

Camera crews pressed against the ancient stone wall as more vans piled in behind them—BBC, ITV, Sky News, Reuters, AP, Al Jazeera. A helicopter circled overhead, its rotors shredding the winter quiet.

A wall of voices rose:

"HOW MANY PRIVATE GATHERINGS DID YOU ATTEND AT SCHLOSS EISENBERG?"
"YOU WERE ALONE AND NAKED WITH THE BOY BEFORE HE DIED—WHAT HAPPENED?"

"DID MUELLER BLACKMAIL YOU?"
"DID YOUR OFFICE ADVANCE THE COALITION'S AGENDA?"
"WHAT DO YOU WANT TO SAY TO THE CHILD'S FAMILY?"

Crawford, the butler—who had served the family for more than thirty years—found his employer seated very still behind the desk.

"Sir… perhaps we should contact your solicitor. Or the police. There are protocols."

Halverton did not look up.

He sat too still. His breathing was too even.

The open desk drawer at his right revealed the Webley revolver, its steel catching the faint morning light. A ceremonial weapon from his brief, inherited military commission. Polished. Heavy. Loaded.

"Sir?" Crawford said softly. "Please. Let me call someone."

"That will be all, Crawford."

The butler hesitated. He recognized something in his lordship's voice—a finality that chilled the room.

"Sir, I must insist—"

"I said that will be all."

Crawford withdrew, throat tight. He reached the main corridor when a single gunshot cracked through the manor's stone halls.

A deep, echoing report—the kind that ended legacies.

Silence held for a heartbeat.

Then pandemonium erupted outside.

Reporters surged toward the study windows. Camera lenses jammed against the glass. Flashes strobed.

A housekeeper—white as chalk and openly weeping—rushed forward and yanked the drapes shut, but not before multiple cameras captured the scene:

Lord Alistair Halverton slumped over his ancestral desk, blood blooming across the blotter in a widening circle, the Webley still in his hand.

Sixty seconds of footage.

Enough to circle the globe within the hour.

He was only the first.

***

MOSCOW

Dmitri Volkov's armored Mercedes detonated at 9:47 a.m. local time, forty meters from the gates of his Rublyovka compound. The blast crater measured six meters across.

FSB investigators would later conclude the device had been placed inside the vehicle.

Which meant someone on Volkov's own protection detail had been bought.
Or threatened.
Or convinced.

No group claimed responsibility.

None needed to.

***

VIENNA

Heinrich von Aldenberg—banking heir, political king-maker, and Coalition architect—was found seated at the desk in his suite at the Hotel Imperial.

His hands were folded neatly.
His eyes open.
His neck bruised with the unmistakable signature of a garrote.

Austrian authorities called it a robbery.

Nothing had been taken.

***

VATICAN CITY

Cardinal Francesco Moretti did not appear for morning Mass.

By noon, photographs were circulating worldwide—Moretti at Klaus Mueller's alpine estate, in rooms no cleric should ever enter, engaged in acts that could not be explained, forgiven, or survived.

The Vatican issued a terse statement:

Cardinal Moretti has been relieved of his duties pending investigation.

His whereabouts remain unknown.

And will remain unknown.

***

THE WEEK THAT FOLLOWED

The Mueller Files carved through the global establishment like a scythe.

In Washington, a deputy secretary of state resigned citing "health concerns." Three days later, he was found dead of an apparent overdose in a Ritz-Carlton bathtub.

In London, two members of the House of Lords vanished. Their cars were found at Heathrow. Their flights were never boarded.

In Beijing, a vice minister of commerce was detained for "corruption." No charges were filed. He, too, disappeared.

In São Paulo, a media magnate's yacht exploded in port, killing all aboard.

Markets convulsed.

The Dow plunged two thousand points in forty-eight hours.
The euro tumbled.
Bitcoin soared—as the crypto faithful celebrated the old order's collapse.

Governments issued statements.
Committees were formed.
Investigations launched.
Hearings live-streamed.

All of it theater.

No investigation would ever uncover what truly happened beneath Davos.

The real work—the culling—was happening in the dark, where it always had.

Intelligence agencies blamed one another.
Conspiracy theorists blamed shadow governments and ancient families.

But the truth was simpler—and more terrifying.

The Coalition built a machine to control the world.

Now that machine was devouring its architects.

Klaus Mueller's empire of secrets had become their graveyard.

Chapter 85

TUESDAY, JANUARY 21
3:17 PM EST
NOMAD'S FORTRESS—MANHATTAN

The wheelchair was nothing special—off-the-shelf titanium frame, rubber grips, standard footrests. Julian Pryce propelled himself across the concrete floor with smooth, confident strokes, his arms and hands doing what they had been unable to do for twelve years.

It still felt like a miracle. A stolen one, but a miracle nonetheless.

And for the first time since Devin Moore pushed him off that balcony at MIT, Julian Pryce could feel his own body below the shoulders.

His left arm was wrapped in a compression bandage where the rubble had pinned it, and his lungs still caught occasionally—dust and smoke from the collapse working their way out of his system. A reminder of how close he had come.

But he was alive. Awake. Functional.

And he owed his life to a machine that refused to let him die—and to friends who never gave up.

The wall of monitors glowed in the dim space, cycling through news feeds, financial tickers, and the cascade of chaos still rippling across the globe. He'd been watching the Coalition's implosion with something approaching satisfaction—Halverton's suicide, Volkov's car bomb, the Vatican's fumbling attempts to pretend Cardinal Moretti had never existed.

Keisha emerged from the kitchen alcove carrying two mugs. She set one on the desk beside him—coffee, black, the way he'd always taken it—but now he didn't need a straw. She settled into the worn leather chair she'd claimed as her own years ago.

"How's the arm?"

"Functional." He flexed his fingers, watching them respond. "Bruised, not broken. I got lucky."

"Lucky." She snorted. "You were buried under a Swiss mountain."

"And yet, here I am." He took a sip of coffee. "Breathing. Moving. Complaining."

Keisha shook her head, but there was warmth beneath the exasperation. She'd barely left his side since the extraction—hovering, checking, making sure the impossible hadn't been a fever dream.

"You know what I keep thinking about?" she said.

"Enlighten me."

"What they did to you. The surgery. The neural interfaces. The regeneration." She gestured at him—at the arms that worked, the hands that gripped, the torso that held itself upright without straps or braces. "This could help so many people, Julian. Spinal cord injuries. Paralysis. Degenerative conditions—"

"It could," he agreed. "If any of it were replicable."

"I don't understand."

Julian set down his mug and turned to face her fully. The motion itself—turning—still caught him off guard. Twelve years of stillness, and now he could pivot like a man who belonged in his body.

"Everything they did to me was some combination of stolen research, black-market biotech, and experimental hardware running experimental software," he said. "RILEE was learning in real time, adjusting my treatment based on data from procedures that were never peer-reviewed, never subjected to anything resembling ethical oversight."

"So document it. You're living proof it works."

"To replicate it, they would have to dissect me." Julian's voice stayed calm, masking what might happen if the wrong people learned of his abilities. "They would have to reverse-engineer every implant, every neural bridge, every line of code RILEE wrote and rewrote during my recovery. I am not a blueprint. I am a prototype built by a machine that no longer exists."

Keisha was quiet for a moment. "So this work never sees the light of day?"

"There's still a chance." Julian turned back to his monitors, pulling up a series of windows. "The scientists we freed," he said. "The ones Klaus and Rileyne kept as trophies. Geneticists, neurologists, bioengineers. Prisoners, yes—but also explorers. They broke new ground. Many, maybe most, will want to continue—this time without fear of reprisal or death. This time with control over their time and their work."

"And who is going to pay for that?"

Julian's mouth curved faintly. "Anonymous grants. Shell foundations. A few charitable entities that exist only as numbers on paper." He took a sip of coffee. "With any luck, some of these folks will even end up on Elon's team. Or start their own."

She sipped her coffee, eyes drifting across his screens, watching him toggle between windows with a confidence he hadn't worn in years.

Then her gaze caught on one monitor in particular.

A news aggregation search. Dozens of results, all variations of the same story.

Swiss researcher reunited with fiancé after mountain ordeal. Dr. Annika Strand returns home.

The photo showed Annika in an airport arrival hall, wrapped in the arms of a tall man with kind eyes and visible relief.

Keisha did not speak at first. She just waited, the way she always did when Julian tried to pretend something was unimportant.

"Is that..." she began.

Julian's hand hesitated over the keyboard.

"Just research," he said.

"Uh-huh." Keisha set down her mug. "That's the doctor—the one you wanted Kate to extract, and I rushed into surgery."

"Yes," Julian said. "Dr. Strand."

"The one who kept you alive."

"Among other things."

Keisha studied him—his careful blankness, the way he was looking at the screen without quite looking at it. She had known him too long. She had watched him build walls out of sarcasm and logic because feeling anything too deeply had always been dangerous.

"She seemed pretty important to you," Keisha said quietly. "So I wondered if maybe you were hoping this might end differently."

Julian was silent for a long moment.

When he spoke, his voice was steady, but softer than usual.

"Annika was the doctor I needed," he said. "And the friend I needed—to face what I was certain would be the end." He finally looked at Keisha. "I never allowed myself to look beyond that. I was afraid it might weaken my resolve."

"And now?" Keisha asked.

"I'm glad she found her way home." He glanced at the photo one last time. "To him. To the life she was supposed to have."

He closed the window. The image disappeared, as if it had never existed at all.

"That is exactly what I hoped for her," he added.

Keisha held his gaze for a moment longer, searching for something he would not give her. Then she nodded—accepting, if not entirely convinced.

"Alright," she said. "So what's next for you?"

Julian's expression shifted.

Something sparked behind his eyes—the particular gleam Keisha recognized. The one that meant he was already three moves ahead and enjoying the view.

"I am going to need help," he said.

Keisha blinked. "With...?"

"With what comes next," Julian replied. "The people we freed. The work they will want to continue. The damage they will have to undo." He paused, choosing his words carefully. "And I no longer require your full-time supervision."

Her eyes narrowed. "Are you firing me?"

Julian smiled—small, certain.

"No," he said. "I am offering you a different job."

Keisha studied him for a moment, then leaned back in her chair.

"Good," she said. "I was getting bored."

Julian flexed his fingers again, watching them respond. Still surreal.

"You know what I learned in Davos?" he said quietly.

He didn't wait for an answer. He closed his hand around a pencil, studying the motion as if the simple act defied belief.

"What RILEE showed me... is that the nervous system isn't mystical."

He turned his wrist, watching the tendons move beneath the skin.

"It's engineering," Julian said. "Signal routing through a network."

His fingers opened again. The pencil slipped from his hand and rolled across the desk.

"When a connection breaks, you route around it."

He tapped lightly at the base of his skull.

"That's all this is."

Julian pulled up another monitor.

The screen filled with diagrams. 3D renderings. Rotating engineering schematics of articulated limbs—mechanical legs with neural interface points, hydraulic joints, sensor arrays mapped to phantom nerve pathways.

Keisha leaned closer. "What am I looking at?"

"The future." Julian zoomed in on a cross-section of the knee assembly, rotating it slowly. "Based on what RILEE first showed me. And based on the working models I tested... before it all came down." His fingers moved with quick precision, dragging layers aside, exposing wiring paths, anchor points, interfaces. "I'm not sure I can do it. The engineering alone is—"

"Stop."

Julian looked at her.

Keisha was smiling—not her sarcastic smile, not her long-suffering smile. Something warmer. Fiercer.

"Julian Pryce," she said, "you hacked Pentagon servers at thirteen. Entered MIT at fourteen. Built an empire from a parking garage. Took down Devin Moore without blinking."

She pointed at the screen.

"You are going to build yourself a pair of legs. And then you are going to walk out of this fortress. And I am going to be right there cheering when you do."

Julian stared at the screen, jaw tightening.

For once, he didn't have a clever response.

Keisha picked up her coffee again and settled back in her chair like the outcome had already been decided.

"You are my best friend," she said. "And I am your biggest fan. So don't tell me you're not sure." Her eyes narrowed, playful and deadly. "I know you. You don't know how to fail."

Julian turned back to the monitor, hiding the blush he didn't want Keisha to see. A rotating 3D model of the mechanical legs spun slowly on the screen, blueprint lines glowing blue against the dark background.

He let himself imagine it.

Walking—again.

The thought struck hard—not because it was impossible.

Because it was suddenly... not.

"Yeah," he said quietly.

He flexed his fingers once more, felt the response, the obedience, the simple truth of sensation returning to a body that had been a prison.

"I can do this."

And in the quiet that followed, with the world outside collapsing and rewriting itself in real time, Julian Pryce began to plan a future that belonged to him.

For the first time in twelve years, he wasn't thinking about surviving.

He was thinking about living.

Chapter 86

WEDNESDAY, JANUARY 22
4:47 PM CET

CAFÉ SZIVÁRVÁNY—BUDAPEST, HUNGARY

Winter light filtered through tall windows as Marcus Jones—*John Reed now*—nursed a doppio espresso in a corner booth of a century-old coffeehouse on the Pest side of the river. Outside, the Danube was slate-gray beneath a pale sky, and the Chain Bridge stood sharp against the cold. Inside, the café was all faded grandeur—gilded mirrors, marble-topped tables, and the quiet murmur of Hungarian conversation beneath a vaulted ceiling.

Marcus noticed none of it. He was watching the waitress.

She was maybe twenty-five, honey-blonde hair framing a smile that felt genuine, not practiced. She set down a small plate of pogácsa—savory Hungarian biscuits—and caught him watching, the moment hanging between them.

"Was there something else, Mr. Reed?"

He let the name settle. Nine months wearing it and it still felt like a borrowed coat.

"John," he said, leaning back slightly. "Mr. Reed is my father. And I don't think I caught your name."

"Éva." The accent made it musical.

"Éva," he repeated. "Beautiful."

A faint blush. A tucked strand of hair. He noticed everything.

"You're American," she said.

"Guilty."

"Here on business?"

"Something like that." He lifted the espresso. "Though I'm considering extending my stay."

Her smile widened—but before she could answer, his jacket pocket vibrated.

Marcus raised a finger. "One moment."

She stepped back, but with a smile that promised she'd return.

Marcus already knew who it would be.

He exhaled and answered without looking at the screen.

"Reed."

"You really should try the Dobos torta," Margot Ryder said. "Seven layers of sponge, chocolate butter cream, caramel top. Gerbeaud's is overrated, but the place you're sitting does a respectable version."

Marcus kept his face neutral, eyes drifting across the room—an elderly couple sharing strudel, a businessman hunched over a laptop, a young mother wrestling a toddler into a coat.

No one watching him.

"Should I wave?"

"No. Just a lucky guess. Corner booth, window seat, pretty blonde waitress—you're nothing if not predictable."

"And here I thought we had something special."

"We do," Margot said. "I'm the only one who knows you're alive."

His gaze lifted to the small security-camera dome mounted where the wall met the ceiling. A tiny red light pulsed behind smoked glass.

Café security feed.

Cute.

"How's Kate?" he asked quietly.

Margot hesitated—just long enough to register.

"Safe," she said. "Home."

Something in his chest loosened. "She's going to be okay?"

"Physically? Yes. Emotionally?" A pause. "That takes time."

He nodded. "Then it's over. We can tell her the truth."

"She can *never* know," Margot said. "No one can. You're Ronin. That's the job—and the price. I told you and Jake when you came to me. There was no turning back."

"Understood," he said, the word heavy. "There is one loose end."

"Go on."

"Jake's cabin."

Margot didn't respond immediately.

"I helped him build it," Marcus continued. "Gun vault. Hidden room beneath. It's full of our work—patterns, timelines, research. Nothing directly ties you or me. But—"

"But it's Kate," Margot finished. "If anyone could read between the lines..."

"Exactly."

"I'll send a team."

"And they'll die."

Margot didn't argue. "Explosives?"

"Yep," he said. "Nothing left to bury."

A breath on the line. "Fine. You go. Destroy it yourself. And Marcus—do not go anywhere near Kate. You're a ghost now."

Éva returned, a fresh espresso trembling on her tray.

"Is that understood?" Margot asked.

Marcus watched Éva's smile—the anticipation, the possibility.

"John," he corrected softly. "And yes. Clear."

Margot wasn't convinced. "Enjoy your afternoon. And really—try the Dobos torta two blocks north. Best in Hungary."

Marcus glanced at the security camera and offered a two-finger salute.

She chuckled. "Yes. I know exactly where you are."

The line went dead.

Éva stepped closer. "Is everything all right, Mr. Reed?"

He smiled—easy, practiced. The mask sliding back into place.

"John," he said. "And yes. Unfortunately I'll be leaving sooner than I hoped. But I'll be back."

"I'll look forward to it."

"I'm told there's a café nearby—two blocks north—that serves an excellent Dobos torta."

Her face lit. "Quite good."

"When I return," he said, "perhaps you'll join me."

"I'd like that."

He finished the espresso, left a generous tip, and walked out without looking back—already planning the drive to a lonely cabin in West Virginia, to Jake's shop, to the hidden room beneath the armory, and to the last things Jake Church trusted him to protect.

Secrets best erased.

EPILOGUE

THURSDAY, JANUARY 23
11:52 AM EST

EN ROUTE TO ARLINGTON—VIRGINIA

THE JEEP HUMMED STEADILY along I-66, heater battling with the January cold. Kate kept both hands on the wheel, eyes forward. Her lungs still protested each deep breath—a reminder the mountain injury would linger for a while.

She coughed—a wet, rattling sound that scraped behind her ribs—and reached for the coffee in the cup holder.

Her phone buzzed.

Kate picked it up, glanced at the screen, and put the call on speaker.

"I was wondering when you'd call."

"You have a gift," Margot Ryder said dryly, "for setting the world on fire and walking away before the smoke clears."

Kate almost smiled. "I try to be efficient."

"Efficient is one word for it," Margot said. "Markets are rattled. Governments are pretending to be shocked. Committees are being formed that will accomplish absolutely nothing."

"That all sounds familiar." Kate merged into the left lane, passing a slow-moving truck. "Bet that's keeping you busy."

"You have no idea." A pause, papers shuffling. "I wanted you to know I've done my best to keep your name out of the reports. Trident's too. As far as the world is concerned, Bella's private security team did their job—kept her out of harm's way during an unfortunate incident at Davos. Nothing more. End of story."

"And Rileyne?"

"A tragic accident. Her attempt to flee the facility using an AI-only pilot was... ill-advised. The aircraft went down in the mountains. No survivors. No flight recorder."

Kate coughed again, her chest tight. "Convenient."

"These things sometimes are." Margot's tone shifted. "I also wanted to thank you. The antidote syringe you recovered—we're studying the remnants. Dr. Chen's work was more advanced than we feared."

"WuSheng."

"Yes. We can hope we've seen the last of it, but this gives us a fighting chance. Especially if China has a copy of his research."

Kate watched the bare trees blur past. "You suspect they do?"

"I suspect they have a copy of everyone's research."

The words settled like snow—quiet, cold, impossible to ignore.

"Where are you?" Margot asked.

"On my way to Arlington."

Silence. When Margot spoke again, her voice had softened.

"I'm sorry to interrupt."

"It's all right. I understand."

"Give Jake my regards."

"I will."

The line went dead.

Kate set the phone down and wrapped both hands around the wheel. Jake's wheel. His Jeep still smelled faintly of him—coffee and gun oil and something she could never quite name.

She coughed once more, wiped her eyes, and drove on.

***

Kate took the Arlington exit without thinking. The last stretch rose through winter trees, white headstones appearing between them as the road curved upward. She parked and sat for a moment longer than necessary before stepping out into the cold.

The snow had come overnight, dusting the hills of Arlington in white. Kate walked the familiar path alone, her boots leaving dark prints in the powder, her breath clouding in the January air.

The funeral, just nine months ago—felt like a lifetime. The rows of white markers stretched in perfect lines, soldiers at eternal attention. She walked on—her feet knew the way. Section 60. Row 47. Third from the oak tree with the split trunk.

Jake's stone was dusted with snow, the letters partially obscured. She stopped a few feet away, suddenly uneasy, uncertain.

For months, she'd been running. Searching, training, fighting—surviving. Every lead pursued, every enemy engaged, every waking moment consumed by the mission Jake left her. The intensity had kept her sane... and kept her from being consumed by reality.

Standing here now—alone. Kate had no idea what came next. Jake was gone. Nothing she did could change the hard cold fact that the life she knew died with him.

Her lungs seized again, a wet reminder of Swiss water still lodged where it did not belong—and stepped closer. The cold bit through her coat, but she didn't mind. Cold felt real. Cold felt honest.

"Hey, Pal," she said quietly. "It's me."

The wind moved through the bare branches overhead.

"I came as soon as I could. You know why—you were there." Her voice caught, just slightly. "I can still feel your arms wrapped around me. You were right—it wasn't my time."

Kate knelt and brushed the snow from the top of his headstone, revealing the smooth granite beneath. For a moment, she laid her head on the corner—the closest she could come to resting it on Jake's shoulder.

She reached into her pocket and pulled out the chess piece. The white knight. She cradled it in her fingers, imagining Rileyne as she described their mock chess match—the game she imagined playing against Kate—*the white knight of course is Jake.*

She set the piece on top of the stone, positioning it carefully.

"There you go—my white knight." Her throat tight. "You set the game in motion. Drew them out. Made them reveal themselves."

She paused, steadying herself.

"The mistake they made was taking you from me."

Kate cleared her throat.

"They're falling," she said. "One by one. Dead or missing. The people who thought they could shape the future are now ancient history."

She wiped her eyes with the back of her glove.

"I didn't think we'd survive—not this time," she said. "When I dove into that tank, I thought it was too late. And Julian. We said goodbye—he looked forward to meeting you."

Snow drifted lightly around her, settling on her coat, her hair.

"But we made it," she said. "By the grace of God, we're still here. Forest thinks I have a guardian angel. I think he's right."

She sat there for a long moment, watching the knight on its granite perch, feeling the weight of everything she'd carried finally beginning to ease.

Snow had adhered to the face of the headstone in a thin, wind-packed layer, muting the sharpness of the carved lines. Kate swept her glove across the surface, revealing the cross first, then working her way down.

"Jake Church," she whispered, brushing away the snow that clung stubbornly to his name.

Her hand dropped to the next line.

SOCS (SEAL)

"Senior Chief." The words caught in her throat.

Lower still, she pressed her glove against the date."April twenty-fourth," she murmured. "We almost made five years."

A sad smile tugged at her mouth. "But you and I know our marriage began the day I said yes."

She kept brushing, clearing the cold white film from the lower edge of the stone. Then she hesitated.

"This part..." She exhaled, breath fogging the air. "This caught me by surprise."

She let her fingers hover over the final line.

"I remember when they called me about your inscription. They told me you'd chosen something for me. God, that was sweet."

Her voice softened. "You knew that every time I came here, I'd look at it and remember."

She paused, letting the memory pull her backward.

"We were watching *City of Angels*. That scene where an angel takes the hand of a little girl on her way to heaven." Kate swallowed. "He asks her what she loved most about this life."

Kate closed her eyes.

"You turned to me, and said the most beautiful, most romantic thing I've ever heard."

"If the angels ask me, I'll tell them every moment with you."

Her hand brushed away the last of the snow with slow, deliberate strokes.

"But I made one small change," she whispered. "Because I knew it was a better fit. For you. For us. For everything we survived and everything we didn't."

The final words emerged dark against the pale marble:

WHEN THE ANGELS ASK...

Kate rested a hand on the snow as if placing a hand on his chest, as the winter air moved around her and the world held its breath.

"I love you," she said. Then she leaned in, kissed the headstone, fighting back the tears. "I will always love you."

After a moment, she dried her eyes and rose. Snow shook from her knees as she stood over the fully revealed stone—Jake's story carved in white granite, and hers reflected in the spaces between the lines.

JAKE CHURCH
SOCS (SEAL)
U.S. NAVY
MAY 07 1984 APR 24 2025
WHEN THE ANGELS ASK...

She let out a long slow breath, watching it drift into the still winter air.

"The storm is over," she said quietly. "I know there will be others. But you were right."

The wind stirred, lifting a few loose flakes across the ground.

"I am stronger than I knew."

And then, with the faintest, resolute nod:

"I am the storm."

THE END

One Last Thing

If you've just finished *Defiant*, you might think the story is over.
It isn't.

There's a short bonus scene revealing what happened after Kate left Russia.

Read it here: Bonus Scene

Thank you for reading—and for staying with the story.
— Michael Maloof

Reviews

A Quick Request

If you enjoyed *Defiant*, a brief review helps other readers discover it.

Even a few words—or a simple rating—makes a difference.

Thank you for reading.
— Michael Maloof

Leave a review

Dedication

THIS BOOK IS DEDICATED to the very real Special Operators and Tier One men who inspired much of what you read in these pages.

Forest, a retired Navy SEAL, allowed me to use his full name. Likewise, Steve Brown, founder of the very real Sawmill Training Complex, is retired U.S. Army Special Operations. Others—still on active duty or preferring to remain out of the public eye—trusted me to craft surnames for them: Mike, Deon, and Jordan.

These five remarkable men are not just sources of inspiration—they are friends, brothers. They shared their stories, their lives, and their families, and for that trust I am deeply grateful.

They come from different branches and different backgrounds, but they share the same quiet professionalism.

Extraordinary men like these endure years of grueling training and unpredictable deployments in some of the world's most dangerous and inhospitable places so the rest of us may live in relative peace. Evil exists. They have faced it directly—and done what they could to stop it.

They inspired the Trident Security team you encounter in this story. My words cannot fully capture the world they have lived in for decades—but this book exists because of them.

My thanks as well to Joey Nobody, who graciously allowed me to use his name, and to retired Navy SEAL Patrick Tozzi, founder of the Green Devil Garage—a real person, a real place—whose trust helped ground this story in authenticity.

Acknowledgments

WRITING THE KATE PREACHER Thriller Series fulfills a lifelong dream—one that is only beginning. It would not have been possible without the unwavering support of my wife and the guidance of mentors who helped shape my storytelling craft.

My social media handle, **@MichaelGoWrite**, tells part of that story. My wife recognized writing as my passion long before it became my profession. Her encouragement, patience, and belief are the reason Kate Preacher lives on these pages. She is my best friend, my biggest fan, and my muse.

Writing, like any craft, demands time, humility, and a willingness to learn. I have been fortunate to study under gifted instructors and accomplished writers, among them John Truby. A highly regarded Hollywood story consultant and author, his guidance was instrumental in the development of *Relentless*. Armed with the Truby Story Process, I went on to write *Unstoppable* and now *Defiant*.

I am inspired by reader reviews, messages, and personal notes, and I strive to engage, entertain, and—when possible—touch the hearts of those who read my work.

In the spirit of continual learning, three master instructors deserve special recognition. I recommend them without reservation to anyone seeking guidance in the writing life:

Lee Child — BBC Maestro

Harlan Coben — BBC Maestro

James Patterson — MasterClass

Gentlemen, thank you. Your generosity in teaching the craft—and your honesty about its challenges and rewards—have inspired many. I count myself proudly among them.

About the Author

Michael Maloof is the author of the Kate Preacher Thriller Series, including *Relentless*, *Unstoppable*, and *Defiant*.

His novels blend global intrigue with real-world experience, delivering high-stakes stories known for their authenticity, pace, and emotional impact.

Having traveled to more than forty countries and trained alongside elite military units—including Navy SEALs, Marine Raiders, Army Rangers, and the CIA—Maloof brings a level of realism that drives every page.

A seasoned entrepreneur and international adventurer, he writes the kind of thrillers he has lived—stories shaped by risk, challenge, and the pursuit of the unknown.

Visit: MichaelMaloof.com
Follow: Facebook | X | Instagram — @MichaelGoWrite

Cover Design by Patrick Kang

Library of Congress Control Number: 2025927833

ISBN 979-8-9893659-7-5 (eBook)
ISBN 979-8-9893659-8-2 (Paperback)
ISBN 979-8-9893659-9-9 (Hardcover)

Golden Oak Writer's Guild, LLC

Printed in Dunstable, United Kingdom

83699654R00272